"RIDE THE BULL AT YOUR OWN RISK."

"How bad could that thing hurt you?" Bud asked. Bud could feel Sissy move her eyes from the bull to him. "Be careful, Bud."

When he reached the center of the bullring, Bud hesitated for a moment and then vaulted aboard the bull. Suddenly he realized that he didn't know where to sit, didn't know how to hold on, didn't know anything about bull riding. He wished they would stop staring at him.

The motor came on with a snort. And suddenly the mechanical bull put its headless head-end down and its legless rear came up in the air.

Bud hit the mattress with his right shoulder first. Getting up furious, Bud pulled two more dollars out of his pocket. "I wanta ride it again."

Paramount Pictures
presents

A ROBERT EVANS/IRVING AZOFF PRODUCTION
A JAMES BRIDGES FILM

JOHN TRAVOLTA

in

URBAN COWBOY

Executive Producer
C. O. Erickson

Based upon the story by
Aaron Latham

Screenplay by
James Bridges & Aaron Latham

Produced by
Robert Evans & Irving Azoff

Directed by
James Bridges

URBAN COWBOY

A Novel
by
Aaron Latham

Based on a Screenplay
by
James Bridges and Aaron Latham

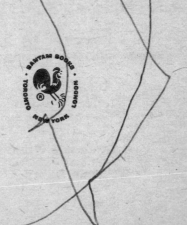

URBAN COWBOY
A Bantam Book
June 1980

ACKNOWLEDGMENTS

*Grateful acknowledgment is made for permission to reprint the
following copyright material:*

*HERE COMES THE HURT AGAIN by Jerry Foster & Bill
Rice. Copyright © 1978 by Jack and Bill Music Company c/o
The Welk Music Group, Santa Monica, California 90401. International copyright secured. All rights reserved. Used by permission.*

*MY HEROES HAVE ALWAYS BEEN COWBOYS by
Sharon Vaughn. Copyright © 1976 by Jack and Bill Music
Company c/o The Welk Music Group, Santa Monica, California 90401. International copyright secured. All rights reserved. Used by permission.*

*LOOKIN' FOR LOVE by Bob Morrison and Debbie Hupp.
Copyright © 1979 by Southern Nights Music. Used by permission of Southern Nights Music.*

*MAMMAS DON'T LET YOUR BABIES GROW UP TO BE
COWBOYS by Ed Bruce and Patsy Bruce. Copyright © 1975
by Tree Publishing Co., Inc. and Sugarplum Music Co.*

*THE MOON JUST TURNED BLUE by John David Souther.
Copyright © 1975 WB Music Corp. and Golden Spread Music.
All rights reserved. Used by permission.*

*LONG HAIRED REDNECK by David Allan Coe. Copyright
© 1975 by Windo Music Publishing Co., Inc. & Lotsa Music.
All rights reserved. Used by permission.*

ISBN 0-553-13826-X

Published simultaneously in the United States and Canada

PRINTED IN THE UNITED STATES OF AMERICA

0 9 8 7 6 5 4 3 2 1

DESIGNED BY MIERRE

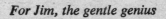

For Jim, the gentle genius

"What giants?" said Sancho Panza.

"Those that you see there," replied his master . . .

"But look, your Grace, those are not giants but windmills . . ."

"It is plain to be seen," said Don Quixote, "that you have had little experience in this matter of adventures."

MIGUEL DE CERVANTES
Don Quixote

BOOK
ONE

Twang Twang

1

The Windmill

Bud climbed the windmill slowly and carefully in the dark. The metal rungs of the ladder were pleasantly cool to his touch on the hot summer night. Bud often climbed the windmill when he wanted to be alone to think. Tonight he wanted to think about leaving the farm. And as he rose higher and higher, the farm beneath him grew smaller and smaller, like a memory diminished by time. Bud's foot slipped on the ladder for an instant, and he stopped climbing and just hung on for what seemed a long time, halfway up in the sky. He was more frightened than he needed to be, but he couldn't help it because he remembered the other time. He knew how treacherous his old friend the windmill could be.

Regaining his calm, Bud continued on up the cool metal rungs that lifted him high in the night. At the end of his upward journey, he reached the small wooden platform, which was just large enough to lie down on. He crawled into place and lay face down on the platform with the huge metal wheel of the windmill suspended just above his back. He still cringed slightly beneath the wheel even though this time he had checked to make absolutely certain it was locked before he began his climb.

Suspended in the West Texas night, Bud blended into it. He had inherited his dark hair from his great-great-grandmother, the Comanche Indian. He owed his deeply tanned skin to working outside every day. And his face was further darkened by a full black beard. Only his eyes seemed made for the day instead of the night. They were undiluted blue. Tonight those eyes were watered—and made more vivid—by memories and apprehensions.

Easing himself to the edge, Bud looked over at the world he was preparing to desert. From this height, that world looked unusually snug and well ordered, for he was too high to see the blemishes, the peeling paint, the rusting farm equipment, the chores to be done. Up here, it was hard to remember why he had ever thought of going. A gust of wind made the giant wheel creak, and Bud half turned as if to meet an attack.

And as he turned, the memory of that other night made his stomach feel as if he were falling. After it happened, Bud had stayed away from the windmill for months, afraid of it. The place at the top of the windmill, which had once been his quiet haven, had become the place he feared most. The accident had happened in the fall. It was not until the following spring that he had forced himself to climb the fearful tower again. And every step up the ladder he had remembered—as he remembered now.

On that night, over a year ago, he had climbed the windmill to his high refuge to think about a football game. He had gone to bed early to be well rested for the game, but he had not been able to sleep, so he had gotten up, dressed, and made his way to the tower. By then, it was after midnight. In the dark, he thought he saw the lever pulled down that locked the giant wheel with its sharp blades, but he was wrong. In those days, he climbed the steel ladder fast and carelessly. And then he sprawled on the wooden platform beneath the silent wheel. Spur would play Matador the next day, and the success or failure of his life seemed to depend upon who won that game. If Matador won, the season would be over for Bud. But if Spur won, he would go on to the bidistrict playoffs and maybe even to the regionals. Bud, who had big, sure hands, played right end. On that night, staring down at the dark farmhouse, he tried to see the world in perspective. He told himself that the house he lived in was just a small house and that the town he lived in was just a small town and the game he would play in was just a small game. But he didn't believe it. He belived the game, won or lost, would be the biggest memory of his life. It would stand out over everything else the way the windmill rose high over the farm.

A gentle wind began to blow on that night so many months ago. And the wheel began to turn! Rolling quickly onto his back, Bud stared up at the circle of knives that rotated slowly above him. Now he realized that the brake below had not been set and he was in danger. Guided by a wind vane, the slowly spinning wheel changed positions slightly to face directly into the breeze. If it moved again, it could easily knock him off the tower, especially if it moved quickly and violently, as it often did. Catching the light of the half-moon, the dangerous blades actually looked almost pretty against the black sky. They spun gracefully like silver batons in the hands of short-skirted twirlers on a high school football field. Bud was terrified of the wheel and yet somehow drawn to it.

In a long-regretted instant, Bud felt he had to do something or ultimately be driven over the edge, so he reached out. He reached out with his right hand as if to catch a pass thrown just a little too long. What he had intended was to try to stop the wheel before it gained too much speed. But the wheel, which weighed hundreds of pounds, was already spinning faster than he thought, and a sudden gust of wind spun it even faster. Bud seemed to feel a sharp pain in his finger long after that finger had been severed and was dropping from the top of the windmill all the way to the ground.

The whole finger was not lost. The blade caught it about midway between the first and second joints. It cut cleanly. The fingernail and one joint dropped away, down and down. Bud stared in horror at his right hand. It was the little finger that was partially missing. As he looked, blood squirted out, dampening his face and his neck. With the wheel still spinning above him, Bud felt he had to find the piece of him that was gone. Turning slowly back onto his stomach, he peered cautiously over the wooden edge, but he could not see his finger lying in the dirt below. From that majestic height, the lost finger was too small and trivial to be noticed. It was one of the surface blemishes that Bud had always climbed the windmill to escape.

Now, at last, Bud did what he should have done in the beginning. He moved carefully toward the ladder. To reach it, he had to pass within inches of the wheel, which now spun so fast that it was only a blur. He told the wheel: don't move, stay there until I'm safe. He concentrated on the wheel not moving the way he had once concentrated on catching passes, with all his energy. And as he crawled and slithered, he started to cry, his tears falling away into the black and becoming invisible long before they hit the ground. The wheel seemed to suck at him, and he thought he felt it touch—even tug at—his hair.

When he finally reached the ladder, Bud was almost too weak to make the long climb down. He clung for a moment to the very top and rested. But the longer he stayed there, the more he bled. He imagined that if he bled much more, he would faint, let go, and fall, so he began his descent. His missing finger hurt him unmercifully. And each time he was forced to grip a rung with his right hand, even though he never used that stub of a little finger, it still hurt all the more. Now blood stained the ladder of what had always been a kind of steel tree house to him. The steel tree had not liked being so used and had tried to shake him out. The climb down was the longest of his life: the windmill seemed to be growing like a living tree.

By the time he reached the bottom, he loved the ground and hated the heights. He began looking for his missing finger as soon as he felt secure on the earth. He almost expected it to draw him right to it, as though it missed the body, as though the finger and the body could still communicate even though the nerves were severed. But it actually took him quite a while, crossing and recrossing the ground under the windmill, to find it. When he did see it, he almost wished he hadn't. It lay dirty and bloody and dead in the dust. He picked it up and carried it into the house.

Bud washed his finger in the kitchen sink before going to wake his parents. His father drove him to the hospital, not the one on Main Street where he was born, because it had been torn down, but a smaller new one on the outskirts of town. In a big-city hospital, an ambitious surgeon might have tried to rejoin the dying finger to the hand, but Spur was a small town. The doctor in the emergency room just threw the finger away.

Bud couldn't play in the game that Friday night, but Spur won anyway.

Now, lying on the wooden platform high up in the night sky, remembering that game not played in, Bud scratched his stub of a little finger. At first, he scratched it unconsciously. Then he realized what he was doing, but he kept right on scratching anyway. It itched the way the memory of that night itched. He kept returning to it, couldn't stay away from it, especially on nights when he climbed the windmill. And this would be his last night to climb the windmill for a long time. He planned to get an early start in the morning. There wouldn't be any windmills in Houston, but he supposed there were probably other ways to get hurt. On his last night at home, Bud wanted to go and was afraid to go and so had climbed up into the night to think it over. Staring up at the cruel wheel, he thought of pulling its blades off one by one, like petals, repeating, I will go, I won't go, I will go, I won't go . . .

The wind was getting stronger now. The old wheel creaked and complained.

2

Leaving Home

Bud woke up to his last farm dawn. While he was packing hurriedly, he heard his mother fixing breakfast downstairs. He had been out on the windmill so long last night that he was sleepy this morning. He could use some of his mother's coffee to help him wake up. But that was all he wanted, just coffee, and an early start. And yet he knew his mother would do everything she could to delay his leaving home. She would put eggs in the way of his going and bacon and biscuits and probably even red-eye gravy.

"Bud, your breakfast's gettin' cold," his mother called from below.

"I don't want no breakfast, Mama," Bud called back. "I gotta get goin'."

Closing his suitcase, he came noisily down the stairs, carrying it in front of him. In the hall, he took an old straw cowboy hat off a peg and put it on his head. The hat was beat-up from shading him through too many months of working in his daddy's cotton fields. It felt comfortable on his head, because it was broke in good, broke in to the point of breaking down, just the way he liked it. He carried his suitcase into the kitchen.

"Take that ugly thing off your head," his mother said, "and sit down."

"I don't have time," Bud said.

"I made gravy."

"I'll just have coffee."

Still standing, he reached for an empty cup.

"Bud, your mama made gravy," his father said.

Bud took off his hat and sat down at the table. His mother passed him the eggs and the bacon and the biscuits and the red-eye gravy. He drank three cups of coffee. He was in a hurry but he could not help enjoying breakfast. It was his favorite meal of the day. No one said much. It was not a family that talked much even on regular mornings, and it got quieter the more special the event. They all just looked at each other and thought about how tomorrow's breakfast table would be different. Bud's parents looked at him sadly, but his two younger brothers, Gene and Billy, looked at him enviously, or so he thought. His baby sister, Sharon, looked at him the way his parents did.

"You gonna miss me?" Bud asked, breaking the silence.

Suddenly everyone spoke at once, assuring him how much he would be missed, how a day wouldn't go by that . . .

"No!" said his youngest brother, Billy, above the general murmur.

"Why you . . .!" Bud yelled.

He threw half a biscuit at his youngest brother, hitting him in the chest, staining his shirt front with red-eye gravy.

"Boys!" said the father.

After breakfast, the family followed Bud out to his brand-new black Ford pickup with a roll bar. He had bought it to make the trip in. And now that he owned it, the truck helped him remain steady in his resolve to go, for he knew he wouldn't be able to keep up the payments if he stayed in Spur, where there was no work and no money anymore.

"Here's some chicken for you to eat on the road," his mother said.

She handed him a brown paper sack.

"Thanks, Mama," Bud said.

Then she handed him another bag, this one made of cellophane.

"And here's some field peas for your Aunt Corene. You cain't get good vegetables in Houston. You'll see."

Bud's father stepped forward and extended his hand. The son took it and squeezed it. Then the farm father sent his farm son off to the city with this advice . . .

"Good luck, Bud."

Bud kissed his little sister on the cheek and shook hands

with his two brothers. Then, when his mother tried to kiss him, he tried to pull away.

"Don't embarrass him," said Billy in his teasing tone. "You know cowboys don't kiss their mamas on the lips."

"That don't matter none," said the mother. " 'Cause he ain't no cowboy. He's a dirt farmer, and he better not ever forget it, especially not where's he's goin'."

Of course, Bud's mother succeeded in kissing him on the lips. He instinctively wiped his mouth. Then he got in his truck and stuck his head out the window.

" 'Bye," he said.

"Now, you be careful," his mother said.

"I will, Mama."

"Don't drive too fast."

"I won't, Mama."

"Call me the minute you get there."

"Yeah, Mama . . ."

Bud pulled slowly away from the farmhouse and then let his pickup loaf down the narrow clay road that stretched through the green cotton fields like a wound. The last farm sound he heard was the windmill clanging a melancholy metallic good-bye as a breeze rose. When the truck rolled onto the blacktop, Bud turned on the radio, drowning out the windmill, and stepped down hard on the gas. His new pickup had quarter-horse acceleration. The summer cotton fields jolted by faster and faster, blurring like a memory.

Bud's long journey almost ended at the beginning. Mounting a slight rise, Bud was startled to see a Brahma bull sunning himself in the middle of the road. It was as though the animal had been placed there to prove that the speeder's mother had been right about going slow. Bud slammed down his brake and skidded to a sideways halt about five yards from the bull, which did not move. The Brahma just stared suspiciously at the black truck as if it were some iron bull come to steal his cows from him. Bud was a little afraid the bull might charge, but one honk of the horn started him moving toward the ditch. Another honk started him running.

And as he ran, the bull's balls swayed from side to side like the clapper of a giant bell. As Bud watched the bull's balls retreat, he unconsciously scratched his own.

Soon Bud's truck was entering Spur. He was the only traffic on Main Street. As he passed the dying stores, he remembered stories his parents had told him about Spur in the days when they were growing up. Back in the twenties and thirties, families had driven their cars into Spur before dawn on Saturdays so they could find a place to park on Main Street. Once you had your parking place, then your car became your portable parlor where you could entertain friends during the day-long party that took place every Saturday the length and breadth of Main Street. But that Main Street party had been over for a long time now. It had moved to the city where Bud was going to look for it.

At the red light on Main Street, Bud, who was speeding again, did not even slow down because the traffic signal had been turned off for over a year now. Spur did not even have enough cars and trucks anymore to support a stoplight, but it still hung suspended over Main Street as a reminder of past glories, like a decoration won in a long-ago war.

Spur lasted less than the length of a country song on the radio. Soon Bud's hometown was only a jumble of low buildings in his rearview mirror. Then he saw the familiar sign cut in the shape of a spur:

YOU ARE NOW LEAVING
SPUR
POPULATION 2000

And that figure was actually too high, just another tall Texas brag. Bud's hometown was fast becoming as much an anachronism as the cowboy equipment for which it was named.

Bud was speeding past cotton fields again. The cotton stalks were stunted and emaciated. Every year the farmers told themselves that they would make a good crop if it would just rain. And every year it seemed to rain less than the year before. Every year the cotton stalks seemed smaller, like the town.

After Bud had been on the road for a couple of hours, he switched his radio from a fading Lubbock station to a swelling Abilene station. The change gave him a sense of making progress. The land rolling by outside still looked the same. The cotton was still stunted and the only trees were mesquites. His eyes gave him no encouragement, but his ears assured him that he was not standing still. He had moved from one place on the dial to another.

3

The Rich Valley

Once he began picking up the Houston radio stations, Bud became more and more anxious to reach this city that he could hardly imagine. He had been patient for hundreds of miles, but now he could actually hear the end of his journey, and he wanted it to be over. He speeded up to ninety. Soon he was passing shopping centers the size of Spur, then shopping centers bigger than Spur. All around him, the city gradually thickened. And he kept having to turn his radio down as he drew closer and closer to the source.

When he first saw the skyscrapers of downtown Houston in the distance, they looked as shiny and fresh and clean as stacks of new money. As long as they were small and far away, Bud liked to look at these new buildings, but as they began to loom closer and larger, he began to find them intimidating.

And then Bud realized that he was lost. With all the tall buildings rising around him, he could not tell north from south. All his life he had known which direction was which until now. Bud wished he could climb up on his windmill and look around and find himself, but he knew that even if he could have, the windmill would not have reached very far up these buildings. He tried to find the sun, which would have sorted out the directions for him, but he couldn't because the buildings were too high. From his pickup windows, the only sky he could see was reflected in the glass of the skyscrapers.

The headquarters of the oil companies rose around him like the walls of a glittering, expensive prison.

Struggling awkwardly, Bud tried to read a map and drive at the same time. Every street name was familiar and yet unfamiliar. The streets were named after the heroes and the battles of the Texas Revolution, which he had studied year after year in his Texas history classes. Travis. Fannin. Houston himself. San Jacento. Bud knew them historically but not geographically. He knew everything about them except where they went.

Pulling over to the side of the road, Bud stopped beside a fire hydrant. He sat there for a long time studying his map. He thought about asking directions, but his pride wouldn't let him. Besides, all the people on the street seemed to be wearing suits and carrying fancy briefcases. So Bud eased his truck back into the flow of traffic, still lost.

He finally stopped at a Roy Rogers fast-food drive-in that he happened on accidentally. It intimidated him less than the surrounding landscape. He bought a fried cherry pie and asked directions of a waitress in a white cowboy hat.

When he topped the great arching bridge on 610 that spans the Houston shipping channel, Bud saw his new home spread out before him in a vast panorama. His forefathers had had similar experiences as they had moved west. They had come up over mountains and seen rich valleys below where they would begin new lives in new homes on new land. But Bud, as he crested his concrete mountain, saw before him a shimmering landscape where ranches had been replaced by refineries all the way to the horizon. The trees had been cut down to make way for cat crackers. The ponds had been drained to make room for oil tanks. It was a very rich valley. Bud saw it, if anything, as a landscape spotted with jobs. His uncle had written him that there was plenty of work in these ugly, smelly petrochemical plants.

Shortly after he came down off the bridge, Bud saw the sign for the exit onto 225. Once he was on 225 headed east, he pulled over to the side of the road and stopped. He got out his uncle's letter again. It gave instructions on how to find the house from this point on. Bud read it twice, moving his lips the first time, and then drove on. He continued on down 225 for miles, past Charter Oil, past Arco, until he finally reached the Shell Refinery, where he turned right onto the

East Belt. In his rearview mirror, Bud saw the flare over Shell blazing like a bonfire at a high school pep rally. At St. Augustine Street, he turned right.

Uncle Bob and Aunt Corene lived in a new development off St. Augustine. Driving through this development, Bud heard the sound of power saws and power drills and concrete mixers. The whole neighborhood seemed still to be under construction. There had not been time to plant grass in the yards yet. Children played outside in the dirt. Bud was driving through a boomtown, like those that sprang up around railheads during the days of the cattle drives, like those that sprang up around mining claims during the gold rushes, and now this one was springing up at the foot of an oil refinery. Bud derived from all the buildings a sense of prosperity. In Spur, people occasionally did a little remodeling, but a new house had not been built in a long time.

Turning onto Westwood Drive, Bud started studying the numbers. He drove slowly down the instant street past all the instant houses, reading the addresses. Uncle Bob and Aunt Corene's house turned out to be the one on the very end, where the street stopped in an abrupt dead end. It was red brick, like all the others, with a gravel and tar roof, like all the others. All the houses in the new subdivision were as alike as cakes baked from the same mix. The shapes varied a little and so did the icing, but that was all. As Bud approached the house, the Shell flare seemed to hover over it like a pillar of fire leading him to his destination.

The place had a herd of vehicles parked out front. An old black Oldsmobile. A green pickup with a toolbox mounted on the back. A pickup with a camper. And a boat on a trailer. Bud pulled up in front, swelling the herd by one. He honked twice before getting out of his truck.

His Aunt Corene came hurrying out of her new house to meet him. He was her favorite nephew. She threw her arms around him and hugged him.

"Hurry up and get in here," Aunt Corene ordered. "We've been waitin' dinner on you."

Aunt Corene looked something like a Hereford cow, with that same broad, flat face and eyes wide apart. She had bovine breasts that now flattened out against Bud. She was his favorite aunt.

"How do you like my beard?" Bud asked.

"I hate it," Aunt Corene said.

"I knew you would."

Uncle Bob appeared in the doorway.

"Hey, Bud!"

"Hey, Uncle Bob!"

Uncle Bob was Bud's daddy's little brother. Whereas Bud's daddy had stayed hard and slim working the farm, Uncle Bob was growing a city beer belly. He had black hair that looked as if he lubricated it with some product produced at the refinery where he worked. He had a deep, affectionate laugh and a wonderful wink.

"I sure do like your new place," Bud said.

"Come on in," Uncle Bob said, "wait till you see the inside. It's got all the modern conveniences. Course I ain't never gonna get outa hock now—overextended myself real good this time."

And then the uncle laughed and the nephew laughed, too.

"How's ever'body back in Spur?" Aunt Corene asked. "Your mama all right?"

"Just fine," Bud said.

In spite of herself, Aunt Corene kept glancing down at Bud's truncated finger. And Uncle Bob kept noticing it, too. They knew all about the accident from letters, but they had never actually seen the results before. They both felt an urge to ask him if he was all right, but they didn't want to draw attention to his hand, didn't want to embarrass him. They said nothing.

"Hey, who's this?" Bud asked.

A redheaded girl about thirteen years old and a black-haired boy of three stood in the doorway.

"You remember Lou Sue," Uncle Bob said. "And that's Willie. I don't guess you ever did meet him. He's too new. Come on out here, kids, and say hello to your cousin Bud."

The cousins all shook hands. Lou Sue was at an age where she was too shy to say anything, but Willie wasn't.

"What's the matter with your finger?" Willie asked. "Somebody eat it all up?"

Willie's parents were always telling him that they were going to eat him all up. And they would put his fingers in their mouths, pretending to start there. Now his parents cringed at his question. And yet somehow they were still proud of him for being so observant.

"No," Bud said. "I was playing around with a windmill and got in an accident."

"What's a windmill?" asked Willie.

"It looks sorta like an oil derrick," Uncle Bob explained to his son. "Only it's got this big wheel on top that goes around when the wind blows. And it pumps water 'steada oil."

"Oh."

"Come on, let's eat," Aunt Corene said.

She led the way into the new house. Uncle Bob carried Bud's suitcase.

"We ain't decided yet where you're gonna sleep," Uncle Bob said. "We thought we'd let you make up your own mind. You can either sleep in the same room with Willie. Or you can sleep in the camper. We sorta think of that as our fourth bedroom."

"Camper sounds good to me."

No one talked much during dinner. Almost the only sound came from the television, which was still going in the living room although no one was watching it.

"You make real good chicken," Bud told his aunt. "It's real different somehow. But good."

Uncle Bob laughed his affectionate laugh, and then Aunt Corene started laughing, too. They shared a secret.

"What's the matter?" Bud asked. "Did I say something wrong?"

"No," Aunt Corene said. "It's just that we saw this funny ad on TV for a pressure cooker that makes chicken taste just like takeout. Now if that don't beat all. We both laughed. But then Bob went and bought me one for my birthday. The kids love it. And to tell the truth we do, too. But still . . ."

Bud ate four pieces, a drumstick, a thigh, a breast, and a wing. As he ate, he noticed that Willie kept watching the little finger on his right hand. But he didn't really mind. He was just glad finally to be where he was after a long day's drive.

"One more?" asked Aunt Corene.

"No, I cain't eat no more," Bud said. "I'm full."

"You must be tired, too?"

"Not really."

"No?"

It was Bud's first night in the big city. He had come a

long way to see what that city had to offer. And he was anxious to begin. But he was too polite to say so.

"Course he's not tired," laughed his Uncle Bob. "He didn't come all the way to Houston to be tired—did you, Bud?"

Bud shook his head.

4

The Saloon

Bud's black pickup followed his uncle's green pickup down the Spencer Highway past alternating fast-food places and car repair shops. Bud watched the silhouettes of his Uncle Bob and his Aunt Corene in the truck up ahead. He could tell that there was a lot of laughter as they rode along by the movement of their bodies. When they laughed, Bud smiled, as if not to be left out of a joke that he could not hear. He saw the green truck slowing down.

From the road, Gilley's Club looked like a shack nailed together out of unpainted boards. The only hint that it was something more came from the parking lot, which was so huge and so crowded that it looked like a mechanical trail drive—with thousands of cars and trucks and even semis bedded down for the night. Uncle Bob parked his green pickup at the edge of this great herd of iron beasts, and Bud pulled his black truck in alongside.

As they walked across the sprawling parking lot toward the entrance, they could not help overhearing an argument going on one row of cars over. Someone was warning someone else to stay away from his woman. And then the someone else told the someone to keep his woman away from him. The woman was crying.

"Just keep walkin'," Uncle Bob said. "And if they go to shootin', just fall to the ground."

And then the uncle laughed his affectionate laugh, so the nephew did not know whether to be frightened or amused or both. The parking lot was pockmarked by years of rains and even floods. No one had ever even considered paving it. Aunt Corene stumbled occasionally, and Bud did, too, once or twice. By the time they reached the entrance, the argument in the parking lot had developed into a fistfight.

"Five dollars each," said the young woman at the door.

"I got it," said Uncle Bob.

He handed the young woman a twenty and got back a five.

As Bud walked into Gilley's for the first time, his lips formed the words *Jesus Christ*, but he said nothing aloud. The honky-tonk, which looked like a shack on the outside, opened up into a vast indoor landscape that seemed to stretch on and on to the horizon, like the Great Plains brought indoors. The place had about fifty pool tables, which made it roughly equal to half a hundred dark bars under one low roof. It was as noisy as fifty bars, as energetic as fifty bars, as teaming as fifty bars. And Bud had just come from a town where there was only one honky-tonk with one pool table and one jukebox and one girl to dance with.

"Why, shit," Bud said, "this place is bigger'n my whole hometown."

"Yeah," said Uncle Bob, "I bet you could put Spur in here two or three times."

And in a sense, it was as though someone had. The honky-tonk was like a small West Texas town with everyone dressed in cowboy clothes—in boots, in jeans, in cowboy hats, in shirts with mother-of-pearl snaps, in belts with first names tooled on the back. It was as though that party that used to take place on Main Street in Spur every Saturday had somehow been moved to a Houston bar. Only the bar was more western—more cowboy—than Spur had ever been. It was less like Spur than it was like the Dodge City that Mat Dillon presided over in "Gunsmoke." Seeing all the other cowboy hats, Bud adjusted his own beat-up straw hat. He was glad his uncle had suggested that he wear it.

"What're you drinkin'?" Uncle Bob asked as they neared the long front bar.

"Bourbon and Coke," said Aunt Corene.

"Beer," Bud said.

"Lone Star all right?"

"Sure."

While they were waiting for their drinks, Bud read a sign suspended above the bar that proclaimed:

WELCOME
TO GILLEY'S CLUB
WORLD'S LARGEST NIGHT CLUB
THREE AND A HALF
ACRES OF CONCRETE PRAIRIE

There were other signs that advised patrons to be careful or they might have a good time. And another said that Gilley's had the warmest beer and the coldest waitresses in town. While he was reading, Bud felt Aunt Corene touch his arm. She wanted him to look at her instead of around.

"Bob and I used to come here back when it was just a concrete slab," she said. "And we'd *dance*. Lordy, that musta been fifteen years ago. Back before Lou Sue was born."

"Yeah, we did a big percentage of our courtin' right here," Uncle Bob said. "Why, one night we . . ."

"Now, Bob, he wouldn't be interested in that."

"Yeah, I would."

"Anyway, after we started a family," Aunt Corene said, "we sorta stopped comin' out."

"That was about when I started gettin' fat," Uncle Bob said with a laugh.

The bartender brought the drinks. Uncle Bob paid and then handed his nephew a long-necked bottle of Lone Star and his wife a bourbon and Coke in a plastic glass. He drank Lone Star, too. The drinks felt cool in their palms.

"Let's look around," Uncle Bob said.

As he followed his aunt and uncle through the crowd, Bud found himself feeling vaguely superior to the city cowboys—and vaguely afraid of them, too. On the one hand, they just wore country clothes, while he really was country. But on the other hand, this was their saloon in their city, and he was a newcomer, in a peculiar sense, a "tenderfoot." What made him real also set him apart. He had an awkward sense of not belonging, of not fitting in, of being conspicuous. It was as though everyone were staring at his stub of a finger—which he rubbed unconsciously—but actually no one did. Still, he was always on guard, almost expecting someone to come up and take a punch at him just because he was different.

And so he thought about his old straw hat. Thinking about it fueled his sense of superiority, which in turn dampened his apprehension. He was proud of his hat because it was so well broken-in, so sweat-stained, so hard-worked. The other straw hats, which bobbed and nodded about him, were too new, too clean, too crisp. These hats had obviously never done a day's work in their lives. Bud pulled the brim of his old hat down lower over his eyes. He liked it that way and it made him feel more secure.

When they reached the dance floor, Uncle Bob asked Aunt Corene if she wanted to dance. Soon Bud was left all alone. He tugged the brim of his hat down even lower. Then he decided to move closer to the stage where Mickey Gilley, who lent his name to the club, was singing to the slowly milling herd of dancers . . .

> Here comes the hurt again,
> You'd think I'd learn,
> The more I believe in love,
> The more I get burned . . .

As always in a honky-tonk, the dancers were forgetting their hurts by dancing to hurting music. Bud caught himself rubbing his little finger—and stopped.

As he watched the singer, Bud had a sense that someone was watching him. Looking around, he noticed a cowgirl standing about ten yards away who was quite simply staring at him. He glanced away and then glanced back. She was still staring. Bud found himself wondering if she was staring at him because she admired him or because she saw that he didn't belong. He didn't know whether to be flattered or embarrassed.

In the darkness of the bar, Bud could not see the cowgirl well enough to tell if she was pretty. But he could see that she was wearing a brown felt cowboy hat, which he thought was silly. Wearing a felt hat in the summertime just wasn't practical. It was too hot to work in. Bud judged her hat harshly—just in case she was judging him harshly—and felt better for it.

Even in the dark, Bud could not help noticing something else about the cowgirl, her eyes. In the half-light, they seemed almost demonic, like coyote eyes. It was because of those eyes that he started moving toward her, but then he heard his uncle calling to him.

"Bud, come on over here," Uncle Bob raised his voice. "Like you to meet somebody."

Bud walked over to where his aunt and uncle were standing with a cowboy in his late thirties or early forties. One of his front teeth was missing. And he was dressed in black from his felt hat down.

"Bud, this here's Steve Strange," Uncle Bob said. "Steve, this here's Bud. My nephew from Spur."

They shook hands.

"Glad to know you, Bud."

"Glad to know you, too, Steve."

"Take care of him, will you, Steve?" said Uncle Bob and then laughed his affectionate laugh, which sounded something like *haw, haw, haw, haw.*

"Sure, be glad to," said Steve, who then laughed, too, but his was more of a menacing laugh, *heh, heh, heh, heh.*

Steve Strange led Bud over to a group of regulars who showed up every night at the south end of the dance floor just as predictably as milk cows show up every evening at the barn. He motioned to a pretty girl with red hair and a T-shirt that proclaimed: COWGIRLS RIDE BETTER BAREBACK. Bud nodded and touched the brim of his beat-up straw hat. Steve introduced Bud to Shari and told her to take care of him, *heh, heh, heh, heh.* He said this new cowboy had just gotten into town from Spur.

"Where's Spur?" asked Shari.

At that moment, at the outermost edge of his peripheral vision, Bud noticed the cowgirl with coyote eyes walk up to a cowboy and unsnap his cowboy shirt all the way down the front in one motion. The cowboy reached for her shirt, but she was too quick for him. She disappeared into the cowboy crowd.

"Hey, I asked where's Spur?"

"West Texas."

Bud was surprised that she did not know.

5

The Lord's Day

Bud woke up to a radio preacher preaching a cowboy-church sermon on a country-and-western station. The minister said God watched over his children the way a cowboy watched over his herd. And so God always knew when one of his calves strayed. Bud reached out and his hand touched a breast. Raising up and opening his eyes, Bud found himself in a tangle of naked bodies. A nude cowboy lay on the floor, hugging a Justin boot in his sleep.

"He never sleeps," the radio preached. "He never nods in His saddle."

Climbing over bodies, Bud got his feet over the edge of the bed. He stood up and headed in the direction of the radio, which was in the other room. He walked through the door and found himself in a kitchen.

Shari, dressed in a loosely tied robe, was making coffee. Steve Strange, fully dressed in his black outfit, was sitting at the kitchen table sipping Pearl beer from a can. Bud stood in the doorway with his blue jeans in his hands. His underwear had been lost past all recovering.

"Hi, Bud," Shari greeted him.

Bud started trying to pull his pants on. He staggered against the doorjamb. He was embarrassed because he realized that Shari was staring at him the way he had stared at that bull in the road.

"Where'd you learn to do all that?" asked Shari.

"Heh, heh, heh, heh," laughed Steve.

"Farm animals," Bud said.

Bud had a cup of Shari's coffee.

A television preacher was preaching in Uncle Bob and Aunt Corene's new living room, but they were not paying him any attention. Uncle Bob was reading the Sunday funnies to little Willie. And Aunt Corene was talking on the telephone.

"No, Ethel, you cain't talk to your little boy just now," Aunt Corene said. " 'Cause he ain't here. Must still be at church, I guess."

She winked at her husband and he laughed, his happy belly making Willie bounce. Then they heard a pickup outside.

"Sounds like he just drove up," Aunt Corene said into the phone. "Hold on, I'll see."

She put the phone down and walked over to the living room window, where she peeked out through the venetian blinds. She saw Bud getting out of Steve Strange's pickup. And she wondered why he had needed help getting home. She returned to the phone.

"He'll be here in a minute."

When Bud entered the living room, it was obvious that he was in pain. He had been beaten up by a couple of bottles of tequila. His eyes were swollen and red, as if the Mexican cactus drink had landed real punches.

"It's your mama," said Aunt Corene. Then she covered the phone. "I told her you went to church."

"Oh, no, I promised to call," Bud said.

"I know."

Aunt Corene handed him the phone.

"Hi, Mama," Bud said as soberly as he could. "No, I'm fine . . . I know I promised, I'm sorry . . . No, I don't have a job yet, it's Sunday . . . Yes, ma'am . . . No, I didn't drive too fast . . . I gave her the field peas, I cain't help it if she didn't say nothin' about it . . ."

When he finally hung up the phone, Bud slumped in a living room chair.

"Get out the Alka-Seltzer," Uncle Bob told Aunt Corene. Then he asked, "Where you been, Bud?"

"I dunno," Bud said. "Cain't remember nothing. Lost my truck. I'll go back for it later."

"Your truck?"

"Yeah, no tellin' where I left it."

"You better lay down," Aunt Corene said.

"Yeah."

Bud got up and headed for the front door.

"Where you goin'?" Uncle Bob asked.

"Camper."

"You can lay down on a real bed in the house if you want to."

"Camper's fine."

"Just a minute. I'll have to unlock it."

The uncle accompanied his nephew out to the camper, which sat in the bed of an International Harvester pickup. When the door was unlocked, Bud crawled inside. The tiny room suited him this morning. It was like a shell. Uncle Bob left him.

But not long after, Bud heard a knock at the camper door. And then it opened. His Aunt Corene put her head in and handed him a bottle of Budweiser.

"This works better for me than alki," she said.

"Thanks," But said.

He raised up enough to take a sip and then collapsed backwards again.

"You gonna live?" asked Aunt Corene.

"I hope so," said Bud. Then he smiled for the first time that Sunday morning. "So I can do it again tonight."

When his aunt left, Bud lay on his back trying to pass out. He watched a fly crawl across the ceiling. He heard Willie playing cowboys and Indians in the front yard.

6

The Cowgirl with Coyote Eyes

Leaning back against the long front bar at Gilley's, Bud surveyed the wide-open indoor spaces. He was feeling a little better now. His hangover had almost passed. His uncle had helped him find his truck. He was a little more at ease with his surroundings on his second night in the honky-tonk. And he was ready to fall in love again. Sipping from a bottle of Lone Star, he watched the dancers glide by, the cowgirls dancing with their fingers hooked through the cowboys' belt loops, the cowboys dancing with the cowgirls' hair gripped in their right hands.

"Hey, Bud!" Steve Strange called from a dozen feet down the bar. "Anything I can do for you tonight, heh heh heh heh?"

"Not yet," Bud called back.

He smiled and shook his head. Then he took another sip of beer.

"Ever find your truck?"

"Yeah, it was over at the high school. Don't remember why."

Bud went on sipping and looking. He was not really looking for anyone in particular, but it had occurred to him that he might see Shari again. He scanned the acres of cowgirls but didn't see her. Still he couldn't be sure she wasn't there because she could easily be lost in the multitude.

26

The Sunday night crowd was almost as big as the one on Saturday night. Then he thought he saw her, but he was wrong. He was a little surprised to discover how disappointed he was.

While he was still looking for Shari, Bud saw the cowgirl with the coyote eyes coming toward him. And she was staring at him as she came. Once again, Bud's emotions alternated—as uncertain as a broken weather vane—between being flattered and being embarrassed. He had thought he had gotten over feeling out of place until he saw her coming toward him. Now he was back on guard. He tugged the brim of his hat down lower over his eyes, a honky-tonk knight adjusting his visor.

As she got closer, Bud saw that she was nice-looking. She had freckles, long curly brown hair, and aggressive breasts that thrust themselves forward. She was not beautiful, but she was as cute as a saying on a T-shirt. Bud was glad she was pretty, and yet her looks made her more of a threat. In the dim light, her eyes now seemed disembodied golden globes. He wondered what they saw.

When she reached the bar, she put her elbows on it and rested for a moment. She seemed simply to have come to order a drink, after all. Then she looked up at him.

"You a real cowboy?" she asked.

Bud was relieved and flattered by the question. He told himself that she had seen that he was different but that she had understood the meaning of that difference. She saw that he was real country, while the others were just playing at being country. But being country was slightly different from being a real cowboy. He thought the question over.

"Depends on what you think a real cowboy is," Bud said.

"Know what?" she asked.

"No."

"If I was you, I'd get me a new hat."

"Who asked you!"

She had wounded him in his pride, his hat. Now he could see how wrong he had been about her. She didn't see and appreciate what he was. She just saw that he didn't belong. She had been laughing at him all along. Embarrassed, he turned away from her and rubbed his little finger.

"Know how to two-step?" asked the cowgirl with the critical coyote eyes.

"Yeah," he said.

"Wanta prove it?"

"Well, all right."

He followed her to the edge of the dance floor. Before he reached for her, he put his bottle of Lone Star in his hip pocket. She hooked the index finger of her left hand through a belt loop on the side of his jeans. And he took hold of her hair. They danced the cowboy two-step.

"Ever'body calls me Sissy," Sissy said.

"They call me Bud," Bud said.

"My real name's Priscilla. What's yours?"

"Well, my whole name's Buford Uling Davis. See, my initials spell out Bud. B.U.D. That's where I got the nickname."

Along with all the other dancers, Bud and Sissy moved in a giant circle around the dance floor. Most of the time, he moved foward while she moved backward. That was the cowboy way.

"You ain't married or nothin'?" Sissy asked.

"No, ma'am," Bud said. "How 'bout you?"

"Nope, me neither. But I was engaged once. Just didn't work out. Twang, twang."

"Huh?"

"Oh, that's just somethin' that fellow I was engaged to used to say. He played guitar in a country band, just on weekends. And he got where he liked to talk like his guitar. When you'd say somethin' reminded him of a country song—you know, somethin' sad—he'd say *twang, twang*. Guess I picked it up from him."

"Oh."

When the music ended, and cowgirls and cowboys started separating, having been friends for a dance, this tide tugged at Bud and Sissy. They both considered moving away from each other, but neither of them wanted to. Sissy let go of Bud's belt loop but then reached out for it again. He wanted to reach out and take her hair but instead he reached for her with words.

"How long you lived in Houston?" he asked.

He hadn't known what else to say.

"All my life," she said.

"I just got here."

"That's what I figured."

Bud took a half step away from Sissy, and her finger slid from his belt loop. Her *figured* made him once again feel like an outsider. The coyote eyes had seen right away that he was not a member of the pack.

"Why?"

"Oh, because I hadn't seen you in here before. Besides, you look real different."

"You mean my hat?"

"That's part of it."

"What's wrong with my hat?"

Bud took another half step away. And he looked around. He was looking for Shari.

"It's too dirty," Sissy explained. "But that's not what I mean. It's not just your hat. It's you. I don't like your hat, but I like you."

Bud looked back down at Sissy. He smiled.

"You're real direct, ain'tcha?"

She nodded.

"I like a direct person."

"Know how to cotton-eyed Joe?"

The fiddle music was just starting. It signaled a stampede toward the dance floor. Soon Bud and Sissy were being jostled. Twice as many people wanted to dance the cotton-eyed Joe as had wanted to two-step. Lines began forming. Sissy, who knew everyone, was soon drawn into a line, and she drew Bud after her. They were all kicking and screaming.

On the bandstand, the fiddle player yelled into the microphone: "Stepped in what?"

And the dancers bellowed back: "Bullshit!"

He asked: "Smelled like what?"

And they told him: "Bullshit!"

He said: "The hell you say."

With the floor so crowded and everyone pushing and shoving as they danced, Bud felt as if he were about to be trampled. And yet he was not afraid, not of being overrun or of anything else. That sense of being the one who did not belong in the pack had lifted, for the moment at least. He hugged Sissy to him. *Stepped in what*? Bud yelled as loud as he could: "BULLSHIT!" *Smelled like what*? And he heard Sissy yell in deep, almost masculine voice: "BULLSHIT!" *The hell you sa*y. He loved shouting it: "BULLSHIT!" And he loved hearing her shout it: "BULLSHIT!" He was somehow very moved and all he could say, all he wanted to say, was *bullshit, bullshit, bullshit*.

After the cotton-eyed Joe, the band slowed down to play another two-step, another sad one. This time Bud and Sissy did not consider drifting apart. She hooked herself to him. And he took hold of her as the singer sang:

> *I was lookin' for love*
> *In all the wrong places . . .*

Now Bud wanted to say something more than "bullshit," but he could not think of what. They spun into a turn.

> *Lookin' for love*
> *In too many faces . . .*

He might have said something about her eyes, but they still made him a little nervous. He might have said something about her breasts—and would have if he had been as direct as she was—but he was too shy.

"You got nice hair," Bud whispered, gripping a fistful of it tightly.

"Thanks," Sissy said. "I wear it long 'cause my daddy loves long hair. He's got TB. I don't plan to cut it till my daddy dies. Twang twang."

"You say that a lot."

"Uh-huh, I know. It's just the way I feel a lotta the time."

" 'S that how you feel now?"

The demon eyes looked up.

"No."

As they spun and turned again, Bud saw Shari standing alone under a light. She was waiting for someone to ask her to dance.

> *Hopin' to find*
> *A friend and a lover . . .*

Bud could see that Shari was prettier than Sissy. He felt disloyal for making the comparison, but he made it anyway.

> *I bless the day I discover*
> *Another heart lookin' for love . . .*

Shari's beauty tugged at him, but he went on dancing
with Sissy. Shari couldn't frighten him. Sissy could. She
looked up at him and her eyes seemed to float toward him
in the dark.

By two o'clock in the morning, the honky-tonk was
almost a ghost town. The air conditioning had been turned
off and the band had gone home. A few couples still sat at
rickety tables, finishing their last drinks. But Sissy still wanted
to dance. Bud followed her to a jukebox. She knew what
she wanted to play, but she had trouble getting out her quarters because her jeans were so tight. When she finally succeeded, she inserted the money and pushed A-24.

> *I grew up a dreamin' of bein' a cowboy,*
> *Lovin' the cowboy ways.*
> *Pursuing the life of my high-ridin' heroes,*
> *I burned up my childhood days . . .*

Sissy no longer held Bud's belt loop, she held him. And
he no longer held her hair, he held her. They danced with
their arms around each other and their bodies against each
other.

> *I learned all the rules of the modern day drifter.*
> *Don't you hold onto nothin' too long.*
> *Just take what you need from the ladies,*
> *Then leave them, with the words*
> *Of the sad country song.*

They danced with his leg between hers. The night crew
was already beginning to clean up. The rattle of their mop
buckets blended with the music of the song.

> *My heroes have always been cowboys,*
> *And they still are it seems.*
> *Sadly in search of, and one step in back of,*
> *Themselves and their slow-moving dreams.*

While the jukebox and the buckets played, Bud realized
that he was going to kiss Sissy, but he wasn't sure just how

because her hat was in the way. The hat would not make a kiss impossible, but it would make it awkward, that damn felt hat.

"I don't like your hat either," Bud said.

And he reached and took it off her head. Then he held it behind her back so he could go on hugging her.

"But I like you."

He kissed her. And she kissed him back. It was a long kiss because she wouldn't let go, not that he wanted her to. She opened her mouth and seemed to draw him down into her. And he was drawn gladly. While he was still kissing her, he opened his eyes long enough to see wide coyote eyes staring at him.

7

Climbing Texas History

By the time Bud and Sissy walked out into the parking lot, most of the mechanical herd had moved on. Only a few maverick pickups and stray cars dotted the rutted field. The couple paused for a moment under a giant lighted sign that said: WELCOME TO GILLEY'S. The apostrophe was a musical note. While they were standing there, someone turned off the sign and it went dark.

"Sure you don't need a ride?" Bud asked.

"Nope, I got my own car right over there," Sissy said.

But neither of them moved from beneath the sleeping sign.

"Where do you live?" he asked.

"With my mom and dad," she said.

"Oh."

"Where do you live? Got your own place?"

"Not yet. I'm staying with my aunt and uncle till I do."

"Twang twang."

"Huh?"

"Well, see, we wouldn't have no place to go even if I did need a ride."

"Guess not."

She leaned over and bit his arm. It only hurt a little.

"Come on, let's go," she said.

"Where?" he asked.

She rode with him to show him the way. They drove back down the Spencer Highway, past all the fast foods and car repairs. Then they took the East Belt to 225, turning right at Shell. They kept going until they came to a beer joint named The Barn, where they turned left. This road led them onto the almost sacred ground where the Battle of San Jacento had been fought over a hundred years ago, where Sam Houston's small army had defeated Santa Anna's hordes, where Texas had won her independence. Now the battleground was a park where people with no place to go often went at night. On this marshy ground, the nation of Texas was born and many later generations of Texans had been conceived. The San Jacento Monument, a huge stone tower with a star on top, dominated the park. As they approached this monument on a narrow paved road, Bud studied it. He had seen pictures of it in all his Texas history books, but now he was seeing *it* for the first time.

"Looks sorta like a crackin' tower," Bud said.

"That ain't all it looks like," Sissy said.

They both laughed.

"Why don't you park down by the reflectin' pool," she suggested.

Lovers gravitate toward water as if moistness had a special attraction for them. Love loves liquids—lakes, rivers, reflecting pools, secretions. Bud parked his truck.

"You never did tell me where you're from," Sissy said.

Bud put his arm around her and she relaxed against him.

"Spur," he said. "Ever hear of it?"

"No, what's it near?"

"Well, Lubbock's seventy miles away. Ever since the drive-in blew over, that's the nearest show."

Bud was playing with the hair that Sissy's father loved. And he was wondering if he dared unsnap her cowboy shirt. Snaps were so nice and easy they were almost like automatic transmission. He thought automatic transmission was just plain too easy, but he wasn't sure Sissy's snaps would be.

"How come Spur?" Sissy asked.

"What?"

"How come you lived in Spur? I been through a lotta little towns like that. And I always wondered how the people got there."

" 'Cause my folks do."

"And how come they do?"

In a sense, Bud was thankful for the question. It gave him something to think about besides those maddening snaps.

"Well, it was my great-granddaddy that come to Spur. He used to live in Sterling County. That's where he grew up."

"Uh-huh."

"But one day ridin' home he comes across a stray cow. So he roped it and tied it to a tree. And then he went to get his brothers to help him drive it home. But when he got back to the cow with his brothers, he found the cow's owner and a lotta the owner's friends. They gave my great-granddaddy and his brothers a choice—a rope or the road."

"You've told this story before."

"Yeah."

"Go on."

"Well, that's when my family headed for Spur."

Sissy thought the story over, trying to sift out the meaning.

"So your great-granddaddy was a real cowboy," she said at last.

Bud reached for the snaps. Sissy's shirt popped open like a cotton boll in late summer, but her expression did not change at all. She wore no bra. Bud put his hand out and his fingers closed around a breast the way his great-granddaddy's rope had encircled a cow that did not belong to him. But the owner did not complain. She did not flinch. She did not pull away. The expression on her face did not even record the encroachment. Bud told himself that he had never met anyone like Sissy before. She guarded her breasts the way an apple tree guards its apples, which is not at all.

"What's your—*oh*—daddy do?" asked Sissy.

The *oh* was her first comment on the massaging of her breasts. Still she didn't flinch. She simply responded involuntarily when he gently rotated her right nipple.

"He's a cotton farmer," Bud said, his voice coarsening. "And he drives a school bus to make a little extra."

Bud was so intent upon Sissy's nipples that he did not notice the first change in her expression. She was a little disappointed.

"My daddy's—*oh*—got a wrecking yard," Sissy said. And then she added proudly, "My great-granddaddy was a blacksmith."

Bud gently eased the cowboy shirt back off Sissy's shoulders. Again, she did not resist in any way. It was not like undressing a mannequin because she was somehow warm and encouraging without ever moving. She conveyed to him that she expected him to undress her, that she liked it, that she wanted it, all the while totally still except for her eyes. Bud sensed that she was a cowgirl who did not flinch at anything, *ever*. It excited him and it intimidated him. When you are given the license to do anything, it can be a rather disturbing challenge.

Then Sissy did react, at last. She put her hand on his crotch, not to excite him, but to see if he was excited. Satisfied, she pulled her hand away.

"Know what we used to do?" Sissy asked.

"No," Bud said in a whisper.

"We used to climb the letters on the monument."

"What?"

"I'll show you."

And suddenly the cowgirl who didn't move was all action. She flung open the door of the pickup, jumped out, and went running along the reflection pool toward the monument—wearing nothing on the top half of her body. The rush of night air turned her nipples even harder as she ran.

After a stunned moment, Bud ran after her. He caught up with her easily, but he did not try to stop her. He wanted to see where she would go and what she would do. He ran beside her, watching her breasts jump on her chest, playful as coyote cubs.

"What the hell's goin' on?" Bud asked.

"I told you I'd show you," Sissy explained.

As they ran up the stairs, the breasts that never flinched jumped higher than ever. Bud wanted to reach out and touch them as he ran. He felt that she would let him. But he didn't. They were not still until they reached the very base of the monument.

Sissy just stood there for an instant looking up. Then she started climbing up the sheer vertical face of the granite. Her ladder was the writing that had been carved deep into the rock. She put the sharp toe of her boot in the S in SANTA ANNA while she dug her fingers into the U in SAM HOUS-TON. Then she pulled herself up one "rung." And as she did so, her breasts pressed against the cold granite and she said, "Oh."

Bud watched Sissy step up to the E in TEXAS while she reached up to the J in SAN JACENTO. She ascended another "rung." And she kept going, up and up, climbing from the I in INDEPENDENCE to the G in BATTLEGROUND, from the *X* in MEXICO to the *V* in VICTORY, from the *L* in GLORIOUS to the first *E* in HEROES. And all the way, her nipples rubbed along the granite, occasionally finding momentary shelter in the groove of a letter. Her legs spread wide in climbing, her body pressed close against the writing, it was as though Sissy were making love not just to the tower but to Texas history itself.

Sissy was almost eight feet off the ground before Bud started after her. He was confident that he could catch up with her because he did not see how climbing a monument could be that much more difficult than climbing a windmill. And he had plenty of practice at that. But climbing history turned out to be harder than he had imagined. It required a knack and he had no previous experience. He tried to hurry and only succeeded in having the tip of his boot slip out of the *A* in WAR. He almost fell. He was forced to climb methodically while all the time Sissy rose higher above him.

"Hey, wait for me," Bud called.

"At the top," Sissy said.

When she reached a ledge, she did sit down and wait for him. There was no more history to climb. The rest of the way up to the star the granite was a sheer, impossible wall, unbroken by the word. Sissy stared down at Bud's struggles. She was touched by his doggedness.

"We started climbin' up here when we was in grade school," Sissy said. "I ain't tried it in years. I wondered if I still could."

When Bud reached her at last, Sissy gave him a hand up onto the ledge. And then they sat there side by side, the cowboy and the bare-breasted cowgirl, brightly lit by floodlights meant to illuminate Texas's glorious past. In the glare, they kissed and Bud reached for the unflinching breasts. He dusted them off. Bud was happy and excited and a little ashamed that he hadn't climbed better. He wanted to impress Sissy.

Relaxing back against the monument, Bud put his truncated little finger in his mouth. The contact with the granite on the climb up made the finger tingle. Sissy saw what he did, but she did not ask any questions. And Bud saw that she saw, but he did not offer any explanation. He was shy about his injury. Now he wished that he had resisted the urge to soothe the finger—since she had noticed—but he went right on sucking.

And as he sucked, Bud studied the panorama all around

him. He looked at the reflection pool that stretched below him. Then he lifted his gaze to the darkened trees of the park. Then he raised his eyes to the refineries along the black horizon. Then he looked back at Sissy's breasts.

Bud was surprised to discover how large they looked in the glare of the floodlight. In the darkened pickup, they had appeared small. But on the bright monument ledge, they were huge. It was as though they had grown during the climb. It almost seemed that Sissy could change the size of her breasts the way she changed the size of her eyes, now squinting, now large and round and dramatic.

"Let's go back down," Bud said.

"All right," Sissy agreed.

"Any easier climbin' down than climbin' up?"

"Harder."

This time, Bud led the way, stepping on HEROES, grasping VICTORY, descending onto SAM HOUSTON and SANTA ANNA. Although he had a head start, Sissy easily caught up with him and passed him on the way down. She waited for him at the base of the monument.

"I'll race you to the truck," Sissy challenged.

"Okay," Bud agreed.

As they ran back along the reflecting pool, Bud was surprised at how fast Sissy could run. He could run faster but it required an effort. Since she was behind him most of the way, he could not really see her, but he imagined how her changeable breasts were behaving during the race. When he touched the fender of the truck, he spun around and she ran into his arms at almost full speed.

"Okay, you won that one," she said.

Breathing hard, they climbed back into the cab of the pickup. He sat behind the wheel while she lay down with her head in his lap as if to rest. Bud reached down and unzipped her blue jeans. Sissy did not flinch. Then he tried reaching inside. Still she did not resist, but the jeans themselves did. They held her so tightly that there was no room for his probing fingers. But he did descend far enough to make a discovery.

"You don't have on no panties," Bud said.

"I've got some," Sissy said, "but I don't ever seem to get around to puttin' none on."

Bud continued his struggle.

"Goddamn pants," he complained with a slightly embarrassed laugh. "They're too damn tight."

"I know," she said seriously, "but that makes it all the more excitin' once you get in."

When he decided it was time to move to the back, Bud picked Sissy up in his arms, like a groom gathering up a bride, and lifted her over the tailgate instead of the threshold. Returning to the cab of the pickup, he reached behind the seat and removed a sleeping bag. He tossed it into the back. And then he, too, vaulted into what is generally called the bed of the pickup.

Sissy helped him unroll the sleeping bag and spread it out, helped him make the bed. When they were done, she tore open all the snaps down the front of his cowboy shirt in a single motion. They lay down together. And he felt what SAM HOUSTON and SANTA ANNA had felt, her bare breasts pressed against him. Then Bud got to his knees and finished undressing her, pulling off her boots and peeling off her jeans. The jeans were so tight that at first her pubic hair looked as if it had been ironed on, like a decal.

Sissy lay on her back, waiting for him, but before he made love to her, he felt he had to explain. He lay down next to her and held up his injured right hand against the night sky. They both studied the silhouette with its one irregular feature. But had tried to be careful not to touch Sissy with his half-lost finger because he was afraid it might frighten her. But now, at this last moment before they became lovers, he felt he owed her more than just keeping his flawed flesh from pressing her unflawed skin. He felt he had to show her his injury and explain it to her—in case she did not want to make love to a cripple.

"I know you've been lookin' at my finger," Bud whispered.

"You've been lookin' at me, too," Sissy said.

"It happened over a year ago."

"What happened?"

"A windmill cut it off."

"I'm sorry."

He turned his hand slowly and his fingers rotated against the night sky like the blades of a windmill.

"I know it's ugly."

"No."

"But it never touched you."

"You thought I was worried about that?"

"And it never will."

Sissy reached up and took Bud's hand in both of her hands. She pulled it down out of the night sky and hugged it to her breast.

"I love your hand," she said. "I love when it touches me. It makes me feel pretty. I love all of it."

And then she raised his hand to her lips. She kissed the palm and each finger in turn, ending with the injured finger. Now Bud—who had been afraid of making her shudder—shivered. He closed his eyes because he was afraid to watch and opened them again because he could not stand not to see. He was more afraid of his injury than she was.

"See, I love it."

She put the half-ruined finger in her mouth and sucked on it. He tried to withdraw it, but she held him firm. He was a little afraid of someone who was so unafraid. And yet he was touched by what he saw as her kindness and her courage. He felt her tongue playing over his scars.

"Thank you," he said.

She actually bit him. And he withdrew his finger.

"Don't ever thank me," she said, "not when we're in bed."

"I just . . ."

"I know."

Sissy took Bud's hand again and lowered it down her body.

"I love it," she said.

And she pressed the injured finger through her pubic hair, between the lips, and into her.

8

The Refinery

When Bud entered the big front gate of the refinery the next morning, he instinctively measured the rows and rows of metal towers against the windmill back home. These towers were taller. Which made him smaller. The refinery itself was bigger than his daddy's farm. It was more like a small ranch with metal trees (cracking towers), metal underbrush (tangled pipes), and metal lakes (giant oil tanks). Bud parked his black truck beside his uncle's green truck in the huge parking lot and got out.

"Sure stinks," Bud said.

"Pay don't, though," his Uncle Bob said.

Following his uncle toward the administration building, Bud looked up at a giant winged horse, as big as a pickup, which hovered over the refinery. It reared high on its hind legs at the top of the tallest cracking tower in the plant. This was the flying red horse, the Mobil Oil Company's old trademark, which was now almost extinct, having been replaced by a new logo. It had been removed from filling stations across the land, but it continued to find a home at the refinery. It was as though the metal horse had been put out to pasture on this metallic range. Bud remembered the flying horse that had stood in front of the station back home years ago. When he was a boy, he had dreamed of riding it.

Uncle Bob held open the door for Bud. Inside, they passed a glass cabinet filled with safety awards and bowling trophies before they came to the receptionist. She made a

41

call, and then a short man with a military bearing came out to meet them.

"Hi, Bob," said George Bradley, extending his hand. "This the boy you told me about?"

"That's right," Uncle Bob said. "Sure appreciate your seein' him."

"Any time."

Uncle Bob introduced Bud to the superintendent, then left the two alone. The superintendent gave Bud a job application to fill out. He hated forms because he wasn't very good at them. He had to ask the secretary several times what information was wanted in different blanks. Then he had a terrible time finding his Social Security Card. When he had finally finished filling out the sheet of paper on both sides, he returned it to the receptionist, who looked it over and then showed him into the superintendent's office.

"Sit down," the superintendent said.

The words sounded like a military command. George Bradley was less warm to Bud alone than he had been when Uncle Bob was there. He sat down behind his desk and studied the application with a sergeant's scowl. While he did so, Bud turned his old straw hat around and around in his hands.

"They call you Buford?" the superintendent asked without looking up.

"No," the applicant said, "they call me Bud. See, that's what my initials spell out. Buford Ul—"

"I can spell," the superintendent cut him off.

Bud was crushing the already crushed brim of his hat. The superintendent kept studying the application.

"I don't like to do this," the superintendent said with a military frown. "Play favorites. It's just not the way we operate around here. But your uncle's a good man, been here a long time. So I'm gonna make an exception. I reckon we can use you if you really want to work." Then the superintendent looked up for the first time and glared at the young man who needed a job. "You know what a 'go-fer' is, Bud?"

"I s'pose it means you go fer things," Bud said seriously. Then he added with a nervous laugh, "Or else you're an animal."

"Well, around here," the superintendent said without a smile, "they're right on about the same level."

The superintendent turned Bud over to a foreman named Ray Slater, who walked him over to the shop, which looked like a huge hangar. Inside, the dozens of workers were dwarfed by the size of the gigantic building. They looked like Santa's elves busy constructing toys that were as big as or bigger than themselves. There were valve toys and furnace toys and pump toys. Once again, Bud was feeling the outsider. He tried hard to look as if he belonged, but he knew he didn't.

"The first thing you'll have to do," said Ray as they walked along, "is lose that beard."

On his first day, of all days, Bud wanted to make his new foreman like him. He wanted to be accepted. And yet he cared about Sissy liking him—about being accepted by her—much more than he cared about any boss. And she liked him in a beard. She had parked with a bearded cowboy and had made love to a bearded cowboy. What if she didn't like her cowboy without a beard? What if she didn't like his face? Bud had to risk displeasing someone, and he chose the foreman.

"Why?" Bud asked. "There are lots of guys with beards."

There were. The shop was spotted with beards. Most of them showed more signs of pruning than his did, but he wouldn't mind trimming his beard. He just did not want to shave it off completely.

"They don't work on my crew," Ray said. "There's a washroom and a razor right through that door."

They stopped walking while Ray pointed.

"But . . ."

"But nothing. I just plain don't like beards. First of all, you boys only grow 'em to chase girls. And then you come to work tired all the time. And second, they're dangerous. If you ever have to wear a gas mask, a beard gets in the way."

Bud just stood there thinking about Sissy.

"You make up your own mind," Ray said. "You want a job or you want a beard. I don't give a damn."

The foreman abruptly walked away from Bud. Bud hesitated for a moment and then headed toward the washroom. He told himself that he could not afford to be in love with Sissy, or anyone else, unless he had a job. Besides, he would lose his truck.

The washroom was a tiny cell that kept taking more and

more dirt from the workers without ever getting rid of any. It washed an army but no one ever washed it. Staring into the smudged mirror, Bud took a last nostalgic look at Sissy's bearded cowboy lover.

In the medicine cabinet behind the mirror, Bud found a pair of scissors and a crusted razor. He went to work with the scissors first, mowing his beard as if it were hay on his father's farm, black hay. His beard fell in the dirty sink beneath him. It fell on the dirty floor. It fell down the front of his work shirt and added to his discomfort. It itched.

And the face below came slowly into a fuzzy focus. The eyes were not at all sure that they liked the face out of which they now stared. With the beard falling away, the nose seemed to grow larger. Bud wondered if Sissy could ever love such a huge nose. Actually, of course, Bud's nose was a normal size, but its relative weight on his face had changed. To Bud it looked as prominent as the lone chimney of an abandoned house that still stands long after the walls have collapsed.

After washing the caked razor as well as he could, Bud touched it to his face and stroked gently. In the wake of the razor, his skin was almost as white as the shaving cream. He thought his skin looked dead. He wondered if Sissy could ever bear to kiss dead flesh.

When he finished shaving, Bud looked in the mirror and saw an unfamiliar face, half tan and half white, with a large nose, and a moustache. He had not been able to bring himself to remove this last reminder of his bearded days. He hoped Sissy would like it. Perhaps it would make him seem less changed.

Bud dried a stranger's face and went out to face all the other strangers. Emerging from the washroom, he saw Ray over in the far corner of the huge shop. Now Bud was suddenly more interested in how everyone looked. He noticed for the first time that Ray had a ravaged red nose, which he probably owed to alcohol. The new face walked in the direction of the tired old one. And the closer he came, the uglier that other face grew, in part because a scowl was deepening.

"Are you deliberately tryin' to make me mad," Ray said while Bud was still ten feet off.

"No, sir," Bud said.

"I thought I told you to *shave*."

"I did."

"You know what I mean."

The other members of the crew chuckled as Bud instinctively raised his hand to his moustache to stroke it. Their laughter embarrassed him. Bud was almost glad to be able to escape back into the dirty washroom. When he finished shaving, his upper lip tingled and felt too big. He was going to have to learn to wear his face all over again.

"Fix him up with some gear," Ray ordered when he returned.

"Say, 'New Hire,' come with me," said a worker just a little older than Bud.

"My name's Bud," he said, putting out his hand as they walked toward the tool shed. He didn't like being called "New Hire."

"I'm Marshall," said the boyish old hand.

Marshall had sandy hair, a handsome face, and a body built like an oak tree. Bud was more like pine. They studied each other in the shadowy tool shed.

"Let's start from the top and work down," Marshall said in a voice that was much louder than necessary. When he talked, he always seemed to be on the verge of shouting. "Here's your hat."

Marshall handed Bud a gray hard hat. When Bud tried it on, it was too small, so Marshall showed him how to adjust the band inside to make it fit. As soon as the hard hat was settled comfortably on his head, Bud felt more as if he belonged.

"Put these on," Marshall said.

He handed over a pair of goggles that looked like aviator glasses with totally reflective convex lenses. Bud raised them to his face, set them on his nose, hooked them over his ears. Then he stared out through the mirrored goggles at Marshall, who was also wearing mirrored goggles. The facing mirror lenses reflected each other infinitely, like the mirrors opposite each other in the barbershop back home in Spur. Bud saw himself in Marshall's eyes—and laughed.

"What's so funny?" Marshall shouted.

"I look like a grasshopper," said Bud.

"No, you don't. You look like something from outer space."

"I like that better."

"This goes over your nose and mouth."

Marshall handed Bud a kind of cup that fit over his face

like a surgeon's mask. It was made of a porous plastic. And it was held in place by elastic straps.

"That's a fresh-air mask," Marshall explained. "It'll keep the foam glass from gettin' in your lungs."

"What's foam glass?" Bud asked.

"You'll see. How's it feel?"

"Funny."

"Wear it a while. You'll get used to it."

"You'll also need a tool belt and some tools," Marshall said.

Soon Bud had a leather tool belt strapped around his waist like a gun belt—weighted down with a hammer and a hacksaw instead of six-guns. He liked the snug feel of it. Like that hat, it gave him more of a sense of belonging. He felt more secure, almost as if he really were armed.

"That oughta do it for right now," Marshall shouted.

Staring into Marshall's mirror eyes, Bud studied his new armor. He looked like a modern knight or some old crustacean.

"Oh, better take some gloves," Marshall said, tossing him a pair. "Now let's go."

Leaving the tool shed, Bud returned to face Ray with his new refinery face. Ray scowled but found nothing to criticize.

"Show him how to cut foam glass," the foreman told Marshall.

Bud followed Marshall to a workbench covered with what looked like a gray styrofoam. It was actually foam glass insulation—a kind of fiber glass—which had to be cut into just the right shapes and sizes to cover a tower that was being refurbished.

"This here's nasty stuff," Marshall warned in a loud voice.

Marshall showed Bud how to measure, mark, and saw the foam glass.

As he sawed, Bud could not help spraying himself with a fine sawdust that was actually ground glass. It worked its way inside his shirt. It got in his hair. It got on his face. It touched him everywhere. He scratched. That ground the glass deeper into his skin. He scratched again.

"Just makes it worse," Marshall warned.

"I cain't help it," Bud said.

Bud could feel that oil work was different from farm work. For farm work only took a part of you, your hands,

your arms, your back, sometimes your legs, but it left other
parts of you to yourself. But the refinery took all of him,
even to his very skin. It seemed to invade every cell without
even an apology, because it owned every cell. Every cell
itched.

Bud took off his hat and scratched. The top of his head
itched. He took off his goggles and rubbed his eyes. His eye-
balls itched in spite of the mirrors that were supposed to protect them. He scratched his arms and his legs. He scratched
his ass and his crotch. The ground glass seemed to be slicing
away at his balls. He even felt that the glass dust had passed
through the fresh-air mask into his lungs and his throat, but
there was no way to scratch them.

Ray Slater walked over and watched Bud saw and
scratch. The new hire tried to do more sawing and less
scratching with the foreman studying him, but he did not
succeed very well. He reached down and scratched his crotch
again.

"How you doin'?" asked the foreman in an accusing
tone.

"Not too good," Bud said. "This here foam glass is eatin'
me up."

"Course it is," Ray said, " 'cause you're jumpin' on it like
it was pussy. Ease up, for Christ's sake. And you'll ease up
on the pussy, too, if you're smart."

Bud glared angrily at Ray from behind his mirrored
goggles. The foreman, like the foam glass, chafed him. And
he began to feel that he would eventually have to scratch,
even if it did make it worse.

At lunchtime, Uncle Bob sought Bud out. They left the
shop together and walked out into the blinding Texas sunshine. They were both dirty by now.

"Your Aunt Corene's gonna be happy," Uncle Bob said.

"About what?" Bud asked.

"The beard."

"Oh, yeah."

Carrying their lunches—Uncle Bob's in a tin lunch box,
Bud's in a brown paper sack—they walked between the tow-
ers. Looking up at them, Bud was reminded of the San
Jacinto Monument.

"How're you gettin' along?" Uncle Bob asked.

"All right," Bud lied.

Uncle Bob led the way to where a dozen workers were eating lunch inside a small pen. It looked as though the men had been rounded up in a corral. Actually, the fenced-off area was simply for smokers. In a refinery, it can be dangerous to light up just anywhere. All the workers had come there of their own free will instead of being driven there like cattle. Or rather their habit had driven them. Uncle Bob lit up a cigar. Bud didn't smoke. He was just there for the company.

"Place sure is noisy," Bud said.

"Yeah," Uncle Bob agreed.

They both raised their voices to be heard above the constant roar of the refinery. It sounded like a jet plane that was always warming up its engines but never took off. Inside the shop, Bud's ears had been protected from the sound, but out in the open he was constantly assaulted. Perhaps the greatest difference between his life before and his life after was this: a farm is always quiet, a refinery never is.

"What makes all that racket?" yelled Bud.

"Oh, about a hundred fires," Uncle Bob yelled back.

"Huh?"

"Look at them towers over there." He pointed with a half-eaten sandwich in his right hand. "See them fires at the bottom?"

"Yeah."

Bud could see the fires glowing through iron gates at the base of the great towers. He had always associated fires with quiet settings—the peacefulness of a campfire, the snugness of a fireplace. But what he heard all around him was a caged inferno.

"Well, that's a big part of your noise right there," said Uncle Bob with a mouthful of bologna and bread and mayonnaise.

"What's it for?" shouted Bud.

"Basically," his uncle said and then swallowed, "what them towers are doin' is separatin' the various differ'nt products from the crude oil itself." He took another bite. "Them fires, well, they heat up the oil there at the bottom, turn it to steam. And the steam rises and condenses at various levels and differ'nt products come off. Gasoline is bein' distilled right up there at the top." He swallowed. "Works just like a regular whiskey still. All these things have differ'nt boilin' points—just like people."

Uncle Bob grinned at Bud, who nodded. They just ate

for a while, saying nothing, as if they were tired of competing with the roar.

"You know Ray?" Bud finally shouted.

"Yeah, long time," Uncle Bob yelled.

"He seems to have a pretty low boilin' point."

"He givin' you trouble?"

"Well, I don't think he likes me too much."

Uncle Bob finished chewing and swallowed. He wiped his mouth with a big, dirty napkin of a hand.

"Ray's just a son uva bitch. I never liked him. Sorry you got stuck with him. Used to be a guard at the prison in Huntsville. Oh, he's real proud a that. Killed one a the prisoners. He's real proud a that, too."

"What happened?"

"You wait, he'll tell you all about it. Like I say, he's real proud a it. You'll see."

The roar of the refinery came between them again.

"Yeah, he was always mean," Uncle Bob said with a curious twinkle that did not seem to fit his words. "But he's been worse ever since one a the boys out here knocked up his daughter."

When he finished delivering this news, his laughter drowned out the roar. The laugh was more than affectionate this time. It was a little malicious. And his eyes danced with a light that had nothing to do with refinery fires. He liked spreading good news.

Above the roar, they heard the whistle. Lunch was over. Uncle Bob stubbed out a second cigar and stood up.

"I gotta go to the head," the uncle announced.

"Me, too," said the nephew.

Again Uncle Bob led the way. As they were walking through the steel forest, Bud felt drops falling on him. At first, he thought it must be some chemical, one of the towers must have sprung a leak. Then he realized that it was water. It was raining. He would come to learn that rain was as common in Houston as it was uncommon in Spur, where it was needed.

"Let's go," Bud said.

And he broke into a run. But he had only gone a few steps before he felt his uncle's hand on his arm, pulling him to an abrupt stop.

"Don't ever do that!" Uncle Bob said, stern for the first time.

"Do what?" asked Bud, surprised.

"Run."

"Huh?"

"Around here," Uncle Bob said, calming down, "if one runs, they *all* run. So don't run unless you mean it."

They walked on through the rain, getting soaked. All Bud's instincts told him to hurry, to sprint, but he walked mechanically at his uncle's side. He felt unnatural and he felt wet.

Inside, the uncle and his nephew took up positions side by side at the urinals. Bud tried to piss but it hurt him. Wincing in pain, he looked down.

"What's the matter?" asked Uncle Bob.

"I don't know," said Bud.

Uncle Bob edged over closer. He looked down. And he grinned.

"You got the clap, Bud."

Instinctively, Bud pulled his hand away as if he were afraid it might catch the disease. The hand reached for the beard that he had so often stroked when he needed comfort, but there was nothing there, neither comfort nor beard. Standing there over the urinal, his whole body dripping, and every drip seemingly infected, he shivered. Now he knew that he would be changed in Sissy's fierce eyes forever. He would have to go to her with what seemed like an unnatural face and make what felt like an unnatural confession. His whole body itched and he heard the roar of a hundred fires in his ears.

9

Telling Sissy

The huge honky-tonk was almost empty. It always was on Monday nights. Tonight it fit Bud's mood, the emptiness, the sense of desertion, the melancholy that seemed to echo through the place. He stood at the back bar in the farthest corner of the saloon all alone, drinking tequila gold as if it were a cure. From time to time, he would lift his eyes from his drink to search the empty acres. When he glanced up, he was looking for Sissy, but he was relieved each time he did not find her.

"Careful, don't hurt yourself," advised the bartender.

"I already did," mumbled Bud.

Maybe she wouldn't come tonight. She had told him that she came to Gilley's most every night, so he had assumed he would find her here. But perhaps Monday nights were just too slow for her. He found himself hoping that they were. Maybe she was at the drive-in tonight. At work, a lot of the boys had been talking about going to the drive-in since Monday night was dollar night. He imagined her in someone else's pickup—not flinching under someone else's hand. Now, when he looked up, he almost hoped to see her. And yet, when he did, when he saw her coming toward him, he did not feel better, he felt worse.

Sissy walked toward him, exactly as she had the night before, with her coyote eyes almost seeming to precede her as she came. It was as though the hunting eyes bore down on him even faster than she did. He did not want those eyes to

51

see him as he was now. She stopped directly in front of him, about an arm's length away.

"I liked you better before," Sissy announced. "With a beard."

"I'm sorry," Bud said.

"You looked more like a cowboy."

"I know."

"So how come you to shave it off?"

"They made me at work so I could wear a fresh-air mask."

Sissy walked on over to the bar. The cowgirl leaned back against it and studied her new cowboy. Then she turned to the bartender.

"I'll have what he's havin'," she said. "But I need a chaser. Gimme a Lone Star."

She didn't say anything else until she tipped back her shot of tequila and swallowed it in one gulp. Then she held out her arm for Bud to look at.

"See," she said, "it gives me goose bumps."

She took a sip of beer. The alcohol warmed her physically and emotionally.

"What I don't understand is this," she said in what was supposed to be a joking tone. "I liked your beard and I didn't like your hat. So you kept the hat and got rid of the beard."

Somehow Bud missed the joking tone. Perhaps it was because Sissy's voice was always so deep that it always sounded serious. Perhaps it was because he had had too much to drink. At any rate, he suddenly got mad.

"Goddamn it," Bud said, "will you shut up about my hat."

The alcohol had warmed his temper and had made him bolder. Besides, he instinctively preferred a fight to a confession.

"I say what I think," Sissy said, a little startled. "Anyway . . ."

"Anyway your hat's a lot worse than mine."

"Jesus, Bud."

It was as though he wanted to drive her away from him so he wouldn't have to tell her. He wanted to pick a trivial fight so he would not have to tell a story that would not be trivial at all.

"What's wrong with my hat anyway!" he attacked, reaching up and pulling down the brim. "I like it."

"I don't wanta talk about it," Sissy said.

She was staring at him as if she didn't know him. It wasn't the missing beard only. It was the temper.

"Come on," Bud insisted, "what's wrong with it!"

"Well, it's just all wore out," she said. "That's all. Let's fergit it."

Bud took a sip of tequila. He couldn't forget it. If he did, they would have to talk about something else. He took his hat off and studied it.

"Hell!" he said, "it ain't wore out, it's just broke in."

"Come on, Bud," she tried to stop him. "You're drunk."

"That's how it's supposed to be," said Bud, admiring the dirty straw. "Not like yours."

For the first time, Sissy felt a hint of anger. She knew it was silly, but he had started it.

"What's wrong with mine, huh?" she asked.

"It ain't wore out enough," he said. "And besides, it's felt," he added with contempt.

"Felt?" She was incredulous. "What the fuck's wrong with felt?"

"Nothing." He was drunk. "Just it's dumb to wear in the summertime."

"Why?"

" 'Cause they're too hot to work in."

Sissy turned away from Bud and put her elbows on the bar. She motioned the idle bartender over.

"Another shot," she said.

She downed it in one swallow again. And again goose bumps covered her arms. But this time she kept them to herself. She folded her arms.

"Bud," she said at last in a calm voice, "a cowboy hat ain't no work hat."

Sissy picked up her Lone Star and walked away from Bud toward the dance floor. As he watched her go, Bud sensed that he had succeeded. He had put off his confession. He felt relieved and sad. Putting his hat back on his head, he didn't like it that much any more.

Bud watched Sissy dance with other cowboys. She never danced more than a dance or two with one, then she would move on to the next, then the next. She was busy pollinating the whole honky-tonk garden. Bud was jealous, but he took some perverse pleasure in telling himself that she would probably give them all the clap, his clap.

Sissy was briefly between partners when a young woman, who was trying out for a job, sang from the bandstand:

> *Darlin', I'm feelin' pretty lonesome,*
> *I'd call you on the phone some,*
> *But I don't have a dime . . .*

Sissy, who stood beside an upright I-beam that helped support the ceiling, dipped her shoulders to the beat of the music. And Bud could see her moving her lips, singing quietly along or perhaps simply pantomiming.

> *Darlin', you're so far behind me,*
> *Tomorrow's gonna find me*
> *Farther down the line . . .*

When she saw him watching her sing, she stopped. She ducked her head so the brim of her felt hat hid her eyes. Bud could almost hear her say: twang twang.

The music seemed to propel Bud in Sissy's direction. He was carried along by the sad love song. Much of what he knew and expected of the world he had learned from country singers. And now this country singer seemed to be telling him that Sissy was moving irretrievably away from him. The song moved him literally. He stopped in front of her. She still kept her head down.

"Know how to two-step?" he asked.

"No," she said.

She still would not raise her head. It was as though he had not only changed in her eyes but ceased to exist for them. He felt he had to make her see him again.

"Look at me," Bud said.

"No," Sissy said.

"Why not?"

" 'Cause I cain't figure out what's wrong with you tonight."

"Dance with me and I'll tell you."

Sissy looked up at him for the first time. He flinched slightly.

"You mean there is somethin' wrong?"

"Uh-huh."

She studied him. "Yeah."

He looked puzzled. "Huh?"

"Yeah, I can two-step."

They danced, but this time she did not hook her finger through his belt loop, and he did not grab hold of her hair. Now that they knew each other a little better, they were more cautious than they had been when they were total strangers. He put a hand behind her back. She put one on his shoulder. Neither of them spoke at first. Bud could barely hear Sissy singing along with the singer on stage: *Darlin', I'm feelin' pretty lonesome* . . . The song echoed in the lonesome emptiness of the Monday honky-tonk.

"I don't know how to tell you," Bud said.

"You don't know how to tell me what?" asked Sissy.

"That I got the clap."

Sissy momentarily forgot how to two-step. She moved one way as he did another. They lost it. And then they struggled to regain their dancing composure.

"You didn't get it from me," Sissy said fiercely.

Her coyote eyes were ready to devour him.

"I know," Bud said.

" 'Cause I don't have it," she said.

"You didn't," he said. "But you do now."

"Oh, my God." She paused. "Well, twang twang."

Bud tried to draw her closer to him as they danced, but she pulled away from him completely. He followed her off the dance floor, struck, in the middle of everything, by how long her strides had suddenly become. Sissy walked up to a table and asked a lone cowboy for something. Bud could not hear what it was. By the time he caught up to her, she already had it in her hand.

"Gimme your hat," Sissy ordered.

Stunned, Bud reached up, removed his old hat, and handed it to her gingerly. As she took it with her left hand, her right fist opened to reveal a cigarette lighter. She ignited a flame and held it to the brim of the hat. The old straw blazed immediately. When everyone looked around startled—as if it were a fire in a refinery—Sissy let the hat fall to the concrete floor. It burned there, upside down. And Bud's and Sissy's shadows danced on the wall of the saloon.

10

Church

While he was waiting at a red light, Bud caught a glimpse of a finger pointing at God. The light changed and he rolled forward. The finger turned out to be attached to a hand, which was attached to the steeple of a large red-brick Baptist church. At first, Bud thought the hand was making an obscene gesture, but a closer look changed his mind. No, the finger was simply pointing. Evidently the church fathers had not had enough imagination to suspect that anyone would think anything else. Then Bud saw Sissy waiting for him on the steps of the church. He was late and owed her another apology.

Bud parked in the church parking lot, jumped out of the cab, and ran—sweating inside his one suit. It was dark blue. Sissy's dress was light blue. As he ran toward her, Bud sensed that there was something different about her. At first, he thought it must simply be the newness of seeing her in a dress, but, as he drew nearer, he was not so sure.

"Sorry I'm late," Bud panted. "I got lost. How do you feel?"

"Fine," Sissy said. "Guess them pills worked. I still don't have no discharge or nothin'. What about you?"

"A lot better. The pus is all gone."

Bud opened the church door for Sissy, who passed in ahead of him. They walked into a hymn. *Rock of Ages cleft for thee.* Sissy saw that her parents had saved a couple of seats for them in the fourth row, but she led Bud to the nearly deserted back row of the church. *Let me hide myself in thee.* They sat down together and opened a hymnal. *Be of sin the double cure.* Bud kept his eyes on the songbook, not because he did not know the words, but because he could feel the stare of parental disapproval. *Save from wrath and make me pure.* He unconsciously scratched his recovering crotch.

After the song, the collection plate was passed. All during this ceremony, Bud kept studying Sissy, trying to discover what was different about her. He stared at the dress, which had a fullish skirt and a sculpted bodice. Nothing distinguished the dress. Its owner had given little thought to picking it out. She had simply bought it to wear to church, to please her father and mother. The dress was in no way an extension of her. Perhaps the dress made her look a little awkward, but it did not really change her. The difference Bud had noticed went deeper.

"Your eyes are blue today," Bud said in a surprised voice too loud for church.

"Shhhhh," Sissy said. Then she whispered, "Course they're blue today. They're always blue. You mean you never noticed my eyes before?"

"Course I noticed."

"Then what're you talkin' about?"

"They're not always blue."

Sissy stared at Bud with large, round blue eyes that were handsome but not fierce. They were not coyote eyes at all. Bud's seeing Sissy without her golden eyes was like her seeing him without his black beard: at first, he hardly felt he knew her. And maybe he did feel a little cheated.

"What's wrong?" asked Sissy.

"When I first met you," Bud said, "your eyes were gold."

She just stared at him with her blue eyes.

"Don't look at me like that," he said. "I'm serious. They were gold that first night. And ever night since. I swear."

"You can ask my mama 'n' daddy," she said. "My eye've always been blue."

She opened them even wider to show him.

"No . . ."

The collection plate was suddenly thrust into Bud's hands by an usher. He reached into his pockets but found no change. He did not wear his suit often enough for silver to collect in its pockets. So he reached for his wallet, knowing, sadly, that he would have to give a dollar. He could not ignore the collection plate, not with Sissy watching, not even if her eyes were blue.

Toward the end of a boring sermon, Bud was mentally and physically restless. He squirmed in his seat and in his mind he did much worse. This was not the first time he had been unable to sit through a morning in church without thinking about taking someone's clothes off. There was something about the dignity of a religious service that seemed to send his mind stumbling off in the opposite direction. Now, sitting so near Sissy in the pew, he wanted to reach over and open the bodice of her dress like a hymnal.

Sissy was squirming, too. As he watched her moving on the seat, he so wanted to lift her skirt, to see . . . And then it occurred to him that he was not sure what he would see. Suddenly Bud desperately wanted to know if Sissy wore underwear in the house of God. He fought the urge to find out, but his curiosity ate at him like foam glass. He just had to know.

"Do you," he whispered, bending down close to her ear, "wear panties to church?"

Sissy looked up at him with a mischievous child's blue eyes. But she didn't say anything.

"Well?" asked Bud.

"Not very often," Sissy whispered.

Bud stared at her skirt in search of a hint, but he still could not be sure. He raised his eyes and saw her father looking back over his shoulder at him. So he immediately lowered his eyes again.

"Is this very often?" Bud asked.

"That's for you to find out," Sissy whispered.

Bud looked into her face, then down into her lap, then back up at her face again. They both giggled in church.

"Come on, tell me."

"No."

Bud looked around the church like a teen-age shoplifter about to steal a copy of a dirty magazine. Sissy looked, too. A middle-aged couple, who sat a good ten feet to their right, appeared intent on the sermon. And an old man, who sat even nearer them on their left, seemed to be dozing. Bud lowered his hand to the edge of Sissy's skirt. She did not flinch. His hand crept a few inches under the skirt. Still she didn't flinch. His fingers crawled slowly up her thigh. She was as motionless as the Rock of Ages in the hymn.

The old man yawned and looked around. Bud, afraid to move, sat with his hand paralyzed under Sissy's skirt, halfway up. Bud was more nervous about their being caught than she was. The hand under the dress trembled slightly, but the thigh did not.

When the old man closed his eyes and lowered his head again, Bud crept deeper into the dark. His crippled hand probed what seemed an eternal refuge cleft only for him.

11

The Wrecking Yard

Bud squinted into the sun as he surveyed the rusting landscape. Sissy was giving him a tour of her family's wrecking yard. He thought it was ugly, but she seemed somewhat proud of it. There was a wrecked Mustang in the middle of the yard. Just beyond it was a smashed Pinto. A little to the right lay the twisted remains of a Colt. There were all kinds of wrecks—pickups, convertibles, just cars, and even one diesel truck. It was like a mechanical horses' graveyard. In the background, a few miles away, loomed the towers of a refinery.

"My mama works in the office," Sissy explained. "I work out here with my daddy."

She was still in her light blue dress and he was still in his dark blue suit. After church, neither of them had wanted to go home, so neither of them had changed. They had eaten lunch together at a McDonald's. Then they just drove around for a while, feeling slightly foolish in their church clothes. Finally, Sissy told Bud she wanted to show him where she worked, but she wanted more, really, and so did he. They were both wondering if they were well enough to make love again. They needed someplace where they could be alone in the daytime, someplace like an empty wrecking yard. But neither admitted out loud why they were there.

"You like workin' here?" Bud asked.

"I don't mind," Sissy said. "Like bein' outside."

She sat down on the fender of a pickup that somebody

had probably died in. It was badly crushed and the windshield was shattered.

"Course," she continued, "I really wished I lived back in the old-timey days. Back when there were real horses 'stead of all these old wrecked cars. And real cowboys."

Bud sat down on the fender beside her. The decaying metal complained under his weight.

"You sure talk a lot about cowboys," he said.

"I reckon," she admitted. "In fact, I know. I once even tried to write a song about cowboys."

"You did? I didn't know you wrote songs."

"I don't. That was back when I was engaged to that guitar-picker. The one I told you about, remember?"

"Sure."

"Lemme see if I can remember some of the words. A cowboy knows how to play pool. And a cowboy knows how to drink. And a cowboy knows how to dance. Come on, help me out, what else?"

"Well, let's see," he said, stalling as he considered the question. "Okay, a cowboy knows how to fight."

"Oh, yeah," she said, laughing, "and a cowboy knows how to brag, too."

She laughed even louder.

"And a cowboy knows how to fix a truck," he said to quiet her.

"And a cowboy knows what to do with a cowgirl," she said. "Who knows? Mighta been a good song, but I broke up with my musician before he got around to writin' the music. Twang, twang."

As the sun dropped lower, its red afternoon rays made the spreading rust all around them look all the redder. When he stood up, Bud had rust on his blue suit. Sissy helped him brush some of it off, but a stain remained.

"I don't give a damn," Bud said.

Then he helped brush the rust off Sissy. She didn't give a damn either.

"Come on, lemme show you the rest of the place," she said.

And she led the way deeper into the wreckage. They made their way through the twisted metal underbrush, stepping over broken axles, walking around dislocated transmissions, taking care not to trip over bumpers. Bud bent over and picked up an abandoned rope, curled like a rattler. Pausing, he tied a small loop in one end.

"What're you doin'?" asked Sissy.

"I'll show you," Bud said.

Quickly fashioning a lasso, he spun it around his head while he was searching for a likely target. He chose the trailer hitch of a dead pickup and let fly. The circle of rope whirred toward the steel ball—and fell just short. He started reeling the rope in again.

"Close," Sissy said.

"I'm gettin' outa practice," Bud said.

He spun the rope around his head again and let it snake once more in the direction of the trailer hitch. This time the lasso dropped over its target.

"Nice one," said Sissy.

Bud pulled the rope taut and dug in the heels of his boots as if he had roped a rank horse instead of a truck. Then he let it go slack and gave it a flip. The loop jumped off the trailer hitch. And Bud began coiling the rope in his hand once again.

"Watch this," he said.

Bud made a loop about the size of a tire on a pickup. He adjusted it a little fussily. Sissy could not imagine what he had in mind. Then suddenly in one motion, he was spinning the loop in front of him. He was doing a rope trick. She had never seen anyone do rope tricks—nobody but Will Rogers in old movies. Maybe Bud really was a cowboy, after all.

"Where'd you learn to do that?" Sissy asked.

"From my daddy," Bud said, "back home in Spur. I'm kinda rusty. Looks like I already been away from Spur too long."

This turn in the conversation troubled Sissy. She did not like the idea of his pining for Spur when he was with her.

"You miss Spur?" she asked.

"Oh, sure. It's real differ'nt from here. There's more space than people, more animals than people. It's great."

"You make Spur sound like a damn Garden of Eden. How come you left?"

"Cause you cain't get a job in the Garden of Eden no more."

Bud was silent while he enlarged his loop. He stepped into the loop and started spinning it around his body, around his blue suit.

"If I'da stayed in Spur, I'da lost my pickup. But when I get some money ahead, I wanta move back. I wanta buy myself my own piece a dirt. Dirt's the only thing worth puttin' your money into. Dirt's the only thing don't rust or break down."

"I don't mind rust," Sissy said.

Lost in his rope spinning and his reveries about his hometown, Bud did not notice the shift in Sissy's mood. He did not realize that she considered Spur, in a sense, a rival. All that worried him was the rope, which had developed a lopsided spin. Then it collapsed completely. He went to work rebuilding his loop.

"I got my eyes on this little piece a dirt near my daddy's place," Bud went on. "Nearest neighbor's five miles off. Still real Texas. I just cain't get used to livin' so close to people. It's a constant shock to my system."

"Uh-huh," Sissy said unenthusiastically.

Soon the cowboy in the dark blue suit had his rope spinning around his body again. He did it better than before. He was improving.

"Spur's sorta like what you were talkin' about," Bud said. "The old-timey days. They drive pickups, but they ride horses, too. I cain't wait for you to see it."

So she was included in the dirt dream, after all.

"That sounds so good," she said in a changed voice.

"Oh, yeah, you're gonna love it."

Sissy studied Bud's rope spinning through changed blue eyes.

"You're good," she said with genuine admiration. "Teach me to do that."

"It's real hard," Bud said.

"Bet I could learn."

"It ain't really for girls."

"Aw, come on, please."

Bud kept spinning while he thought it over. Then he stopped, letting the loop slump to the ground. He gathered up the rope, made a smaller loop, and swung it around his head. Sissy looked at him quizzically. He surprised her by letting the rope fly in her direction. She did not flinch as the loop tightened about her body.

"Come on, get over here," said Bud, pulling on the rope. "I'll teach you."

Sissy turned out to be a good pupil, better than he had imagined or hoped.

The sunset gilded the wreckage.

"Do you think we could?" asked Sissy.

"I don't know," Bud said.

"You *are* better?"

"Uh-huh."

"Maybe we could try."

"Maybe."

"I know a place."

"Where?"

"There's an old Rambler over there. It don't run no more. But the seats still recline."

They made love in the wreckage.

They began slowly, gently, gingerly, in first gear, afraid of their own bodies. Their hands asked questions in a touching sign language all their own: are you whole? are you well? am I hurting you? And the bodies always answered no. Which meant, yes, go on.

As they grew less fearful of their own parts, they grew bolder, speeded up, shifted gears, rocking the old car slightly as if it had come back to life. In a sense, they were coming back to life, too. And they were hungry after their week-long fast.

At last, they rushed head on at each other at top speed. They crashed into each other. They smashed into each other, collision after collision after collision, in the wrecking yard. It was as though they were trying to put dents in each other. They seemed to be testing their bodies to see if they really were as well as they felt. And then they collapsed side by side on the old rust-dusty seats.

"Did we make the finals?" Sissy asked when she got her breath.

Bud smiled and lay still with his arms around her while the dusk was deepening all around them. They lay in a gray grotesque world of twisted metal shapes. Bud lifted himself up onto one elbow and looked down at Sissy. His blue eyes contracted into a squint.

"Jesus Christ," he said.

"What?" she asked.

"Your eyes're gold again."

And they were. Her eyes, which had shown blue in the

sunshine, now glowed gold in the moonlight. It was as though she were one person by day and another by night, as though she were one person in church, where he had first seen her blue child's eyes, and another person in the giant saloon, where he had discovered her golden coyote eyes, as though her eyes took the color of the sky in the daylight and the hues of the moon in the dark of night, now.

12

The Punching Bag

As he walked into the saloon, Bud felt those same old feelings again, awkward, peculiar, conspicuous. Since he felt that everyone was looking at him, he put his hands in his pockets, so no one would be able to stare at his cut-off finger. But his finger was not the root of his uncertainty tonight. Rather, it was the new weight on his head. It was a black shadow over him. He pulled the brim down as if it were a black mask.

"Where'd you get the hat?" Steve Strange asked at his elbow.

"Sissy picked it out," Bud said defensively.

"It's a nice one," Steve said.

"Thanks," Bud said, relaxing a little.

"Cost fifty dollars," Sissy said. "On sale."

She was proud of her ability to spot value, but he thought she was telling too much. He ducked his head.

"Well, maybe I'll get me a new one," Steve said. "This one's gettin' kinda old."

"Uh-huh," said Sissy.

"Come on over here, you two. I wanta show you somethin', heh, heh, heh, heh."

Bud and Sissy followed Steve in the direction of a crowd gathered at the far end of the bar. They pushed their way into the throng until they could see what had drawn everyone. It was a machine that consisted of a punching bag and a

66

dial. When a cowboy hit the bag, the dial measured the force of the punch.

"Do you win anything?" asked Bud.

"Just satisfaction," said Steve. "And maybe a broke hand."

A cowboy named Norman stepped up and threw a punch that sent the needle on the dial all the way up to 300. That was as high as it would go. The machine lit up and a siren went off. And everyone clapped.

"Way to go."

"Nice one, Norman."

He responded to the praise by spitting chewing tobacco on the concrete floor.

"Who's next?"

Bud made a fist. He wanted to fight the machine. But he could not help remembering what had happened to him the last time he fought machinery. He wondered whether he should try with his left hand or his crippled right.

"My turn," said Bud.

He stepped forward and put a quarter in the machine. When he pressed the button, the punching bag dropped down into position. He studied it, selecting his spot. While his eyes were on the bag, he could feel *her* eyes on him. With her watching, he now knew that he would have to use his right hand, his stronger hand, no matter how crippled it was. He drew back his right arm and swung at the punching bag as hard as he could. But he tried too hard. He hit the bag off center and the dial only went up to 150. The siren did not go off. It was then that Bud first noticed another feature of the fighting machine: his weak punch lit up a picture of a woman who was fully clothed.

"It'll work better," Steve said, "if you'll take a couple of steps back."

Bud retreated. He cocked his arm again and then looked back at Sissy. She smiled and made a muscle. He lunged forward with a high overhand haymaker that caught the bag in its midsection. This time the hand on the dial swung up to 250—and a picture lit up showing a woman in her underwear.

"That's better," said Steve. "Now put your whole body into it. Really rare back."

Glancing quickly back at Sissy, Bud actually took a little jump into the air as he swung. He came down with all his weight behind the blow. It was a knockout punch. The arm on the meter made a complete revolution, all the way from 0 to 300, and still kept going until it came to rest on 5. It looked as if he had only scored 5 points, but he had actually scored 305. The siren blew and a picture lit up showing a woman with no clothes on at all. Bud looked around proudly at Sissy, expecting some sort of praise.

"I wanta try it," Sissy said.

"You'll hurt yourself," Bud warned.

"No, I won't."

"Sissy."

"I gotta quarter. And I don't s'pose that damn machine cares if it's a girl quarter or a boy quarter. Huh?"

Sissy hated being told not to do something. Because she always knew she was being told not to do it because she was a girl. So she naturally had to prove that she could do whatever she had been told not to do. She walked over and jammed twenty-five cents into the punching machine.

"Be careful," Bud warned. "That bag's a mean un."

Stepping back and taking careful aim, Sissy swung as hard as she could. Her fist hit the bag the slightest bit crooked. Her knuckles skidded on the bag. And her wrist seemed to give, like a cracked drive shaft. Sissy flinched slightly. Bud flinched even more and rubbed his own fist. The dial read less than 100. She did not light up the picture of any girl at all.

"That's enough," Bud said.

"Fuck you," said Sissy.

More and more cowboys and cowgirls crowded around the punching bag. Word had spread quickly in this small town named Gilley's that a girl was fighting the machine. They all wanted to see. Bud was worried about Sissy and a little jealous of the attention she was receiving.

"Come on, Sissy!"

"Atta girl!"

Above all the shouting, Sissy heard only one voice, Bud's, cautioning her to be careful. And she knew he was cautioning her because she was a girl. So she swung even more recklessly than before. This time the dial showed 175 and a girl with her blouse off lit up. Sissy smiled through a grimace. Her wrist hurt.

A cheer went up from the crowd of cowboys and cowgirls. Now Sissy was more determined than ever to make that siren blare. She took several steps backwards so she could get a running start. Then she launched herself at the bag with all her cowgirl courage. But she hit the bag crooked again and the dial only went up to 125.

"You all right?" asked Bud, moving in her direction.

"Sure," Sissy said indignantly, retreating before him.

Sissy did not want him to see the damage she had done to herself. She was now as sensitive about her own right hand as he was about his. He pursued her, catching up to her in a few steps. He reached out his injured hand and took hers. It was the first time she ever flinched and pulled away from him.

13

The Fight

In the glare of the fast-food lights, the hand looked even worse than it had in the dimness of the saloon. Bud sat beside Sissy in a bright booth, examining her injuries. Her hand was swollen from her wrist to the tips of her fingers, the skin had been knocked off three of her knuckles, and her whole hand was spotted with dry and drying blood.

"Can you move your fingers?" Bud asked.

"I—*oh*—think so," Sissy said, moving them slightly.

After Gilley's closed at two in the morning, the couple had driven down the Spencer Highway to an all-night omelet joint called Stonie's. On the way, they passed dozens of fast-food places, all decorated to look like bright packages in a supermarket, the highway itself being the shelf. Stonie's, with its bright orange-and-blue exterior, was not the prettiest box on this shelf, far from it. Nor did it serve the best food. And yet it was the traditional next stop after the giant honky-tonk shut down. Sissy had been eating at Stonie's for years. And tonight she wanted another of his middle-of-the-night breakfasts because her pain had turned her thoughts to food.

"I better clean it up a little," Bud said. "Don't want it gettin' all infected."

"Okay," Sissy agreed.

Bud dipped the tip of his napkin in a glass of water. Then he used the napkin to begin cleaning Sissy's wound.

"Oh," she said.

"Hurt?" he asked.

"No, just cold," she lied.

While Bud continued to work over Sissy's hand, another couple approached the booth. They were Norman Tucker, who had been the first to sound the siren, and his young wife, Debbie. They stared respectfully at the injured hand for a moment before making their request.

"Can we siddown?" asked Norman.

"All right," Bud said unenthusiastically.

The couple crowded into the corner booth. Then Norman held up both his fists, clenched.

"Look at my knuckles," he said. "I hit it with both hands, see?"

Some skin had been barked off the knuckles on both hands, but his wounds were not nearly as deep as Sissy's. Still she studied the hands appreciatively.

"I guess," she said, "that makes you twice the cowboy I am."

Bud was jealous of the attention that Norman was receiving.

"I broke my hand once," he said, anxious not to be left out, "in a bar fight in Oklahoma City."

"That where you lost your finger?" asked Debbie Tucker.

Everyone else in the booth recoiled slightly at Debbie's frank reference to Bud's missing part, but she did not appear to notice. She simply said whatever came into her mind. She thought of this habit—whenever she thought of it at all—as being direct.

"No," Bud said, "I lost it in a fight with a windmill."

"What?" asked Debbie.

Sissy decided to try to come to Bud's rescue. She would tell the story so he wouldn't have to. She knew how sensitive he was on this one subject.

"He climbed up on a windmill," Sissy explained, "to think about somethin'. And the wind started blowing. You can figure the rest out for yourself."

"I'll bet he was doin' more than just thinkin' up there," Norman laughed. "And if I know what it was, he's lucky just his finger got cut off 'steada his pecker." He laughed again. "Or maybe it got cut off, too. You'd know about that, wouldn't you, Sissy? Is his pecker a little on the short side?"

"Shut up," Sissy said.

She took Bud's crippled right hand in her bruised right

hand and began caressing it. The bloody hand sought to heal the spotless one. Bud was immensely touched by the touch of the swollen fingers.

While this crippled finger play was going on, Bud happened to notice someone moving on the periphery of his vision. He looked up. It was Shari. She noticed Bud's glance and smiled at him. And then he smiled, too, as if by reflex.

Sissy looked up to see what Bud was smiling at. When she saw, her jealousy rose quickly.

"Go on!" Sissy said.

"What?" Bud asked.

"Go on, get out!"

"What're you doin'?"

"I seen the way you looked at her."

"Huh?"

"So go on, just go on. I'll get somebody else to take me home."

"I cain't go around with my eyes closed. I just looked up and there she was."

Meanwhile, Shari paid her check and passed on out of the all-night restaurant, lingering outside long enough to stare at Bud through the big fast-food window. She smiled at him again.

"Go on," Sissy ordered, "go with her."

"You're jealous," Bud said.

Reaching over playfully, Bud started tickling Sissy. He was trying to coax her out of her jealousy, to make her laugh herself into a better mood. Sissy could absorb almost any amount of caressing, but she could not stand any tickling at all. She not only flinched but recoiled and fought his hands.

"Stop it!"

"You're jealous, Sissy's jealous."

What she was was very ticklish.

"Don't, Bud! Don't tickle me! I'll wet my pants! Bud! Stop!"

Bud was too drunk or having too much fun to realize that Sissy was getting madder. He kept on tickling her until she reached over and pinched him on the thigh. Her hand might be bruised, but it was still strong. Working in the wrecking yard kept it that way. Her fingers felt like wrecking-yard pliers. She must have hit a pressure point. The pain in Bud's thigh, being so unexpected, seemed almost unbearable.

"Ow!" Bud yelled. "That hurts."

The pain seemed to madden and blind him. It was as if he no longer recognized Sissy, no longer knew who was hurting him, only knew that *something* was. Without thinking, acting on reflex again, he struck out at this *something*. He slapped *it* across the face. Sissy reflexively raised her injured hand to her injured cheek.

"Oh!" Sissy cried. "You hit me!"

"Shit!" Bud explained. "You pinched me hard."

"You're not supposed to hit girls."

Sissy felt cornered and injured. She had to get out of that booth, but Bud was in her way, hemming her in. She half got to her feet, hitting the table a shuddering blow as she did so, spilling coffee and bruising the tops of her thighs. She was like a rodeo bull gone insane in the chute. She was trapped but she was determined to find a way out. That way was over Bud. She simply hurled herself at him, half sitting on his lap, half pushing him aside, until she was free of him and out of the booth.

Stunned, Bud sat for a moment and watched her walk toward the door. He had never seen a girl with longer strides, and tonight they were longer and more determined than ever. Suddenly, he jumped up out of the booth and rushed after her.

Sissy hit the door as hard as she would have liked to hit Bud. By the time Bud reached the door, it had already rebounded shut again.

"Hey!" Bud called after Sissy across the muddy parking lot.

"I ain't talkin' to you!" she yelled back.

She was heading for the highway. Out-of-doors, her strides seemed to get longer still.

"Where you goin'?" Bud yelled.

"Home," Sissy shouted back.

"Hey, how you think you're gonna get there?"

"I got a thumb." Sissy stuck her thumb up in the air as if she were hitchhiking. "And I got a middle finger." This bruised finger stood up all alone on her hand.

"Hey, come on, Sissy! I didn't hit you that hard."

When she reached the highway, Sissy turned and thrust her arm out with her thumb raised. Her whole body shook with anger and defiance. Below the hitchhiking thumb, the fist was clenched tight. Bud could not help noticing that her breasts heaved with each angry breath. They were maddeningly sexual. And yet at the same time they were like twin banners bearing the battle cry: DON'T TREAD ON ME!

"If that's how you feel," Bud said angrily, "that's just fine with me."

"Fine," Sissy said, flipping him the finger again, "fergit it."

"Fine, fergit it," he echoed in a softer voice.

And then he flipped her the finger, too.

Bud turned and ran toward his pickup, got in, and started the engine. His truck burst out of the parking lot the way Sissy had burst out of Stonie's. Bud pulled up in front of Sissy and stopped so fast that his machine quivered—as if it were angry.

"Get in!" Bud ordered.

"Fuck you!" Sissy said.

Furious, Bud stepped down hard on the accelerator. He left a part of his tires on the pavement in front of Sissy to mark the place where they had broken up. The wheels hurled gravel back at her like angry words.

Then the truck shuddered to a halt. It started backing up. Bud did not seem to care about the chaos he was causing on the Spencer Highway. Brakes squealed. Tires skidded. Horns honked. It was as if the entire highway had taken Sissy's side in the quarrel—all the cars and trucks were screaming at him.

But Bud hardly seemed to notice. He was concentrating on Sissy, whom he watched through the truck's rear window. When he drew alongside her, he brought his truck to another trembling stop.

"Goddamn it, Sissy!"

When she ignored him, Bud jumped out of his pickup and headed straight for her. She turned and ran back toward Stonie's. He ran after her. It was another race. They ran alongside a huge puddle, left by a sudden afternoon storm. It was a corrupt version of the reflecting pool, which they had run along on that first night, now thickened by mud and even the grease and oil of a parking lot. Attempting to dodge Bud, who was almost within reach of her, Sissy veered into the muddy water. She gained a few steps, but soon she heard him splashing into the water behind her. The splashing grew nearer. She turned to look just as he lunged at her. He tackled her as if he were finally playing the big game he had not been able to play in so long ago. Their hats fell off almost simultaneously and dove into the awful water. Their boots were flooded. They rolled over and over in the water and the mud. She tried to scream, but her mouth filled with puddle. She sputtered, choked, and coughed.

Bud was spitting up dirty water, too. He tasted fury and disappointment and mud. Sissy was flailing at him, bruising him as she bruised her own hand worse. To try to stop her, he grabbed a handful of the hair her father loved. It felt coarse and muddy and wet in his fingers.

"Damm you!" Sissy choked.

Now they were wrestling in the brown water. Bud was trying to pick Sissy up in his arms. He was going to carry her to his truck. He got to his knees, cradling her roughly, but she kept hitting him and kicking wildly until they both collapsed back into the sludge again. Several snaps gave way on her shirt and one muddy breast rolled lazily out and looked up at him. Even its unblinking stare seemed reproachful.

Then Bud looked up and saw a big red pickup barreling into the parking lot. It was coming right at them. The driver did not see the couple in the mud until they were almost beneath his wheels. Then he threw on his brakes and skidded toward the angry lovers. He stopped so close that they could feel the heat of the engine.

"Jesus Christ!" yelled the cowboy in the truck, "I almost killed y'all."

In the glare of headlights, Bud and Sissy looked like Adam and Eve in that moment just before life was breathed into them, when they were still mud instead of flesh. The lights stunned them for a moment, but then the mud Adam and the mud Eve continued their battle, the eternal battle. They rolled in the water as if they were making violent love or violent hate. Sissy reached up and clawed Bud's face. He wiped his cheek and looked at his hand.

"Goddamn," Bud said, "I'm bleedin'."

Struggling to his feet, he looked around him for his missing hat. When he saw it, crushed and half submerged, he walked over and picked it up. Now that it was injured—destroyed—he realized for the first time that he had come to love that hat. He tried to brush off the mud, but it was useless. He blamed *her* for what had happened to it. He stared angrily down at her and walked away.

"Bud!" Sissy called after him.

Getting to her feet, Sissy grabbed her own soaked hat and hurried after Bud, but he just walked faster. When he reached his truck, he slammed his drowned hat on his head and flung himself onto the seat behind the wheel. Then he studied his injured face, which was beginning to hurt, in the rearview mirror. A long scratch ran across his cheek, vivid as a neon sign.

"Bud!"

Catching up, Sissy placed her own muddy hat on her head and crawled sullenly up onto the pickup seat on the passenger side. Water from her hat trickled down her face like muddy tears as she slammed the door on her side of the truck. Bud slammed his door, too. With the truck still quivering, he suddenly turned on her with wounded, distorted features which frightened her.

"You wanta get married?" Bud asked.

BOOK
TWO

The Bull

14

The Wedding

Bud sped too fast toward marriage. Gripping the wheel too tightly, he rushed past cars that were less desperate. Edgy and exhausted, he watched for exit twelve. He also watched himself in the rearview mirror, which he had adjusted for just this purpose. He was trying to get to know himself in a white tuxedo. It was as white as the White Sands that his great-great-grandfather had once crossed on horseback, going snow-blind and almost dying on the way. Bud was having trouble with his eyes, too, but for another reason. He simply had not gotten enough sleep.

After he had gotten home from Gilley's the night before, Bud had wished for a windmill to climb to think over what he was about to do. Since he had none—but still needed something to do—he decided to take apart his carburetor. The problem was that once he got it taken apart, he couldn't put it back together. He had worked on carburetors dozens of times before but never when he was this nervous. Bud labored over his machine until three o'clock in the morning. Then he gave up and went to bed. If he couldn't get his truck running, well, he just wouldn't get married.

At six o'clock in the morning, Bud had his wrenches out again. The curburetor still would not go back together. And he simply would not get married without his pickup. He even wondered if perhaps he couldn't fix his carburetor because he didn't want to get married. He worked on the carburetor all morning. He didn't get his truck running again until shortly

79

before noon—and he was supposed to be at the wedding chapel by twelve-thirty. The man at the chapel had warned him about how important it was to be on time.

Just as he was beginning to believe that, in his hurry, he had missed it, Bud saw exit twelve. He turned the wheel sharply to the right and began pumping his brake. The wedding chapel was just off the Gulf Freeway, the exit ramp practically leading right to the front door. The name "Harmony Wedding Chapel" was painted on the side of the building in faded red. The whole building was faded, its white paint peeling, giving the impression of a bridal gown that the moths have been after.

Bud was one of the last to arrive. There was already a long line of pickups strung out in front like cavalry ready to charge. The prodigal groom was welcomed and rushed inside.

The wedding chapel had a very low ceiling, which made Bud duck instinctively although he was in no real danger of hitting his head. Everything was painted white, the floor, the walls, the pews, the altar, the ceiling. Bud was in rented white. It was as if he were some endangered animal whose protective coloration helped him survive by blending into his surroundings. Above the general chatter Bud could hear Steve Strange's *heh heh heh heh heh.*

No one really wanted the couple to get married in a wedding chapel. Bud wanted to get married in Gilley's, and Sissy was willing, but her mother refused even to consider such an idea. Her mother wanted them to get married in the Baptist Church, like decent folk, but his mother was opposed. His mother wanted them to get married in the Methodist Church. In the end, they had compromised. They would get married in a wedding chapel and have their wedding reception at Gilley's. Bud wanted them to ride horses from the chapel to the saloon because he felt sure no one would dare paint JUST MARRIED on a horse, but the mothers were against it.

In the back, somewhere out of sight, the preacher put on a recording of "Here Comes the Bride," which thousands of weddings had worn and scratched. Surprised by the suddenness of the music, Bud hurried to the front of the chapel to wait for his bride at the altar decorated with white plastic flowers. Half turning and looking back over his shoulder, the groom saw the bride appear on the arm of her father, who wore a black tuxedo. The bride grinned ever so slightly as she saw her groom flanked by his ushers and her bridesmaids. The ushers were all in identical black tuxedos, all rented from the same shop on the Spencer Highway. Sissy saw Marshall from the plant and Norman from Gilley's and Uncle Bob, who was the best man. The bridesmaids were all in flowing green dresses the color of green Jell-O. There stood a bartender from Gilley's named Marshallene and a cousin named Betty Jo and Aunt Corene, who was the matron of honor.

The bride was halfway down the aisle when everyone in the chapel heard a resonant baritone voice outside questioning a new arrival.

"Are you here for the twelve-thirty wedding," the resonant voice asked, "or the twelve-forty-five?"

No one could hear the soft-spoken reply.

"I'm sorry," the resonant voice boomed again, "but you'll have to wait out here till this one's over."

Then the man with the resonant voice appeared at the back of the chapel carrying a bible. This wedding mill was a one-man business. He put on the record, he guarded the door, and he performed the ceremony. While the bride continued her slow march up the center aisle, the minister hurried up an outside aisle. His unnatural hair was shoe-polish black. He reached the altar only a few steps ahead of the bride. Bud heard *heh heh heh heh heh.*

Bud smiled at Sissy. She looked beautiful and funny and radiant and strange. She wore more yards of clothing than he had ever seen her wear before, and she looked more feminine than he had ever seen her look before, except when she was nude. The veil made her appear slightly distant and unattainable. She was his Sissy and she was someone he had never seen before. He had known her always and he wanted to meet her. She carried a bouquet of lavender flowers and she had blue eyes.

"Hi," the bride said through the veil.

"Hi," the groom said.

And then he just had to know. He had thought he would be able to wait until after the ceremony to find out, but now he found he couldn't wait. His curiosity simply overpowered him.

"Do you?" he whispered. "You know."

He could not help glancing down at the skirt of her flowing gown. She knew instantly what he meant.

"No," she whispered back.

Then they both started giggling at the altar. He tried to stop, but the sound of her laughter reignited him. And when she tried to stop, his laughter kept her laughing, too.

"You don't?" he laughed.

"No," she laughed.

"Really?"

"You want me to prove it?"

"No!"

"Shhhhh."

The minister did not wait for them to stop laughing. He did not like to waste time. After all, there was no time to waste.

"Do you, Bud, take this woman, Sissy," he intoned over the giggles, "to be your lawfully wedded wife, to have and to hold, in sickness and in health, for richer, for poorer, for better, for worse, keeping only unto her till death do you part?"

"I—*hah hah*—do."

"And do you, Sissy, take this man, Bud, to be your lawfully wedded husband, to have and to hold, in sickness and in health, for richer, for poorer, for better, for worse, keeping only unto him till death do you part?"

"I—*hah hah hah*—do."

"You may now place the ring on the bride's finger."

Uncle Bob handed the gold wedding band, lit with a single tiny diamond, to Bud. And the groom slipped the ring onto his bride's finger. He was beginning to regain control of himself now.

"Repeat after me: With this ring I thee wed."

"With this ring I thee wed."

As the groom held the bride's hand, they could both see that their fingers were still lightly spotted with oil, hers from the wrecking yard, his from the carburetor.

"You're a married man now," the minister told Bud. "And I'd never tell a married man what to do. But I might just mention that a wedding kiss is traditional."

Perhaps it was because the whole ceremony had seemed so funny to the groom. Perhaps it was actually because he took it so seriously that he needed some humor to lighten the moment. Perhaps it was simply an impulse. Perhaps he just wanted to make Sissy laugh again. At any rate, for whatever reason, Bud stepped forward and tried to kiss the preacher. Above the general laughter, he heard *heh heh heh heh heh.*

After the laughter died down, the groom raised the veil and kissed his wife. Then he led her out of the chapel past a sign painted in big unfaded red letters:

NO
RICE
ALLOWED

15

The Reception

Bud wanted everyone to like the big saloon. He wanted his little brothers to be impressed by it. He wanted his baby sister to enjoy it. He wanted his father to love it the way he loved it. He even wanted his Methodist mother, who had always preached against roadhouses and honky-tonks, to have a good time in Gilley's. Somehow he felt that his worth had been fused to the worth of the bar. It was as though he were a member of Gilley's Junior Chamber of Commerce. He studied his family and his friends carefully for signs of approval.

"How you like it, Mama?" Bud asked.

"It's big enough," his mother said.

"We met right over there," said Sissy, pointing, "at the bar."

She did not yet know her mother-in-law well enough to know that she flinched at words like *bar*. But Bud's mother made an effort to make her flinch almost imperceptible. She felt a need to fit in and not embarrass her son.

"Oh, yeah," said Uncle Bob in a booming booster's voice, "this here's the marriage capital of Texas."

"Sure is," said Aunt Corene in another loud voice.

The aunt and uncle wanted people to like the saloon, too. After all, they were the ones who had first introduced Bud to it.

"And the divorce capital, too," Bud's mother said in a low voice, "I'll bet."

84

"Oh, Mama," Bud said.

"I'm sorry," she said.

This conversation was interrupted by the arrival of the official wedding photographer, who had been rented along with the tuxedos. He wanted to start with a wide group shot of the two families, the bride's and the groom's. He lined them up in front of the bandstand. The bride and groom stood in the center, flanked by all their relatives.

They made a curious picture, in part because of what they wore. On Sissy's side of the frame, many of the men and boys had boots on. But on Bud's side, no one wore boots. On Sissy's side of the photo, there were lots of western suits, cut with slanting pockets. But on Bud's side, there were none. Sissy's side of the picture was all city people while Bud's side was almost all country people, but the city mice looked like country mice and the country mice looked like city mice.

"All right," the photographer said, "now just the bride and groom, please."

The rest of the family drifted to the sidelines while the photographer focused on the newlyweds alone. The groom put his arm around the bride's waist.

"Kiss her!" yelled Bud's littlest brother.

He did. He took her in his arms and kissed her, a longer, slower kiss than when he kissed her in the wedding chapel.

"Come on, Velma," Sissy's father whispered to his wife, "you didn't cry at the wedding. How come you're cryin' now?"

"It's such a pretty picture," Sissy's mother said. "I cain't help it."

The wedding ceremony had been rushed, but the picture-taking would not be. In a sense, the ceremony could be fast because the photographs would be forever slow. In the future, the wedding pictures would become the wedding.

"Come on, smile," called Aunt Corene.

Flash. Bud and Sissy kissing, his eyes closed, her eyes open, her cheeks sunk in from kissing so hard.

Flash. The groom standing behind the bride, reaching around in front of her, grabbing her breasts, both of them laughing.

Flash. The groom taking a dip of Skoal tobacco, the bride making a face.

Flash. The groom spitting tobacco juice.

"I wanta try it," said the bride.

"Sissy!" scolded her mother.

"Oh, all right."

Flash. The bride pouting.

"Show us your garter," yelled Uncle Bob.

"I cain't," Sissy said. "I don't got no stockings on."

"Aw, come on."

Flash. The groom raising the skirt of the bride's wedding dress high enough to reveal an ankle and a calf, the bride looking apprehensive.

"Bud, not too high," Sissy cautioned. "You know."

Flash. The groom raising the bride's white skirt high enough to expose a knee, the bride concerned.

"Bud!"

Flash. The groom raising the bride's dress high enough to show a thigh and a white-and-blue garter, the bride laughing.

"All right, if you wanta go all the way."

Flash. The wedding dress descending.

Flash. The bride and groom kissing again, both with their eyes closed.

Sissy led the way to the jukebox. Bud followed and behind him trailed several others. They all crowded around to look at the selections. Several called out their favorites but to no avail. The bride placed a slightly oil-stained finger on a number and turned to her groom.

"This one okay with you?" Sissy asked.

"That ain't no weddin' song," complained her cousin Betty Jo.

"I didn't ask *you*," the bride said.

The bridesmaid frowned to show that her feelings were hurt.

"It's fine with me," Bud said.

"Gimme a quarter," Sissy said, "there ain't no pockets in this thing."

Bud found a quarter in his white tuxedo pocket and handed it over. Sissy pushed it into the machine and touched the button she had selected. The groom led the bride to the center of the giant deserted dance floor at the heart of the giant, nearly deserted honky-tonk. He took hold of her hair. She reached for his belt loop but found only a cummerbund.

My heroes have always been cowboys,
And they still are it seems.

The bride and groom's light footsteps echoed softly in the Gilley's ghost town. They looked around them at their family, at their friends, at their saloon, but they kept looking back at each other, the way people in love do. And then they only looked at each other in the artificial darkness of the midday honky-tonk.

"What color are my eyes?" asked Sissy.

"Gold," said Bud. "They're always gold in Gilley's."

Sadly in search of, and one step in back of,
Themselves and their slow-moving dreams . . .

On the edge of the dance floor, cousin Betty Jo was still complaining that the song wasn't a wedding song.

"It ain't even a love song," Betty Jo said.

"Yes it is," said Uncle Bob.

As the bride and groom fled the saloon, they were finally showered with rice. It came like a white gusher, spraying them all over. They ran as fast as they could, hand in hand, toward Bud's pickup, which was festooned with greetings from their friends: SUCKER! MISTAKE! JUST MARRIED!

In midflight, Sissy paused to throw her bridal bouquet into the crowd. Tall, lanky Norman caught it. Everybody laughed at him. He just didn't know any better.

The bride got into the pickup on the groom's side, sliding under the steering wheel. Then the groom climbed in and they roared off, the tires throwing gravel back at the rice-throwers. A half dozen old cowboy boots and a colorful assortment of beer cans followed them out of the parking lot.

"Bud," Sissy said.

"Yeah," Bud said.

They were just pulling out into the Spencer Highway and he was speeding up.

"Would you be real disappointed if . . ."

"If what?"

They had to stop at a traffic light.

"Well, if we didn't . . ."

"Didn't what?"

In the daylit cab, the groom studied his blue-eyed bride. Her gown seemed to fill the entire truck.

"Well, if I didn't want to . . ."

"Didn't want to what?"

Sissy's wedding dress made her even harder to read than usual—a blank white page. The light changed, but Bud did not notice.

"Didn't want to drive all the way to Huntsville right now," she said.

"We don't have to go," he said.

"Maybe we could still go tomorrow," she said, "if we want to."

"Uh-huh."

A car behind them honked. Bud looked up and saw that the light was green. He eased his truck forward. He was in no hurry because he didn't know where he was going.

"I know you went to a lot of trouble about the reservations and all. But it'd take us almost two hours to get here."

"Yeah."

"And I just can't wait that long. Let's just go home."

Bud speeded up. He kept accelerating all the way to Allen-Genoa Road, where he turned left. The ride away from the wedding was turning into as much of a race as the ride to the ceremony. Once they had made up their minds, neither of them could wait, but an occasional red light forced them to. They passed shopping centers and brand-new apartment houses and people working in their yards who yelled and waved at the newlyweds.

When they finally reached the trailer park, Bud passed an eight-miles-per-hour sign going forty miles per hour. All the mobile homes were arranged in a giant circle, like a wagon train circled up for the night. Kicking up dust on the circular dirt road, the truck passed trailer after trailer until it reached number 64, which stood out conspicuously.

"Goddamn it," muttered Bud.

The newlyweds' new rented mobile home was decorated just like their pickup. Their friends had covered it with signs that said: SUCKER! MISTAKE! JUST HITCHED! Old boots were tied to the doorknob. The truck and the trailer were a matched set.

"Come on," Sissy said.

They both got down from the truck.

"You gonna carry me?" asked the bride.

"Sure," the groom said.

He reached out to scoop up his new wife.

"Not like that," Sissy said. "Ever'body does it that way. I wanta do something different. I wanta ride piggyback."

Sissy jumped up on Bud's back, clasped her arms around his neck, and he grabbed her legs. The groom piggybacked the bride over the threshold of their new mobile home. When he got inside, he didn't put her down. He kept right on going through the miniature living room, down the pinched corridor, and into the bedroom, which was almost all bed. Bud and Sissy were home.

16

The Honeymoon

Bud and Sissy spent what honeymoon they had at the Huntsville Prison rodeo. High in the grandstand, where they sat in the hot sun waiting for the rodeo to begin, they kept looking around at the guards holding shotguns. Sissy put her arm through Bud's. The newlyweds wore matching cowboy shirts, tan with flowers. She had picked them out. It was as though they were in uniform, too, like the prisoners and the guards. They both wore brand-new cowboy hats.

Across from their seats, there rose another grandstand, this one surrounded by a chain link fence with barbed wire on top. Male prisoners in white suits were filing into the giant pen. Sissy reached over and took a pair of binoculars out of Bud's hands. She raised the glasses to her eyes to get a better look at the outlaws.

"Some of them are kinda cute," said the bride.

"Yeah, the cute ones're rapists," said the groom.

It took some twenty minutes for all the male prisoners to file in and seat themselves behind the wire. Bud looked down at his program. He was studying pictures of calf roping and bull riding when he heard a great shout go up from the far stands. He looked up to discover the cause of the trouble.

A couple of dozen female prisoners, dressed in bright costumes, were being led to a small pen down below. Bud knew from the program that these were inmate contestants who would compete in the greased pig chase. The male prisoners welcomed the females with cheers, shouts, and a stamping of feet. It sounded like a prison riot.

"*Take it easy,*" blared the announcer over the public address system. "*This is as close as you are gonna get for the next ten to twenty.*"

Bud and Sissy hugged each other. Then he took the binoculars from her. Pressing them to his eyes, he studied the newcomers.

"Some of them are kinda good-lookin'," the groom said.

"Yeah, the good-looking ones all killed their husbands," the bride said.

Then there was a great knocking and rumbling as the bulls were driven into the rodeo chutes. The convict cowboys, who would try to ride them, climbed up on the chutes and began working over the animals, getting ready. All the cowboys, since they were all prisoners, wore striped prison uniforms. But they were not the traditional horizontal prison stripes. Rather, these stripes were vertical. And they were wide. The outlaws appeared to be dressed in black-and-white-striped pajamas. In addition to the pajamas, they wore cowboy hats, chaps, boots, and spurs. Bud laughed.

"What's so funny?" asked Sissy.

"They sure don't look much like cowboys," Bud said, "do they?"

"They are though."

"Really?"

"Course. Outlaws make the best cowboys."

"Well, I . . ."

"Sure they do. 'Cause they just don't care. Don't give a damn. If they get hurt, they don't have to work at their prison jobs no more. It's like a vacation. Besides, most of 'em are lifers anyhow and ain't got nothin' to lose."

"*We like to start big here at the prison rodeo,*" boomed the announcer. "*So we're gonna open all ten chutes at the same time. And you're gonna see ten cowboys tryin' to ride ten bulls without bumpin' into each other. It's quite a sight. And anybody who gets trampled to death gets time off for good behavior.*"

While the crowd was still laughing, all ten gates to all ten chutes were thrown open. Ten bulls carrying ten striped cowboys came exploding out. They bucked and kicked and spun and jumped and hooked with their horns. The ten bells around their necks clanged like a jangling burglar alarm. Sissy grabbed Bud's arm and squeezed.

Watching through the binoculars, Bud could follow only one rider at a time. Without the glasses, Sissy could watch all ten. She saw a lot of violence far off, he saw a little close up. She saw three riders go down almost simultaneously. He saw only one of those cowboys fall, but he saw something she didn't, the expression of pain on the cowboy's face when a hoof landed on his shoulder. A few bucks later, Sissy saw one prisoner being butted while another was being kicked. Bud only saw the cowboy who was kicked, but again he saw something she didn't, the blood coming out of the cowboy's nose.

The object of this event was to ride the bulls all the way from one end of the arena to the other. The first cowboy to reach the far wall would be the winner. Sissy saw which cowboy won. Bud didn't.

"Jesus," said Bud, lowering the binoculars. "Those bulls're rough."

"They weren't that bad," said Sissy. "I seen worse."

When the calf roping started, Bud passed the binoculars to Sissy. Then he watched the cowboys, the horses, and the calves. She watched mainly the calves. He admired the coordination of the horses and riders working together. She was shocked at how roughly the calves were treated. With the ropes tight around their necks, their eyes would bug and their tongue would loll out of their mouths.

"Those poor calves," Sissy said.

"I don't think they much mind," Bud said. "They're used to it."

Next, the female prisoners in the brightly colored uniforms were released from their pen. Once again, a cheer went up from male prisoners in their fenced-in bleachers. The women had been divided into teams of two. You could tell the teammates because they wore the same colors. There were two in pink, two in yellow, two in purple, two in red . . . They matched, like Bud and Sissy.

"It says here," Sissy read from the program, " 'the girls often steal the show.' "

"You like it when that happens," Bud said. "Don'tcha? When the girls steal the show. I know."

The groom put his arm around his bride and hugged her. They both laughed on their honeymoon. And then they kissed quickly high up in the stands.

The greased pigs were released from a pen. They came squealing out into the arena, where the women in bright colors squealed after them. Each team carried a gunnysack. They were supposed to catch a greased pig, put it in the sack, and rush it to the judges. The first one to reach a judge with a sacked pig would win. The gaudy rainbow of women ran and fell in the dirt and got greasy from the pigs and ran some more.

"Gimme those binoculars," Sissy said. "You're enjoyin' this too much."

The team dressed in hot pink won the greased pig contest, to the immense pleasure of the grandstand dressed in white.

"See, they 'stole the show,' " the bride said.

The newlyweds enjoyed their rodeo honeymoon. They drank beer and ate hot dogs. They fought playfully over the binoculars. Bud saw big, jarring bareback broncs while Sissy watched tiny toy horses bucking far below. And then she was treated to monstrous saddleback broncs while he had to be satisfied with watching merry-go-round figures in the distance.

"What's next?" asked Bud.

Sissy opened the program again and riffled through the pages.

"The hard-money event," she reported.

"That's the one you told me about."

"Yeah."

Another pen was opened and a herd of prisoners in white pants and red shirts came pouring out. Then they scattered all over the arena at random like wild flowers.

"I cain't hardly believe it," Bud said.

"I know," Sissy said.

She did not have to be told that he was not talking about the rodeo—he was talking about being married.

"It's like I know you," he said, "and I don't know you."

When he looked at her, sometimes she seemed distant and strange. Other times she felt close and familiar. Sitting there beside him, she would seem small and weak, then large and strong, then small and weak again. He kept trying to adjust his mental focus, but he could never see her sharply, clearly, well defined. She kept growing and shrinking, approaching and receding, being magnified and then reduced.

"Let me introduce myself," his bride said. "I'm Mrs. Buford Uling Davis. But you can call me Sissy."

"The next event is unique to the prison rodeo," blared the announcer. *"We load a Bull Durham tobacco pouch with a hundred dollars. And then we tie that pouch between the horns of the meanest old bull we can find. It's up to those boys in the red shirts to take the money away from the bull. That's why this is called the hard-money event. Takin' money from a bull can be a whole lot harder'n takin' it from a liquor store, ain't that right, boys?"*

"I'm proud to meetcha," said Bud.

And he was proud. Sissy had danced with all the cowboys at Gilley's, but she had married him. In his mind, at least, she was like the prize between the bull's horns. A lot of cowboys had had a chance at it, a lot had touched it, a lot had done more, but he was the only one who had taken it home with him as his. He put an arm around her and drew her to him.

"All right, boys, here he comes. And it don't look to me like he likes the color of your shirts."

The bull that came trotting into the arena had horns almost four feet long. The red shirts in its path divided like the Red Sea. Sissy pressed her fingernails into Bud's thigh.

As the bull ran here and there, most of the red shirts fled before the prize. The bolder ones would approach the horns, even lunge at them, but they would always flinch at the last moment. The bull loped at will among the outlaws, who did not have the nerve to take its money.

"Come on, boys, don't be shy."

"I'd like to try that," Sissy said.

Bud didn't say anything. He just gave her a curious look. Once again, he felt her receding. She was not a little bride on a honeymoon anymore. She was something else.

"Bet I could do it."

An unflinching black cowboy in a red shirt darted out of the pack and plucked the Bull Durham sack neatly from between the bull's horns. He ran toward the fence waving it high in the air. He was a most happy prison cowboy.

"Now we know what you're in here for. Looks to me like you're a pickpocket."

"Didn't look that hard."

The bull and the red shirts returned to their pens.

"He says, no, he's no pickpocket. He's just a purse-

snatcher. Well, I think we're gonna let him explain that to the bull hisself, how he thought ol' El Toro was carryin' a purse. Just whisper it in his ear."

Bud leaned over and spoke softly to Sissy.

"Let's go find some quiet place," he said. "Okay?"

"You wanta fuck?" asked the bride.

"Well, yeah . . ."

"But I wanta see the bull-riders."

It was the first time she had ever refused him since they had met. He was a little jealous of the bull-riders even before he saw them. His new wife was going out of focus again.

"And now the final event of the day."

Sissy always felt the same way about the riding of the bulls. It was her favorite event, but it meant that the rodeo was almost over. The bulls made her happy and sad.

A couple of rodeo clowns rolled a red barrel into the center of the arena. They would hide in the barrel if the bulls came too close. They looked happy and sad, too. They had happy faces painted on, but they were still prisoners.

"And now, ladies and gentlemen, if you'll direct your attention to chute number ten. The cowboy is Wayne Hodges. It says here that his home's Sweetwater, Texas, but that ain't quite accurate. It'd be more like it to say his home's Huntsville since he ain't never gonna leave here for the rest of his life."

When the chute opened, Wayne Hodges, the lifer, lasted less than four seconds. The bull spun and bucked at the same time, and the outlaw went off sideways halfway through his ride. An outlaw clown rushed to his rescue and almost got gored for his kindness. The bull chased both the bull-rider and the clown to the fence. The clown made the audience laugh by climbing the fence with no hands. He ran up it like stairs.

Between riders, Bud reached over and removed the binoculars from Sissy's eyes. He didn't want to look through them. He wanted to kiss her. After all, it was their honeymoon. They were still kissing when chute number nine opened. She opened her eyes.

She was just in time to see the first spin catapult the prison cowboy from the bull's back. But he could not untangle his right hand from the rigging. It was as if his hand were manacled to the bull. He was dragged and kicked and trampled. Sissy bit Bud's lip.

When the outlaw finally freed himself from the rigging, he slipped to the earth and did not move. The rodeo clowns were the first ones to reach him. The kiss ended.

"What happened?" Bud asked.

"He got drug," Sissy explained.

"Prob'ly a suicide wrap."

"Uh-huh."

"Not too smart."

"That ain't it. That's just how prison cowboys are."

An ambulance rolled into the arena. A stretcher was removed from the back of the hearselike vehicle, and the broken prisoner was lifted onto it.

As the ambulance drove slowly from the arena, the next rider was already lowering himself onto the next bull. Then there came a sudden hammering of boards. The sound made Bud shift his binoculars from the long white car to chute number eight, where the bull was trying to throw the cowboy even before the gate was opened. The animal's head and shoulders came up out of the top of the chute—and the rider disappeared completely.

Suddenly Bud and Sissy were both on their feet. Lots of people were standing. Bud lowered his binoculars so that he could hug Sissy, as if she were the one in danger. And she hugged him, as if he were. There was a sense of wanting to do something but not being able to do anything except hold onto each other.

Then the fallen cowboy erupted from the chute. The other prison cowboys dragged him violently up and out. There was no time to be gentle. They hurled him over the edge of the chute and let him fall in a heap on the ground. But he got up and dusted himself off. As Bud and Sissy sat down, he climbed back up on the chute and prepared to get back on the bull.

A few deep breaths later, the cowboy lowered himself once more onto the unreliable back. Through the binoculars, Bud studied the rider as he performed his preride ritual, adjusting his glove, testing his grip on the rigging, then wrapping the rigging around his gloved hand again and again. The free cowboy in the stands watched the prison cowboy in the chute to see if he could see any fear. But he saw none, at least none he could recognize, not even under magnification. He saw nothing out of the ordinary except a curious pin on the cowboy's hat. It was a gold number: 13½.

Suddenly the chute was thrown open and the bull came twisting into the arena. The outlaw rolled expertly with the punches. He kept his feet high and floated. *One second.* Sissy reached over and took hold of the binoculars. Bud let her have them. *Two seconds.* She smiled as she pressed the glasses to her eyes. As she watched, she wondered what it would would be like actually to ride a bull. She had always wondered. *Six seconds.* If she ever did ride one, she wanted to ride it like this cowboy. He moved with the bull. He didn't fight it. He didn't try to overpower it. *Buzzer!* The cowboy let go the rigging and slid to the ground, somehow escaping without falling under the freight train's wheels.

Sissy watched the cowboy for a moment to make sure he was all right. Then she turned the glasses back to the bull, which kept on bucking, all alone in the middle of the arena, trying to dislodge a burden that was no longer there, spinning around and around, like the wheel of a windmill.

17

The Bull

Like the wheel of a windmill, the machine spun in a cruel circle. And as it turned, it bucked. It was a headless, legless, automated monster. This hybrid of animal and engine had been created out of leather and plastic and gears. It had the body of a bull but the heart of a pickup. A piston, rather than sinews, made it buck.

Even before they saw the machine—while they were still paying at the door—Bud and Sissy sensed that the saloon was different. It was louder, more excited, and somehow meaner. They looked around warily, but there were too many cowboys and cowboy hats in their way for them to be able to see the source of the changed mood.

"Wanta beer?" Bud asked.

"No, let's go see what's goin' on," Sissy said.

They joined a whole herd of cowboys all moving in the same direction. As she walked, Sissy occasionally raised herself up on tiptoes, but she still was not tall enough to see over the bobbing field of hats.

"Can you see?" asked Sissy.

"Yeah," said Bud.

"What is it?"

"I dunno."

They kept crowding their way forward, closing in on the new and rather ominous curiosity. Bud took Sissy's hand. When she first caught a glimpse of the machine, her gilded eyes grew rounder. Then a cowboy stepped in front of her

and she lost sight of it again. Pressing on, she saw it again.
She sensed that it could hurt people, which made it more
magnetic. Propelled by her long strides, Sissy bore down on it
the way she had born down on Bud that first night they
danced together.

"What the fuck is that thing?" Sissy asked.

"How many times am I gonna have to answer that question?" asked Steve Strange.

"Least once more."

"It's a mechanical bull."

"What?"

"It's what they train bull-riders on. It's a buckin'
machine."

Sissy bit a finger as she studied this machine that had in-
vaded her saloon.

"Looks mean," she said.

"Uh-huh," he agreed. "Heh heh heh heh heh."

Once she knew what it was, it was as though she had always known. It was a mechanical bull, of course. At first, she
was acutely aware of its being a machine, but she grew less
and less so as she watched it buck. The longer she studied it,
the more she thought of it, not as a piece of machinery, but
simply as a bull. This engine came to life in her coyote eyes.

"Who's gonna be the first to ride it?" asked Steve. "Heh
heh heh heh heh."

The bucking bull had a clanging bell tied to its ass.
Mattresses were spread all around it on the concrete floor to
break falls before the falls broke bones. Chairs had been arranged in a circle around the mattresses. And at the eye of
the circle, the bull spun and bucked and rang its bell, chal-
lenging all the cowboys in the bar to prove that they were
worthy of the name.

"Come on, who's gonna be my first customer?"

Bud's eyes left the bull long enough to focus on Steve
Strange, who sat on the perimeter of the bullring operating
the bull by remote controls. Curious about the controls, he
moved a few steps closer. The bucking was controlled by a
simple on—off switch. Turn the machine on and it bucked,
turn it off and it stopped. It was like the ignition switch in a
car. Then there was a miniature steering wheel that controlled the spinning. When Steve turned the wheel to the left,
the bull spun to the left. When he turned it to the right, the

bull reversed directions, bucking all the while. Steve noticed Bud's interest in the controls.

"Come on, Bud," the bull master said, "ride the bull. You're tough. Heh heh heh heh heh."

"No," Bud said, "lemme see somebody else ride it first. I ain't no test pilot."

"I'll ride it first," Sissy said.

"No, you won't," her new husband told her.

Sissy did not protest, but she pouted. Now she found the bull more magnetic than ever because it had been denied her—more magnetic and more dangerous.

"How much does it cost to ride the damn thing, Steve?" Norman called out.

"Two dollars," Steve announced.

The crowd grumbled. That seemed high.

"For how long?"

"Eight seconds. Just like in the rodeo."

For the first time, Bud noticed a sign lettered in red and nailed to a nearby wall: RIDE THE BULL AT YOUR OWN RISK. This warning naturally added to the sense of menace.

"How bad could that thing hurt you?" Bud asked.

"Pretty bad," Steve Strange said, "but it'll make you a cowboy."

Bud could feel Sissy move her eyes from the bull to him. He glanced down into the gold. Then suddenly he took two dollars out of his pocket and moved up to the table.

"Be careful, Bud," Sissy said.

"First, you gotta sign a release," Steve explained, "sayin' you won't sue Gilley's if you bust your ass."

Bud signed the release without reading it, as the crowd around the bull continued to grow.

"You ever been on a bull before?" Steve asked.

"Nope," Bud admitted. "Rode some calves."

"Well, this here's a little bit differ'nt. You right-handed or left-handed?"

"Right."

"Okay, put this glove on your left hand. I wantcha to ride left-handed, see? 'Cause that way, if your hand gets broke, you can still work. Right?"

"Okay."

Steve handed Bud a rough leather glove, which was supposed to be a bull-rider's glove but which was actually a day laborer's glove. He had bought it down at the hardware store at the corner of Spencer and Shaver.

" 'S all yours," said Steve, nodding toward the bull.

Bud started out across the mattresses. He wobbled a little on the soft footing, like a toddler, but he kept going. He could feel Sissy watching him. Everyone was watching him. He felt conspicuous again, but not in an unpleasant way. People weren't looking at him because he was out of place but because he was doing something special. Still he was a little uneasy. With all these people staring at him, Bud didn't want to look foolish. He wobbled again on the mattresses, and his nerve swayed slightly, too.

"Don't hurt him now, Steve," Sissy cautioned.

"It's on real low," Steve reassured her.

"What?"

"It's got differ'nt speeds. I got it on low, so I don't kill somebody right off."

"Promise?"

"Course. I got it set on three. It'll go all the way up to ten. Heh heh heh heh heh."

When he reached the center of the bullring, Bud hesitated for a moment and then vaulted aboard the bull. Suddenly he realized that he didn't know where to sit, didn't know how to hold on, didn't know anything about bull riding. He tried to remember what he had seen at the prison rodeo, but it didn't help. The satisfaction he had originally felt at being the center of attention was turning into worry. He wished they would stop staring at him. At first, he had wanted to show off for Sissy. Now her coyote eyes frightened him as much as the bull did.

"Hey, Steve," Bud said with a little laugh to cover how he really felt, "how the hell do you ride this Goddamn thing?"

"Put your right nut in your left hand," Steve explained, "and hang on."

Everyone laughed. Bud did, too. But it was as though they were all laughing at him. He put his right hand up in the air the way he had seen bull-riders do, but it did not make him feel more secure on the bull's back. Instead, he was all too aware that this was his crippled hand. He seemed to be holding up his cut-off finger for everyone to look at. *Look! Can you see? I'm not like you.*

"You ready?" yelled Steve.

"As I'll ever be," Bud called back.

Steve pressed the button that brought the machine to life. The motor came on with a snort. And suddenly the bull put its headless head-end down and its legless rear came up in the air. Bud was pitched forward onto his balls. He felt as if they were going to crack like robin's eggs.

Bud's manhood crashed into the rigging—which was supposed to help him in his ride, but which was actually a hammer banging between his legs. This rigging was a hard leather handle that would not give a fraction of an inch—or forgive. The bell tied to the bull clanged maddeningly in Bud's ears. He was frightened. He was afraid he was being neutered at the very beginning of his marriage. His sexual organs were taking a terrible beating. Since the mechanical bull had no testicles, it seemed to want no one else to have them either. The pain soaked Bud with sweat.

"Ride 'em!" yelled Sissy, excited.

All the cowboys and cowgirls were cheering and jeering. Steve spun Bud first to the right, then back to the left, then to the right again, punctuating each turn with *heh heh heh heh heh*. He understood better than the others what Bud was going through.

"Hold on!" Sissy shouted above the others.

Then Steve put the bull in a dead spin, never changing directions, whirling Bud dizzy. It was like trying to ride a spinning windmill. Bud felt the same falling sensation he had felt on the windmill *that* night. Yet on that other night, he had caught himself, he had saved himself—only a part of him had fallen. Tonight all of him was falling and he could do nothing about it.

Bud hit the mattress with his right shoulder first. Getting up, furious, Bud pulled two more dollars out of his pocket.

"I wanta ride it again," he announced.

Moving unsteadily back to the table, Bud lay down his quaking money.

"Okay," said Steve. Then he added, "Hurts your nuts, don't it?"

Bud did not say anything, but his walk was answer enough. He limped toward the mean machine. Rather than vaulting, he crawled onto the bull's back.

"Ready?"

"As I'll ever . . ."

Suddenly the bull was bucking again. And Bud's manhood was once again crashing against the rigging, time after time, like breaker waves.

"Hang on!" yelled Sissy.

Bud felt his ass coming unstuck from the bull's back. It rose higher and higher in the air. Then he pitched forward. He went head first over the "head" of the bull—and as he did so the rigging clawed at his balls.

"That's just about the worse way to get off a bull there is," Steve said as if he were holding class. "Good way to lose your nuts and never find 'em again."

Sissy started out across the mattresses to Bud, but he did not see her. He just got up hurting and clawed his way back onto the bull. It was as if he thought the machine must be getting tired. He would wear it out.

"You didn't pay," Steve called to his victim.

"Sissy, give him two dollars," Bud yelled.

As she walked toward the table, Bud felt his stomach spinning. He was dizzy and afraid he was going to throw up with everyone watching. He was sick from his knees to his eyes. The pain throbbed with a mechanical regularity, as if it were run by a motor, too.

"Keep your knees up," Steve said. "And snuggle up as close to the rigging as you can get. That'll keep you from slammin' into it."

When the rider scooted up, Steve turned on the bull. The rigging still was not kind to Bud, but at least it did not have an opportunity to deliver any more haymakers.

"Ride it, Bud!" Sissy yelled. "Ride it! Ride it!"

Bud began moving with the bull instead of trying to fight it off. When the bull's "head" went down, he leaned back. When the "head" came up, he leaned forward.

"You're doin' it, Bud!" yelled Sissy. "You're doin' it! Come on!"

Bud almost lost his balance, lurching to the right, but somehow he pulled hard and saved himself. As he crashed back into position, the big leather fist hit his balls again, hit hard enough to register 300 on any meter, hit firmly enough to set off sirens inside his head.

"Okay!" Steve called. "Eight seconds."

As the bull stopped bucking, Bud slid down off its back. He just stood there a moment, leaning against the machine to keep his balance. He was surprised to hear everyone applauding. The sound made him look up. Sissy was clapping and smiling at him. He staggered toward her.

"Fuck, that was the longest eight seconds I ever knew about in my life," Bud said.

"I wanta ride it," Sissy said.

"No, ma'am," said her husband.

"Why not?"

"It's too dangerous."

"No, it ain't."

The saloon was beginning to spin as if Bud were still riding the windmill bull. He sat down on the mattresses and put his hands between his legs. He was afraid he had been crippled again.

18

Sore Balls

When they reached home, Bud and Sissy heard the radio playing in their trailer. The newlyweds had kept the radio going in their new home constantly, even when they weren't at home, ever since they got married, tuned to KIKK, the self-proclaimed "kicker spot on your dial." The truck radio was also set on KIKK. So when they came home—or left home—they never had to miss part of a song. As the truck stopped with a soft crunch in the driveway, the two radios sang:

> *Mamas, don't let your babies*
> *Grow up to be cowboys . . .*

Bud's soft moan mingled with the dual voices of Waylon Jennings and Willie Nelson singing together. He was still in pain.

> *Don't let 'em pick guitars*
> *And drive them old trucks . . .*

Leaning over to turn off the truck radio, Bud moaned even louder.

"I'm sorry," Sissy said.

"Ain't your fault," Bud said.

"I know. Still wisht I could do somethin'."

While they whispered in the dark pickup cab, they heard the radio in the trailer softly singing:

> *Let 'em be doctors*
> *And lawyers and such.*

They both opened their doors and got out. Bud closed his door and leaned against it. Sissy hurried to him. She put her arm around him. He smiled as if it were a joke, but actually it hurt worse standing up than it had sitting down. His pride kept him from leaning on Sissy the first few steps. Then he put his arm around her and leaned. The stairs hurt him. The walk across the living room and down the narrow hall was only slightly less painful.

By the time they reached the bedroom, Waylon and Willie were nearing the end of their song:

> *Mommas don't let your babies*
> *Grow up to be cowboys.*
> *They'll never stay home . . .*

Bud lay down on his back with his balls cupped in his hands. That didn't help so he raised his legs in the air. Sissy was getting undressed.

"They gettin' any better?" she asked.

"Worse," Bud grimaced. "I think they're swellin' up."

Looking down at him, Sissy tried to keep from grinning, but she couldn't.

> *And they're always alone,*
> *Even with someone they love.*

"What's so funny?" Bud asked.

"Nothin'," Sissy said.

Then they both laughed out loud.

"Aw, that hurts," he said. "Don't make me laugh. It pulls somethin'."

They laughed harder than ever. They were the way they had been at their wedding, each keeping the other laughing.

"Want me to kiss 'em," Sissy said, out of breath, "and make 'em all better?"

"No!" Bud said.

And they laughed some more.

"You didn't brush your teeth," she laughed.

"And I'm not gonna," he laughed.

"Well, I am."

Bud's naked wife went in the bathroom and started cleaning her teeth. At first, she laughed even with toothpaste in her mouth, but slowly she calmed down. And in the bedroom Bud did, too. Then Sissy returned with the toothbrush in her mouth. A drop of toothpaste fell on her left breast and stayed there.

"You rode real good," Sissy said, her words distorted by toothpaste.

Then she hurried back into the bathroom to rinse the paste out of her mouth. Bud could hear her gargling. He winced as he heard her returning.

Crawling onto the bed, Sissy knelt between his raised legs. She put her hands on his knees. Looking down at him from the traditional male perspective, she was no longer laughing. She looked concerned, sympathetic, worried.

"Ain't we gonna do nothin'?" she asked.

"I don't know if I can," he said.

Bud felt a throbbing in his crotch as though his heart had descended to his scrotum. And this scrotum heart was in distress. Pain radiated down into his legs, up into his abdomen.

"Be the first night," Sissy said, "since we got married that we ain't done nothin'. Twang twang."

She stared softly down into his reddening eyes. He shifted on the bed and winced.

"Okay," Bud said, "but we'll have to take it easy."

Sissy helped Bud out of his clothes. The shirt was easy. The boots were harder. When she pulled on them, each boot felt as if it were attached to a ball. The jeans were a little easier but not much. Bud almost expected to see blood on his jockey shorts, but there was none. Sissy removed those, too. Sissy turned out the light. Bud could barely see her as she moved toward him. Then he felt her hand. He flinched.

"Ow!"

"I hardly touched 'em."

"Maybe we better not . . ."

"Lemme try this."

Gently, carefully, tenderly, she put one of his crippled balls in her mouth, just as she had once put her mouth around his crippled finger. At first, it hurt and Bud flinched again. *Ow!* But then the cool bath began to soothe the pain.

"That's better," he said.

Sissy relaxed him. And then she aroused him. And then she mounted him. In the beginning, they made crippled love.

"Am I hurtin' you?" asked Sissy.

"Yeah," winced Bud.

Sissy tried to be more careful, but she didn't stop. As they slowly gained momentum, it kept on hurting, but Bud cared less and less about the pain. He began bucking rhythmically beneath her. Perhaps it was this motion that made her think of it. Or perhaps it was something else entirely. At any rate, in the middle of their lovemaking, Sissy thought about the bull. She promised herself that she would ride it. And it wouldn't flinch and it wouldn't tire.

19

The Boiler

Bud walked with a slight limp that was actually a secret swagger. It was his way of reminding himself and others of what he had done the night before. He limped to the tool shed. He limped to the workbench where the foam glass patiently awaited him. He limped past Ray.

"I hear you're a real honky-tonk hotshot," the foreman said.

Somehow word had spread through the shop that Bud had ridden the honky-tonk bull last night. They all knew that he had been bucked off but had kept on trying until he stayed on. Everyone was interested in the new bull and the cowboy who had ridden it. Now, he sensed, the other workers accepted him as they never had before. Some were even a little jealous of him. He was no longer the new boy, the new hire, he was a bull-rider.

"Nope," Bud said.

He could deny that he had done anything special because he knew he had.

"That's not what I hear," Ray persisted.

Bud shrugged and limped over to the band saw. He pushed a piece of foam glass toward the whirring blade. Soon the air was filled with itchy mist. When he finished cutting the piece of insulation, Bud paused to scratch.

"What's the matter?" asked Ray.

"Stuff itches," Bud said.

"You don't like cuttin' foam glass?"

"It's all right."

"Well, I guess it really ain't no job for a hotshot, is it?"

"I didn't say nothin'."

The other workers were watching and listening now. Ray had been picking on Bud—what they called "riding him"—ever since he came to work at the refinery. They were almost used to it. But now they knew more about Bud, were more interested in him, and so paid closer attention.

"Come with me," Ray said. "I gotta job for you. You, too, Marshall. Come on."

Bud followed Ray with a slight limp. When he had gotten up that morning, his balls had been better, but he had found a black bruise six inches long on his right thigh. He favored his right leg as he walked.

"What's the matter with your leg?" Ray asked.

"Nothin'," Bud said.

Marshall caught up to Bud. They exchanged puzzled looks.

"I used to work up to Huntsville, you know," the foreman said as they walked. "And the boys up there were always gettin' stove up like that, one way and another. Oh yeah, they used to pull some real dumb stunts just to get outa workin'."

Bud made an effort to stop limping and succeeded to a certain extent.

"Worse was one day this guy just started walkin' off the cell block. So I started closin' the big doors. Real heavy. But he just kept acomin'. So I didn't have no choice but to close the damn doors right on his pukin' head. Pinched it right in two. Guess he got what he wanted though. Never had to do another lick a work in his life."

Ray chuckled at his own story. Marshall laughed a dry laugh. And Bud just tried to keep from limping. Ray led the way out of the shop into the sunshine—which did bring a faint smile from Bud. Maybe it wasn't going to be so bad, after all. He liked working in the out-of-doors.

Bud and Marshall followed Ray across a dirt road and on through an acre of dirt used to park heavy equipment. They kept going until they came to the foot of a metal ladder that led up to a raised platform twenty feet in the air. All three of them climbed the ladder, one after the other—Ray, then Bud, then Marshall. When they reached the top, they stood in a little group, like friends.

"Marshall," Ray said, "I want you to show your buddy how to clean a boiler."

The sun never shines in a boiler. It was a long cylindrical tank with what looked like a submarine door at one end. The inside was coated with tar. There was little light and less air. It was as though Bud and Marshall had been swallowed by a dirty, metallic whale.

Bud felt trapped, caged. He took shallow, hurried breaths of stale, stuffy air. He sweated hard in the hot tin can. And he itched. Even here he could not escape the foam glass. He used chunks of it, like synthetic steel wool, to scrub the tar collected on the imprisoning walls. Wiping his hand across his wet face, he ground foam glass deep into his skin. Then he scratched his sweaty, itchy face. The pressure was building in some inner boiler buried in his brain, the needle edging toward the red zone.

"I cain't stand this much more," Bud said.

"Me neither," Marshall said.

The difference was that Bud meant it. He felt all the frustrations of all his days on the job coming to bear upon him at this moment. The pressure inside the curved walls of his boiler skull now threatened to set off some kind of explosion at any moment. And it kept mounting.

While he waited for the relieving bang, Bud kept on scrubbing at the collected tar with the gnawing glass. In the half-darkness, he barked his knuckles against the hard hide of his enemy. Then he badly scraped the tip of his cut-off finger. It not only hurt him, but it seemed to humiliate him as well. After the pain, a wave of anger surged through him. The pressure was intolerable now. He angrily threw down the mean foam glass.

"Shit!" Bud snapped. "I quit."

"You don't mean it," Marshall said, a little worried.

"Yeah, I do."

Bud headed toward the air lock at the end of the boiler, which looked too much like a prison door. Marshall followed him. They moved in single file toward the light.

"Wait."

"No, I gotta get outa here."

He had to get out of the giant boiler before the boiler in his head ruptured. He had to get out of the refinery. He had to get away from the foreman before the door clanged shut.

"You know you're doin' just what Ray wants you to."

"I don't give a fuck."

Bud was almost to the light.

"What about Sissy?"

Bud half turned, his hand on the air lock.

"What about her?"

"You're married now. You cain't just do what *you* want no more."

Bud thought it over. Had he forfeited the right to quit impulsively because he had proposed impulsively?

"See what I mean?"

"Maybe."

Bud stood half in the darkness and half out. He didn't move. Marshall could see that he had checked his friend's flight.

"Come on back," Marshall said. "I wanta hear all about that damn bull. How hard is it to ride?"

"Well, it ain't easy," Bud said with a half-smile in the half-light.

Then he slowly walked back into the darkness as a heavy door seemed to close behind him.

At quitting time, Ray returned to check on his young men in the boiler. The boiler was marginally cleaner and they were incredibly dirtier. The foreman stuck his head into the blackness of the iron whale, looked around, and motioned them out. They emerged from the world of shadows, looking like shadows themselves. Seeing them, Ray was pleased with his day's work. At the same time, he softened slightly. He was glad that they were so tired, and yet their exhaustion touched him. Ray smiled a good-humored smile, which Bud took to be a mocking smile.

"How do you like boiler work?" Ray asked.

The foreman meant the question as a kind of joke. He asked it in the spirit of someone who asks if a hot day is hot enough for you. He laughed and clapped Bud on the back. The new hire misunderstood.

"Just fine," Bud said defiantly.

Ray recoiled not at the words but at the tone. Just when he was softening, Bud seemed to harden. In a sense, the foreman felt betrayed.

"Don't get cute with me," Ray snapped. " 'Cause you're still on probation. You know what that means?"

"What?"

"That means I gotcha by the honeymoon. And I'm gonna hang on good 'n' tight."

Bud, who had almost forgotten his injuries of the night before, suddenly remembered how sore his balls were. He limped.

20

The Stranger

When they walked into the saloon that night, Bud and Sissy headed straight for the bull without even stopping at the bar. As they went, Bud scratched at the foam glass, which no amount of soap and water could wash from his skin. At first, he scratched hard, then more gently, then only lightly and absentmindedly. By the time he reached the bullring, Bud was no longer scratching any more at all. Now the only itch he felt was to ride the bull again. He wanted to try it on a higher speed.

The couple nodded at Steve Strange, who was in his place at the bull controls. Steve touched the brim of his hat. They walked over to his table.

"How you been?" Bud asked.

"Cain't complain," Steve said.

"Hurt anybody tonight?"

"A few. Heh heh heh heh heh."

Steve, who in his earlier days had been hurt repeatedly by bulls, seemed to enjoy hurting others. He evidently believed that what had happened to him should happen to all the Gilley's bull-riders.

"I'm gettin' pretty good at this," Steve boasted. "I can throw the hat off a cowboy and then throw the cowboy in his hat."

"Betcha cain't throw me in mine," Bud boasted.

"Heh heh heh heh heh."

A drunk cowboy paid his two dollars, signed his wobbly

signature on the waiver, and staggered toward the bull. Steve, who had spent years of his life in bars, had grown to hate drunks. He winked at Sissy as if to say that they were in for some fun. Reaching the machine, the drunk had no idea how to mount it.

"How you go about this?" asked the drunk.

"Hurry up," Steve yelled.

The drunk cowboy tried to crawl aboard, but he kept slipping and sliding back to the mattresses.

"Get a ladder," Steve called.

The drunk cowboy's girl friend appeared out of the crowd and with her help, the cowboy finally mounted the bull.

"Ready?" asked Steve.

"Look how he's sittin'," Sissy said in a low voice.

"Heh heh heh heh heh."

The drunk cowboy was sitting far back from the rigging. The first buck would obviously send him roller-coastering down the bull's back directly into the hard leather grip. Understanding the danger, Sissy could not help giggling.

"Here goes," Steve said.

The bull master pushed the button—and the cowboy came crashing down onto the rigging with a terrible vengeance. The bull rider screamed in pain, Steve laughed, and Sissy could not stop giggling.

"Don't kill him!" yelled the drunk's girl friend.

But it was too late. The drunk went headfirst over the "head" of the bull. Then he lay on the big bed with his knees pulled up, clutching his balls.

"What've you done to him?" cried the girl friend.

Everybody laughed.

"Twang, twang," giggled Sissy.

Bud strode out to the bull as the cowboy with the wounded balls crawled from the bullring. Vaulting aboard, he began tugging on the work glove.

"What's it on?" Bud yelled to Steve.

"Three," Steve called back.

"Turn it up to four."

A little fussily, Steve Strange left his place behind the bull controls and walked out across the mattresses to the bull itself. There he knelt down as if before some mechanized altar, but he was not praying to the bull, he was making it meaner. The speed control was located at the base of the bull. Reaching down, Steve turned a small handle to the right—from three up to four. Then he retreated to the comfort of the controls. As he was adjusting himself in his seat, he sensed a woman bending toward him.

"I wanta ride it, Steve," Sissy whispered. "Any girls rode it yet?"

"Just Jessie," Steve smiled. "She rode it this afternoon. Heh heh heh heh heh."

Sissy looked over at Jessie, who grinned. Jessie had the long, thin, nose-dominated face of a bronco. She wore boots and jeans but a halter instead of a cowboy shirt.

"Jessie rode it?" Sissy asked.

"Yep," Steve said.

"I wanta ride it, Steve."

Waiting on the bull's back, Bud began to grow impatient. He was anxious to prove that he was still the best bull-rider in the honky-tonk. He was wise enough not to make that boast out loud because he knew he would get an argument. But he nonetheless thought he was. And he knew Sissy thought so, too.

"Get closer to the rigging," Steve called humanely.

"I'm already tryin' to hatch it," Bud said.

Then the bull master pushed the buck button. Next he turned the miniature steering wheel, and the bull began to spin. First one way and then the other.

"Ride it!" Sissy yelled, thinking all the while how much she would like to ride it.

This ride was Bud's roughest yet. He knew he was not riding gracefully, but at least he was riding stubbornly. The bull's bell was more maddeningly loud than ever—as he was tossed back and forth like a human bell clapper, his insides ringing, his brain seeming to clang within his skull.

"Eight seconds!" yelled Steve Strange.

When the machine stopped, everyone applauded. The sound of the clapping seemed to restore some self-control to Bud's body. He slid down off the bull and staggered forward —self-conscious and grinning. Sissy put two fingers in her mouth and whistled.

"Pretty good," Steve said.

"God*damn*!" Bud said.

While Bud was still grinning shyly and proudly, another cowboy walked up to the table and laid a bill on it. The motion had considerable authority. The hand that held the money had extravagant confidence in itself. It was a ten-dollar bill but a hundred-dollar gesture.

"Hello, Steve," said the newcomer. "How you doin'? Remember me?"

"Sure, Wes," Steve said. "I'm doin' okay. How about you?"

"Cain't complain. Betcha ten bucks you cain't throw me."

Bud's gaze moved from the confident hands up to the arms, which were tattooed. A green snake slithered down one forearm, ready to strike. A red scorpion crawled up the other, ready to sting. A little higher up, a miniature pair of handcuffs floated on a proud bicep. Glancing around, Bud noticed that Sissy was studying the stranger, too.

"Sorry, Wes," Steve said. "I cain't do no gamblin' around the bull. Gilley don't like it."

"Steve," Wes said in a scolding tone, "ten bucks."

Now Bud was staring Wes straight in the face, which he found oddly familiar. He looked away but soon looked back. For some reason, Bud found himself measuring himself against this new cowboy. Bud was younger, maybe ten or fifteen years younger. Wes was in his middle thirties, at least, with little wrinkles beginning to form around his eyes. Bud was looking for weaknesses.

Sissy looked at the stranger through other eyes. She saw his strengths, the straight nose, the handsome brown eyes, the muscles beneath the tattoos. And he had the perfect straight teeth you do not expect to find in a man with pictures on his arms.

"All right," Steve said, "ten dollars."

The bull master tried to hand Wes a work glove, but he would not take it. Reaching in his hip pocket, Wes pulled out a real bull-rider's glove. He tugged it onto his right hand, taking his time, doing it right, because he well understood the importance and the drama of close attention to detail. Once the tight-fitting glove was on the hand, he took out a leather thong and tied it in place, wrapping it around and around his wrist, knotting it with his left hand and his straight teeth. Then he flexed his leather-covered fingers. The gloved hand looked more self-assured than ever. It was a hand with presence.

"What's it on?" Wes asked.

"Four," Steve said.

"I'm gonna turn it up to six."

As Wes walked out toward the bull, he swayed a little on the mattresses but not much. Then he knelt before the bull. Once he had turned it up, he vaulted aboard. Then he slipped his hand into the rigging. He spent even longer adjusting his grip than he had adjusting the glove. He opened his fist and then closed it, opened it and then closed it again. It was as if he were riding for big prize money instead of a ten-dollar bet. Every movement was professionally exact. When he was finally ready, Wes looked up at Steve.

"Okay," Wes said.

Steve turned on the bull like a light, bringing it to life. It began hammering unmercifully at the rider, but he did not seem to mind. It was quite beautiful the way he rode, his body arching in the rhythm of the bull. He rode it as surely as a spur rides a boot, as confidently as a six-gun rides the hip of a movie cowboy, as gracefully as a weather vane rides a windmill. No one had ever ridden the bull at Gilley's like this.

Watching from the sidelines, Bud was jealous. He tried to study how the stranger did it. He was already half aware that he would soon be borrowing this style. And yet he hated the teacher. He sensed that his stature in Gilley's was shrinking buck by buck, spin by spin. He had been the fastest gun in town, but a faster gun had just arrived.

Wes was even pretending to spur. He raked the imaginary bull's sides with his imaginary rowels. It was a graceful but nonetheless gratuitous motion that seemed to say that he did not need his legs to hang on. Bud hated those spurs that weren't there.

Steve was working hard at bucking Wes off, twisting the wheel of the bull controls first one way and then another, as if he were driving a getaway car down a twisting dirt road. But the rider easily rode the bounding, twisting back. He even smiled down at the bull master.

The cowgirls, who were gathered around the bull, were excited by the sexual power of the ride. Some of their bodies mimed, ever so slightly, the rhythm of his riding. The bucking machine had great sexual energy—and the tamer of that machine inherited some of that energy.

Even Sissy was attracted to him. It was obvious even to her prejudiced stare that Wes could ride much better than Bud. Taking her eyes off the rider momentarily, she glanced at her husband. She could see that he was trying to hide his jealousy. Then she looked back at the rider.

The grace of Wes's ride was in the fluid movement. In a sense, he conquered the bull by surrendering to it, by going any way the bull wanted to go. He moved with the bull the way a lasso moves with a roper's hand, up and back and round and round.

The crowd began applauding even before the ride was over. When the bull finally stopped, and Wes slid painlessly down, the applause built into an ovation. Bud stuck his hands deep in his Levi's pockets. Wes walked over to the bull master's table, where he picked up his money with his gloved hand. Then he walked off toward the bar, untying his glove as he went. Sissy watched him go, which made Bud clench his fists in his pockets. From the outside, it looked as if his balls had taken a beating and were swelling.

"I'm gonna ride it again," said Bud in a fit of competitiveness.

"*I* wanta ride it," Sissy protested.

"You get me another beer," Bud ordered.

Sissy started to refuse, but then she moved off toward the bar. She was following Bud's orders, but she was also following Wes. Bud immediately regretted sending his wife on this errand. At the bar, Sissy waited in line behind Wes to be served.

"That's the best bull ridin' I ever saw," Sissy said. "You a real cowboy?"

As Wes was turning, half smiling, Bud appeared behind his wife. He took her by the arm.

"Come on," Bud said.

"What's the matter?" asked Sissy. "What about your beer?"

"I ain't thirsty no more."

"How come?"

"I want you to quit that flirtin'."

"I wasn't flirtin'. I was just payin' him a compliment. I don't call that flirtin'."

"Well, I do. Let's just dance."

Bud led Sissy to the dance floor, farther and farther from the best mechanical bull rider either of them had ever seen. When they reached the other dancing couples, she put her finger through his belt loop and he grabbed her hair, but he took hold of it a little too firmly, pulling it, hurting her, as he acted out a painful possessiveness.

While they danced, Bud and Sissy both noticed Wes walk over and stand at the edge of the dance floor, drinking a Lone Star. His eyes with little wrinkles around them squinted each time a pretty woman danced by. When Sissy passed, he squinted at her, too. Then he nodded and touched the brim of his black hat. Bud stared back angrily at the gesture and at the hat. It was decorated with a curious gold pin. Looking more closely, Bud saw that it was a number: 13½.

Sissy looked at Wes and then beyond him. She focused on the bull, which was still bucking in the background. She wanted not only to ride it but to ride it the way the stranger had ridden it.

21

Stonie's

Sitting in a booth in the back of Stonie's, Bud took another hot gulp from the silver-colored flask. It was too late to buy a drink but not too late to borrow one. And Bud was not ready to stop drinking yet. Wiping his mouth, he noticed his reflection mirrored in the flask's shiny surface. He looked distorted, his nose crooked, one eye bigger than the other, his mouth a smear. The cowboy in the flask did not look the way Bud looked, but he did look the way he felt. In that sense, it was a perfect likeness. It was as though the flask mirrored feelings rather than mere surface features.

At three o'clock in the morning, Bud *was* distorted. He was distorted by drink. His balls were swollen and distorted from riding the bull—although they were not nearly as bad as they had been the night before. Worst of all, his image of himself was distorted. He was no longer impressed with his own bull riding, which meant that he was no longer impressed with himself. He felt a little foolish for having believed that he was better than he really was. But now he knew.

"Give it back."

"Huh?"

"The flask—give it back. I want some."

Looking up from his own image, Bud grinned drunkenly at Marshall, who was seated across from him in the booth. It was his flask. Marshall had gone to Gilley's that night to ride the bull, but he had never quite worked up the courage. Perhaps he should have felt even worse than Bud, but he didn't. Beside him sat Crystal, his girl friend, who dyed her hair blonde and wore her cowboy shirt tied in a knot under her breasts.

"Sorry," Bud said, handing over the flask.

Marshall lifted the flask to his lips. Then he passed it to Crystal, who in turn handed it to Sissy. Goose bumps came up on Sissy's arms, but she didn't notice because she was studying Bud.

"Come on, cheer up," Sissy said. "I know, tell 'em the one Norman told you, the one about how you get to be a cowboy. That's a good one."

"Well," Bud said, "I dunno . . ."

"Aw, come on."

Bud did not feel like being funny, but he would try. He leaned forward and rested his elbows on the counter.

"All right," Bud said a little too seriously, "this here's how you get to be a cowboy. What you do is you get yourself a big handful of marbles and you put all them marbles in your mouth." Pausing in his story, Bud puffed out his cheeks as if his mouth actually were full of marbles at this moment. He amused himself with this gesture and felt a little better. "And, you see, ever time you ride that damn bull, you spit out one a them marbles." He paused before his punch line and then got it wrong. "And by the time you've spit out all your marbles, you're a cowboy."

"That ain't it," Sissy said. "You're drunk."

"Whaddaya mean that ain't it?"

"You're s'posed to say '*lost* your marbles.' "

"Oh, yeah, that's it."

Marshall and Crystal finally laughed. And Marshall passed the flask back to Bud. When he saw his reflection this time, it was a clown's distorted laughing face.

"Hey, Jessie," Sissy called.

Jessie, who was on her way to the jukebox, stopped to see what Sissy wanted. She was rubbing two quarters together.

"Yeah," Jessie said.

"You really ride that bull?"

"Uh-huh." Jessie smiled with crooked teeth. "Steve let me in there this afternoon and let me ride it as much as I wanted. I'm sore as hell, but I rode it up to three."

"Damn, I wanta ride it."

Glancing up from the flask, Bud looked angry. The alcohol had fueled his temper.

"Now don't start that again," he told his wife.

"Well, she rode it," his wife protested.

"I don't give a damn."

Suddenly Bud got even angrier. His fist hit the Formica top of the table, rattling the coffee cups. He was staring in the direction of the long counter.

"What the hell was that?" Bud asked.

"What?" answered Sissy.

Her husband was glaring at Wes, who was lowering his hat onto his head. Preoccupied with his own reflection, Bud had not seen Wes enter the restaurant with Steve. Now Wes, his hand still on his hat, smiled in their direction. His features distorted by anger, Bud looked from Wes to his own wife.

"What's he doin' tippin' his hat at you?"

"Shhh, Bud."

"Don't he know we're married?"

Bud grabbed Sissy's hand and held it up, pointing to the wedding band. Embarrassed, she struggled to pull her hand away, but he held it tight.

"Hey, Tattoo!" Bud called. "See this ring?"

Wes pretended not even to hear the question, but everyone else in the small restaurant did hear and looked up. Bud, who normally hated being conspicuous, was too drunk and mad to care. But Sissy cared. Still trying to free her hand, she looked around at all the staring faces. Then she stared down at the Formica tabletop, hiding.

"That's a weddin' band. That means we're married. Okay? She's my old lady, and she don't want nothin' to do with you. Got it?"

Ignoring this outburst completely, Wes turned to Steve and said something so softly that no one else could hear. Then Wes and Steve took seats at the counter.

"Don't act silly, Bud," Sissy scolded.

Pulling hard, she finally managed to wrest her hand out of her husband's grip. She hid it and her ring under the table. She hoped Bud would calm down now, but he didn't.

"She belongs to me, okay?" Bud called.

"I don't belong to nobody," Sissy said in a much lower voice. " 'Cept myself."

When she looked up to punctuate her declaration, she saw not only Bud looking at her but many others as well. She looked down again. Normally, she was not easily embarrassed, but tonight she felt especially sensitive, perhaps in part because of Wes's presence.

"You hear me, Tattoo!"

Swiveling on his counter stool, Wes looked back at Bud. Smiling, he reached up with his middle finger and touched the brim of his hat in a gesture of mock courtesy. Then he turned away.

"Did you see that?" Bud asked.

"What?" asked Sissy, looking up again.

"Did he just give me the finger?"

As he waited for an answer, Bud's eyes moved from Sissy to Crystal to Marshall.

"I didn't see it if he did," Marshall said.

"Calm down, Bud," Sissy said, "or I'm leavin'."

They were interrupted by a waitress who arrived, loaded down with plates. She had them balanced all up and down her arm. She looked tired and harried.

"Ham 'n' cheese," the waitress said. "Who gets that?"

When Marshall raised his hand, she banged a plate down in front of him.

"Cheese omelet?"

Crystal raised her hand.

"Bowl a chili?"

Sissy nodded.

"Burger, extra slice a onion?"

"That's me," Bud said, still angry. "And it better be well done now. If that cow's still movin', I'm sendin' it back."

Unimpressed by his threat, the busy waitress hurried away.

"Pass the ketchup," Crystal said.

"I think he flipped me the finger," Bud said.

"He didn't know we were married," Sissy said. "You're just jealous."

Taking a bite of his hamburger, Bud chewed unhappily. Then he studied the meat that he held in his hands. He thought he saw blood.

"Wait a minute, honey," Bud called to the waitress, who was picking up another order at the counter. "This thing's still alive."

Sissy looked down.

"I cain't help it," said the exasperated waitress. "Whaddaya want from me?"

"I want you," Bud said, rising to his feet, "to put it back on the fire!"

Looking up, Sissy saw his nostrils flare, his jaw jut forward, his eyes narrow. She did not remember until later where she had seen that expression before: that was how he had looked when he proposed to her.

"Bud!" she said.

Suddenly he hurled the bleeding hamburger at the waitress. He knew as soon as he let it go that his aim was off, way off. He felt disappointed, cheated, but only momentarily. The soggy lump of meat and bread missed the waitress and struck Wes in the middle of the back, bull's-eye. Perhaps, without knowing it, Bud had hit what he was aiming at, after all.

"Jesus!" Sissy said.

Wes got slowly to his feet.

22

Shadows in the Parking Lot

In the darkness of the parking lot, Bud faced not only Wes but other frightening shadows. He could not help remembering stories of other predawn fights, stories he had heard all his life, stories always told as a warning. Since his mother had been the storyteller, he had not always taken her warnings seriously. He knew all about a mother's fears. Sometimes he laughed. Even now he managed a smile when he thought of how worried she would be if she knew that he was about to revive a family tradition. The shadow came toward him.

Bud clenched his fists, but Wes's hands remained open, confident, in no hurry. As the shadow drew closer, Bud took a swing at it, but it ducked. He swung again and missed again. It was as though he really were fighting a shadow that he could never hit or hurt. Perhaps that was because he was so drunk. Growing frustrated, Bud charged like a bull, but Wes handled the human bull as easily as he had the mechanical one. He stepped out of the way and watched Bud rush by.

Bud had heard the story of his great-great-grandmother over and over. She was an unfortunate woman. Her first husband, whose name was Goodall, liked to spend his Saturday nights at the saloon in Spur. He was not a naturally argumentative man, but he was proud. One night some cowboy insulted him, or, at least, he thought he had been insulted. This insult led to angry words and then blows. Goodall won the fistfight, but he lost later on. Riding home after midnight, Goodall suddenly found himself facing the cowboy whom he had beaten. Seeing a gun in the cowboy's hand, he pulled a knife. They rode toward each other like knights in the lists, armed with uneven lances.

Bud charged Wes again, but again the shadow stepped out of the way. Drunk, Bud stumbled and fell in the dirt of the parking lot. While Wes waited for him, Bud rose slowly out of the dirt. Then the shadow stepped forward and hit Bud hard on the right cheek. Bud fell.

On that other early morning so long ago, the bullet hit Goodall before he could use his blade, the gun a much longer lance than the knife. Bud's great-great-grandmother's first husband clung to his saddle for half a mile, but the pain and the loss of blood finally loosened his grip, little by little, until he fell. He lay on his back, looking up at the moon, one unblinking death mask staring at another.

"Bud!" Sissy yelled.

She ran toward him.

"Stay out of this," Bud ordered.

Getting up slowly, Bud clenched his fists. The shadow stepped forward, curious to see how badly he had hurt his target. The target swung. Bud hit Wes on the forehead and staggered him back. And then Wes came back at Bud, hurrying now, mad.

When Goodall died, he left behind him an infant daughter who would become Bud's great-grandmother. Two years later, Goodall's widow, after the proper mourning, married a man named Adams. He spent his Saturday nights at the saloon, too. His wife always waited up for him because now she knew what could happen.

Wes stepped forward, punching with his left, then crossing with his right. He fought as expertly as he rode. A left hand hit Bud in the nose and opened the blood faucet. Then a right hand hit him in the throat. He started coughing. Another left hit him in the mouth.

Bud's great-great-grandmother's second husband got into a fight with a cowboy in the saloon. And the cowboy waited for him on the road home. This fight was fairer, knife against knife. They both managed to cut each other, but only Adams died. Bud's great-great-grandmother lost two husbands to fights on the saloon road. Their bodies were found within a mile of each other.

Slumping back against a pickup fender, Bud slowly sank to the ground in a sitting position. And then he just sat there as if he were watching television.

"Okay," Steve Strange said. "Hey, that's enough."

The voice of the peacemaker seemed to remind Bud of where he was and what he was there for. Pulling himself to his feet, he leaned against the pickup for a moment. Then he propelled himself back at Wes, pushing off the truck.

"Bud!" Steve said. "Fight's over."

Sissy rushed up and hugged Bud, pinning his arms to his sides. He struggled in her grasp, but she held him tightly. He could not free himself without hurting her.

"No more," she said.

"I'm bleedin'," Bud said. "Shit!"

Sissy released him in order to examine his wounds. She reached up and touched his bleeding lip. He pulled away from her and headed for the truck. She followed him. They got in the truck and slammed the doors. Bud had trouble getting his keys out of his pockets because his hands were bloody and sore.

Wes stood brushing off his clothes. Steve walked over to him.

"You okay?" Steve asked.

"Sure," Wes said. He thought for a moment before asking, "He won't go to the cops, will he? I don't want no trouble."

"Bud? No, he's a cowboy."

Wes nodded and started to walk away.

"You gotta place to stay tonight?" Steve asked.

"No," Wes said.

"We don't have no room in our trailer, but I got a buncha old cars out back. You can sleep in one of 'em if you want to."

"Appreciate it."

Steve and Wes looked up as Bud's truck spun its wheels, kicking up dirt like a mad iron bull, and then roared angrily out of the parking lot. The truck was soon going eighty miles an hour down the Spencer Highway. Bud was still drunk. Sissy braced herself beside him.

"Slow down, Bud!" she said. "Slow down or let me out."

Bud did not seem to hear her. He just drove faster. Staring straight ahead, her coyote eyes frightened for once, Sissy saw the traffic light up ahead turn yellow.

"Bud!" she yelled.

She saw another car approaching them at a right angle from the cross street. She saw the light turn red. And she knew that there was going to be an accident.

"Bud!" she yelled again. "Look out!"

Bud slammed on the brakes but too late to keep his truck from crashing through the red light. The car approaching from the side street swerved to the left. The truck and the car came so close that they exchanged patches of paint, like blood brothers exchanging blood. Then Sissy grabbed Bud's arm in terror—and he lost control of his pickup completely. The truck spun all the way around. Everything blurred—car lights, the red light, fast-food lights— the way the world looked from the back of the spinning bull. When the truck finally came to a stop, it was in a ditch by the side of the Spencer Highway.

"You okay?" Bud asked.

"I dunno," Sissy snapped.

Catching a glimpse of himself in the rearview mirror, Bud saw that his face was distorted by cuts and bruises. His lips were swollen, his right eye was puffy, his jaw bulged unevenly. It was as though the distorted face he had seen in the flask earlier had been a prediction.

Looking over at Sissy, Bud saw that her face was misshapen, too, made almost ugly by anger. Bud shook his head miserably.

"You coulda killed us," Sissy said.

"I know," Bud said.

The family had almost left more casualties on the saloon road.

23

The Fall

Bud heard the voice and felt the pain almost simultaneously. The voice was coming from out there. The pain was throbbing in here. He desperately wanted to get away from both. His stomach seemed to twist around and around, as if Steve Strange were at the controls.

"Bud, you got to get up," Sissy said. "Come on, it's already six o'clock. You'll be late."

Sissy smiled down at her husband, who was so bruised by fists without and drinks within. She felt sorry for him—tender toward him—and yet she also felt that he deserved his punishment. The conflict between the sympathy and the satisfaction produced the smile. She bit her lip as he opened his eyes.

"Ain't you goin' to work today?" Sissy asked. "Otherwise I'll call you in sick."

"Bring me a beer," Bud ordered.

"If they smell beer on your breath . . ."

"Bring me a beer, Sissy."

"Yes, sir."

When she returned to the bedroom, Sissy carried a Lone Star. She handed it to her husband stiffly. Bud emptied the bottle into himself before he got out of bed. Sissy offered him coffee, but he asked for another beer instead. He drank it while he got dressed. He put on an old pair of jeans, a Spur High School football jersey, and high-topped work shoes. He put on his hard hat, but he did not wear it very long. His head did not feel like holding up a heavy helmet. On the radio, Mickey Gilley was suffering, too.

> *Here comes the hurt again,*
> *You'd think I'd learn . . .*

Bud felt the music was too loud. It seemed to make his headache worse. The hurting song hurt him. Bud turned it down.

"You sure you're all right?" Sissy asked.

Bud did not answer. He was busy forcing four Clorets into his mouth. When he had his breath-fresheners in place, he took another sip of beer.

"Bud, you sure . . ."

"No."

"Then don't go."

Bud slouched toward the door. Sissy bit her lip again.

> *I'm lying right here again,*
> *So close to the flame . . .*

The sound pursued Bud out to his pickup. Crawling gingerly behind the wheel, he turned on the truck radio. It was a reflex. Gilley's voice was louder and closer now.

> *Here comes the hurt again,*
> *But I'm used to the pain . . .*

He turned it down.

"Be careful," Sissy said.

Standing on the steps of the trailer in nothing but a robe, Sissy watched Bud pull out of the driveway. The speed limit in the trailer park was eight miles an hour, but he was soon going forty. He swerved to miss a car backing out. Sissy watched him all the way out of the park.

When he was out of sight, she went back inside the trailer, walked straight to the telephone, picked up the receiver, and dialed. Then she waited, twisting the cord.

"Barbara," she said. "Hi, it's Sissy. Is Steve home?"

She did not have to wait long for him to come on the line.

"Steve," Sissy said, "I wonder if you'd do me a favor this afternoon."

Steve emerged from his trailer carrying a cup of coffee into his backyard. It was a landscape of unmowed grass and broken-down automobiles, great hulks with graceful lines that were almost extinct now, a Nash, a Studebaker, a Packard. They had old-fashioned fins that turned up like old-fashioned horns. Balancing the coffee, Steve made his way carefully through the longhorns' graveyard.

Passing the Nash, Steve glanced inside at a tumble of memories. This old wreck was his attic. He stored everything in it he didn't want to throw away but couldn't fit in his cramped trailer. His wife had complained about the lack of storage space until he showed her that the old cars could be extra closets. Through the cracked window on the driver's side, he saw the dolls his daughter had played with when she was a baby. And he saw an old lampshade that one of the dolls appeared to be wearing. And he saw old shirts and old boots and old family pictures.

Steve moved on to the Packard. There were a few discarded items between the seats, but the seats themselves were still clear enough so that the car could be used as a spare bedroom. Steve saw Wes asleep in the back seat, his body curling under a borrowed blanket. Smiling down at his guest, Steve tapped gently on the window.

As he opened his eyes, Wes brought the gun up. Suddenly Steve was looking through a car window, not at memories, but at what could be the end of all memory. Old clothes were safer to store than old friends.

"Hey, hold on," Steve said. "It's just me. Steve. I brought you coffee."

Wes hesitated. Then he nodded and put the gun down. He stretched.

Speeding into the refinery parking lot, Bud knew he was late. Since he was in a hurry, he had trouble finding a parking place. When he finally located one, he put his hard hat on and limped toward the gate. He hoped it would be an easy day. He wished for one spent entirely indoors in the shop. He didn't want to lift anything heavy or climb anything tall.

Bud nodded to the guard in his booth as he entered the plant. The guard booth was there to keep people out, but it looked no different from ones built to keep people in. The same was true of the high fence and the barbed wire. It was supposed to fence people out, but it would have looked no different if it had been fencing people in. The refinery was no prison, but it would not have needed many changes to make it one.

This morning, Bud felt like an unwilling inmate in the plant. The smell made his stomach feel worse. The constant roar made his head hurt worse. He wanted to get away, but he knew he couldn't. He was walled in by truck payments and trailer payments and a new wife. He didn't want to lose any of them.

When he reached the entrance to the shop, Bud hesitated before going in. He knew he would have to face being conspicuous again. He was as embarrassed about having lost the fight as he had been proud about riding the bull. At last, he knew he couldn't wait any longer. He was late. He opened the door and walked in. Crossing the shop, he felt like a stranger with a strange face.

"You're late," Ray said.

"Sorry," Bud said.

Then the ex-prison guard took a closer look at his new hire.

"What happened to you?"

"I tripped."

"I'll bet."

Looking around, Bud was aware of the other members of the work crew studying him. He could feel that they were not jealous any more. He missed their envy.

"How you doin'?" Marshall called from the other side of a workbench.

"Okay," Bud lied.

"Really?"

"Sure."

When Bud smiled to show that he was all right, it hurt his swollen lip.

"I gotta job," Ray said, "I been savin' just for you. Come on."

Steve Strange drove up to Gilley's and parked in the vast parking lot, which was as empty as the Texas sky. Wes was with him. They walked around back of the honky-tonk to where an old trailer stood slowly rusting. It was silver with rounded corners, which made it look a little like an old-fashioned dirigible.

"I lived here for a while before I got married again," Steve said. "It's real convenient bein' right out back here."

When Steve found the right key, they went inside to look around. The interior was covered in old-fashioned wood paneling, now water-stained. The paneling sagged and bulged, but it also gave off a golden glow that warmed what was otherwise a wreck of a home. Thanks to this glow, the light in the trailer seemed to be the color of pale tequila.

"Well?" Steve asked.

"Beats sleepin' where I been sleepin'," Wes said.

Wes stared at the couch, which had too many chevron-shaped tears in its upholstery, like service stripes. Then he looked back at Steve.

"I sure appreciate this," Wes said. "A place to stay, a job."

"Well, you helped me once," Steve said. "Besides, I can really use another hand around the bull."

"Good."

"Just be straight with me, Wes. Don't make me sorry I helped you."

Wes walked back to the tiny bedroom in the rear of the trailer. He smiled inexplicably. Steve wondered what was so funny. He was a little afraid Wes might be laughing at *him*. Then Steve saw his old friend reach down and pick something up off the floor.

"Somebody lost somethin'," Wes said.

He held up a pair of faded lavender panties.

"Like I said," Steve chuckled, "it's real convenient."

"I'd like some of that convenience right now," Wes said. "I ain't been convenienced in so Goddamn long."

He raised the panties to his face, like a mask.

Sissy was stripping chrome from a wrecked Chevrolet, but her mind was not on her work. She labored over a worn-out machine while she daydreamed about a new one: the bull. As noon approached, she moved over to where her father was working, patiently rewinding a starter.

"Daddy," Sissy said, "I'm gonna take off this afternoon. Okay?"

"It's all right with me," her father said, "if it's all right with your mama."

Sissy rubbed her dirty hands on her jeans as she headed

for the office. Entering through the back door, she came up behind her mother, startling her.

"Mama, I'm gonna take the afternoon off, okay?" Sissy said.

"It's okay with me," her mother said, "if it's okay with your daddy."

Bud looked down at a miniature world. He could see the worker ants moving back and forth below. Above him towered the huge flying red horse. Some company executives were arriving tomorrow for a meeting, and the whole refinery was being given a general cleaning and polishing. Down below, tiny men were sweeping and shoveling and fixing. Up above, it was Bud's job to groom the winged stallion.

The flying red horse rode the cracking tower the way a windmill wheel rides a windmill. Bud stood beneath the horse on a small platform that was similar to the platform beneath a windmill's blades. He felt strangely at home up here, and yet the view was very different from the view from his windmill. Farm after farm after farm had been replaced by refinery after refinery after refinery. All the way to the horizon stretched towers and tanks and derricks. Way over there, Bud could barely see the trailer park where he lived, but he could not be sure which one was his trailer. And out there was Gilley's, looking impossibly small.

While he studied the landscape, Bud methodically scrubbed the horse's red hide with a chunk of foam glass which worked like steel wool, only better. Every few minutes, Bud paused in his cleaning to scratch. He was sick at his stomach, his head hurt, he was bruised, and he itched.

The tower seemed to sway slightly in the rising wind. The horse strained at the cables that secured it, as if it longed to fly away from its refinery home. Remembering another rising wind, Bud grabbed one of the cables and hung on tighter than he needed to. Accidentally dropping a piece of foam glass, he watched it fall and fall and fall.

Driving east on the Spencer Highway, Sissy reached in the back seat and felt around. It did not take her long to find her cowboy hat. She put it on and pulled the brown felt brim down low over her eyes. Then she reached into the back seat again, looking for something else. Keeping her eyes on the road, she felt here and there until her fingers touched freshly ironed cotton. It was a white cowboy shirt with the sleeves cut out of it. She laid the shirt on the front seat beside her.

When she stopped at the red light at the intersection of Spencer and Shaver, Sissy unbuttoned the greasy blue work shirt quickly, the buttonholes loose from years of use. Then she wriggled out of the soiled shirt and tossed it in the back seat.

As she was picking up the clean shirt, the light changed. She just stared at it, undecided. The pickup behind her honked and helped her make up her mind. She put the shirt aside and stepped down on the gas. Her old Mustang coughed through its exhaust pipe as it rolled forward. Sissy drove down the Spencer Highway with her uncovered breasts pointing straight ahead, like miniature headlights. She didn't care. She wasn't self-conscious. She might have been shyer if her breasts had not been so well shaped. Sissy was not a beautiful woman, but she had perfect breasts suspended beneath perfect eyes. She drove along smiling. After all, with her hat on, she felt dressed.

When she reached the intersection of Spencer and Strawberry, Sissy stopped again at another red light. She reached for her cowboy shirt as a motorcycle pulled up beside her. She could feel the rider looking at her. Then she heard him tapping on her window.

Sissy did not panic. Nothing concerning sex or sexuality ever seemed to frighten or embarrass her. She didn't even attempt to cover herself. Instead she placed a clenched fist between her breasts where she knew he was looking. And then she slowly raised her middle finger.

Bud climbed down from the steel horse to have lunch. His uncle met him at the foot of the tower. They walked together to an area of the plant that looked like a miniature trailer park. Dozens of tiny trailers—the size of campers— were huddled together. They served as storerooms for the workmen, overgrown lockers. Uncle Bob poked his head into one of these mobile storerooms and grabbed his lunch box.

"Where's your lunch, Bud?" Uncle Bob asked.

"Didn't have time to make it," Bud said.

"What about Sissy?"

"She's not that kinda wife."

"Well, your Sissy didn't make you nothin'. My Corene

made me too much." He rubbed his paunch. "You can have half a mine."

They sat down on wooden sawhorses and stared into the lunch box.

"I ain't too hungry," Bud said.

"You better eat somethin'," Uncle Bob said. "You're liable to get sick."

"I'll be all right."

"I dunno. You don't look too good."

Bud watched Uncle Bob eat. He ate two bologna sandwiches, taking big bites. Then he opened a pack of Twinkies.

"How about one a these?"

"No thanks."

Shaking his head, Uncle Bob attacked the sweet buns. The whipped cream filling smeared his lips. A part of him enjoyed the taste, but he never smiled. He was growing more concerned about his nephew. When he finished the Twinkies, he reached back into his lunch box.

"See what she does to me," Uncle Bob said.

He pulled out a can of vanilla pudding. Grabbing a small metal ring, he gave it a tug and the whole top came off. He found a plastic spoon. Before he took a bite, he held out the pudding in Bud's direction more as a courtesy than as a hope. Bud just shook his head.

As he attacked the pudding, Uncle Bob felt a little embarrassed. It bothered him that he was eating so much while Bud wouldn't eat anything. So he ate fast to get it over with. He swallowed the whole pudding in half a dozen bites.

"I guess it's about that time," Bud said wearily.

"Afraid so," Uncle Bob said.

They stood up, stretched, stowed the lunch box, and started back toward their jobs. They walked along in silence for a while, then Uncle Bob finally felt compelled to give some advice even though he knew how unlikely Bud was to take it.

"If you're too sick to eat," Uncle Bob said, "then you're prob'ly too sick to be workin' way up there."

When she entered the closed saloon, Sissy saw Jessie riding the bull. She could see her plainly because the side doors had been thrown open, letting some sunlight into Gilley's dark world. Sissy was so preoccupied by the sight of the bullrider that she did not, at first, notice who was at the controls. She simply hurried toward the bullring, passing empty bars, empty pool tables, and empty rows of tables and chairs. Her strides grew longer and longer as she drew closer and closer to the bull. She couldn't wait.

Then Sissy saw who was running the bull and stopped. Wes looked up at her and nodded. Suddenly the bullring seemed more dangerous. Sissy was unsure what she should do. She wanted to approach the bull, but she was reluctant to come any nearer the new bull master. After all, he had beaten up her husband. Sissy told herself that Bud's enemy was her enemy, and yet she did not turn to go.

"That's enough," Wes called.

Turning off the bull, the bull master smiled at Sissy. She felt that he understood her uncertainty—and was amused by it. For some reason, she didn't want him to think she was a coward, so she started forward again.

"Hi, Jessie," Sissy said.

"Hi, Sissy," said Jessie, surprised.

The bull-rider slid down off the bull and walked stiffly across the mattresses.

"How you doin'?" Sissy asked.

"You really wanta know?" asked Jessie.

"Sure."

"I'm glad I'm not a guy."

Jessie put her hand between her legs and rubbed. Watching, Sissy felt something tighten between her own legs. Then she glanced at Wes, then looked away again.

"Me too," Sissy said. "I'm glad I'm not either."

Steve Strange seemed to materialize out of nowhere. Actually, he emerged from a storeroom.

"Hi, Sissy," Steve said. "You remember Wes?"

She nodded.

"He's workin' here now. Livin' out back."

"Oh."

Sissy and Wes studied each other. She wondered if she should say something about what had happened the night before. He wondered if he should. Neither of them did.

"You still wanta ride that thing?" Steve asked.

"That's why I'm here," Sissy said.

"Good, hop on."

"Who's gonna run the bull?"

She had almost not asked the question. She did not want

anyone to think that she was afraid of Wes. She did not want anyone to think that she thought of him at all.

"I s'pose Wes will," Steve said, "if that's okay with you."

Sissy looked at Wes, who was waiting for her answer. She felt that it was not all right. She sensed that it would be wrong to let Wes run the bull for her on the day after he beat up her husband. Sissy hesitated—weighing her disloyalty to Bud—before making up her mind.

"Sure," she said, at last.

Walking across the mattresses, Sissy was afraid of the bull and yet anxious to mount it. She imagined that it might hurt her and yet she was impatient to feel whatever it would do to her. She approached the bull the way she had approached sex the first time.

"Atta girl," said Jessie.

Sissy vaulted easily onto the bull's back. She had been afraid she would have trouble—it was so tall—but she didn't. She took to the bull naturally from the first moment.

"Now what?" Sissy asked.

Getting up from the controls, Wes moved unhurriedly over the mattresses. He came up on the bull's left side, as if it were a horse, as if this machine cared which side people stood on.

"Move up as close to the rigging as you can get," Wes said.

He patted her on the ass to encourage her to move forward, and she wriggled up closer to the rigging handle.

"How long you been married?" Wes asked.

"Not very long at all," Sissy said.

She was surprised that he would ask such a question. She wished she had told him that it was not any of his business.

"Good."

"Why?"

" 'Cause I want you to ride this bull like you was still on your honeymoon."

The tower was harder to climb the second time. The higher Bud rose into the sky, the dizzier he felt. The fumes made the refinery all around him seem to wiggle. Pausing halfway up to rest, Bud thought he felt his tower sway, but he was not really sure whether it was the tower or him. He hung on tight and wished he had eaten something.

Bud started his climb again, but he paused again and again. He wanted to stop completely, to give up, but his pride, which was as hard as his hat, would not let him. Three-quarters of the way up the tower, he located his trailer park. A few feet higher up, he saw Gilley's. At that height and distance, Sissy's car was only an unrecognizable dull red dot.

When he finally reached the platform at the top of the tower, Bud looked down and was afraid he would throw up on all the men and machinery below. The possibility appalled but also amused him. He could imagine the panic below. He smiled down at the little men who did not know their own peril.

Then Bud went to work. Picking up a block of foam glass, he started scrubbing the bronco once again. The longer he worked, the thinner the air at that altitude seemed to become. It might have been his hangover. It might have been his hunger. It might have been the sulfur fumes. Bud or his tower—or both—seemed to sway more and more often.

The wings were the hardest to reach. Leaning out over the platform, Bud brushed at them ineffectually with the foam glass. He could see that he was doing no good, so he leaned more and scrubbed harder, and some of the collected pollution began to give way. He was making progress until the foam glass slipped out of his hand once again. He grabbed for it but missed. When he looked down, his tower seemed to change into a steel axis on which the earth spun. He felt his dizzy grip loosening.

"Help!" Bud screamed.

But no one could help or even hear him at that height. Thrown by the flying steel horse, he fell through the vast Texas sky.

The bull spun on its axis. Sissy was dizzy. She felt her fingers losing their grip. Suddenly the bull changed directions. It was as though the earth suddenly began to spin backwards. Sissy felt herself falling through the whirling air.

All her life, Sissy had dreamed dreams about falling. They were the nightmares that always woke her up. In those dreams, her stomach seemed to fall faster than the rest of her body. It fell within her body as her body fell, a fall within a fall. And now Sissy felt herself falling down another dream.

Bud, who had dreamed the same dreams, kept trying to wake up from his fall, but he couldn't. The world seemed to spin inside him and all around him. His stomach spun on its axis, and he spun around it. He remembered the windmill.

After falling less than ten feet, Bud hit the pipes. One struck him a cruel blow across the back. Another pounded his thighs while a third caught him hard behind the knees. His senses were flooded by pain and relief. Wincing, he reached to try to get a hand on one of the pipes to steady himself. Then he felt himself slipping. His right hand brushed one of the pipes but too late. He was falling again, clawing at the blue sky.

Sissy landed on her back on the mattresses. The blow drove most of the air out of her lungs. She lay there trying to breathe. Wes rushed up to her and bent over her. Seeing him indistinctly, she reached out a hand to him.

"You okay?" Wes asked.

"Jesus," Sissy said.

"Lemme help you up."

Wes lifted her onto her unsteady feet. She reached for the comb in her pocket to fix her hair, but her hands were trembling too badly to use it. A tremor also ran through her thighs. And her stomach felt as if it had been punched.

Sissy hurt in many places, and yet she felt an incredible sense of elation, having ridden the bull and survived. She was so happy to be alive and unbroken that she could hardly believe it. Later on, thinking back on it, she would imagine that soldiers felt the same way after they survived their first battle. She felt lucky and excited and special.

Riding the bull was like sex, only better in a way because it was dangerous. It was like making love to an outlaw.

"I wanta do it again," Sissy said.

When he landed, Bud felt as if all his bones were shattering. Lying there, he was surprised to be alive. He could not understand how he had been reprieved. Looking around, slowly and carefully, he realized that he was still high in the air. Bud had landed on a scaffold that had been attached to the side of the tower by a maintenance crew. This scaffold was only two two-by-sixes wide. Afraid to move, Bud lay very still at the edge of the void.

24

After the Fall

They used the bright yellow crane to lower Bud. Strapped into a stretcher, he was suspended from a steel cable. The crane moved him through the sky as if he were an I-beam or a steel pipe. Rocking gently in the air, Bud felt not so much afraid as simply sleepy.

Down below, a group of men waited to receive him. Among them was his uncle, who chastised himself for ever having brought his brother's son to the refinery. He raised his hands over his head to steady the stretcher while Bud was still twenty feet in the air. When it finally came within reach, Uncle Bob helped guide it safely to the ground.

"Bud," Uncle Bob said, "you all right?"

"I think so," Bud said with a sleepy, embarrassed grin.

The uncle studied his nephew the way a father studies a newborn infant, counting the fingers and toes, staring into the eyes, making sure all the right parts are there.

"Can you move ever'thing?" Uncle Bob asked.

"Far as I know," Bud said.

Looking around, Bud saw that he was surrounded now. Workers crowded around on all sides, staring down at him, asking how he was, laughing, looking concerned, worrying about him, kidding him. The company nurse, plump in her white uniform, pushed her way through the crowd. She bent over him with a blood-pressure sleeve.

"Don't try to get up," the nurse said. "Just relax while I make sure you're all right."

Bud was embarrassed by all the attention. He felt a little foolish, as if he had been thrown by something that he should have been able to ride.

"You okay?" asked Ray.

Wincing at the familiar voice, Bud looked around for the face. He found the foreman standing at the foot of the stretcher.

"Sure," Bud said.

"You're damn lucky."

"I know."

"Was still a damn fool thing to do."

"Know that, too."

Turning in apparent disgust, Ray walked away from the stretcher. The ex-guard almost seemed to believe that Bud, like a lazy prisoner, had gotten himself hurt just to get out of work. The foreman was not going to waste any more time on his new hire. He had work to do. He had not gone very far before he heard someone behind him.

"How you doin'?" asked Uncle Bob.

Bud's uncle put his arm around Ray as if the two of them were old friends, but he squeezed a little too hard for friendship. They walked along together, side by side.

"All right," said Ray, a little startled.

"I been meanin' to have a talk with you."

"About what?"

Uncle Bob took his time. He just walked and squeezed. He wanted to make sure they were out of hearing of the others. He waited until he was ready.

"I want you to stop ridin' my nephew," Uncle Bob said at last, giving the foreman a special squeeze.

"What're you talkin' about?" Ray asked.

"You heard me."

"What?"

"And there's one more thing." Uncle Bob leaned close to Ray as if this were a secret to be shared only by the two of them. "I hold you responsible for what happened to Bud today."

"I dunno what you mean."

"I mean Bud better not be bad hurt."

"You threatenin' me?"

The uncle answered by giving the foreman an especially hard squeeze and a shake. From a distance, they looked like old friends who were *so* happy to see each other. When the one old friend finally released the other, they just stood there looking at each other. It was obvious, even from a long ways away, that this was an emotional meeting. Then one old friend took a hammer out of his tool belt.

"Jesus!" said Ray. "You're crazy."

"I've had this a long time," Uncle Bob said. " 'Bout as long as I've worked here."

The foreman took a couple of steps backward. Then he turned and walked quickly toward the shop. He kept listening for the sound of footsteps, but no one was following him.

Uncle Bob just stood there with too much water in his eyes. He was angry at the foreman, but he was also angry at himself. The foreman had ordered Bud up that tower, but the uncle felt that he still could have stopped him—should have stopped him. After all, he had seen how bad his nephew felt at lunch. And yet he had let him go. Worse, he had brought Bud to the refinery in the first place. Somehow Uncle Bob had believed that if it was good enough for him then it was good enough for his nephew, without stopping to consider how terrible it really was. Now the uncle could not understand how he could have brought his brother's son to such a loud, smelly, dangerous, evil place. He held the foreman responsible for what happened to Bud, but wasn't he even more responsible?

Swinging the old hammer in an arc, Uncle Bob brought it down hard on a gurgling twelve-inch pipe. The blow was fueled by all the emotion he felt at that moment. He was striking out at Ray, at the whole refinery, at himself. The pipe rang loudly and the hammer broke. Everyone turned and looked. Uncle Bob just stood there, holding the broken hammer, staring up in the air in the general direction of the flying red horse.

Pulling away from the nurse, Bud hurried toward his uncle. His back hurt him but he tried not to show it. He was relieved to discover that he could walk at all.

"What's the matter?" asked Bud as he approached.

"Nothin'," said Uncle Bob.

"You okay?"

"Sure."

The uncle grinned. He was glad to see Bud walking, too. Dropping the broken hammer, he took out an oily handkerchief and blew his nose.

"Lemme drive you home," Uncle Bob said.

"No, I'm all right," Bud said.

"You sure?"

"Uh-huh."

"Well, get your stuff. I'll walk you to your truck."

"What?"

"I said, 'I'll walk you to your truck.' You're goin' home right now."

Bud looked reluctant.

"I mean it. Get outa here."

It was not quite that simple. Bud had to report to the nurse's office, where he was given a quick physical examination. Nothing was broken. The nurse gave him a vial of pills to take for pain and told him how lucky he was.

Then he went to the locker room. Opening his locker, he hung up his tool belt and reached for his lunch pail out of habit. When he found no lunch pail there, he slammed the locker door.

Uncle Bob walked him to his truck and kept asking him if it hurt to walk. And Bud kept lying. As they walked through the gate in the fence, they nodded at the guard. Uncle Bob followed Bud out into the parking lot. He even opened the truck door for him. Bud got in. Uncle Bob closed the door and leaned on it.

"You sure you can make it home all right?"

"Sure."

As he spoke this rote reassurance, Bud was not looking at his uncle. Instead, he was staring back into the refinery. Turning his head, Uncle Bob glanced in the same direction. It did not take him long to discover that his nephew was looking at the flying red horse.

"Know what?" Uncle Bob asked.

"What?" asked Bud.

He still did not look at his uncle.

"Somebody oughta climb up there some night and cut that damn horse down."

Bud looked at his uncle, but his uncle was not looking at him.

25

Tuna Fish Salad

Bud drove home more carefully than usual. He was still feeling perishable. His legs ached. His back hurt even worse. And he was still hung over and sore from the night before. At the same time, Bud felt a certain exhilaration, for he had come within inches of the end of his life—and lived. He could hardly wait to tell Sissy about it. As soon as he got home, he would call her at the wrecking yard.

When he pulled into his trailer park, Bud saw someone sitting on his stoop. At first, he smiled because he thought it was Sissy. He would not have to call her at work. He could tell her in person. That would be a lot better. But then he looked puzzled. Now he was close enough to see that the woman waiting for him was not Sissy, but he was not sure who she was. At last, he grinned a small grin. Aunt Corene was waving to him.

"Howdy," Bud said getting out of the truck. "What're you doin' here?"

"Bob called and told me what happened," Aunt Corene said. "I come to check on you."

"I'm all right."

Bud unlocked the front door and followed his aunt inside. The trailer was a mess. Male and female clothing embraced on the couch and chairs and floor.

"Sissy at work?" Aunt Corene asked.

"Yeah," Bud said. "I better call her right now."

While he started for the phone, his aunt took her first real look around.

"My God, Bud," Aunt Corene said, "you two live like pigs."

"Sissy ain't too good at keepin' house," Bud said. "I bought her a vacuum cleaner, but she ain't even taken it outa the box. Course she works, too, you know. It ain't like she just sits around paintin' her nails all day."

Reaching the telephone, he picked up the receiver and dialed the number at the wrecking yard. He listened to it ring. He was so anxious to talk to his wife that he grew impatient waiting for someone to answer. It rang three times, four times . . .

"Hello," Sissy's mother's voice came over the line, "Tyler Wrecking."

"Hi, this is Bud," he said. "Sissy there?"

"No, she took off early today. I think she had somethin' to do."

"She say what?"

"Nope."

When he hung up the phone, Bud suddenly discovered how much his back hurt him. He eased himself onto the couch without bothering to remove the dirty clothes that cluttered it. He rested heavily on one of Sissy's cowboy shirts.

"Aw," he complained.

Aunt Corene was busily picking up. She stacked the magazines. And she divided the dirty clothes into white and colored piles.

"Least Sissy picks up her underwear," Aunt Corene said. "Which is more'n I can say for you."

"No she don't," Bud said defensively. "She don't wear none."

Since her nephew was obviously still in pain, Aunt Corene decided to stay with him until his wife came home. While they waited for Sissy, the aunt went on cleaning. She finished picking up in the living room and dusted. Sissy still did not appear. Aunt Corene moved on to the kitchen, which was much worse than the living room, with stacks of dirty dishes and dried chili in the sink. It was a big job and took a long time. There was still no Sissy. Aunt Corene changed the sheets in the bedroom.

Bud was worried.

It was getting dark when Sissy pulled her car into the trailer park, excited. As she approached her home, she was surprised to see Bud's truck already parked in the driveway. When she noticed Aunt Corene's camper parked in front, Sissy began to feel a little nervous. Pulling into the driveway behind her husband's car, she got out—exhilarated and worried. She opened the front door.

"Bud?" Sissy called.

She stopped as soon as she noticed what had happened to her living room. Looking around, she discovered Bud's aunt in the kitchen. She was preparing a meal.

"What're you doin' here?" Sissy asked. "What's the matter?"

"Nothin' much," Aunt Corene said. "He just almost got killed, that's all."

"Bud!" Sissy yelled.

"He's takin' a hot bath," his aunt explained.

Sissy hurried down the short hall and pushed open the bathroom door. Looking inside, she saw her husband sitting in the miniature tub with a Lone Star in his hand. He glanced up and started to say something, but she spoke first.

"What happened?" Sissy asked.

"I fell off a fuckin' tower," Bud said in a proud and at the same time irritated tone. "Two hundred feet in the air. Damn near broke my back. Where you been?"

"Visitin' Jessie," she said. "I forgot about the time."

Aunt Corene came up behind Sissy and looked in at her nephew soaking in the tub. He reminded her of Bob a lot of years ago.

"Bud, now that Sissy's here, I'm going on home. I made y'all both individual tuna salads and put 'em in the refrigerator."

"Thanks, Aunt Corene," Bud said. "I don't know what I'da done if it hadn't been for you."

"You know where we are if you need anything. Just throw a rock."

As Aunt Corene retreated, Sissy watched her go. The wife relaxed a little as the aunt departed.

"Get me another beer, will ya, honey?" Bud asked. "I wanta soak a little more."

Moving back into the kitchen, Sissy unzipped her blue jeans. Then she pulled them half off in front of the refrigerator. With her Levi's wadded around her knees, she examined injuries of her own. The inside of her thighs were turning the color of hail clouds. Her right hand rested comfortably between her legs as she studied herself. She didn't flinch.

"I shoulda known better'n to climb up there feelin' the way I felt," Bud called from the bathroom. "It was the tallest one, the tallest tower, the one with that damn horse on it, you know."

Sissy touched her bruises. She approached them carefully, the way she rarely approached anything. She found her skin sore beneath her fingers. But still she didn't flinch.

"I guess I musta had a dizzy spell. Coulda been the sulfur fumes, I don't know. Add to that a hangover and no lunch. One minute I was all right. The next minute I was fallin'."

Sissy could hear the pride and excitement in Bud's voice as he told his story. She wished she could tell him about her falls, too. She wanted them both to be proud, both to be excited. She would have liked them to compare their bruises one by one. She felt cheated, but she knew she had cheated herself.

"I tell you somethin', honey, your old man's a lucky son of a bitch. A scaffold saved me. If I'da hit it six inches over, I'da fallen all the way, the whole two hundred feet."

Sissy was too absorbed by her own wounds to realize that Bud expected some response from his wife, that now he felt a little cheated.

"You shoulda been there," Bud said in a low voice.

Sissy was struggling now. Pulling her jeans back up was harder than pulling them down had been, since they were so tight. She hurt her thighs.

"Where's my beer?"

"Coming."

Opening the refrigerator, Sissy took out a Lone Star and carried it into the bathroom. She walked in just as her husband was getting out of the tub. Bud seemed to be bruised all over, bull bruises blending into fight bruises blending into refinery bruises.

Sissy and Bud sat at the Formica table in the trailer kitchen, both proud of their injuries, one openly, the other secretly. The individual tuna salads, which Aunt Corene had prepared, sat in front of them. Bud was eating his hungrily, Sissy picking at hers.

"What were you and Jessie up to?" Bud asked. "I thought you didn't like her."

"She's all right," Sissy said. "Just girl talk, you know."

She used her fork to remove a piece of onion from her mouth. She added this to a small pile of onion growing on the side of her plate.

"I like tuna salad better with pecans and apples in it," she said, "and not so much onion."

"We don't have no pecans and apples," Bud snapped. "You ain't been shoppin' and that's all she could find to fix. She asked me what I wanted and I said corn bread tastes real good when you hurt. And she looked and there wasn't even a package of instant. What were you plannin' to feed me?"

Sissy removed another piece of onion from her mouth, this time with her fingers.

"Don't complain against me, Bud."

Bud swallowed a big mouthful.

"We ain't been married long enough for me to do much complainin' yet. Just certain things a man wants his wife to do. Be home when he gets here." He put up one finger. "Pick up after him." He raised another finger. "Fix him somethin' to eat." He unfolded a third finger. "And make good love to him." Bud was painfully aware that the fourth finger, which he extended, was foreshortened.

Sissy stared at Bud with a pained expression on her face, too. She did not even notice her husband's embarrassment. He had hurt her and she was thinking of her own wound.

"Oh, I know that's good," Bud said. "I don't have the slightest complaint in that department. But, honey, we cain't just live on love alone. We'll shrivel up and blow away."

His wife smiled.

"I just thought we'd go to McDonald's."

"Shit."

Sissy spit out a piece of onion. She looked up with a bad taste visible on her face.

"I work, too, you know," Sissy said. "It ain't like I ain't got nothin' to do."

Bud washed down another big bite with a swig of beer. He softened slightly as he remembered defending his wife to his aunt in almost those same terms. When he lowered the bottle, he was grinning.

"I know that, honey," Bud said. "Let's not get in a fight."

"I don't wanta fight neither," Sissy said.

Bud reached over and took Sissy's hand. He never felt more married to her than at this table. They had slept together before they were man and wife, but they had never eaten alone together in their own place. This setting made him want to make up.

"You still wanta go to Gilley's tonight?" Bud asked.

"No, you're hurt," Sissy said.

"It'll make us feel better."

26

The Shoot-out on the Bull

In the pickup, the husband and wife both had their un-
spoken reasons for being in a hurry. Bud was anxious to get
to the saloon so that he could tell his story. He felt that there
was no point in falling off a tower if you couldn't talk about
it. He imagined a ring of excitement around him. Sissy was
anxious to reach the honky-tonk because she wanted to ride
the bull. She wanted to feel it under her again. Like her husband, her imagination was filled with an excited circle, too,
the bullring, with herself at its center.

And so the trip took longer than usual. There were more
fast-food places than ever before. There were more car repair
shops. There were more red lights determined to stop them.
When they finally reached the sprawling parking lot, it took
them longer than usual to find a parking space.

As they neared the big front door, Bud and Sissy both
grew more and more nervous. They both had expectations
and they were both worried about being disappointed. The
new wife was more nervous than the new husband because
she had a bigger secret and hoped to take a bigger chance.
They held hands more tightly than usual as they walked, even
squeezing occasionally, he for his reasons, she for hers.

Bud and Sissy went straight to the bar. They both ordered straight shots of tequila with Lone Star chasers. When
Sissy swallowed her tequila, goose bumps rose as usual on her
arms, but Bud did not notice. He was looking around to see
if anyone had noticed him.

"Hey, Bud!" Marshall called from over by the punching bag. "How you feelin'?"

"Not too bad," Bud shouted back, "considerin'."

Marshall started over toward Bud and Sissy. He wanted to know more about the accident. Maneuvering his way through the cowboy crowd, Marshall kept talking.

"I'm surprised to see you out here tonight," he almost yelled.

"Oh, hell," Bud said in a much lower, more self-conscious voice, "I'da felt worse if I'da stayed home."

Bud glanced down at Sissy to see if she was impressed by Marshall's concern, but she was not paying any attention to him. She was watching the bull.

"Well, it's good to see ya," Marshall said, now close enough to shake hands and slap backs. "You're a lucky son of a bitch. I wanta hear all about it."

And Bud wanted to tell him, but Sissy was growing restless, responding to her own inner imperative.

"Let's go over to the bull," Sissy said.

"I cain't ride it tonight, honey," Bud said. "My back's damn near broke."

"You can watch," she said.

"Well, all right," he said.

Holding her husband's hand, Sissy led him through the crowd toward the bullring. Marshall followed along behind. To Sissy, even this trip seemed longer tonight. As they neared the bull, Bud's hand tightened slowly around hers and pulled her to a stop.

"What's he doin' here?" Bud asked.

He was staring at Wes, who sat at the bull master's table some twenty feet away. His confident hands manipulated the controls that manipulated the bull.

"He's workin' here now with Steve," Sissy said without stopping to think.

"How do you know?" Bud asked suspiciously.

Sissy did stop to think now.

"Jessie told me," she said, at last.

Bud might have pursued his suspicions, but he was distracted by a slap on the back from a calloused hand. Turning, he saw Bubba, who also worked at the plant. Bubba was handsome, with blond hair and a powerful body that had the blunt force of a cinder block.

"How you feelin'?" Bubba asked.

This same question would be repeated all night long.

"Mighty thankful to be alive," Bud said.

"I'll bet," Bubba said. "I seen you fall. I was just one tower over. I thought you was a goner for sure."

"I thought I was a goner, too," Bud said. "Another coupla inches . . ."

Other cowboys were beginning to gather around Bud as if he were some new attraction the saloon had thought up. They wanted to hear the story of how he had almost died. His refinery accident seemed to make him more of a cowboy in their eyes.

"How'd it happen?" asked Gator, a short cowboy with a black moustache, who was one of the best dancers in the club. "Somebody push ya?"

"I dunno. One minute I had my footin', the next I didn't."

"What saved you," said Gator, who was always trying to be funny without much success, "is you landed on your head. Ain't that right?"

"I landed on my back," Bud said humorlessly.

Engrossed in his own story, Bud didn't notice that Sissy was preparing for an adventure of her own. Leaving his side, she walked over to the bull master's table, over to Wes. And even this was a long journey, as she kept expecting her husband to call her back. When she reached her destination, she picked up a glove off the table. Sissy looked at Jessie, who was standing nearby, and they both grinned. Then she glanced down at the bull master.

"I wanta ride it, Wes," Sissy said in a low voice laying down two dollars.

"Get on out there," Wes said with a wink.

"What speed's it on?"

"Four. I'll turn it down."

Wes half got up, but Sissy stopped him.

"Leave it right there," she ordered.

Still in a hurry, Sissy turned and seemed to charge the bull. Her long strides carried her rapidly across the mattresses. Then she vaulted easily onto the bull's dark back. As she slipped on the glove, Sissy glanced over at Bud, but he was still talking about his accident and paying her no attention.

"Mighta been the fumes," Bud told his listeners. "Seemed like they were worse'n ever today."

"Damn right," said Bubba. "I felt sick myself all afternoon."

Suddenly Marshall stepped forward to get a better look at something. When he saw that he was right, he grinned mischievously.

"Hey, Bud," Marshall said, pointing, "you recognize her?"

Bud and all the cowboys gathered around him turned to look. They saw something that had never been seen in the saloon before. A cowgirl sat astride the bull.

"Sissy!" Bud shouted.

Glancing up from the glove on which she had been concentrating, Sissy saw that Bud looked surprised and angry. She had known he would be.

"Don't get mad at me, honey," Sissy said. "I got to. I just got to."

Bud felt confused. A moment before, he had been the center of attention. Now she was. He felt as if she had stolen something from him. At the same time, he could not really believe that she was going to ride the bull. Girls just didn't.

"Hey, get off that, Sissy," Bud called. "You'll hurt yourself. That damn thing's dangerous."

Sissy didn't move.

"She knows what she's doin'," Wes said.

Bud turned and glared at the bull master. Still confused, he was beginning to grow suspicious.

"A girl's on the bull!" a cowboy shouted in a loud, excited voice.

The cry echoed through the huge honky-tonk. *Girl on the bull! Girl on the bull! Girl on the bull!* Quickly the crowd around the bullring swelled. And naturally Bud was jealous. He remembered when he had been the first man on the bull. There had been a lot of excitement then, but he felt that there was more excitement now over the first woman on the bull. The Adam of the bullring had been eclipsed by the Eve—and he did not like it.

"Don't forget what I told you," Wes called to Sissy. "Snuggle up close to the rigging. Keep your head in the well. And don't think about nothin' but the ride."

Now Bud knew where his wife had been that afternoon. He looked angrily from Sissy to Wes and then back to Sissy again. Now the envy he had felt was complicated by a sense of betrayal. Studying his wife, he was surprised to see how much care she took adjusting her grip in the rigging. It occurred to Bud that Sissy was as fussy about her grip as Wes had been.

"Sissy!" Bud called again.

"You about ready?" Wes asked.

Slinging her left hand over her head to balance herself, Sissy expertly arched her back.

"Okay," she yelled.

Wes touched a button that set Sissy's breasts in motion. They bucked along with the bull. Suddenly everyone around the bullring was aware that she was not wearing a bra. *Girl on the bull*! *Girl on the bull*! Bud's emotions and thoughts spun and bucked in unison with the bull. He was surprised Sissy rode so well, not surprised, angry, sort of proud, a whole lot of things, but most of all jealous and suspicious of what had taken place that afternoon.

"Ride it, Sissy!" yelled a female voice.

"Throw her, Wes!" cheered a male voice.

Bud's mind finally found a focus: hatred. He hated the sight of Sissy's wild breasts bucking with no chutes to contain them and all the cowboys, especially Wes, watching. He hated Wes's spinning and bouncing his wife at will. And he hated Sissy's riding so well. But the crowd loved it . . .

Ride 'em, cowgirl! *Look at her go*! *Go, girl*! *Shit*! *Harder*! *HARDER*!

Bud glanced from his wife to Wes. He could see—or thought he could—that Wes enjoyed tossing Sissy. And he hated even more.

Shit! *She's great*!

Out on the heaving bull, Sissy somehow sensed that this was the beginning of a great romance. She had never felt anything this exciting, this powerful, this tireless. It was better now than it had been in the afternoon because so many people were watching and cheering.

"Faster!" Sissy yelled.

Bud somehow sensed the sexual competition and seethed. If he had attempted to sort out his thoughts—which he didn't—he would have concluded that his sexual rival was Wes. And he would have been right in part, but only in part.

Wes decided to see just how good Sissy was. He put the bull into a dead spin. It turned in a complete circle three times. Then he suddenly reversed directions. Sissy lurched sideways.

Bud smiled. His mind had already finished the action. His imagination already saw his wife sprawled on the mattresses.

But somehow Sissy held on. She pulled herself back onto the mechanical bull's back. She still seemed a little off balance, somewhat ungraceful, but she liked the bull even more for being difficult and dangerous.

"Eight seconds!" yelled Steve Strange.

Wes switched off the bull. Sissy slid off happy, excited, and shaking.

"Shit, Bud," said Bubba, "she rides better'n you do."

Bud winced.

"Course she does," said Marshall. "A girl ain't got nothin' to lose."

Bud didn't say anything. He simply reached in his pocket and moved toward the table at the same time. He threw two dollars at Wes—hurling them with more anger than he had thrown the hamburger. But the air caught them and they fluttered helplessly down.

"I'm next!" Jessie protested.

"Like hell you are," Bud said.

He marched out across the mattresses. At first, Sissy thought he was coming to congratulate her, but as he drew nearer she saw she was wrong. The husband brushed past his wife as though he did not recognize her and vaulted onto the bull.

"What's it on?" Bud yelled.

"Bud, you got a bad back," said Sissy.

She still stood on the mattresses only a few feet away from the bull. She waited there as if she expected to be called upon to help her husband down.

"It's on four," Wes said.

"Turn it up to five," Bud ordered.

"Bud," Sissy cautioned.

"Put it on five, Jessie," Wes said.

Jessie moved grudgingly out toward the bull. She still had not forgiven Bud for stealing her ride, but she was willing to turn it up in the hope that he might injure himself.

"You got a bad back," Sissy repeated. "Don't ride it. You'll hurt yourself worse."

"You lied to me!" Bud said.

Sissy turned her back and walked to the edge of the

circle. She had been so happy and now she was so confused.
Her emotions were bucking and spinning, too.

"You forgot a glove," Wes said.

He said it in such a way as to make Bud seem not to
know anything about bull riding. Bud naturally resented the
tone.

"Throw me one," Bud snapped.

"Here, Sissy," Wes said. "Take him a glove."

For some reason, she smiled at the bull master as she
took the glove, but she frowned as she turned toward Bud.
She walked sullenly out across the giant bed to her husband.
When she handed him the glove, he did not thank her.

Adjusting himself on the bull, snuggling up close, Bud
flinched. His back *did* hurt.

"Okay," Bud called.

Lifting his free hand over his head, Bud arched his
back—in imitation of Sissy. Wes pressed the button, which
sent a rush of pain through Bud's injured body. Wincing, he
leaned forward too soon—ruining his balance. Struggling to
regain some control, he crashed into the rigging. His balls
screamed.

Ride it! Show her! Come on!

As she watched, Sissy found that she was worried about
Bud's back and proud at the same time. She was in the habit
of rooting for him and she rooted for him still in spite of his
tantrum. As he crashed into the rigging again, Sissy worried
about more than his back. She wished there were some way
she could shield her husband's balls.

"Ride it, Bud!" she called.

Bud hurt. His balls hurt. His riding hand hurt. His back
hurt doubly because it was injured already. His emotions hurt
him worst of all—the jealousy, the envy, the sense of betrayal.

"Eight seconds!"

Bud slid stiffly—painfully—off the mechanical bull. His
hand went automatically to his back. Sissy started out across
the big bed toward him.

"You all right?" she asked.

Bud glared at her with eyes bloodshot with pain and anger. Pulling off his glove, he thrust it at her as she rushed up
to see if he was injured.

"Okay, now you ride it!" Bud ordered. "You want to
ride it. Ride it! You think you're so good."

Sissy was stunned. She took the glove and looked at it. Then she glanced in Wes's direction.

"It's too fast for her," Wes said.

"No, she wants to show off," Bud snapped at the bull master. Then he turned back to his wife and said in a low, furious tone, "Go ahead. You wanta show how you can ride better'n me. Now's your chance." He reached in his pocket. "Here, I'll put down the two dollars."

Sissy stared at Bud, getting mad. Then she turned away from him and toward the bull. She headed for the machine.

"Bud, that's too fast for her," Steve Strange said.

"She needs to learn a lesson," Bud said.

"She don't have to ride it," Wes said, "if she don't want to."

"They say you don't have to ride it," Bud yelled at Sissy. "That it's too fast for you. Too fast for a girl."

"Fuck you!" Sissy said. "Gimme a good ride, Wes."

She jumped onto the bull's back and started pulling on the glove, her tugs more purposeful this time. As she adjusted the glove, she clenched and unclenched her riding fist.

"Okay!"

Once again, Wes fondled the controls. Sissy slammed forward into the rigging but with nothing to lose. The rigging hurt her but in an ambiguous way. She moved with the bull as if the two of them were dancing a cruel dance together. The bull led and she followed, the way a lifetime of distaff dancing had taught her to do. It was the right way to ride a bull.

As Bud watched her, he unconsciously let his right hand drift to his crotch. The pain in his back had eased somewhat, but the ache in his balls was worse than ever. He rubbed them. When he realized what he was doing, his hand sprang away like a frightened rodent.

Wes did give Sissy a good ride. He lifted her. He lowered her. He lifted her again. It was like making love by remote control.

Sissy rode even better at the higher speed. Her balance did occasionally falter but never enough really to endanger her ride. The crowd, which was growing all the time, yelled louder and louder.

RIDE IT, SISSY! GO, SISSY! I'D LIKE TO RIDE HER!

Bud looked for the offending voice, but he could not find it. He was angry at Sissy for exposing herself to such remarks.

"Eight seconds!"

Sliding down off the bull, Sissy was pulling off the glove before she hit the ground. Her legs shook less this time.

"Put it on seven," Bud ordered.

He shook as if he were the one who had just ridden the bull. He tried to stop, but his anger and frustration and pain would not let him. He walked trembling toward the bucking machine.

"Bud!" Sissy yelled.

But again he simply brushed past her, ignoring her. He was trying to ignore everything, not only his wife, but also the cheers, the jeers, the muscle spasms in his back, the throbbing in his balls.

"Jessie, put it on seven," Steve said.

Bud jumped stiffly onto the bull. While he waited for Jessie to turn the speed up two notches, he found himself staring at Wes. And Wes stared back just as steadily. It was as though they were taking aim at each other.

"That's too fast for you, Bud," said Sissy, protective and angry at the same time. "You hear me? It takes a real cowboy to . . ."

"Shut up!" Bud said. "Okay, let's go."

Wes started the bull bucking and turned it at the same time, so Bud was off balance from the very beginning. He almost fell off to his right. He almost fell off to his left. Then he almost fell off head first. Bud had really had no idea how hard the bull would buck on seven. It bucked so hard that it almost seemed like a different animal, one he didn't know, one he had never ridden before. This strange, new bull frightened him.

"Bud, let go!" Sissy yelled. "You're hurtin' yourself."

The rigging was like a piston driving again and again into his balls. And it drove so much harder than ever before. It pumped pain into every part of his body.

"Bud!"

It was a fistfight—a barroom brawl—fought by remote control. Wes manipulated the controls and knocked Bud to the left. He made another adjustment and knocked him to the right. Left, right, left, right, Wes delivered a fast combination of blows. And there were plenty of low blows.

One low blow made Bud almost pass out. He let go his

hold on the rigging before he even realized what he was doing. A second blow lifted him into the air. He was too groggy to understand the danger he was in. He did not see the bull whirling around to deliver one final blow as he fell. The bull's "head" hit him on the way down—and there was a loud crack.

Sissy was running toward Bud even before he landed. Wobbling like a frightened toddler on the springy mattresses, she hurried to her fallen cowboy. As she bent over him, she was afraid he might say something cruel to her, but she was even more frightened that he might be seriously hurt. She tried to take his hand, but he screamed and pushed her away.

"What's the matter?" Sissy asked.

"He broke my fuckin' arm," Bud said.

27

Get Away!

Sissy drove. The hospital was only a few blocks away. She parked near the emergency room entrance and helped Bud toward the black door. Inside, she filled out the papers while he slumped in a plastic chair. He thought he was going to pass out from the pain—he wanted to—but he could not quite drop over the edge. When she finished with the forms, Sissy came over and sat next to Bud. And they waited. And they waited. And they waited for emergency care.

A siren drew closer and closer. Then suddenly it was out front and a lot of people in white were running. The black doors were thrown open to receive two stretchers. The doctors and nurses were yelling back and forth in a medical code that Sissy and Bud could not understand, but they did understand the urgency. Sissy noticed a boot extending from under one of the white sheets. Two pickups had collided at the intersection of two poorly lighted side streets. Tonight the machines were winning.

The accident meant that Bud would have to wait even longer to have his arm set. In one place, it was turning the color of a puddle of oil. Sissy tried to put her arm around Bud, but he pushed her away. He started to say something but decided to wait. This was not the place to have the fight. There were too many strangers to overhear. There was a soberness about the surroundings. Even the lights were too bright. Bud would wait until they got home to accuse Sissy of betraying him.

After a forty-five-minute wait, a heavyset nurse finally led Bud away to have his broken arm attended to.

Sissy drove again. Bud slumped against the door on the passenger side, staring down at his new cast. The broken bone was in his forearm. The cast extended from his wrist to his elbow. With his eyes on the external evidence of this new injury, his memory went back to the old one. His right side was unlucky. The windmill had taken a finger from his right hand and now the bull had snapped a bone in his right arm. The two hurts had happened a dozen inches apart. His cut-off finger peeked from the end of the cast.

When they pulled into the trailer park, Bud grimaced and shifted his weight. He was brooding. His back was stiff. And every time his wife hit a bump, his balls ached. Sissy drove around the circular drive to their aluminum home. The radio in the truck and the radio in the trailer sang a John David Souther song:

> *Hang up the phone,*
> *And lose my number . . .*

Sissy turned off the truck radio, got out, went around and helped Bud out. Then she tried to get him to lean on her.

"Get away," Bud said.

> *Leave me alone,*
> *So I can cry . . .*

"Just tryin' to help," Sissy said.
"I don't need no help. Not from you."

> *Don't touch my heart anymore,*
> *It's broken and sore . . .*

With his left hand, Bud fumbled with his keys, trying to pick out the one to the front door. Sissy reached for them, but he pulled them away from her. Finally he inserted the right key in the door and opened it. Then he made a point of going through the door first as if she were not there. Sissy followed.

Inside, Bud headed straight for his bottle of Jim Beam,

but he couldn't get the cap off with one hand. Giving up, he held it out to his wife.

"Okay," Bud said, "you wanta help, help."

"You sure you need that?" Sissy asked.

"Just open it."

Sissy took the cap off the bottle, and Bud filled a drinking-water goblet to the brim.

"Bud!"

"You layin' him?"

> *And the moon just turned blue,*
> *Goodbye, goodbye . . .*

"No, I ain't. I ain't layin' him. What're you talkin' about?"

"You lied to me!"

"I *was* with Jessie. I just didn't say where."

Bud took a long drink from the goblet.

"My daddy always says, if a woman'll lie about one thing, she'll lie about another."

> *Go back to town,*
> *With your old boyfriend.*
> *He can take you home,*
> *And I know why . . .*

Turning his back on his wife, Bud headed down the short hall that led to the bedroom. She followed. He sat down heavily on the bed. She sat down cautiously beside him but not too close. Bud tried to take off his shirt, but he had no more luck than he had with the whiskey bottle cap. He was crippled—again.

"Here," Sissy said. "Let me help."

Bud tugged violently at his cowboy shirt and tore it. His shirt hung half on and half off his body.

"I don't need no help from you!" Bud yelled. "I don't want no help from you. And I don't want you showin' off on that Goddamn bull no more."

"I wasn't showin' off."

"What? Whaddaya call it if you don't call it showin' off?"

"I was just ridin' it."

"Ridin' it?"

"That's right, ridin' it. And I'm gonna go right on ridin' it. Again and again. As much as I want."

"Oh, no, you're not."

"Oh, yes, I am."

"I said, no, you're not!"

"You're not my daddy. You cain't tell me what to do."

"I'm your husband. That's the next best thing. And I say you ain't gonna ride it no more. Never."

"You're just jealous 'cause I can ride it better'n you."

Bud had trouble sorting out which hand to use. He started to raise his right hand, remembered the break, and got even angrier. Drawing back his left hand, he glared at his wife next to him on their marriage bed. Now Bud would hurt Sissy where he had loved her so many other nights. The back of his left hand struck her across the mouth. Her hand came up to touch her injuries as his hand withdrew.

"You hit me!" Sissy said.

"Get out!" Bud ordered. "You get out of here."

He expected an argument, but he did not get one. Sissy ducked—fearing another blow—as she scrambled off the bed. She ran down the toy hallway into the dollhouse living room, where she struck a coffee table with her shin. Limping, she ran on.

"Go ahead, run. Get out!"

"You hit me!"

Sissy left the door open. Bud followed her to the door and slammed it. He heard her car start as he kicked the coffee table, knocking it over, breaking an ashtray and an empty Lone Star bottle. Then he limped back into the empty bedroom.

> *Well, you can count me out*
> *Of your triangle.*

Bud tapped his bruised foot to the music.

28

Ain't Workin' Here No More

When Bud woke up the next morning, the radio was still on. It had sung him to sleep and kept him company all night long, moaning of hurts, complaining of unfaithfulness, regretting breakups. As he opened his eyes, Waylon Jennings was singing:

> *My heroes have always been cowboys,*
> *And they still are it seems,*
> *Sadly in search of, and one step in back of,*
> *Themselves and their slow-moving dreams.*

Somehow, associating this song with Sissy, Bud reached out for her, but he did not touch her. Looking around, he did not see her.

"Sissy," Bud called out.

While he waited for her voice to come back from the bathroom or the kitchen, he began to grow uncomfortable. He had not really remembered yet, but he sensed that something was wrong.

"Sissy."

When he did remember, Bud suddenly felt very lonely. And the longer he lay in bed, the worse this feeling became. When he could stand the loneliness no longer, he got up to turn the radio on, but it was on already.

He turned it up. Bonnie Raitt kept him company as he tried to decide what to do.

> *Darlin', I'm feelin' pretty lonesome.*
> *I'd call you on the phone some,*
> *But I don't have a dime.*

The song started him thinking about calling Sissy's parent's house. But he wasn't sure she would be there. And he didn't know what he would say. So he thought about making himself breakfast, but he didn't feel like eating.

> *Darlin', tears are in my eyes now,*
> *Knowin' I should try now,*
> *To make it back to you . . .*

Bud got mad at the radio and turned it off. He finally decided to get up and get ready for work.

Bud went into the compact bathroom, where he was haunted by female paraphernalia. He picked up a tube of lipstick and wrote a scarlet *FUCK* on the mirror. It did not make him feel any better. In the cramped space, his unfamiliar cast kept bumping into things. He knocked over a bottle of Sissy's lotion. It broke and made the bathroom smell like his wife.

On his way to work, Bud drove past Sissy's parents' home. He wanted to reassure himself that his wife had gone to her mother and father—and not to Wes. He did not see her car. Speeding up, he headed for the plant.

As he drove, Bud got angrier and angrier at his wife, at Wes, at the bull, even at the plant. And the closer he drew to the plant, the more he concentrated his anger on it. He told himself that he had never hated his job at the refinery more than he hated it this morning. Actually, he was tricking himself, or attempting to, short-circuiting his fury to make it more bearable, taking emotions aroused by his wife and heaping them on the plant. He thought about how unhappy he was in his work to avoid thinking about how miserable he was in his marriage. He had his emotions totally confused which was what he wanted.

Driving along, Bud started muttering to himself. He was arguing with someone, but he was not sure with whom. *I've had it*. He spoke the bitter words to his wife, his boss, his wife, his boss. *I want out*. But he was not sure whether he wanted out of the marriage or the refinery or both. *I hate you*. He hated Sissy and Ray and foamglass and the noise and the smell. When he saw the flying red horse floating above the petrochemical plant, he hated it personally. By the time he pulled into the refinery's parking lot, he believed he had made up his mind. *I cain't stand it no more.* And he wouldn't, not even one more day.

All the way to the shop, Bud thought about quitting. He imagined what he would say to Ray and how surprised the foreman would be. He relished the idea. It was a time for big changes in his life. He had broken up with his wife and now he would walk off his job. Entering the shop, he said the words over and over to himself: *I quit.*

Then he took one look at the foreman's face and started trying to think of ways to keep his job. He could see that the foreman was looking forward to giving him some bad news.

"There just ain't much you can do around here with a broke arm," Ray said. "You're still on that hunderd and fifty-day probation, you know. So we cain't keep ya on, you understand?"

Bud thought about suggesting that they pay him half a salary for his one good arm, but he quickly rejected the idea. He just nodded.

"Maybe you can come back when the cast comes off. We'll see."

"Okay."

"Course you'll have to start over at the bottom"

Once again, Uncle Bob offered to walk Bud to his truck. They moved together through the forest of distilling towers, passing beneath the flying red horse. Bud wondered when his life would ever get back to normal. He was afraid it never would. Seeing a discarded rag in his path, Bud took a couple of quick steps and kicked it as hard as he could.

"Take it easy," Uncle Bob said.

"Ever'thing was great," Bud said angrily, "till they brought in that damn bull."

He kicked the rag again but without the same violence.

"You'll be all right," his uncle reassured him. "You'll mend."

"Well, I better look for some kinda job. I may not have no wife no more, but I still got truck and trailer payments to make."

"I don't like to hear you talk that way."

Bud slowed his pace as if he were somehow reluctant to

leave this loud, stinking place. He did not like the refinery, but it was somehow better than the unknown. He had no idea what he was going to do to earn a living for the next few weeks. In fact, he did not even know what he was going to do for the rest of the day.

"There's a lotta work around here, Bud," Uncle Bob said. "I'm sure you'll find something to do with one good hand till the cast comes off. I'll ask around."

Uncle Bob tried to look cheerful to make his words of comfort seem more believable, but this expression was forced. He was not really unhappy to see Bud leave the refinery, but he was concerned about something else. The shadow of a tower passed over his face.

"I ain't worried about you findin' a job," Uncle Bob said, "but I am worried about you 'n' Sissy. What're you gonna do about her?"

"Whaddaya mean 'do about her'?" Bud asked. "Nothin', that's what."

More shadows passed over the uncle's features.

"Don't be hardheaded, like the rest of the family, Bud. Apologize to the poor little thing."

"Poor little thing? Shit no. I cain't have no woman lyin' like that. She's the one who oughta apologize, not me."

They were approaching the well-guarded front gate. Bud already felt a kind of nostalgia for the dreaded place. He glanced back over his shoulder at the steel landscape.

"You're just as ornery as your daddy," Uncle Bob said. "Go on, give her a call."

"She can call me," Bud said. "She's the one in the wrong. I'm in the right this time."

Leaving the gate behind them, they walked on into the parking lot. Bud took off his hard hat and held it out to his uncle. For the first time, he felt an attachment to it.

"You better take this," Bud said. "I guess they'll wanta give it to somebody else."

Uncle Bob received the hat solemnly.

"You wanta come over tonight for supper?"

"No. I dunno."

"Well, if you feel like it."

Uncle Bob watched Bud drive away. Then he turned back to the refinery. Looking up at the flying red horse, he gave it the finger.

When he got home, Bud was lonely again. With two people living in it, the trailer had always seemed much too small, but it was somehow much too big for one. Wanting company, he sought out the companionship of Jim Beam. This time he was able to get the top off without any help. He did not even bother to pour it into a glass this morning. Drinking directly from the bottle, Bud managed to make himself drunk before lunchtime. He did not know what else to do.

Lying down on the couch, Bud kept sipping at the bottle. It was just a way of getting through the day. Drinking was something he could do with a broken arm. The bottle was not heavy. Eventually he fell asleep—or passed out—and so got through a part of the afternoon.

When he woke up, Bud turned to his television set for company. The afternoon movie was on. It turned out to be *Red River*. Bud had trouble following the story since he had missed the beginning and since his mind kept wandering. He left the television on but paid less and less attention to it. The people in the story would have to work out their problems on their own while he concentrated on trying to work out his.

Almost absentmindedly—or so it seemed—Bud reached over and took the photo album off the shelf. Leafing through it, he remembered Sissy. The pictures were like that child's game in which you said "freeze" and everyone stopped exactly where he or she was. Only instead of "freeze," you said "smile" or "hold it" or "one two three" or just "click." And these magic sounds stopped time so that nothing moved or changed or aged or betrayed you.

Smile. Sissy posing in the wrecking yard, sticking out her tongue, her face covered with grease.

Hold it. Sissy biting the pink paint off her nails.

One two three. The dark outline of Sissy's right breast hovering against a sunset sky.

Actually, it was hard to see just what this picture was a picture of, but Bud had taken it and remembered. In the viewfinder, it had looked beautiful. The breast had been a white cloud suspended in the sunset. The pink of the nipple had blended into the pink of the sky. But it had come out too dark and a little out of focus. The breast was a black cloud.

Click. Sissy in her bikini drinking a Lone Star at the beach.

Click. Sissy drinking a Pearl at the beach.

Click. Sissy drinking a Bud.

Click. Sissy and a dozen others posing for a group picture around the word *GILLEY'S* spelled out in beer cans on the beach.

Bud remembered how drunk she had gotten that day. He remembered how drunk he had gotten. Now he was drunk again. He wondered about her.

Smile. Sissy taking off her boots.

Smile. Sissy taking off her cowboy shirt.

Smile. Sissy taking off her jeans.

Smile. Sissy skinny-dipping in the San Jacento River.

Smile. Bud diving nude off a freeway overpass into the river.

This place had been one of Sissy's favorite picnic grounds for years. She liked it because it was the only place where three freeways crossed the river and each other at the same time. The freeways made good diving boards.

Hold it. Sissy dancing with a red chicken at an outdoor party given by one of their friends.

Hold it right there. Bud dancing with the chicken.

Bud smiled for the first time all afternoon. He had forgotten about dancing with that chicken. And now he forgot why he had done it.

Click. Sissy posing in her wedding gown with no panties on.

The missing panties did not, of course, show in the wedding photograph, but they were etched forever on a negative in the groom's mind. He smiled again, and then the smile disappeared. He rubbed the back of his hand across his mouth.

Click. Sissy grinning at the prison rodeo, her eyes bloodshot after one night of marriage.

Click. Sissy staring at all the outlaws, trying to imagine their lives, wondering on her honeymoon how much they missed fucking.

The pictures of his honeymoon caused Bud to turn to a honeymoon souvenir. The prison rodeo program was tucked in the back of the photo album. He took it out and started leafing through it. There were the female prisoners chasing the greased pigs. There were the bareback riders being thrown this way and that on the black-and-white pages. There were the saddle bronc riders falling one way and another.

There were the clowns who cavorted with bulls. And there were the bull-riders.

Without knowing anything about it, Bud imagined that the bull-riders were the most desperate criminals in the prison. He supposed that holdup men would ride broncs while killers would ride bulls. So the bull-riders fascinated him more than the other cowboy outlaws. Feeling desperate himself, he studied the faces of these most desperate of deperados.

29

Grudge Dance

It was outlaw night at Gilley's. Like migrating birds, motorcycle gangs passed through the giant saloon a couple of times a year on their way to somewhere. These gangs sat at the long tables dressed in black motorcycle boots, black pants, black shirts, black leather jackets, long hair, earrings, and black cowboy hats. They were hell's cowboys. In honor of their presence, the band was playing a David Allen Coe song that the gangs always requested:

> *The bikers were lookin' at the cowboys,*
> *Who were lookin' at the hippies,*
> *Who were hopin' to get outa there alive . . .*

When he came in that night a little drunk, Bud was surprised and intimidated by the look of the crowd. Once again, he felt like an outsider in his saloon. He had been thinking about outlaws all afternoon and now outlaws were all around him. It was as though they had come to life out of his imagination. It was as if so much dwelling upon outlaws made him see outlaws everywhere he looked. He had come to the honky-tonk that night to find one and had discovered a hundred.

Stopping at the long bar for a Lone Star, Bud glanced over at the bullring. He couldn't pick Sissy out of the crowd, but he nonetheless felt sure that she was there. Holding the beer in his hand like a weapon, he headed for the bull. Pushing through cowboys, Bud saw Wes and Steve seated at the bull master's table. Sissy stood behind them. Bud took a long

173

swallow of Lone Star as he stared in their direction. Then he found himself focusing on the 13½ pin on Wes's hat.

"You ever done this before?" Wes called.

He asked the question of a slightly plump, blond cowgirl named Wanda who sat heavily astride the bull. Since Sissy had proved that cowgirls could ride the machine, they all seemed to want to.

"No, I'm a virgin," Wanda said, "so don't get carried away. Be gentle."

"Anything I make sore," Wes said, "I'll be glad to kiss."

All the cowboys and cowgirls around the bullring laughed. Even Bud smiled in spite of himself, but he thought Sissy laughed too hard.

"Put your arm back," Wes said. "You ready now?"

"Now really, Wes, don't hurt me," Wanda said, putting her arm back. " 'Cause I'm gettin' married on Friday."

The bull began to undulate slowly on its lowest speed. Wanda squealed as she rocked plumply back and forth. And the crowd laughed and cheered.

"Ride it, Wanda," Sissy yelled. "Come on."

Bud was walking in her direction. More or less ignoring the cowgirl on the bull, he concentrated on reaching his wife. The crowd around the bullring was so thick that he made slow progress. Holding his beer in front of him and excusing himself, he kept pushing and nudging his way along. Wanda had finished her ride and the crowd was clapping by the time Bud reached Sissy.

"I gotta talk to you," Bud said.

Sissy ignored him. Leaning down to Wes, she asked, "Need another beer?"

"Sure," Wes said.

"Now don't do this," Bud said. "You talk to me."

"How about you, Steve? Could you use a beer?"

"Yeah, thanks."

"What kind?"

"Anything but a Falstaff, heh heh heh. I just finished a Falstaff, and I never drink the same brand twice in a row. It's sort of a superstition with me."

By ignoring him, Sissy bruised Bud worse than angry words would have. It was as though she had slapped his ego. They were getting better and better at hurting each other.

"Sissy," Bud said, "shut up about that beer and talk to me."

Without a word, Sissy headed for the bar. Bud followed after her. Sensing him behind her, she speeded up. When he caught up with her halfway to the bar, Bud reached out with his good hand and grabbed her arm. He turned her around.

"Goddamn it, Sissy, talk!"

"No!"

"Okay, just listen. I got somethin' important to tell you. I figured out where I seen him before. I went through the pictures. We saw him at the prison rodeo, that's where. He's an escaped convict."

A little out of breath from the rush of words, Bud stood waiting for Sissy's stunned reaction.

"No he ain't," Sissy finally spoke to him. "He ain't escaped. He's out on parole."

"You knew that?"

"He told me. Now leave me alone, Bud. I ain't talkin' to you no more, and I mean it."

Sissy tried to pull away from Bud, but he held fast to her arm. They struggled there in the middle of the honky-tonk.

"Sissy, you're my wife!"

"Take it easy."

The voice belonged to Wes, who had come up behind them. This stranger was telling Bud how to treat his own wife. The husband was furious at the outlaw, but his quarrel at the moment was not with the man out on parole, it was with Sissy.

"Sissy," Bud said, "please . . ."

Jerking her arm out of her husband's grip, Sissy turned away and headed for the bar once more to get the beers. With Wes looking on, Bud did not feel he could pursue and wrestle with his wife again. He let her go.

"Okay," Bud said, "if you won't talk to me, I'll find somebody who will."

Looking around the room in what amounted to a panic, Bud's eyes soon picked out the woman in the saloon who seemed to belong there least. That was why he saw her, because she stood out so. She was the only woman in the honky-tonk who wore a dress. It was red. As he moved toward it, Bud seemed to kick the floor with his boots with every step.

Sissy glanced behind her to see if her husband was carrying out his threat. She saw that he was. As he approached the red dress, she took hold of Wes's arm.

Without a word, Bud took the hand of the woman in the red dress and led her toward the dance floor. She looked back at her girl friends with a quizzical expression on her face. They appeared almost as out of place as she was. One wore beige slacks, the other green slacks. Their blouses were silk. And one of them had on an alligator cowboy hat.

She mouthed, "Good luck."

When they reached the dance floor, Bud grabbed the girl in the red dress by the hair and started spinning her to a fast two-step. She had never been to Gilley's before, but she knew how to do the cowboy dances. She hooked her thumb through his belt loop and spun with him. Her left cheek touched his cast.

Waiting in line at the bar, Sissy watched Bud dance with the dress. She increased the pressure on Wes's arm.

"You okay?" Wes asked.

"No," Sissy said.

"Can I help?"

"Wanta dance?"

"Sure."

She could get the beer later. They walked to the dance floor together. Wes gathered Sissy's hair in his hand and she linked herself to his jeans. They began to spin in the wake of Bud and the red dress as though they were chasing them. As Bud and Sissy turned around and around in other people's arms, they kept turning their heads to watch each other. Bud pulled the red dress closer to him—and Sissy eased in closer to Wes. When he could, the husband watched his wife's breasts, constantly measuring how close they drew to the outlaw. They moved nearer and nearer, then backed away, then edged closer again. Beneath the fabric of the cowboy shirt, the breasts swayed together gracefully, like yet another loving couple dancing to the music. Now they danced away from the outlaw, now they danced up to him again, now they brushed him gently.

Bud pulled the red dress against him. He released her hair and put his arm around her body. He pressed so hard that his cast hurt her back, but he was oblivious to her pain. He was too busy trying to hurt his wife to notice. Feeling the breasts beneath the red dress hugging his chest, Bud looked over at Sissy.

His wife was dancing with the outlaw's leg between her legs. She seemed to be riding the leg the way she rode the bull, her knees slightly bent, her body swaying, her thighs pressing firmly. And it seemed to her husband that she was enjoying it as much. Bud felt as if his manhood were being assaulted, as if Wes were kneeing him between the legs.

Hurting, Sissy's husband pressed his own right knee deep into the red skirt, prying between strange legs. At first, the skirt seemed to resist him, but then it relaxed and let him in. Besides pain and jealousy and a desire to hurt, Bud felt the beginning of sexual desire. As he stiffened slightly, Bud saw Sissy peeking over Wes's shoulder at him. All he could see of her were her coyote eyes full of animal pain.

The band paused and then eased into another song. The new beat was faster, so the dancing couples shifted from the two-step into a whip. The cowboys took the cowgirls by both hands, pulled them forward, pushed them back, turned them in a circle, and popped them like whips. Bud pulled the red dress close so that they almost touched and then sent her spinning away. Then Wes pulled Sissy even closer so that they actually did touch before he sent her whirling.

Ouch! As their hands flew together, Bud's cast hurt the manicured fingers of the girl in the red dress. She let out a little cry and he winced. The cast had not interfered with the two-step, but the whip required precise hand work. Now the cast was in the way. It made Bud feel awkward. Watching Wes spin and whip Sissy so gracefully, Bud felt that he was losing the dance. This dance was a fight, and he was fighting it with only one good hand.

Bud saw Wes begin to spin Sissy like a piece of clay on a pottery wheel, around and around and around. Wes reached out with his free hand as if he were going to shape the clay into something beautiful. As she turned, Wes's hand touched Sissy's spinning waist as though he were molding it.

Then Bud saw Wes's hand begin to move up, mounting higher and higher. The outlaw hand drew ever closer to Sissy's breasts. It molded the lower chest. And then the renegade hand was actually bumping the bottoms of Sissy's breasts as she spun. She did not try to protect herself. Bud wanted to do it for her. Just as, so much earlier, she had wished she could shield his balls on the bull, he now wished he could shield her breasts. But he couldn't.

Nor was there any way Bud could copy Wes's style, not with that clubfoot of a cast on his right arm.

"Oh," said the red dress.

Bud had hurt her again. He was sorry, but he hurt, too. Every time the outlaw hand nudged his wife's breasts, it hurt him. It was as though the hand were pounding into him the way it had in Stonie's parking lot. The sometime bull master went right on turning Sissy the way he often turned the bull, keeping her in a dead spin. And his hand kept rising.

When the music stopped, Bud wanted to say something that would hurt Sissy the way her dance had hurt him. Since he knew his wife would not respond to anything he said to her, he decided to speak his first words to the woman in his arms, the woman in the red dress. He made sure he spoke loud enough for his wife to overhear.

"When're you gonna take me home and rape me?" Bud asked.

The new woman was startled by this opening. She looked worried for an instant, but then her face relaxed into good humor. Tilting back her head, she smiled.

"Whenever you get ready, cowboy," the red dress said.

"He's ready right now," Sissy yelled from a few steps away.

The woman in the red dress stared at Sissy, puzzled. Bud got even angrier.

"I sure as hell am," he said.

Wes laughed softly.

"Let's go," Bud said.

Taking her hand, he led the red dress toward the door. On the way, he pushed his way through a crowd of hell's cowboys in their black uniforms. He was so mad he didn't even notice them, and they were so surprised they didn't do anything.

"Wait a minute," the red dress said, "I have to tell my girl friends I'm leaving."

She pulled away from Bud and walked over to her friends, who were standing on the fringe of the dance floor.

"I got myself a cowboy," she half whispered. "See y'all later."

Then the red dress returned to her cowboy. This time she took him by the hand and led him. She carefully guided him around the bikers in cowboy hats, who seemed to be working themselves into the mood for a honky-tonk range war. When Bud and the red dress neared the door, he looked back over his shoulder.

Sissy was heading for the bull.

30

Your Cheatin' Heart

Passing out of the saloon, Bud and the red dress paused in the Badlands of a parking lot. They looked each other over more carefully now. She thought he looked the way a cowboy should look. He liked her large brown eyes, which gave no hint of ever changing colors. He admired her long, dark hair. She had a straight nose, high cheekbones, and expensive teeth. Bud told himself that his wife was cute but the woman in the red dress was beautiful.

"Who was that?" the red dress asked.

"My wife," Bud said.

The girl in the red dress laughed.

"My name's Pam."

"Hi, I'm Bud."

Pam laughed again.

"Well, what do we do now?" she asked.

"You got a car here?"

"No, I came with my girl friends."

"Good, I got my truck."

Pam followed Bud to his pickup. He opened the door for her and she got in. Then he walked around and climbed in.

"Say, cowboy," Pam said, touching his arm, "you're not just doing this to make your wife jealous, are you?"

"I dunno," Bud said. "Maybe."

Starting the engine, he looked over at her. She was smiling.

"You know where Nieman-Marcus is?" she asked. "I just live around the corner from there."

"Nope."

"Well, I'll give you directions. Take the Gulf Freeway."

As they were bouncing out of the rough parking lot, Pam kept starting to say something and then checking herself.

"What is it?" Bud asked.

"Well," Pam said, "it's just that you must think I'm crazy to go off with you like this."

"Nope."

"But I've just got this thing about cowboys. Drives my daddy crazy."

"Uh-huh."

"He says, 'Why do you like cowboys?' And I say, 'Well, Daddy, most men today are just too complicated.' You see, Daddy goes to an analyst three times a week. So I tell him, 'I like men with simple values. I like independent, self-reliant, brave, strong, direct and open men.' My daddy says, 'You mean dumb.' Daddy's a scream."

Sissy knelt at the foot of the bull, as if it were a totem, turning up the speed. She raised it three notches. Then she vaulted onto the back of the bucking machine, which she squeezed with her legs.

"Come on, Wes," Sissy called. "Run the bull."

"What's it on now?" Wes asked.

"Seven."

She said it proudly but with a mischievous smile on her face. Then the smile gave way to her memory of what had just happened.

"You're gonna hurt yourself," Wes warned.

"That don't matter," Sissy said. "Ain't nobody usin' it tonight anyhow."

"Get off at this exit here," Pam said.

Bud turned the truck off the Route 610 Loop onto a ramp that led to Westheimer Street. The black pickup passed beneath the massive, elegant, moneyed Galleria Plaza Complex, which housed not only Nieman-Marcus but also Lord and Taylor, Cartier, Sakowitz, and an ice-skating rink.

"You get up this way very often?" Pam asked.

"Not very," Bud said.

"This is my favorite city in the whole world. It's got so much *energy*."

"You mean money."

"They go together. Turn right up here."

Bud did not even pause at the red light before turning. He seemed to accelerate going around the corner.

"Be careful," Pam said.

"Better take it easy," Wes said.

"Why?" asked Sissy.

" 'Cause you'll bust your ass."

"It's mine. I'll bust it if I want to."

Wes stopped the bull anyway. He didn't mind hurting her a little, but he didn't want to hurt her a lot. He leaned back and waited for her to climb down.

Sissy did slide down, but she did not leave the bull. She simply knelt before the bull once again—turning up the speed.

"Any girl ever ride it on eight before?" Sissy asked.

"I don't think so," Wes said. "And I reckon there's a reason for that. I don't think it'd be too smart for a girl to try."

"I hate it when somebody tells me a girl cain't do somethin'."

Sissy jumped up onto the bull again. She arched her back and threw her free arm over her head like a ballerina.

"Turn it on, Wes," she ordered.

"Like you say, it's your ass," he said. "If you wanta get hurt that bad. . ."

"That's it," Pam said. "The doorman will park your pickup for you."

Bud looked up at the skyscraper in which Pam lived. He had always lived and played and loved in a horizontal landscape. Spur and his trailer park and Gilley's were all alike in their flatness. The only vertical landscape he knew was a work landscape, the petrochemical plant. But now he faced a home that towered above him like a cat cracker. Actually, it was taller than a cat cracker. Pam lived even higher off the ground than Bud worked. Bud was uneasy, somehow sensing that in Texas a vertical landscape was an artificial landscape.

"You lived here long?" Bud asked, not knowing what to say.

"No, I just moved in," Pam said. "This building's new. Brand-new. I just love new things, don't you?"

"Sometimes. Like old things, too."

Bud followed Pam into a lobby that seemed big enough to hold his whole trailer park. He tried not to look impressed. He wasn't sure why.

"That's another reason I love Houston," Pam said. "It's so new. Brand-new."

Crossing the lobby, Bud was puzzled. He knew that Pam had a better education than he did, which he found intimidating, but she still did not always make sense.

"I don't understand," Bud said in front of the elevators. "If you like new things so much, how come you like cowboys?"

The elevator doors opened and they stepped inside. Pam pressed the top button.

"You're new," Pam said. "Really, you're the newest model."

"What?"

"Believe me, you are."

Bud decided to drop it. When the elevator doors opened, he followed Pam down a wide carpeted corridor. Her apartment was all the way at the end. She unlocked the heavy door and led him into a living room that was almost twice as big as his whole trailer.

"I apologize for how it looks," Pam said. "I'm not really moved in yet. Just sort of camping out."

The huge living room was bare except for a stereo, records, a candelabra standing on a packing crate, assorted bottles of spirits, and paint cans along with a painter's drop cloth. It was not messy, just empty, the way the West had once been. She took his hand and led him toward a wall of windows that were not yet dimmed by curtains.

"Come look at the view," Pam said.

Although he had spent much of his work life high in the air, Bud nonetheless felt a sense of vertigo as he approached the glass wall. He could see farther than he could from the top of his windmill at home, farther than he could from the flying red horse, farther than he had ever seen before. The lights of the city stretched all of the way to where the horizon met the stars. It was as though Houston had been built to decorate Pam's apartment.

"May I offer you a drink?" Pam asked.

"Okay," Bud said.

"What would you like?"

"Tequila's all right."

Pam found two glasses and handed them to Bud.

"Help yourself," she said. "And pour me one, too, would you. I want to light the candles."

While Bud poured neat shots of tequila into the glasses, Pam lit all the candles in the candelabra and turned out the lights. She sat down on the floor, and he sat down facing her.

"Daddy bought me this place," Pam explained. "It's sort of a graduation present."

"What does Daddy do?" Bud asked.

"Daddy does oil," she smiled, "and all that that implies."

Pam held up her glass of tequila to propose a toast. It took Bud a moment to realize what she was doing and what she wanted him to do. Then he raised his glass, too.

"To cowboys," Pam said, "and all that *that* implies."

Sissy knew she was going to have to let go. The bull was slapping her around like an angry lover. She was knocked backwards, caught herself, was knocked sideways, caught herself again, and was bent almost double. The bull hurt her thighs, it hurt her between her legs, but most of all it hurt her hand. The glove was not enough to protect it.

Crying out in pain, Sissy released her grip. The bull threw her to the floor. She just lay there, not even trying to get up, her injured hand pressed between her bruised thighs. She moaned softly.

Jessie hurried out to her. The one cowgirl knelt over the other.

"Leave 'er alone," Wes said.

Jessie looked around, surprised and puzzled.

"You heard me. She got just what she wanted. So don't go feelin' sorry for her, okay? Just back off. She can get up all by herself."

"Wes!"

"I mean it."

"What's got into you?"

"Nothin'. I just don't believe in babyin' cowboys."

Jessie stood up slowly and walked off, leaving Sissy all alone on the mattresses.

Lying on the queen-sized bed, Pam flinched. It happened when Bud touched her left breast with his right hand. He could not be sure what it was that made her wince. Was it the roughness of his cast? Or was it his missing finger? He kept wondering.

Bud could not help comparing Pam's breasts to Sissy's. These new, rich breasts were slightly larger than the ones to which he was married—but they were not as perfectly formed. They were rounder, blunter, seemingly more hastily sculpted. They were also less fearless, less aggressive. Withdrawing his right hand, Bud caressed Pam with his left hand only.

"You did a real nice job in here," he said.

Bud wanted to pay Pam some kind of compliment. He considered saying something about her body but decided to say something about her bedroom instead. He was a little shy in the presence of this kind of woman.

"Thank you," she said.

The bedroom was as finished as the living room was unfinished. She had started with it. The bed was covered with a fur blanket made of beaver skins. A backgammon set was open on a night table. The most unexpected ornament in the bedroom was a black saddle, trimmed generously with silver, that cost more than a car. The silver saddle sat astride its own stand. All Bud's women seemed to love to ride.

"I guess you have a talent for that sort of thing, decoratin'."

"I don't know if I do or not."

"You do."

"A decorator did this."

Bud did not know how to respond to this news. He had meant to pay her a compliment, but it had not worked out as he had hoped. He was a little embarrassed.

"Just about the only thing I brought to this room," Pam said, "is me."

"That's what I like best," Bud said.

Proud of himself for salvaging the compliment, he lowered his mouth to her breast. Pam's nipples did not harden as fast as Sissy's would have. They seemed to know that they were rich enough not to have to do anything in a hurry.

"That's a nice baby," Pam said to the nursing Bud.

Wes was examining Sissy's injured hand. The rigging had rubbed the skin off two knuckles. Blood spotted her fingers. Her hand looked the way it had that first night she had punched the punching bag. They sat together at a small table in the vast honky-tonk. Wes dipped the tip of a paper napkin in a shot of tequila and then used it to clean the wound. Sissy did not flinch, but she closed her eyes as the alcohol stung her.

"If you wanta toughen this up," Wes said, "get a cigar box and fill it with sand. Then, when you're just sittin' around doin' nothin', watchin' TV or somethin', get the box out and pound on the sand with your hand." He made a fist and drove it into an imaginary box of sand. "That'll do it."

The night crew was beginning to clean up. The saloon was closed. With its "head" turned toward them, the bull seemed to watch the bull master and the injured bull rider.

"I'm still livin' out back," Wes said.

Sissy did not say anything.

"It's real convenient."

She was still silent.

"There's a cigar box out there."

"Okay," Sissy said.

Getting up from the table, they walked toward the back door of the honky-tonk. She held her wounded hand in front of her face and blew on it. Her breath felt pleasantly cool and painful at the same time. Just before they reached the door, she lowered her hand.

"If he can go off with somebody else," Sissy said in a near mumble, "I can go off, too." She looked up at Wes. "Besides, I ain't never known a real outlaw."

The cowboy rode the rich man's daughter. Bud could feel that Pam was softer than Sissy. Her arms were softer. Her shoulders were softer. The legs that she wrapped around him were softer.

And Pam could feel that Bud was harder than her college boys. Since he worked with his body, it was also a better tool for pleasure. He felt like a huge hammer on top of her. She felt like a bed beneath him.

"Oh, you fill me up," Pam said.

As he speeded up, Bud realized with a part of his consciousness that the springs were not squeaking. He was beginning to learn about loving money.

"You ever drink this stuff?" Wes asked.

He held out a square bottle with a yellow-and-red label.

"I dunno," Sissy said, "what is it?"

Wes turned the label so that it faced him and read aloud, "Mezcal con Gusano."

"I don't know no Spanish."

"That means Mezcal with a worm. See, that's the worm down there at the bottom. That little white thing. See it?"

Standing in his tiny trailer kitchen, Wes held up the bottle for Sissy to look. The mezcal seemed to belong in this trailer, for it was the same gold color as the old wood cabinets and the varnished panel walls. Sissy saw a white worm floating in the golden drink.

"What's it doin' there?" Sissy asked.

"The Meskins say," Wes explained, "that if you eat the worm you'll see visions."

"You ever see any visions?"

"No, I cain't say that I have. The worm just makes me feel good."

Wes took the gold cap off the top of the bottle and poured mezcal into two kitchen glasses. He took one and handed the other to Sissy. He started to take a drink, but she stopped him.

"What's this to?" Sissy asked.

"I dunno," Wes said.

"To outlaws," she said.

And Sissy drank the whole shot in one desperate gulp. Goose bumps sprang up on her arms. When she looked to see if he had noticed, she saw that he was staring not at her arms but at her breasts. She folded her arms over them.

"Come here," Wes said.

"I'm here," Sissy said.

"Close."

"I'm close. This place is so small, I couldn't be nothin' but close."

Wes reached out, took Sissy's wounded hand, and drew her to him. He put his arms around her and kissed her. Her cheeks sank in. The outlaw hands found her breasts. She let them.

"How many banks you rob?" Sissy asked.

The kiss was over, but the hands still held her breasts,

feeling their shapes, through her shirt. He ignored her question.

"Okay, then, just why?"

The robber hands opened her cowboy shirt one snap at a time.

"You ever kill anybody?"

"Don't talk," Wes said.

When he tried to pull her to him, Sissy resisted for the first time.

"Wait," she said. "I like to do this."

She grabbed the front of his cowboy shirt with both hands and tore open all the snaps in one motion. Then the two open shirts collapsed against each other.

Pam sat nude on her silver saddle. Bud lay sprawled on the bed. They were looking at each other and smiling. With her hand on the saddle horn, she rocked gently.

"Can I ask you something?" Pam said.

Crossing her arms over the horn, she leaned forward.

"Sure," Bud said.

He raised up on one elbow.

"What happened to your finger?"

"Windmill accident."

Pam could tell by his tone that he did not want to say any more about it, so she did not pry into the details of just how he had been hurt. But she could not bring herself to drop the subject completely.

"Maybe you oughta see a specialist," Pam said. "Daddy knows a lotta doctors. He could . . ."

"I think it's too late," Bud said.

"I cain't," Sissy said. "I thought I could, but I cain't do it to Bud. I'm sorry. No . . ."

Pulling away from Wes, Sissy staggered slightly as she headed for the door of the trailer. She put out her hurt hand and steadied herself against the refrigerator. She had consumed a lot of mezcal but had been careful to stay away from the worm.

"Sissy."

"Sorry."

Pushing off from the refrigerator, she steadied herself against the cabinet. She moved along it, holding onto it, all the way to the door.

"Really, I'm sorry."

Looking back, Sissy saw Wes with the bottle of mezcal to his lips. He let the golden drink run into his mouth, some of it spilling down his cheeks, until finally the worm passed into him. Wes caught it between his teeth and smiled at Sissy as he bit it in two.

Sissy slammed the door. She did not mean to. She was too drunk to close it gently. Then she got in her Mustang and slammed that door, too. She knew she was too drunk to drive, but she drove anyway. She was going home to wait for Bud.

31

Moving Out

When she pulled into the trailer park, Sissy could see that Bud's truck was not home. She drove slowly—being overly careful because she knew how drunk she was—around the circular drive to what had been her home. She parked and went inside. Although she knew he was not at home, a part of her still expected to find him there. She listened for him in the dark trailer.

"Bud," Sissy called out.

Turning on the light, she searched the living room for him.

"Bud!" she called louder.

Standing in the middle of the living room, Sissy took off her cowboy shirt and dropped it on the floor. She was suddenly so tired that she knew she had to get to bed. She would wait for him there. The mezcal and the emotions and the late hour had all exhausted her. She left her boots in front of the television set. Her jeans fell to the floor halfway down the short hall. She kept her socks on to warm her feet in the empty bed.

Lying on her back with a twisted sheet between her legs, Sissy wanted to make love before she went to sleep. Perhaps she was still excited from her brush with the outlaw. Maybe it was a feeling set in motion by lying down in this bed. Whatever it was, Sissy wished Bud would hurry.

Listening for her husband, Sissy lay with her eyes open.

189

She had never before noticed so many sounds in the trailer, but none of them were Bud.

Sissy pulled at the tangled sheet. She locked her legs around it. She thought how surprised Bud would be to find her naked in his bed. She imagined how glad he would be to see her—she knew how glad she would be to see him. Sissy needed Bud tonight. Her hand crept between her legs. A truck passed outside, but it wasn't his. The slow wheels on the gravel sounded like slowly gnashing teeth.

Sitting on the couch in the midmorning light, Sissy watched a Western on television. She was paying so little attention that she did not even know the name of the movie. And she was having trouble following the plot because she kept listening for a pickup and glancing out the window. Used car and truck commercials kept coming on.

Sissy was hungry, but she did not get up and make herself breakfast. At first, she had not eaten because she wanted to wait and eat with Bud. Now she was not sure why she continued her fast, but she did.

The black truck finally did pull up outside. Through the window, Sissy could see Bud nervously adjusting his clothes. He had seen her car and knew she was there. Bud took longer getting from his truck to his trailer than he ever had before. Opening the door, he just stood in the doorway looking at his wife on the couch.

Sissy got up and moved past Bud without saying anything. He watched her go into their bedroom, where she picked up a suitcase that she had already packed. Then she came back toward him. When she reached him, she paused for a moment. Reaching up with what at first seemed a tender gesture, the wife took hold of her husband's collar and pulled it open. On his neck was a red discoloration. Sissy did not ask. Bud did not try to explain.

"Twang," Sissy said in a low voice, "twang."

She carried her suitcase to her car without any help.

Bud spent the rest of the day wondering if Sissy would come back. He did not expect her to, but he waited anyway.

While he waited, Bud kept trying to imagine what Sissy was doing at that very moment. He tried to "see" her at her parents' house, but that vision always gave way to a vision of his wife with the outlaw. That day his imagination made him suffer. Bud "saw" Wes unsnapping Sissy's shirt, "saw" his wife defending her breasts the way an apple tree defends its apples, "saw" the outlaw hands touching the unflinching nipples. "Watching" them, he kept pounding his fist into his thigh until he made a bruise. Bud tried to think of something else, but his imagination kept on hurting him. He "saw" Wes taking Sissy into an awful bedroom, "saw" him on top of her, "saw" her on top of him, which was somehow worse, "saw" his wife riding the bull master the way she rode the bull.

Sometime in the afternoon, Bud got so hungry that he got up and opened a can of Hormel chili. He ate it out of the can without heating it. He hated the taste of the congealed grease in his mouth, but he kept on eating anyway. He did not expect anything to taste good today. With grease in his mouth, he "saw" Wes nursing at Sissy's breasts as she continued her ride. And then he "heard" her say: *Did we make the finals?*

Where was she? What was she doing? Who was she with? Was she at home? Was she at work? Was she with the outlaw? Was she happy or unhappy? The questions pounded at him like his unconscious fist. The expanding bruise was like a bull bruise.

Sissy was on the run, like an outlaw. She leaned back in the Greyhound seat, biting the inside of her cheeks. Outside, a landscape hurried by full of trees and fences and barns and windmills and white-faced cows and real bulls. But Sissy hardly noticed. She wanted to get as far away from Bud as she could. The most distant place she could think of was a farm near San Angelo where one of her mother's sisters lived with her husband, Aunt Jo and Uncle Clyde.

Everyone in her family seemed to think the trip was a good idea. Bud had never been popular with them. When they learned that he had hit Sissy, they wanted to put her well out of his reach. Sissy's mother had called her sister. And Aunt Jo said she would love to have Sissy come for as long as she wanted to stay. She could get over her bruised face and broken marriage on a cotton farm. Sissy thought it would be good to get out of Houston.

The Greyhound bus rolled west on Interstate 10. Sissy had taken the bus because she did not think her old Mustang would survive the trip. The ticket had taken almost the last of her money, but her mother had promised to send her some more. At this moment, her car was parked in back of her parents' house. She sort of missed it.

Looking out the moving window with unfocused eyes, Sissy wondered what she would do that evening in San Angelo. She would have to try to talk to her relatives, whom she had not seen in many months. There would be no music. There would be no two-steps. There would be no bull to ride. She missed the bull already.

Perhaps it was the motion of the bus beneath her that kept her thinking about the bucking machine. While the bus's rise and fall echoed the more violent pitching of the bull, she began to feel aroused the way she had the night before. But now she did not want Bud or even Wes. She wanted to ride the bull. She kept imagining herself on its back, crashing up, crashing down, spinning around, the crowd cheering. And then she thought of the bull bucking all night tonight without her.

When she came back, all the other girls would be better riders than she was. She felt jealous, in a sense. It was as though she wanted to be the bull's favorite.

In San Antonio, the bus stopped to take on new passengers. Sissy got off and went to a pay phone in the depot. She placed a collect call.

"Hello, Wes, it's Sissy," she said. "Can you come get me?"

BOOK
THREE

The Rodeo

32

Reunion

The cars and trucks drove right into the store. They braked to a halt in front of Bud and delivered their orders. He hurried off to fetch what they wanted, usually beer. He rang up the orders, sacked them, passed them through the car windows, took the money, and handed over the change. Then they drove out the other side. The Beverage King had a good location, built, as it was, at the intersection of two especially busy roads, Shaver and Allen-Genoa. There was always a steady, rolling line of customers. It was like working in a drive-through honky-tonk.

Bud wore blue running shoes, blue jeans, and a yellow T-shirt that said "Beverage King" on it. His cast was so dirty that it looked more brown than white. He worked with both hands, often carrying a six-pack in each.

All around Bud, the beer was stacked in great mountains. There was a Budweiser peak. And over there was a Coors hill. And down there was a whole range of Lone Star. Bud was moving through a pass between a mountain of Schlitz and a hill of Miller when he saw a white Corvette turn into the market.

"Hello, cowboy," Pam said.

"Pam," Bud said, coming up to wait on her, "what're you doin' here?"

"Shopping."

"I tried to call you a coupla times."

195

"I've been out of town. Just got back yesterday. Went to Gilley's last night."

"You did?"

Bud was surprised. Pam did not seem like the type to spend her first night back in Houston in a honky-tonk.

"Yeah. I guess I thought you might be there. But you weren't."

"I ain't been there for a long time."

"That's what everybody said."

"I've been tryin' to stay outa trouble. I was gettin' crazy. Drinkin' too much."

"I see." She smiled. "Anyway, somebody told me you were working here."

"What can I get you?"

"Two six-packs."

"What brand?"

"Whatever brand you like." Pam paused. "Your wife was there last night."

"I'll get your order."

Hurrying away, Bud disappeared behind the mountains of beer. He picked out two six-packs of Lone Star and carried them to the counter. At first, he had been glad to see Pam, but now he found her presence more and more unsettling. He wished Pam had not mentioned Sissy. He did not want to talk about his wife or even think about her. And yet at the same time he was irresistibly curious. He carried a brown sack and the bill to the Corvette.

"She was?" Bud asked.

"They say she's out there every night," Pam said. "She's getting so good on that bull that she can ride it standing up. She puts all the men to shame."

"They say she's out there every night," Pam said. "She's ride it, far as I'm concerned. That'll be eight oh nine with tax."

Pam opened her purse and took out a twenty-dollar bill. The inside of her purse was well ordered. She was not a woman who carried around a mess inside a sleek, expensive bag. Passing the beer inside, Bud hurried off to get her change. He returned slowly because his curiosity still itched like foam glass.

"She still with that ol' boy?" he asked when he got close enough.

"Uh-huh," she said. "They say they're living together."

"Where?"

"She moved into his trailer." She paused again. "I thought you knew."

"No. I better wait on somebody else. Good to see you."

"You just gonna stay home tonight?"

"Yeah, I guess so."

"Maybe I'll come over and make your wife jealous again."

When he pulled into his driveway that evening, Bud paused for a moment. Looking behind him, he saw Sissy's name still stuck in the pickup's rear window. He had been meaning to take it out for a long time but had somehow never gotten around to doing it. Now he knew it was time. Reaching back, Bud pried "Sissy" loose. Then he held the miniature license plate in his right hand and stared at it:

Texas
SISSY

Tossing it into the glove compartment, Bud got out of the truck and walked the few steps to his trailer.

Bud did not have to wait long for Pam's white Corvette to pull up outside. He invited her in and poured tequila into two glasses. They sat down on the couch and he put his feet on the coffee table. Now the trailer seemed too small again.

"Where were you?" Bud asked.

"Washington," Pam said. "My daddy goes back a couple of times a year to give the government hell."

"Have a good time?"

"Oh, sure, I love Washington. I went out with a congressman while I was there." She looked at Bud. "He was married, too."

"We're gettin' a divorce," Bud said.

While they were waiting to feel comfortable with each other, the telephone rang. Bud got up stiffly to answer it.

"Shit," he complained. Then he picked up the receiver and said, "Hello."

As he listened, the expression on his face brightened slightly.

"Oh, hi, Uncle Bob. What?"

Bud looked over at Pam and shrugged.

"No, it's all right. That's right, I've got company."

He turned away slightly.

"No, it's not her."

He turned back.

"No. No, we're not hungry. Yeah? Well, that sounds good. Let me ask her."

Bud put his hand over the mouthpiece of the telephone.

"It's my Uncle Bob. My Aunt Corene just made a homemade Karo-nut pie. We'll go have dessert if it's okay with you."

Pam shrugged, smiled, and nodded.

"Thanks." He took his hand off the phone and talked into it. "Uncle Bob? We'd love to."

Bud smiled shyly at the next question. Once again, he partially turned away.

"Oh, a coupla hours, at least. Okay, fine. See you then."

Hanging up the phone, Bud returned to Pam on the couch. Still wearing his Beverage King shirt, he felt too soiled to sit next to a woman like Pam. She wore an off-white pants suit that made her look too clean to be touched by workday hands. Bud moved away from Pam slightly. She looked up to see what was wrong."

"I feel like a shower," Bud said.

"Okay," Pam said.

Her expensive smile was even whiter than her suit.

"I'll be as quick as I can."

Bud hurried off down the short hall. In the small bedroom, which was the size of the foyer in Pam's apartment, he pulled the T-shirt off over his head. He jerked off his running shoes without untying them. When he finished undressing, he took a chance and scampered the few feet to the bathroom with nothing on. Closing the door, he turned on the loud water.

With the water pounding in the tin shower like rain on a tin roof, Bud did not hear the door open quietly. He had his eyes closed to keep out the soap, so he did not see the shadow moving on the other side of the shower curtain. Then that curtain opened and she stepped in beside him wearing nothing but a towel wrapped around her head.

"Don't get my hair wet," Pam said.

With two people in it, the shower was as cramped as a coffin. It was much smaller than Pam had imagined when she first conceived the idea of a friendly invasion. She felt a little claustrophobic. Bud was excited.

"Careful," Pam said. "I don't think there's enough room for that."

"I know," Bud said.

There was not enough room, but he did not seem to mind. He seemed intent on proving that he was a sexual Houdini.

"Easy, cowboy."

"Okay."

"We're making a flood."

33

The Old Bull-Rider

Sitting at the table, picking at her Karo-nut pie, Pam could not help thinking that it was too sweet. She had been feeling this way—vaguely critical of everything—ever since she arrived. She tried to stop, but she couldn't. She thought Uncle Bob was too fat and should lose some weight. She thought Aunt Corene was too dowdy and should pay more attention to her hair. She thought the house was too cluttered and should put away most of its tin trophies and trip souvenirs.

"Corene found this just this week," Uncle Bob said.

He was unfolding a wad of tissue paper.

"I was unpackin' some boxes I'd almost forgot about," Aunt Corene explained.

"I won it for bull ridin' back in 'sixty-four," the uncle said. "Won it at that Mesquite Rodeo." Turning to Pam, he added, "That ain't the biggest rodeo in the world, you understand, ma'am."

"Come on, Bob," said the aunt, "first place is first place."

Uncle Bob handed a silver belt buckle to Bud, who studied it carefully. In the center, a raised silver bull was trying to throw a raised silver rider, who had been hanging on stubbornly for over fifteen years. The name "Bob Davis" was engraved on the buckle, along with the year, "1964," and the achievement, "First Place." In Bud's left hand, the buckle felt cool and heavy. He hefted it up and down, weighing the honor.

"Damn, first place," Bud said. "I didn't know you ever won first."

"Oh, sure," Aunt Corene said.

Reaching across the table and the remains of the too-sweet pie, Bud handed the heavy buckle to Pam. She could not help thinking that it was too big.

"You rodeo any more?" Pam asked.

"No, ma'am," Uncle Bob said with an affectionate laugh, *haw, haw, haw.*

Everyone but Pam laughed. She was aware that she was left out of some kind of family joke. And in that moment, she sensed that *he* was more like *them* than he was like *her.*

"Uncle Bob had an accident," Bud said, attempting to look serious. "He mighta been another Larry Mahon but . . ."

"Come on, Bud," Uncle Bob interrupted.

"That's right, another Larry Mahon," the nephew continued, "but he got hurt and had to spend almost a whole year in a cast."

"I got caught in the chute," the uncle explained. "Fell off the bull. Got stomped real good. I got a plastic bone in my leg, a plastic plate in my head, and . . ." He paused, looked at his nephew, and winked. "How well you know this pretty lady, Bud?"

Everyone but Pam laughed again. She felt she didn't know Bud as well as she had thought. She had never seen him in this setting, which made him seem something of a stranger.

"Well enough," Bud said. "Go ahead and tell her. Go ahead."

"Well, in addition to all them other plastic parts," Uncle Bob said with a wink at Pam, "I got one plastic nut."

Everyone laughed while she stared. She felt as if the joke were somehow on her.

"He bullshits a lot," Bud laughed. "But he's tellin' the truth this time."

Pam felt Uncle Bob was too candid, but she still liked him better. She could not help it. His partial castration touched her somehow. Injuries seemed to run in the family.

"Excuse me," said Aunt Corene, getting up from the table, "there's something I've gotta do."

While Uncle Bob stacked the dishes, Bud reached over and picked up the trophy buckle. Pam studied Bud studying the buckle. She felt that there was more between them than the kitchen table. What bothered her was that she cared—cared enough about her cowboy to be concerned about how different they were.

"How about another cup a coffee?" Uncle Bob asked.

"Sure," Bud said.

"Please," said Pam.

The uncle got up and got the pot. He emptied it into three cups.

"You two got any plans tonight?" Uncle Bob asked.

"Yeah," Bud said, "Pam's takin' me to a new club downtown. It's called 'Cowboy.' "

"That's too bad."

Bud and Pam both looked puzzled.

"We were hopin' you'd come along with us," Uncle Bob explained.

"Where you goin'?" Bud asked.

"Believe it or not, we're gonna go to Gilley's tonight. Be the first time since I took you there that first time. Maybe you could come with us for just a little while. Go to that other place later."

"I dunno."

Bud was not anxious to return to the huge saloon at all after all it had done to him. He was especially reluctant to go back with Pam at his side. He did not want to find himself in the same room with Pam and Sissy—even if it was a very big room.

"We're not gonna take no for an answer," Aunt Corene called from one of the bedrooms. "It's gonna be a lotta fun out there tonight."

"Y'all come on now," Uncle Bob said, "go with us."

"Why?" Bud asked. "What's so special about tonight?"

"They're havin'," Aunt Corene called, "a Dolly Parton look-alike contest."

Bud's aunt appeared in the doorway with a platinum blond wig on her head and ten-gallon breasts on her chest. She wore an electric blue pants suit with crimson trimming. She was even padded behind. Posing in the doorway, she reached up and fondled her new balloon breasts.

"Lord have mercy," said Bud, standing up from the

table. He looked from his new aunt back to his new girl friend. "Whaddaya say?" he asked.

"I wouldn't miss it," Pam said, "for anything in the world."

Pam stared at Bud's aunt in astonished disbelief. It was as though Aunt Corene had dressed up in this costume to prove absolutely how different Bud's family was from Pam's own.

34

Betrayed

It looked like a great breast roundup. The milling herd of mammaries bounced and swayed and rolled and bumped into each other. The hundreds of breasts looked like balloons, like squashes, like cantaloupes, like honeydew melons, like pumpkins, like eggplants, like watermelons, like giant mangos, like pillows, like punching bags, like bags of laundry, like sacks of feed. Some of the great breasts danced, some played pool, some punched the punching bag, but more and more drifted over to the bullring to watch. The herd of breasts naturally gravitated to the bull.

Sissy watched all this breathing, undulating flesh with a pout on her face. Occasionally, she would glance at Wes to smile a wry smile.

"All those big tits don't affect me like they do most girls," Sissy told the bull master.

"Oh, no," Wes said.

"Most girls are goin' around like this tonight, hidin' their tits." Sissy crossed her arms over her breasts in imitation of the other cowgirls. "But not me."

"No?"

"No, those big tits make me wanta stick my tits out far as they'll go." She arched her back, as if she were on the bull, and stuck her chest out. "Like this."

Wes took off his cowboy hat, scratched his head, and put his hat back on. He looked at the cowgirl with the arched back and laughed.

"What's so funny?" she asked.

"Sissy, you talk like a guy," he said.

"Huh?"

"You do. Most girls say 'boobs.' See? And most guys say 'tits.' See? But not you. You're a girl but you say 'tits.' "

"So what?"

"Nothin'. It just sounds funny, that's all."

"Well, I never did wanta sound like a girl," Sissy said, still pouting. "I'll bet alla *them* say 'boobs.' "

Sissy's face suddenly hardened as if she hated all those tits out there. The arch went out of her back. Wes noticed and wondered.

"What's the matter?" he asked.

"Nothin'," she said.

Across the honky-tonk, Sissy watched Bud coming into the saloon followed by his Uncle Bob, his Aunt Corene, and the woman he had left with that night. She had not seen him since the day she left the trailer, but she had thought about him every day, wondering how he was doing, if he was happy, if he was unhappy, if he was thinking of her. Now she tried to study his faraway face with the same unanswered questions on her mind.

Bud saw Sissy. Even at that distance, he seemed to be able to see the gold of her fierce eyes. He looked away and then looked back. He was searching for Wes and it did not take long to find him. Sissy had her hand on his shoulder. Bud flinched at the touch.

"What's wrong?" Uncle Bob asked.

"Oh, nothin'," Bud said.

"Oh, I see," his uncle said, following his gaze. "I'll buy you a drink."

As they moved up to the bar, the crowd blocked Sissy from Bud's view. Now he could look around him at all the pale breasts bobbing like whitefaces on a trail drive. He had secretly been looking forward to seeing all the mammary glands spilling out of dresses, but, now that he was actually here, he felt a little different. At first, he was simply overwhelmed. Then he found all the big breasts somehow funny. Then they seemed ridiculous. And finally they were a little sad. When they sagged, it was as though they hung their heads sadly.

In spite of how he felt, Bud kept looking. He even worked up a certain curiosity over which Dollys were padded

and which Dollys were "real." He could usually tell because
the real ones displayed so much of themselves.

"What'll you have?" Uncle Bob asked.

"Tequila gold," Bud said.

"You've growed up some since the first time I brought
you in here."

"Well . . ."

Bud was uneasy for all sorts of reasons, but he was still
glad to be back in the sprawling honky-tonk. He sensed and
absorbed its vast energy. He found himself tapping the top of
the bar with his right thumb in time to the music. His home-
coming had made him feel giddy. Bud kept looking over at
Pam to see how she was responding to the place. He thought
he understood how she felt—like an outsider. He understood
because he had felt the same way when he first started coming to the saloon. But he had desperately wanted to fit in. He
was not sure that she did.

"Come on, let's go over to the bull," Uncle Bob said.
"I've never seen it. I wanta see just what kinda machine that
is."

The uncle knew that his nephew might be reluctant to
approach the bull because his wife was there. But Uncle Bob
thought it might be good for Bud and Sissy to get a closer
look at one another. He hoped that by bringing them closer
together physically they might also be brought closer in their
marriage. Uncle Bob liked Sissy and did not want Bud to lose
her. Besides, he also wanted to visit the bullring because he
really did want to get a closer look at that bull.

"Okay," Bud said without enthusiasm.

Downing the last of his tequila, he led the way through
the crowd. He was halfway to the bullring before he saw his
wife again. Sissy and Wes and Steve were all huddled together at the bull master's table. They were talking and
laughing. Bud wondered what they were talking about. He
hoped it wasn't him.

Seeing her husband approach, Sissy moved slightly closer
to Wes and put her hand on his neck. Wes did not notice the
hand because he was so preoccupied with a Dolly who was
just struggling aboard his bull. She wore a bright blue jump
suit with a neckline cut low enough to reveal all but the tips
of the icebergs. Wes did not find the Dollys sad. He was having a good time. As far as he was concerned, Dollys and
cowboys were made for each other.

"Hey, Steve," Wes said, "I'll bet I can throw her wig and then throw her in it."

"Oh, don't hurt her," Steve said. "Just buck her titties out, heh heh heh heh heh." Then he turned to Jessie who was standing beside him. "Jes, go out there and tell her what to do."

While Jessie made her way out to the bull, Steve got up from the bull master's table. He saw an old friend approaching and wanted to go say hello. He moved along the perimeter of the bullring, just outside the mattresses. The crowd moved back to let him pass. Then he stuck his hand out.

"Hi, Bob," Steve said. "I ain't seen you in here in ages. And Corene! Damn, ain't you a slice a heaven."

Uncle Bob and Steve shook hands. And then Steve hugged Aunt Corene, making her balloons squeak. After greeting the aunt and uncle, he turned to the nephew.

"How ya doin', Bud?" Steve said. "You gonna enter our little contest?"

"What?" asked Bud.

Was Steve making fun of him? Why would he enter a tit contest? Should he laugh or get mad? He could already hear the heh heh heh.

"Ain't you heard?" Steve asked. "We're havin' a rodeo. Bull ridin' and ever'thing. Somebody's gonna win a lotta dough. Ain't you seen the signs?"

Looking around him, Bud suddenly saw the signs everywhere, nailed to the honky-tonk walls, taped to all the steel beams that held up the roof, tacked to the bars. There was even one hung from the bull master's table a few feet away. Since it was the closest, it was the easiest to read:

GILLEY'S RODEO
ENTER NOW!

Gilley's Club is proud
to present the world's
first indoor mechanical rodeo

Uneasy about looking in that direction, Bud only scanned the rest of the poster before looking away. But he did see enough vaguely to understand that there was going to be a dance contest, a punching bag contest, and a bull-riding contest. Top prize in the bull-riding event was $5,000.

"Oh, I'm sorry, I forgot about your arm," said Steve, who had not forgotten at all but enjoyed teasing people about their wounds. "I don't s'pose you could do much ridin' crippled up like that."

"Cast'll be off soon," Bud said. "Who's gonna run the bull?"

"Wes. Gonna try your luck?"

Before Bud could answer, a delighted cry went up from the bullring crowd. Wes had skillfully done just what Steve had told him to. The Dolly's giant breasts were now bucking in the open and free. The bull master should have shut down the bull at this point, but he was enjoying the show too much. He lifted her up and set her down, whirled her one way and twirled her the other, her breasts always following a little behind the rest of her body, trying desperately to catch up. The Dolly attempted to cover herself but then put her arm up again to keep from losing her balance. Her great tits bounced and jerked and kicked like the greased pigs in the sacks at the honeymoon rodeo.

Watching the Dolly flopping on the bull, Sissy made up her mind. She had been trying to decide whether to ride the bull with Bud watching her. On the one hand, she wanted to show off to him how good she had gotten. But on the other hand, she knew he would not enjoy the show. He had never wanted her to ride the bull. And she knew that the better she rode it, the less he would like it. So she had almost made up her mind not to ride when the Dolly's breasts had come galloping out. Now Sissy felt an urge to prove that not all tits were such bad riders. She arched her back and got ready— hating the sound of the laughter, wishing Wes would stop.

"Come on, Wes," Sissy said, "that's enough."

"Okay," Wes said.

Giving her one last bouncing spin, Wes brought the bull and the breasts to a halt. A groan mixed with cheers went up from the crowd as the Dolly scooped her breasts back into her blouse. Wes took off his hat and ran his hand through his hair, pleased with himself.

"I wanta ride it," Sissy said.

Wes looked up at her, disappointed. He was not opposed to her riding the bull, like Bud. Normally, he loved to toss her and turn her on the bucking machine. But at the moment he was having so much fun playing with the Dollys that he hated to give them up. Still he did not try to keep Sissy off the bull. He handed her a glove.

"No, thanks," she said. "I don't need it."

Sissy had been pounding the sand in the cigar box—the way Wes had told her to—until her hand was almost glove-tough. Besides, she knew she would not be using her hands very often on this ride. She planned to trick ride, to show ride, to no-hands ride. She would show Bud and all the rest of them.

As she walked toward the bull, Sissy kept looking over toward Bud. Wes followed her gaze and saw Bud for the first time. Now Wes was looking forward to giving Sissy a ride more than he had been. This would be its own kind of fun. Wes would make Bud feel every buck, every turn.

Vaulting onto the back of the bull, Sissy sat there as confidently as any cowboy had ever sat. She wore blue jeans and an orange spaghetti-strap top with "Gilley's" written across her chest. Her back was arched, her tits were pressed forward as if responding to a dare, her left hand was in the air, and her eyes were turned in the direction of her husband. Sissy stared at Bud to tell him that this ride was for him, but she soon grew nervous and let her vision wander. Her gaze drifted past Bud's new girl friend, lingered briefly on Aunt Corene, and came to rest on Uncle Bob. He smiled at her warmly, and she could not help smiling back.

"You about ready?" Wes called.

"Okay," Sissy said.

As the bull leaped, Bud saw his wife look back at him and stop smiling. He was not smiling either. The husband was completely unprepared for what happened next. While he stared, Sissy released her grip on the rigging and lowered herself slowly backwards until she was actually lying on her back. Bud's wife lay on the bull as if it were a bed, her legs spread, the rigging pounding rhythmically into her. In full view of her husband, the wife was unashamedly making love to the bull.

Nor was he the only one who saw. Everyone saw. The crowd cheered the way they had when the unfortunate Dolly had ridden the bull. Sissy did not have to expose her flesh to arouse the crowd. Bud felt as if he were being betrayed before the multitudes.

Sissy sat back up. Momentarily relieved, Bud relaxed his

fists, which had been gripping air. Then he saw his wife turn around on the bull so she was riding it backwards, facing its "tail." Turning around on the bucking machine was a trick in itself, which the crowd cheered and applauded appreciatively. Reclenching his fists, Bud watched as his wife again slowly lowered herself. She bent down and down, closer and closer, until she lay face down on the bull. Once more the animal was her bed, once more her legs were spread around the riging, once more the hard handle pounded into her. Now Bud could hear her as she rode. The bull would buck and she would say, "Uh." The sounds alternated with the bucks in a steady incantation, buck, *uh*, buck, *uh*, buck, *uh*, buck, *uh*.

The crowd was hushed now as if they were all listening. They had never seen anything like it and were utterly fascinated. The boisterous cheering had given way for the moment to an almost reverent admiration. This mood was not really altered by the occasional whistle.

At first, Bud could not believe that Sissy's hips were moving the way they were. He told himself that he was imagining it. But then the undulation became more obvious. Her hips rose, *uh*, and fell, *uh*, and ground around, *uh*. Sissy was making love to the bull the way it had never been made love to before. Bud thought her face looked intent but happy.

Glancing over at the bull master, Bud thought he saw ecstacy on Wes's face, too. The crowd in general was almost as delighted. With the undulations, the clapping and cheering began to mount once again. It was as though Sissy controlled their responses, taking them up, letting them down again, then building them back up to an even greater frenzy. It was as if she were making love to the whole bullring.

Giving one last hard push, Sissy sat up again. Then she turned sideways on the bull and lay back once more. She rode the bull lying across it like a sack of flour or a bedroll or a victory bouquet. With her curving spine pressed against its spine, her boots and legs dangled on one side while her head and shoulders dangled upside down on the other. When the bull rose, her arms and upside-down breasts swayed in one direction. When it came down again, her arms and capsized breasts swayed in the other. Watching the pendulums of sculpted flesh swing one way and then another, Bud could see that his wife's nipples were hard. As the bull bucked, they moved on her chest like startled eyes looking for someone.

The crowd was hushed again, a part of it seeming to

sway with the rider, this way and that, this way and that. This was a graceful reprieve from the excitement of the previous tricks. It was as if she were getting them ready.

In one motion, Sissy pulled herself back up into a sitting position on the bull's back. She rocked there a moment before she straddled the rigging and started getting to her feet. Suddenly she towered over everyone like some impossible female giant. Sissy rode the bull standing up with both boots firmly planted on its back. From an incredible height, the golden coyote eyes looked down at Bud.

As the cheering and clapping rose, Bud turned and started walking toward the door. He did not ask the others to follow him but they did. They all pushed their way through cowboys and Dollys as they made difficult progress. No one stepped aside because no one was paying any attention to them. Everyone was watching the cowgirl standing up on the bull.

Bud did not stop until he got to the parking lot. Soon Pam and his aunt and uncle were grouped around him. They all looked concerned as if they thought he were ill.

"I'm sorry," Bud said.

"That's okay," Uncle Bob reassured him.

They all stood around looking so unhappy that Bud felt compelled to break the spell, to undo what he had done.

"Why don't we all go up to that other place?" he said. "The one uptown."

Uncle Bob and Aunt Corene looked at each other. He wanted to go because he did not want to leave his nephew feeling the way he felt. She had her reservations.

"Sounds good to me," Uncle Bob said. "How 'bout you, Corene."

"I dunno," Aunt Corene said. "They ain't even had the judgin' yet. Why don't we let them go ahead?"

"Oh, come on," Bud said.

"But I couldn't go dressed like this," Aunt Corene protested.

"Sure you could," Bud said. Then he turned to Pam and asked, "She can go like that, cain't she?"

Pam looked startled for a moment, but she knew what was expected of her.

"Of course," said the girl in the white pants suit.

"See," Uncle Bob said. "Just pop your titties and let's go. Anybody got a pin?"

35

Cowboy

Cowboy was located in a shopping center with stores on each side. It was so popular that it was hard to find a place to park. Just inside the polished front door, the first impression of the club came from its name spelled out in pillows nailed to a wall. There was a pillow in the shape of a *C*, a pillow shaped like an *O*, all the way down to a pillow cut in the shape of a *Y*. Pillows seemed an odd way to spell such a word, and yet they somehow fit the place. This Cowboy was like Pam, soft.

Bud immediately hated the place, but he was not sure for a long time why. As they made their way through the crowd, he disliked each Cowboy cowboy and each Cowboy cowgirl individually. And he was simultaneously intimidated by them all. He knew he was in the presence of money. What disturbed him most was understanding that Pam was more like *them* than she was like *him*. His seeing her in her club was like her seeing him at his aunt and uncle's kitchen table.

"Isn't it great?" Pam said. "Don't you just love it? Hasn't been open a year yet."

As they moved deeper and deeper into Cowboy, it felt more and more like the lobby of Pam's apartment building. There were polished woods, and shiny chromes and well-watered plants hanging from the ceiling and growing in corners. Pam seemed to know everyone, keeping up a constant patter as they made their way toward the bar.

"Hi, darlin'," she said to someone and then moved on.

"Hello, Charlene . . . Hi, Richard . . . I'd like you to meet Bud and . . . Oh, no, I'm sorry, I've forgotten your names, Bob and Corene something . . ."

"Davis."

"Oh, of course, like Bud. I really am sorry. My daddy always says he's surprised I don't forget his name."

They descended four steps and arrived at a horseshoe-shaped bar built of burnished wood. A bartender moved up wearing a cowboy hat and a sheriff's badge. Over his head, hundreds of glasses were suspended in a rack upside down, glittering in the light. The place was pretty.

"Hi, Pam," the bartender said. "How's your daddy?"

"Just fine," Pam said. Then she turned to her guests. "What do y'all want to drink? Order anything you want. I have a charge account here. Corene?"

"Just a beer," said Aunt Corene.

"I'll have a beer, too," Uncle Bob said, "and I'm payin'."

He handed the bartender a twenty-dollar bill.

"Tequila gold," Bud said. "A double."

"A margarita, Joe," said Pam. "No salt."

A woman in an alligator cowboy hat walked up to them. Bud thought she had been with Pam that first night at Gilley's, but he wasn't sure. Perhaps Pam had lots of friends with scaly hats.

"Hey," said the alligator cowgirl, "finally got your cowboy uptown, huh?"

So Bud had been right.

"Uh-huh," said Pam.

Meanwhile, Uncle Bob was whispering to Aunt Corene, "You see how much they charge for just beer?"

Pam's friends kept coming up to say hello to her. She had been out of town and they were all glad to see her back. Bud studied her friends, but he did not try to talk to them. He would not have known what to say since they were so different from him. Feeling isolated, Bud turned to his Uncle Bob.

"I was thinkin'," Bud said, "that I might just enter that rodeo. Whaddaya think?"

"Might be fun," Uncle Bob said.

"Bud," said Pam, "I'd like you to meet Dr. Roy Smith. He's with the Medical Center."

Bud shook hands with a man in his early forties who

wore gold-rimmed glasses, a white cowboy shirt, and a white felt hat. His stomach pushed the front of his cowboy shirt out a little too far.

"I don't wanta do it just for fun," Bud told his uncle. "I wanta win."

"Course," Uncle Bob said.

"Bill, let me introduce you to my friend Bud," Pam said. "Bud, this is Dr. William Ross. Baylor Medical School."

Bud took the hand of a man in his late thirties who wore a blue cowboy shirt with lots of scrollwork, a black string tie, and a white felt hat. His middle looked too much like a pillow.

"I'm serious," Bud said. "You won that belt buckle and all. You think you could teach me? Coach me?"

"Be happy to," Uncle Bob said, pleased at the suggestion. "Now lemme see." He scratched the back of his head.

"Bud, like you to meet Jim Rodgers," Pam said.

The latest arrival wore a green cowboy shirt with a bolo tie and a beige cowboy hat.

"Hi," Bud said, "you a doctor, too?"

"No," said the beige hat, "lawyer."

"You know," Uncle Bob said, "there may still be one a them machines out at the Circle Eight. I ain't been out there in a long time, but there used to be. Maybe we oughta run out there 'n' look around."

"Sure."

"You busy in the mornin' early?"

"No."

"Bob," Pam said, "would you like another beer?"

"No, ma'am," said Bud's uncle, who remembered the price.

Pam took hold of Bud's hand and gave it a slight tug.

"Come on, Bud," she said, "let's go dance."

"Nah," he said.

"Oh, come one."

Gripping his hand firmly, she pulled him toward the dance floor. He followed reluctantly. The small raised dance floor was made of beautifully varnished and buffed wood. It looked like an oversized coffee table. There was no band. The dance music was all recorded. And it was a curious mixture—Loretta Lynn, the Eagles, Boz Skaggs, Jimmy Buffet, Willie Nelson. The dancers looked like a field of daisies in the wind with all the bobbing white hats. Bud balked before entering this field.

"What's wrong?" Pam asked.

She really wanted to dance.

"*They* ain't cowboys," Bud said, raking the dance floor with an angry look. "They're just doctors and lawyers dressed up to look like cowboys. Really burns my ass."

At last, he knew why he did not like Cowboy. It was because he did not see any cowboys in it. Somehow all these soft cowboys debased the name.

"Bud," Pam said gently.

"What?" he snapped.

"Well, don't get mad. After all, you're not a cowboy either. Not really."

Suddenly Bud wanted to run out of this shopping-center saloon. He was sorry he had come. He wished he had never seen it. But instead of running, he simply put his hands in his jeans pockets, hiding his missing finger. And he kept staring angrily at all the cowboys who were not cowboys. Pam was afraid he would turn this anger on her. She took hold of his arm to calm him.

"Maybe not," Bud said in an unsteady voice. "But I bet I can learn to be one. Bet I can."

"Of course," Pam said, relieved that he seemed to have softened. "But right now, let's just dance. Please. For me."

Bud let Pam lead him onto the dance floor. Into the field of daisies flew a blackbird.

36

Circle Eight

"There it is," said Uncle Bob.

Up ahead, a wooden horse reared up on its hind legs. A huge barn of a building—which housed an indoor rodeo every Friday and Saturday night—loomed in front of them. The name, CIRCLE EIGHT, was written across its face in weather-beaten red letters. Bud was surprised by how much the big rodeo barn looked like Gilley's saloon.

"Red's prob'ly around in back," Uncle Bob told his nephew.

Slowing down on the rough ground, the uncle drove on around to the rear of the building, where three pickups were parked in a row. Uncle Bob pulled his truck up beside them and killed the engine. An old man with gray hair and a pot belly emerged from the back of the barn as the uncle and his nephew got down.

"Hey, Red, how you been," Uncle Bob called.

"Why, Bob Davis," Red shouted back. "What brings you out? Don't tell me you're goin' back on the circuit."

"Not hardly."

The three of them met in the shadow of the barn.

"Red, I'd like you to meet my nephew, Bud."

"Glad to know you, Bud."

"Me, too."

They shook hands.

"Red, Bud here wants to learn bull ridin'."

"That's good." The gray-haired man looked the young

216

man over, his gaze lingering on the cast. "We got practice nights ever Tuesday and Thursday. He can come out 'n' ride all the bulls he wants."

"But . . ."

Uncle Bob tried to interrupt Red, but the Circle Eight owner was into his practiced sales pitch now and could not be halted until he finished it.

"He can ride a beginner's bull for three dollars. Better bulls cost a little more. All the way up to twenty dollars. The more you wanta get hurt the more you gotta pay."

He laughed.

"Well, Red, that sounds like a pretty good deal," Uncle Bob said. "Only Bud here ain't interested in bull ridin' on a real bull. He wants to learn how to ride a mechanical bull like you used to have around here. You still got that ol' thing?"

Red took off his straw cowboy hat and scratched his hair, which was wet from sweat.

"You mean that ol' El Toro buckin' machine?"

"That's it."

"Yeah, we still got it. Ain't been used in a while and it's pretty dirty."

"You reckon we could clean it up?"

"Don't see why not. It's over there under that there tarp."

"Sure appreciate it."

Red scratched his hair again.

Bud sat on the back of the mechanical bull, staring into the dull brown eyes of a real bull. The human and the animal seemed to regard one another curiously. The bucking machine stood beside a holding pen that had been built onto the back of the rodeo barn. The real bull waited in the holding pen to be fed. The mechanical bull was plugged into an exterior electrical outlet.

"Now you gotta keep your head in the well," Uncle Bob coached. "When the bull goes to the left, you tilt your head over to the left. Really lean into the turn. See, what throws you off a spinnin' bull is centrifical force. You know what that is?"

"Sure," Bud said impatiently.

"Okay, when you lean into the spin, you cut down on the centrifical force."

"All right."

"Now I'm gonna spin it to the left. You ready?"

"Ready," said Bud, lifting his cast over his head.

Uncle Bob gently turned the controls that started the bull bucking and spinning to the left. Bud tilted his head to the left but straightened it up as he began to feel himself losing his balance.

"In the well! In the well!"

Making an effort, Bud leaned into the spin and saved himself. As he spun with growing confidence, he kept seeing the other bull whirl by. The animal stood absolutely still as if mesmerized.

"That's it! Stay in the well! Atta boy!"

Bud leaned harder. It felt unnatural but seemed to work. His instincts told him to sit up straight, but his uncle told him to lean, so he leaned. And he sat his seat on the bull.

"Okay, that's good," Uncle Bob said.

He shut down the bull and smiled. He was enjoying this more than he had expected to. He even liked the familiar rodeo smells. He seemed to appreciate the company of bulls, real and unreal.

"Okay, now we'll go to the right. Ready?"

"Ready."

"Remember, head in the well."

As the mechanical bull started to buck this time, the real bull suddenly started to buck, too, in imitation of the machine. The two bulls leaped and spun across the fence from each other. Seeing the other bull begin its dance, Bud momentarily lost his concentration and forgot what he was supposed to do.

"In the well! In the well!"

It was too late. Uncle Bob stopped the bull to keep from throwing his nephew. The real bull stopped, too.

"You see that?" Bud asked.

"Yeah, but you gotta keep your mind on your business," Uncle Bob said. "Let's try it again. Ready?"

"Ready."

The mechanical bull spun to its right, and the real bull started bucking again, too. But this time Bud kept his head in the well.

"That's it! That's right! You got it!"

When Uncle Bob stopped the mechanical bull this time, the real bull kept on bucking.

"What's harder to ride?" Bud asked a little out of breath. "This kinda bull or that kind?"

The veteran bull-rider thought for a while.

"In some ways," Uncle Bob said, "I s'pose a mechanical bull's harder. With a real one, you can watch its head and get some sense a whichaway it's gonna turn. With this one, the treachery of the bull depends upon the treachery of the man at the controls."

37

Escape

Early in the morning, Sissy was awakened by a mezcal headache. Her mouth tasted as if it were the breeding ground for those bottom-of-the-bottle worms. Lying there, running her tongue over her teeth, she wondered for a moment what she was doing there. Almost every morning, there was that moment when she asked herself that question. And then she always remembered. She looked over and saw Wes's bare back and an arm and a snake tattoo. Recalling at dawn her outlaw nights, Sissy shut her eyes as if to black out the memory. It didn't work. It never did. She remembered, all right. She remembered saying to him the night before as he bit into her: *I used to fantasize about your head between my legs, your outlaw head.* And she really had had that fantasy, only in her mind it had been different from the way it was in the trailer, and it had not tasted of worms the next day.

Looking around her, Sissy felt the way Wes had felt every morning for the past several years, every morning until recently. She felt she had to escape, had to get out of there. She had felt this urge before but never as strongly. Last night's bruises were especially sore. Making up her mind, she stared at the green snake on Wes's arm as if it were guarding her. As she sat up slowly, trying not to shake the bed, Wes moved. She held her breath for a moment as if it were her breathing that had disturbed him. The outlaw rolled back closer to her, but he did not wake up. He had had a lot to drink the night before, too. She waited to make sure he was settled and then pushed her legs over the side of the bed. She looked back over her shoulder at the green snake, but it lay quietly. As she gathered herself to stand up, she thought: now is the most dangerous part, now the bedsprings will squeak, now he will wake up. Getting up in one quick motion, Sissy expected the coiled green snake to strike. But it lay sound asleep.

Sissy stood there for a moment, with nothing on, looking down at the outlaw whose bed she had shared for too long. She was still impressed by his body, but it no longer mattered. Moving slowly and carefully once again, she took a few tentative steps toward the kitchen. The old trailer creaked, and she stopped, but the snake did not stir. She took a few more steps, this time more deliberately, and reached the kitchen. She leaned on the refrigerator, the door cold against her right breast.

Sissy was halfway to her clothes. They were strewn about the living room where he had undressed her. She remembered his sudden overwhelming hunger and his explaining that he was making up for all those nights in prison. Tiptoeing into the tiny living room, she found her jeans crumpled on the floor, her cowboy shirt reclining on the couch, and her boots hiding playfully under the coffee table. She got dressed much more slowly than she had gotten undressed because she did not want to wake the man who had undressed her. Her legs seemed incredibly loud as they crept into her Levi's, but the bedroom remained quiet.

When she was ready, Sissy opened the door stealthily and broke out. Her Mustang was parked out front. Waiting for her now, it looked like her oldest friend. She reached for her keys, which dangled from a clip that hung from a belt loop. Getting in, she started the engine. The old car snorted loudly but she did not care anymore whom she woke.

Even at that hour, the Spencer Highway was full of pickups going to work. Sissy passed little families of trucks parked in front of the Waffle House, Dunkin' Donuts, McDonald's, even Stonie's. Turning left on Shaver, she continued on south through a residential neighborhood having breakfast. Soon she would be home having breakfast, too. She tried to think of toast and eggs on her own kitchen table instead of the taste of last night's worm.

When she reached the trailer court, Sissy saw Bud's

black pickup parked in the driveway beside their mobile home. She had expected it to be there, and yet she had been afraid it wouldn't be. She told herself that he had not spent the night somewhere else, that he was home. The truck made her happy until she noticed that her name was missing from its rear window. Bud's name was still there but hers was gone. As her hangover hit her another blow in the stomach, she felt like driving right by her old home. But she did not know where she would go.

Bringing her car to a halt, Sissy got out quietly. She was still being cautious. She felt that breaking into her own home was going to be as precarious as breaking out of Wes's. Climbing the stairs almost noiselessly, she thought about knocking but decided on a surprise instead. It occurred to her that he might have someone with him, but she would take the chance. Removing her keys from the clip, she unlocked the front door and opened it slowly. Stepping inside, she saw that the trailer was a mess.

"Bud," Sissy almost whispered.

She listened.

"Bud," she said louder.

She listened again.

"Bud!" she almost shouted.

Sissy knew Bud was not at home, but she moved into the bedroom anyway to look. It was empty and dirty. Returning to the living room, she looked around her. Smiling, for some reason, she picked up two beer bottles in each hand and carried them to the trash basket under the sink in the kitchen. Then she returned for another load.

When she had conquered the clutter, Sissy went into the bedroom and opened the sliding door of the closet. In the corner stood a large cardboard box that had never been opened. Its undisturbed staples gleamed in the midmorning light. Sissy wrestled the big box out onto the bed, where she knelt over it. She broke one of her badly kept nails opening the box. A brand-new vacuum cleaner—which had almost given up waiting for her—peeked out at her through the brown packing paper. She touched the long, cool barrel hello.

Sissy started vacuuming. She minded it less than she had expected. After all, she had always liked to work with machinery. While she cleaned, she kept listening for Bud. She loved the idea of his coming in and finding her using the machine that she had not even unwrapped while they were living together as husband and wife. She listened for him as she vacuumed the bedroom. She listened as she moved down the hall. She listened as the machine roared in the living room. She was still listening as she used the special attachments to get in the corners and around the windows.

When she finished vacuuming, Sissy dragged the vacuum cleaner back into the bedroom. She returned it to its place in the corner of the closet but without its box. She listened still, but all she heard were children and dogs and other vacuum cleaners in other trailers.

Sissy lay down on the bed to rest from her cleaning. She had hoped Bud would be at home when she got there. Then she had hoped he would find her cleaning the trailer. Now she did not know what to hope for. But she looked around for something to write on.

She found several unused thank-you cards. They had bought them to send to friends who gave them wedding presents, but they had somehow never gotten around to writing or mailing a single note. She found a black felt-tipped pen, her favorite kind, and wrote to her husband:

Dear Bud,
    I woke up this morning and felt awful about life and other stuff. Maybe its cause you were with Uncle Bob (and Aunt Corene) and I wasn't.
    I think we could be friends, maybe even more.
    I still want to see Spur. If you want to call, I'll be at Gilley's ALL AFTERNOON waiting.
                                    Love,
                           your not yet X-wife
                                    Sissy

P.S. I liked vacuuming today but I still ain't making no promises.

When she finished writing, Sissy looked around for a place to put her letter where Bud would be sure to see it. She decided to lean it against the radio. She felt sure he would find it there. Looking at her note reclining against the speaker, she was proud of her work, all of it. She thought her note looked as clean and neat as the trailer that held it.

Sissy felt it was time to go, but she lingered on. He still might come home. The day before, she had promised Jessie that she would meet her at the saloon to practice on the bull. They would run it for each other. Sissy was already late, but she found that she didn't mind. Perhaps she wouldn't go at all. She wanted to ride the bull, but she did not want to see Wes, and he might just come in. She was still trying to make up her mind whether to go or stay when she heard footsteps on the stairs.

"Bud," Sissy called.

She wished she had not put the vacuum cleaner away. She wished she had left it right in the middle of the trailer.

38

Moving In

When there was no answer, Sissy hurried to the door and opened it. Her feelings plummeted from love to hate, she changed from hard to soft, she had been turning in what seemed a good direction when everything stopped and spun back the other way. She felt dizzy as she stared at Bud's new girl friend standing in the doorway holding a hatbox. She didn't know her name or want to know it. The two women faced each other for a moment like old-time gunfighters who were somehow lost in time and gender.

"Oh," Sissy said, at last, "I was just leavin'."

"Good," Pam said.

Sissy hurried into the living room to retrieve what little she had brought in with her. She picked up her hat and thrust it on her head. She grabbed her keys. Then she pushed past the woman standing in the doorway and went on out.

Moving deeper into the trailer, Pam looked around herself in a kind of disoriented dismay. Bud's home was so changed that she hardly recognized it. She was so absorbed in how altered the place was that she did not hear Sissy coming up behind her.

Sissy kicked Bud's new girl friend from behind. When her victim turned, she kicked her again as hard as she could between the legs. The hatbox fell noisily to the floor. As the new girl friend sank to her knees, the outlaw girl turned and walked out of the trailer.

"Funny," Pam called after her. "Very funny."

When she reached her car, Sissy got in noisily and slammed the door so hard the window rattled. She was not creeping away from or back to anything anymore. She turned on the engine and gunned it. The old car backfired. It sounded like a shoot-out in the trailer park. Then she put the car in gear and roared angrily away toward the exit and whatever lay beyond it.

Sissy's dust still hung in the air when Uncle Bob and Bud pulled into the trailer park. Bud was excited from his first day of training on the bull. Although he was bruised, he was also a better rider than he had been when he set off that morning. He was looking forward to a hot shower. His wife did not happen to cross his mind.

"Well, do tell," Uncle Bob said as he drove. "Looks to me like you got company."

"What?" Bud said.

"Ain't that Pam's car?"

"Sure looks like it. Wonder what she wants."

"Beats me. I just hope I didn't bruise you up too bad, that's all."

Laughing his affectionate laugh, the uncle braked his pickup to a halt behind the white Corvette.

"Wanta come in?" Bud asked. "Have a cup a coffee?"

"Oh, no thanks," Uncle Bob chuckled. "See ya in the mornin'."

Bud got out and hurried up his steps. As his uncle drove off, he opened the door. Stepping inside, he looked for Pam. She was standing in the middle of the living room with angry tears making her eyes glisten.

"Hi," Bud said, "how'd you get in?"

"The door was open," Pam said.

Bud thought he must have been more sleepy this morning than he had realized, forgetting to lock the door like that. He noticed the curious expression on Pam's face as he moved toward her.

"What's the matter?"

"Nothing."

Pam tried to soften her expression and smile. As she seemed to relax, so did he. He looked around him at his trailer.

"Damn!" Bud almost yelled. "You cleaned up the place."

Turning, he hurried down the hall to the bedroom.

"You even changed the bed," he yelled from the other end of the trailer. "And vacuumed!"

Pam picked up the fallen hatbox and started back toward the bedroom, too.

"That's real nice," Bud went on. "I just love a woman's touch around the place."

Unbuckling his pants, he pulled them down to examine his bull bruises. His thighs were red, but they did not look as mean as they had when he had gotten hurt at Gilley's. Looking up, he saw Pam coming down the hall toward him with something hidden behind her back.

"What're you doin'?" Pam asked.

"I been out practicin' on the bull," Bud explained. "Just checkin' the damage. What're you doin'? What've you got there?"

"Close your eyes," Pam said. "Go on, close 'em. Trust me."

Bud slowly closed his eyes. Then he peeked. But he closed them again. Pam took something from behind her back and set it on his head. She adjusted it. Then she turned his head so that he was looking directly into the mirror over the dresser.

"Now," Pam said.

Bud opened his eyes and stared at himself in the mirror. He was wearing a white felt cowboy hat. Bud liked the hat, but he felt out of place in it. He immodestly believed he looked good in it but thought he did not belong in it. Grabbing Pam, Bud hugged her and kissed her thank you. During the kiss, she accidentally knocked the hat off his head.

"Know what's great about you?" Bud asked.

"What?" Pam laughed.

"You took the vacuum cleaner outa the box. I mean, I bought it for Sissy and she never even opened it. That's what I love about you."

Bud kissed Pam again. Thank you for the hat. Thank you for the cleaning. Thank you for being different from Sissy.

After they made love on the clean sheets in the clean bedroom, Bud wandered out to his truck. He felt around in his messy toolbox until he found a small handsaw. Carrying the saw back to his stoop, he sat down on the third step and studied his cast with a businesslike expression. Pam came and stood in the doorway behind him.

"I thought we might drive down to Galveston," Pam said. "Spend the afternoon. Have dinner by the water. Maybe go to a show."

"I got to work at the Beverage King tonight," Bud said. "It's Friday. I work the late shift Friday. It's a big beer night, you know."

"What are you doing?"

Sitting on the stoop, Bud was busy sawing away at the cast on his arm. White sawdust was snowing all over his boots. The saw made an irritating, grating, scraping sound as it moved back and forth.

"Doctor says this cast can come off tomorrow," Bud said. "Just takin' it off a day early and savin' a little money."

"Yes, but . . ."

"Look, I'm not you. I don't have all your money. With me ever little bit helps."

It was as though the saw were another voice in the conversation: *grate, scrape*.

"I know."

"Course things'll get a little better when I go back to work out at the plant next week. Uncle Bob says they'll let me work the double shift to make up for the time and money I lost. Overtime I can make almost twenty dollars an hour. Get me back on my feet. Say, turn up the radio, will ya? That's one a my favorite songs."

The saw said: *grate, scrape*.

Walking into the bedroom, Pam reached for the radio and saw the note propped against it. She picked it up and read it quickly. She knew what Bud would think of her if he ever saw the note. She could try to explain—talk about the kick, talk about how mad it had made her—but he would still know that she had taken credit for something someone else had done.

"Come on, Pam," Bud called. "Turn it up. It's almost over. What're you doin' in there anyway?"

"Nothin'," Pam lied.

When she turned up the radio, Johnny Lee could be heard singing loudly and clearly:

I was lookin' for love
In all the wrong places,

Looking for love
In too many faces . . .

Holding the note behind her, the way she had hidden the hat, Pam moved back down the hall into the living room. Her purse was on the couch. She picked it up and hurriedly stuffed the note into it. Then she returned to the doorway.

"I didn't realize you could make that much," Pam said a little distractedly, "working at the refinery."

While the saw continued to grate and scrape, the radio went on singing:

> *Don't know where it started*
> *Or where it might end.*
> *I turned to a stranger,*
> *Just like a friend . . .*

By now, Bud had managed to cut through the cast in one place. Pieces of it had chipped and fallen away.

"Sure, it pays good," Bud said. "Why do you think I come to Houston, anyway? Not for my health. If I was worried about my health, I'da stayed home where you can breathe the air. See, the idea is, you come down here, you get a job, and you save up enough to go back home and buy some land. That's the deal."

Grate, scrape, said the saw.

"Course, with the high cost a livin' and inflation and gas and breakin' my arm and my pickup and trailer and divorce and payin' little bills I didn't even know about that she run up, I ain't been able to save a dime. But I'm gonna. Been thinkin' a takin' up underwater weldin' so I can work on them offshore rigs. It's dangerous work, but it pays better. Get me home faster."

"Bud, I never met a cowboy who didn't talk about going home to the country," said Pam. "But something always keeps them here. Something or someone."

"Don't have to be like that."

Scrape, grate.

Pam sat down behind Bud on the steps of the stoop. She leaned forward and massaged his shoulders.

"Bud, I think I'm gonna bring some clothes down here," Pam said. "Move in for a while. You need a woman to take care of you. All right?"

"Suit yourself."

Bud scraped the saw across the cast one last time. Putting the sharp teeth aside, he began wrestling with his old plaster-of-Paris enemy. It was a struggle.

39

A Day

The alarm went off in the dark. Pam heard it but knew even in her sleep that it could not have anything to do with her. It just couldn't. It must be a noise in someone else's life that she was just overhearing. The sound finally stopped, as she had known it would. Someone had taken care of it.

"Pam," Bud said. "Get up. Make coffee."

She had ignored the alarm, which had to be for somebody else, but she could not ignore the voice.

"Uh, what time is it?"

"Five o'clock. Now come on."

Pam sleepily opened her eyes and was shocked by how close the walls were. She yawned lazily, not bothering to cover her mouth. Then she felt a hand slap her hip. It was not hard but it was still recognizable as a slap.

"Coffee," Bud ordered.

Groggily, languidly, Pam sat up in bed. She was wearing a short beige gown. Stretching, she lowered her legs over the side of the bed. She had lovely legs marred by no bruises. Rising, she moved off down the hall toward the kitchen. It was the first time in her life that she had gotten up at five o'clock in the morning to make coffee.

In the kitchen, she found all the pieces of the coffeepot in the dish-draining rack. When she had the parts fitted together, she got down the red can of Folger's coffee. A plastic top covered the can to keep its contents fresh. She removed the top and reached for the small plastic measuring spoon inside. Her hands were still groggy as she spooned coffee into the pot. She was almost finished when the can slipped from her grip and fell with a loud clatter. The kitchen floor was covered with coffee grounds.

It was Bud's turn to drive. As he approached his uncle's house, the sun still was not up. The only light in the sky was the refinery flare, which seemed to hover over Uncle Bob's home. As he pulled into the driveway, the old bull-rider came bounding out the front door as if it were a chute. He suddenly seemed to have farm energy in the middle of the city. He got in next to his nephew.

"You're lookin' pretty wide-awake," Bud said sleepily. "What's got into you?"

"That's what Corene keeps askin'," Uncle Bob said. "She says I'm too much for her all of a sudden. But I think she really likes it. Maybe I just like gettin' up early the way we used to. I dunno."

The sun was coming up by the time they finally saw the rearing wooden horse that advertised the Circle Eight Rodeo. Mist still hung in the air.

Bud had gone only a few steps toward the mechanical bull when he saw something that made him slow his pace. This morning, there was no bull in the holding pen, but there was another bull roaming free and unpenned near the bucking machine. The animal was grazing on a stray clump of grass and paid no attention to the visitors at first, but Bud watched it closely. Growing up in Spur, he had been taught to fear bulls the way other children were taught to be afraid of the boogeyman. If he wasn't careful, the bull would get him. As a child, he had had nightmares about bulls. In these dreams, he was always trying to get away from them. He would usually try to escape by climbing something—a roof, a tree, the windmill.

"The trick to handlin' bulls," Uncle Bob said, "is not to let 'em know you're afraid of 'em."

Bud was afraid that trick might be beyond his powers. He doubted he was that good an actor. To reach the mechanical bull they would have to pass within a few feet of the real one. And the real bull had longer than average horns. Bud felt a little ashamed of his fears, but he could not deny them, at least not to himself, although he did hope to conceal them from the bull and his uncle.

"What's he doin' out like that?" Bud asked.

"I dunno," Uncle Bob said. "Red don't keep his fences up too good. I reckon he figures his bulls know where home is so it don't matter if they get out."

As they drew within a dozen feet of the bull, it raised its head and stared straight at them. It moved its right foot, scratching the dew-bright earth.

"Easy now," Uncle Bob said.

Bud was not sure whether his uncle was talking to him or the bull. With the morning fog all around him, he felt as if he were walking in a dream. When they moved within ten feet, the bull shook its head. They were so close that Bud could read the number on the orange tag clipped to its ear, 81. All the while, Bud was keeping a running calculation of how close he was to the bull as compared to how close he was to the fence. Taking another step, he felt that he was crossing into that no-man's-land where the fence was farther away than the bull. And all the time, he felt so pitifully childish for thinking this way.

"Easy," Uncle Bob said again.

As they passed the bull, Bud quickened his pace slightly now that every step carried him farther away from the bull instead of closer to it. He felt that he had never been so anxious to reach the bucking machine in his life. He had to restrain himself to keep from running the last few feet. When he finally reached *his* bull, Bud climbed it the way in his dreams he had always climbed a roof or a tree or the windmill. Somehow he felt safe now.

"You know," Uncle Bob said, leaning against the black machine, "even back when I was rodeoin', I never got used to bein' around them damn critters. They're just so damn mean."

For the first time, it occurred to Bud that his uncle might have been as afraid as he had been. After all, Uncle Bob had suffered more from bulls than he had and had more reason to fear them. The thought somehow relaxed him.

"I don't feel too comfortable around 'em neither," Bud admitted.

For some reason, he patted the shoulder of the mechanical bull.

"Well, let's get to work," Uncle Bob said. "Now, seems to me you've got a pretty good grasp of the fundamentals. I mean you ain't gonna fall off. Least not too often. So what we gotta work on now is improvin' your style. That's how you score points."

"Uh-huh," Bud said.

"Now what I want you to do this mornin' is try to spur a little bit. Rake it a time or two. You know, just pretend, just go through the motions. Maybe by the time the rodeo rolls around we can find you a pair of old spurs. We'll see."

"That sounds good."

"Now in a regular rodeo you ain't required to spur a bull the way you are a horse—but it always makes a good impression. Makes you look like a mean son of a bitch who knows what he's doin'. Whether you do or not."

Laughing softly, Uncle Bob retreated to the controls. He looked up at his nephew.

"You ready?"

"When Bud nodded, his uncle started the machine. The snorting and leaping of the mechanical bull frightened the real bull, which loped away with its balls banging between its legs.

"Rake it!" yelled Uncle Bob. "Rake it! Rake it a coupla times."

As he stepped down on the clutch, Bud used the same motion and muscles as he had to "spur." He could feel that he was tired and bruised. Releasing the clutch, he started his truck rolling toward the refinery. He was going to work having already done the equivalent of a day's work.

By the time they reached the refinery, it hurt Bud every time he had to "spur" his pickup to change gears. When he parked in the plant's parking lot, Bud got out limping.

"You gonna be all right?" Uncle Bob asked.

"Prob'ly," Bud said.

"Feel like workin'?"

"No, don't feel like it, but I reckon I will."

"Well, today's payday. Almost makes it worth it."

Bud, who had been back at work at the plant for a week now, would be collecting his first refinery paycheck in a long time. He had fallen so far behind while the cast was on his arm that he needed this payday badly.

Arriving a little early, he sat down on a sawhorse to rest his weary muscles until starting time. Marshall came over and sat beside him.

"How you doin'?" Marshall asked.

"Not too bad," Bud said.

"You don't look too good. What is it? Is it that new girl I seen you with?"

Bud smiled and shook his head.

"Maybe you oughta try to stay outa bed and get some rest," Marshall said, clapping him on the back.

Just at starting time, Ray appeared. He gathered his crew around him to give them their instructions for the day. Bud instinctively took up a position near the back. He unconsciously rubbed his bruised left thigh as he listened.

"We got some more big shots comin' in next week," Ray announced. "So we gotta police up this place."

There was general groaning. They had cleaned enough already. They hadn't gone to work here to be housewives. They were men, not cleaning ladies. Bud didn't say anything.

"All right, all right," Ray said, "hold it down. You'll be cleanin' ladies if I say you're cleanin' ladies. Now listen up."

One by one, the foreman assigned cleaning jobs to his men. Some would sweep out the shop. Some would clean and organize the tool shed. Some would scrub the smoke marks off a tower that had recently suffered an accidental fire.

"Bud, you're goin' back in the boiler," said the ex-guard, making it sound like solitary confinement. "Don't see how you could fall offa one a them."

This time, Bud went back into the iron whale alone, like a true Jonah. He scrubbed its black walls in the black day of a boiler's bowels. The boiler was shaped something like a mobile home, about the same length, about the same width, about the same amount of room inside. Cleaning it was like cleaning the dirtiest, foulest trailer that ever was. He worked all day on it and still wasn't finished.

"Tired?" Uncle Bob asked.

They were driving home together along Route 225. Bud was stiff in new places now. He had bull bruises and boiler bruises competing with each other.

"Mmmmmm," Bud said.

They saw the Barn up ahead. It was a huge beer joint located between two plants on refinery row. The parking lot was crowded with cars, pickups, and semis. It was always especially popular on paydays when it exchanged money for paychecks, taking a commission.

"Wanta stop?" Uncle Bob asked. "Have a beer and cash your check?"

"I don't think so," Bud said. "I'm just too tired. If you don't mind."

The nephew drove his uncle straight home and dropped him off. Waving a last good-bye, he pointed his pickup in the direction of his trailer court. He was so exhausted that the steering wheel felt heavy in his hands. When he stopped at a red light, he closed his eyes and rested his forehead on the wheel for a moment. He almost went to sleep. Behind him, an impatient horn served him as an alarm clock. He drove on.

Reaching the next red light, Bud was about to close his eyes again when he saw a familiar sight that sent a surge of energy through him. It cleared his mind. It opened his eyes. It lifted him out of his sag. Across the street, Sissy was standing on the back of her wrecker, working hard. She had her hook into the front end of a stalled car. And she was cranking it up by hand.

Sissy's face was smeared with grease the way it was in the picture in the photograph album. Her biceps were bulging under the strain. She braced herself by sitting astride the arm of her wrecker as if she were riding it. She had on old torn, patched, and retorn blue jeans. Her breasts pushed hard at her red shirt as if they were working, too. Bud loved seeing Sissy trying so hard.

Without thinking, Bud honked the horn of his truck. Sissy looked up, but she did not know which direction to look in. He could see her searching. He honked again. When she stared in his direction, he waved and smiled.

Sissy was surprised by the sound of the honking horn. When she discovered where it was coming from, she was even more startled to see Bud waving at her. Anger surged in her the way energy had surged in Bud. The day she had cleaned his trailer, she had waited all afternoon for his call, which never came. She had waited just where she said she would, at Gilley's, but all her work had not even earned her a thank you. Time after time, she had gone into the office to ask if they were sure Bud hadn't called. Time after time, they were sure. And time after time, she told them she would be out by the bull if he did call. While she waited for what did not come, she rode the bull over and over. She rode it so long and so often that she reinjured her hand. She had been so sure that he would call. When he didn't, she had no choice but to go back to Wes.

And now there was Bud waving at her. He hadn't gotten around to calling but now he was honking. He couldn't go to the trouble of dialing a number when she needed him, but if he just happened to run into her by accident, he would say hello. His feelings toward her might be that casual, but hers toward him were still intense.

Sissy gave Bud the finger. Her gesture stunned him, bruised him, and angered him. He stopped smiling, glared, and raised his middle finger to her. Husband and wife remained locked in this fuck-you shoot-out on the highway until the light changed. Then he sped away with her looking after him.

Pushing the hair out of her eyes with a curt motion, Sissy went back to work. She cranked harder than ever, as if she were trying to raise the front end of the Battleship Texas.

When he got home, Bud went straight to the small bedroom and collapsed across the bed. Pam, who had been waiting for him all day, was hurt. She wondered if he had even forgotten that she was there. She would remind him. Getting up from the couch in the living room, she went into the kitchen. She opened the refrigerator and looked for a Lone Star. There was one way in the back. She reached way in and fetched it out. Finding an opener, she popped off the top. It made a happy sound and she smiled resignedly.

Pam was still smiling as she carried the bottle of beer down the hall toward her cowboy. She had already made up her mind to hide her hurt as she handed him the beer and welcomed him home.

Stepping through the bedroom door, Pam looked down at Bud, who was sound asleep in all his clothes, passed out, sprawled diagonally across the bedspread.

"Bud," she said.

When he did not move, Pam lifted the beer to her own unsmiling lips.

40

Stroganoff

Uncle Bob's green pickup slowed down and stopped in front of the trailer. Bud got out carrying his lunch bucket. The afternoon wind was blowing harder than usual. Bud put his hand on his hard hat to keep it from blowing off. Whenever the wind blew like that, he seemed to hear a windmill—the blades racing, the gears complaining, the sucker rod clanging. But the trailer park had no windmills. It was just a sound he heard in his memory when the wind rose.

"See you at midnight," Uncle Bob called through the open window. "Get some sleep. Say hello to Pam."

"Thanks," Bud said.

Bending into the wind, he headed for his front door. As he mounted his steps, he looked back over his shoulder. He was still searching for the windmill that was never there. Opening his front door, he walked in out of the wind.

"Howdy," Bud called.

"Hello," Pam returned his greeting from the kitchen.

Coming down the hall, he saw her stirring something on the stove.

"Smells good. What is it?"

"Stroganoff."

"What's that?"

"Come and taste."

Crossing the living room, Bud walked on into the tiny kitchen. He dropped his lunch bucket on the Formica table

238

and opened the refrigerator to get a beer. Then he gave Pam a peck of a kiss.

"Here," she said.

Pam held up a wooden spoon, which contained what looked like ground meat in some sort of gravy. Bud opened his mouth and she fed him.

"Mmmmmm," he said.

"There's a party at Cowboy tonight for a couple of friends of mine," Pam said. "Daddy might go."

"You go on," he said, swallowing. "I cain't. I'm workin' the graveyard tonight."

"Oh, no," she said, disappointed, "not again. You worked all day."

Bud popped the top off his beer. This time it made a surprised sound. Lifting it to his lips, he took a long drink.

"I know," he said, at last. "They've got a cat cracker down. And they've got ever'body workin' eight hours on and eight hours off till they get it cranked up again. Besides, it pays time 'n' a half."

"Oh."

"I'm gonna lay down now. Take a nap."

"Aren't you hungry?"

Bud took another drink of beer and wiped his mouth with his hand. Pam looked at him, waiting for an answer.

"I ate a barbeque at the Barn. I'll eat again just as soon as I wake up. Then I've gotta go to Gilley's."

"What?"

To make her feel better, Bud took the wooden spoon out of her hand, scooped up another bite of Stroganoff, and lifted it to his mouth. He talked while he chewed.

"Yeah, I gotta, mmmm, watch that son of a bitch run the bull for a coupla hours. Uncle Bob's idea. He says I oughta study his technique so I'll know what to expect come the rodeo. Ever'body does it a little differ'nt and I don't want no surprises. Mmmmm, sure is good."

"Thank you."

"Now I gotta get to sleep. Wake me in two hours, all right?"

In a hurry, Bud put down the spoon and left the kitchen. He disappeared down the little hall. Soon Pam heard water running in the bathroom. She turned down the fire under the Stroganoff and went after him. When she reached the bathroom, she leaned in at the door. He had soap all over his face.

"Bud," Pam said, "I don't want you going to Gilley's without me."

"Honey," Bud said, speaking not to her but to her reflection in the bathroom mirror, "I gotta study his technique on the bull."

"All right, I'll go," she said suddenly. "I'll just be late to Cowboy." She paused. "You don't care if I go to the party? You won't be jealous?"

Bud spit out some soap.

"Nope."

"Not even a little?"

Bud splashed water on his face and then reached blindly for a towel. Finding one, he hugged it to his face for a moment, then lowered it.

"I hope I learned a lesson about jealousy with Sissy," he said. "I hope I'm the kinda person that learns by experience."

"Not everyone does," she said with a smile.

"Well, contrary to what you or your daddy think," he challenged, "all cowboys ain't dumb. Some cowboys got the smarts real good."

"I'm sure," she retreated.

Dropping the towel to the floor, Bud made his way out of the bathroom. Passing Pam rather coldly, he walked into the bedroom. He started to sprawl across the bed but stopped himself in time.

"What've you done now?" he asked.

His tone was both affectionate and accusing. It was as though he were speaking to a child who did not know any better.

"What?" she asked.

"You bought me another new shirt," he said.

It lay sprawled diagonally across the bed.

"I had it made for you," she told him.

The shirt was on a wire hanger. Picking it up by the hook, Bud studied it. The shirt was blue with lots of red, white, and green scrollwork on the pockets and the yoke. He remembered where he had seen others like it.

"You bought it for me to wear to Cowboy."

"I just want you to look nice."

Treating the shirt a little roughly, Bud carried it fluttering to the closet and hung it up with an abrupt motion. As she watched him, Pam's eyes glistened with hurt expectations. She told herself that cowboys were too hard to be nice to.

"It's real pretty," Bud said too sharply. "Now don't forget to wake me."

Sprawling across the bed where the shirt had been, he did not even bother to reach for a pillow or to take off his work boots. He was exhausted and vaguely unhappy.

Studying him, Pam leaned against the doorframe. Her eyes were still bright with disappointment. She was unhappy, but she tried to appreciate how tired he was. Glancing at the window, she decided to pull the cheap curtains. She thought he would sleep better in a darker room. Moving to the window, she looked out. She saw the murky light and the bruise-colored clouds.

"It's going to storm," Pam said.

But Bud was already asleep, dreaming of windmills.

41

No Escape

Sissy's old Mustang bounced across the giant parking lot beneath a sky that looked like her bruised thighs. The car snorted to a stop in front of the decaying blue-and-silver trailer. Getting out, Sissy pulled her brown cowboy hat down lower on her head to keep it from blowing off. Stooping, she reached inside the car and took out two brown paper bags of groceries. Since her hands were full, she closed the car door by backing into it and giving it a little push with her behind. On her way into the trailer, Sissy looked back at the wind blowing across the vast, empty parking lot and felt some of the melancholy of a pioneer woman watching the wind howl across the vast, empty plains.

She had trouble opening the door. She had somehow to balance the bags, insert her key in the lock, turn the knob, and pull on it—all without dropping anything. She thought Wes might hear her fumbling and come to her aid, but he didn't. Perhaps he wasn't home. Finally, she managed to get the door open, but at the same time a roll of paper towels came tumbling out of the top of one of the bags. Holding the door awkwardly with her foot, she bent down for the towels.

When she stepped through the door, all loaded down, Sissy noticed the bottle of mezcal and two glasses sitting on the coffee table in front of the couch. Struggling on into the kitchen, she lowered her burdens onto the counter next to the sink.

"Wes," she called.

Hearing no answer, Sissy walked over to the sliding door that separated the kitchen from the bedroom. Placing her hand on the door, she hesitated a moment. Then she slid it open and looked into the bedroom.

Wes was sitting on the bed. He had his jeans on but no shirt. He was pulling his boots on. Looking up, he smiled at Sissy.

"Home a little early," Wes said, "ain'tcha?"

"No," Sissy said.

Reaching over, Wes knocked loudly on another sliding door, one that separated the bedroom from the cramped bathroom. Someone began sliding the door slowly from the other side.

"Marshallene was just leavin'," Wes said.

The bathroom door slid open about four inches and stopped, revealing a thin strip of Marshallene, one eye, a piece of one breast, a part of one leg. Sissy knew her. She was one of the bartenders at Gilley's. The one eye looked frightened.

"Excuse me," Marshallene said. "I'm sorry, Sissy. I . . ."

"Don't matter," Sissy said, shaking her head.

Marshallene slid the door open the rest of the way and stood there, framed in the doorway, redheaded, big-breasted, freckled, and embarrassed.

"Like I say," Wes said, "she was just leavin'."

Tucking her Gilley's T-shirt into her cutoff Levi's shorts as she went, Marshallene left the sanctuary of the bathroom and nervously began her escape. Sissy, who blocked the bedroom door, stood aside and let her pass.

"Really, I'm sorry," Marshallene said.

Once she was past Sissy, the redheaded bartender speeded up and almost ran to the front door. She threw it open and was gone. The door slammed hard. Either Marshallene had slammed it or the wind had caught it.

Leaning against the bedroom doorframe, Sissy stared down at Wes. He was calmly snapping up his cowboy shirt without apology or embarrassment.

"Well, honey," Wes drawled, "you cain't expect a man like me to be faithful to any woman."

"Twang twang," Sissy said.

"What?"

"Nothin'."

Sissy could feel her hands trembling. She needed to do

something, something mechanical, something that would momentarily occupy her mind and hands. Turning away from Wes back into the kitchen, she started unpacking the grocery bags. Her quivering fingers closed around a bottle of ketchup. She wanted to throw it and make an angry red mess, but she forced herself methodically to place it on a shelf in the refrigerator. Then she wondered if an unopened bottle of ketchup really needed refrigeration. As soon as this thought crossed her mind, she was irritated at herself for thinking about anything so unimportant at this moment. And yet she did not want to think about *this moment*.

Reaching back into the bag, Sissy's unsteady hands grappled with two cartons of milk, quarts. She carried them to the refrigerator, too. As she was arranging them on the shelf, she took another look at the ketchup, which looked somehow out of place. She turned back to the bag of groceries for whatever consolation it could offer.

As she withdrew a carton of eggs, Sissy heard Wes getting up off the bed. He moved into the kitchen and stood looking at her. She tried to keep her eyes on her groceries as if she did not see him standing there, but she was acutely aware of his presence. Suddenly the trailer was smaller than it had ever been before. She felt that they were cramped together, crushed together. Sissy had never felt so all alone and so crowded at the same time.

"You got cigarettes?" Wes asked matter-of-factly.

Nodding, Sissy reached into one of the grocery bags. She pulled out a carton of Marlboros and stood there holding them. Then she suddenly threw the red-and-white box at Wes as hard as she could. It bounced off his chest, fell to the floor, and spilled open.

Wes reached for Sissy as calmly as if he were reaching for a quart of milk to put away. He took her by the hair, gripped tightly, and forcefully lowered her head toward the burst carton of cigarettes. In spite of herself, she let out a whimper. She knew she sounded just like a girl, but she couldn't help it. He pulled her hair tighter and she whimpered again. The hurt sound echoed in the box that held them.

"Don't," Sissy yelled.

"Pick 'em up," Wes said in a calm, polite voice.

"No!"

It was a child's *no*, the *no* of a tantrum, an absolute *no* with no thought of ever changing. It was the same *no* that she had hurled at Bud in front of Stonie's when he told her to get into his pickup on the night he ultimately proposed. Into this *no* were compressed all her *no*s: *No I won't do it, no you cain't make me, no you cain't push me around just because I'm a girl.*

Pulling her by the hair, Wes dragged Sissy one way and then dragged her back the other. It was as if he were doing a cruel version of a cowboy dance, holding her in the traditional fashion by the hair, leading her one way, turning, and leading her the other, turning again. They danced to the sound of Sissy's hard breathing and her involuntary whimpers, which kept fighting their way up out of her chest.

"I said," Wes repeated with more authority but still polite, "pick 'em up."

He emphasized his words by giving her hair and head a hard shake. Her head hit the stove. Suddenly her consciousness seemed to be a ball of pain. Her skull hurt. Every hair hurt.

Reaching down, Sissy picked up the wounded red-and-white carton. Wes relaxed his grip on her hair slightly and put his free hand out to receive his cigarettes. Sissy drew them back and threw them at him once again. This time she had much less power behind her throw. The cigarettes glanced off his wrist as she whimpered again.

Wes dragged Sissy's head in a great arc and brought it crashing back into the oven door. There was a metallic shudder. Sissy was finally more frightened than she was angry. The blow and the pain dimmed her eyes, but she reached out almost blindly and fumbled until her hand found what was left of the carton of cigarettes. She lifted it toward Wes. He took it.

"Thank you," Wes said with good manners.

Feeling the mean hand loosen its grip on her hair, Sissy shook her head to make sure she was free. Convinced that she was, she raised up slowly. She did not look at Wes. She folded her arms across her heaving chest and stared down at the stray packs of cigarettes that still lay scattered on the floor.

"Now make me somethin' to eat," Wes said.

"Fix it yourself," Sissy snapped.

Wes grabbed her by the hair and threw her against the sink, which struck her hip a bruising blow. Sissy wanted to turn and rush out of the trailer, but she was sure he would not let her go. She might have tried to fight her way past him anyway, but she had nowhere to run to. Holding onto the edge of the sink because she had to hold onto something, Sissy felt that the outlaw's trailer was now her prison.

Turning in her tiny cell, Sissy opened the refrigerator door. She took out three eggs and carried them back to the counter. She placed them on a small plate, where her nervous fingers toyed with them, rolling them restlessly back and forth, the shells making a faint rumbling sound against the dish like tiny thunder.

Outside, a flash of light brightened the air and a moment later real thunder shook the trailer and the eggs. Wes walked over and looked out the porthole window set in the front door. He smiled at the bruised clouds.

"Gonna storm," he said.

Sissy broke one egg against another.

42

Cold Night

"Goddamn ol' smelly thing," Uncle Bob said. "You know, sorta looks pretty tonight."

"Uh-huh," Bud said gruffly.

Rolling toward a hard night's work in the black truck, they saw not the refinery itself but its lights stretching before them. Darkness had blacked out all the towers, leaving just the bright bulbs that the towers supported. The awful plant looked like a glowing forest of Christmas trees—heavy with Christmas tree lights—growing all the way to the horizon. The refinery seemed to be a terrible landscape by day, an enchanted landscape by night. It was two creatures, as changeable as Sissy's eyes.

"Always surprises me."

"Huh?"

"How good it looks at night."

"Oh, yeah."

"You're still pissed off, ain'tcha?"

"Yeah."

The refinery lights provided the only brightness in the night, for clouds, now invisible, blocked out the moon and stars. The wind was still blowing hard. From time to time, an especially hard gust made the black truck swerve. Bud's mood seemed an extension of the weather, and his uncle simply could not cheer him up, but he kept trying.

"Maybe she just forgot," Uncle Bob tried. "You know how the time gets away from you sometime."

247

"Like hell," Bud snapped. "She did it on purpose."

"Maybe she didn't·understand."

"Come on. I specific'ly asked her to wake me in two hours. She understood, all right. She just didn't want me goin' down there 'n' hangin' around where Sissy is."

"Well . . ."

"Well, nothin'. She knew how important it was to me. I told her why I was goin'. Explained it all. But I don't s'pose she much cares if I win or not."

Uncle Bob tried not to say anything. He knew he should not take sides, but he could not help it. He had feelings, too.

"Well, a lady like Pam wouldn't," Uncle Bob said. "Now Sissy . . ."

"Now don't get started on Sissy," Bud cut him off. "I saw her the other day. Just by accident. And we did our conversin' with our middle fingers. I don't wanta hear no more about her."

The older man looked at his nephew and then looked away out the window. He was remembering something that blurred his view of the refinery lights—making them look more and more romantic—even as he felt worse and worse.

"Aw, Bud," Uncle Bob said, still staring in the other direction, "even a hardheaded cowboy has to swallow his pride once in a while to keep somebody he loves. In my lifetime, I've lost a couple a people I loved that I shouldn't a lost just cause a pride." He turned toward Bud. "Pride's one a the seven deadlies, you know."

The affectionate laugh warmed the cab of the pickup.

"Damn!" Bud said.

Uncle Bob wondered if his nephew had even been listening to his speech. His thoughts seemed to be somewhere else entirely.

"What's the matter now?" the uncle asked a little impatiently.

"I'm just lucky it started thunderin'," Bud said with tight jaw muscles. "Otherwise I mighta slept right through work. You'd still be sittin' home waitin' for me to come pick you up. Shit."

As the pickup pulled into the company parking lot, a bolt of lightning lit up the night enough to show how ugly the refinery really was.

A huge urn of coffee sat at the foot of the ailing cat cracker. The company was willing to make this investment in keeping the men on its graveyard shift awake. Workers in hard hats and goggles were clumped around it.

"How's the coffee?" Bud asked his uncle.

For the past hour and a half, they had been working on the tower, each at a different level. Now, during coffee break, they were both drawn to the urn and each other.

"Kinda cold," Uncle Bob said.

"Couldn't be half as cold as I am," Bud said.

Bending down to fill his styrofoam cup, he shivered. He was surprised at how cold it was. Somehow he had expected the Houston nights to be as mild as the Houston days. They weren't. Besides, the wind was blowing hard that night. Up on the cracker, he had been so cold that he had trouble holding his tools. He kept being afraid he was going to drop something. Now his coffee trembled slightly in his hand. It was so *damn* cold.

"You're plum freezin'," Uncle Bob said, "ain'tcha?"

"Sorta," Bud said.

"I don't s'pose you brought nothin' warm to wear?"

"Didn't know it was gonna be this cold."

"Well, after midnight it gets pretty nippy around here."

Uncle Bob started taking off his red-and-black plaid lumberman's shirt. It was wool. He wore it over his khaki work shirt.

"What're you doin'?" Bud asked.

"Here, put this on," said Uncle Bob.

The uncle held out the shirt, but the nephew did not take it.

"No, I'm fine."

"No, you're not. Do what I say. Take it."

"I couldn't . . ."

"Don't be silly. I don't need it. I got my thermal underwear on. I've worked graveyard before."

Bud took his uncle's wool shirt. As he slipped into it, he seemed to shiver worse than ever. Now that relief was on the way, he momentarily gave in to the cold.

"Thanks," he chattered.

As he was buttoning up the wool shirt, doing it awkwardly, holding the cup of coffee at the same time, Bud noticed his foreman moving in his direction. Ray paused at a trash can, which was located next to the urn, long enough to deposit a used styrofoam cup. Then he walked on over to where Bud and Uncle Bob were standing together.

"It's about time," Ray said. "S'pose you could crawl back up there without fallin' off?"

"Ray, ol' buddy," Uncle Bob said.

"Yeah, Bob?"

"Shut up."

The foreman turned around and walked away toward the cat cracker. The uncle and his nephew watched him go. Then they smiled at each other.

"I better get back to work," Bud said.

"Yeah, me, too," Uncle Bob said. "You know, I was thinkin'."

"What?"

"We'll be gettin' off around sunup. Wanta run back out to the Circle Eight? Think you'll be up to it?"

"Sure."

"Time's runnin' out, ya know."

They parted, moving off in separate directions. Over his shoulder, Bud heard someone shout.

"Hey, Bob," the unknown authority called, "we need somebody to check the pressure on the five tank 'fore we try to start this baby up."

"I'll go," Uncle Bob shouted back.

Reaching his station on the catwalk, Bud looked down and saw his uncle crossing the road. He appeared small and somehow a little funny way down there, marching along, his pot belly leading, his arms swinging in exaggerated arcs. He was like a purposeful toy.

Picking up a rounded piece of insulation, Bud started wiring it in place around an exposed pipe. Since he was warmer, he worked faster now. The next time he looked up, he saw his uncle climbing the stairs that wound up the side of the huge white storage tank. Once the cat cracker was reactivated, it would draw crude oil from this tank number five, but before the valves were opened, someone had to do a routine pressure check. Bud imagined that he could see his uncle breathing hard as he carried his extra pounds up the curving stairs, higher and higher.

"Could you pass me one a those?" Marshall asked.

Bud looked around.

"Sure."

He picked up a molded section of insulation and handed it to Marshall.

"Thanks."

Suddenly lightning once again dispelled the becoming darkness to reveal the ugliness of the refinery. This time, the bolt was closer and brighter than before. It lit up more awful details. An instant later, the thunder rolled in to shake the catwalk under Bud's feet.

"Damn," Marshall said, "I don't like it up here when that happens. Makes me nervous."

The closeness of the lightning made a lot of people nervous. Soon word was passed to get everyone down off the cat cracker. It was just too dangerous to have men working up there during an electrical storm. The order was circulated quietly so that no one would panic. Ray came walking unhurriedly down the catwalk, informing the members of his crew.

"Let's take a little break," the foreman repeated over and over, "till this thing blows over. Be careful goin' down."

There was a general migration towards the ladders and a steady flow down them. Bud and Marshall joined this stream. When they were halfway down, lightning once again lit the ugliness and made everyone hurry a little more. Marshall reached the ground just ahead of Bud.

"Buy you a cup a coffee?" Bud asked.

"Thanks," Marshall chuckled.

They moved off toward the urn together. Bud filled a cup and handed it to Marshall. Then he ran one for himself. As they moved aside to make way for others at the urn, Marshall studied Bud in his oversized plaid shirt that made him look like a little boy playing dress-up.

"Nice shirt," Marshall said. "Too bad they didn't have one big enough."

Suddenly Bud turned toward tank number five. He had forgotten all about his uncle. Everybody had. Uncle Bob was still up there on the big white tank taking pressure readings in an electrical storm. Bud saw him from below now instead of from above. He didn't look funny anymore.

Suddenly, lightning lit the plant brighter and uglier than ever before. And then there was a roar louder than thunder as flames came clawing up out of tank number five. A small, rounded figure turned away from the burning lake and tried to outrun fire.

As the flames from tank number five mounted higher and

higher into the night sky, the plant got uglier and uglier, impossibly ugly, as ugly as anything ever could be. Then suddenly tank number six caught fire and it grew uglier still.

It was not cold anymore.

His too-big shirt flopping sloppily, Bud ran toward the noise and the light and the heat and his uncle. He kept bumping into bodies because everyone else was running the other direction. He pushed and shoved, afraid and angry, unable to understand why people kept getting in his way. He did not even see the men he ran into because he was looking at a man burning to death.

"Uncle Bob!" Bud screamed. "Uncle Bob!! Uncle Bob!!!"

"Bud," a voice shouted behind him. "Bud, stop! Stop! Stop him!"

He did not know or care who was yelling at him. He just kept running, his face getting hotter and hotter, brighter and brighter, glowing more and more insanely.

"Uncle Bob!"

"Bud!"

The burning man's mouth was open in pain. It was as if the deafening roar came up out of his lungs. He seemed to scream with the voice of the fire itself.

"Bud!!"

Suddenly his foreman's prison guard face was in front of him, the features distorted, the mouth wide open, screaming Bud's name. The fire burned like a cruel sun behind the intruding head. The yelling face was in the shadow, like the dark, cold side of the moon. Bud was trying to see his uncle, but that hated head kept getting in his way. And hated hands grabbed at his wool shirt.

"Stop, you bastard!" Ray screamed. "Get out of here! Get out! Damn you!"

Bud swung as hard as he could at the offending face.

"Uncle Bob!"

His hand hurt as it crushed into some bone, which gave way before it.

"Bud!"

The screaming voice sounded choked.

"Uncle Bob! Uncle Bob!"

The face dropped away, its nose broken. The foreman's body collapsed. Now Bud had a clear view of the top of tank number five, but he could not see his uncle. He searched in panic until he found him. Uncle Bob had fallen, too.

"Uncle . . ."

Someone tackled Bud from behind. He lay on the ground sweating and crying. It was so *damn* hot.

43

Warm Day

Bud was too warm in his black wool suit. He had bought it especially for the funeral. It had cost him most of the first refinery paycheck, so now he was deeper in debt and Spur was farther away than ever. He wondered if he would ever get home or if his dirt dream would end up amounting to no more than a plot of soggy dirt in a cemetery like this one. He told himself to stop thinking about himself. He should think about his Uncle Bob, but such thoughts were hard, especially since he had been the one who identified the body. Standing behind the coffin in his warm wool, Bud could not help remembering that his aunt had brought his uncle's wool suit to the mortuary for him to be buried in. No one had had the nerve to tell her that there was not enough of him left to wear it.

Bud and the other pallbearers wore white rose boutonnieres pinned to their lapels. They stood in a crooked line facing the other mourners across the casket. The others were seated in green chairs, each of which bore the cemetery's name to cut down theft. Bud looked from one face to another, trying not to stare at any man or woman or child too long, not wanting to make anybody self-conscious. Aunt Corene's red face was crying behind a black veil. Lou Sue's face, which seemed too young for makeup, was stained by the mascara mixed with tears. Little Willie was fidgeting on his chair. Bud's mother looked sad and worried. Sitting in the back row, Pam appeared somehow out of place, too beautiful, too well-groomed in her simple black dress and single strand of pearls, too clear-eyed. She was simply different.

A young woman in a gray flowered dress, who was slightly overweight, began singing an a cappella solo:

> *Softly and tenderly*
> *Jesus is calling . . .*

While she sang, Bud was surprised to find a different and seemingly inappropriate song running through his mind, as if his head were some sort of jukebox, a jukebox filled with nothing but profane music, a jukebox over which he had little control, a jukebox that played:

> *My heroes have always been cowboys*
> *And they still are it seems . . .*

The young woman's voice was clear and unafraid in front of all those people. She had grown up singing in church.

> *Calling to you*
> *And to me . . .*

The voice inside Bud's head was little more than a mumble, but it was an insistent mumble.

> *Sadly in search of, and one step in back of,*
> *Themselves and their slow-moving dreams . . .*

Bud could see Aunt Corene's lips moving with the words of the church song she knew so well, the song she herself had selected for the service.

> *There on the ramparts,*
> *He's waiting and watching . . .*

And Bud moved his lips, too, ever so slightly, so that no one saw, but he could feel them open and close.

> *Cowboys are special,*
> *With their own brand of misery,*
> *From being alone too long.*

You could die from the cold
In the arms of a nightmare,
Knowing well your best days are gone.

In the middle of the song—songs—an old car came rolling down the paved cemetery road toward the grave. The machine rumbled irreverently as it came.

Looking in the direction of the disturbance, Bud saw Sissy's rusty old Mustang. Now, mixed with all the other emotions, there was anger. By arriving at this moment, Sissy had added one more feeling than he could possibly handle, possibly absorb. He was angry not so much at her but at her doing this to him, overloading him, overwhelming him, making him feel emotionally helpless.

"Let us pray," said the preacher. "Our Father Which art in heaven, hallowed be Thy name, Thy kingdom come, Thy will be done . . ."

Bud found himself looking from Sissy's car to Pam, back at the car, then back to Pam again. That was when he noticed that Pam did not know the words to the prayer. She was trying, but she kept going wrong and having to drop out. Sissy's car stopped and the door opened with an unlubricated creak. She got out wearing black jeans and a white eyelet blouse with no sleeves. Taking off her cowboy hat, she tossed it back inside the car.

"For Thine is the kingdom and the power and the glory forever. Amen."

Bud saw Sissy walking toward the grave and the service and him. He wondered what she was doing dressed that way. Her clothes made him even angrier. It was as though she were trying to embarrass him in the middle of his grief. After all, she was still his wife, even if they were not living together, and her actions must reflect upon him. He told himself that Sissy had ruined the funeral for him without stopping to think what that might mean.

"Pallbearers," the preacher said, "would you please leave your boutonnieres on the casket?"

Bud unpinned his white rose, reached out, and placed it carefully on the coffin. The service was over. People were getting up and filing away. Bud made his way to his Aunt Corene and put his arm around her. As he was helping her away from her husband's grave, he felt a light hand on his arm. It was Pam's. The three of them—Bud, Aunt Corene, and Pam—walked together over the cemetery lawn. Lou Sue and Willie followed behind them.

Bud felt protective of his aunt so he was very irritated when Sissy rushed up to her and intruded on her grief. Bud's wife threw her arms around his aunt, held her close, both of them making little noises that had meanings without being words.

"I'm so sorry," Sissy finally managed to say. "I didn't know. Nobody called me. I just came in what I had on when I heard."

"Oh, Sissy, sweetheart," Aunt Corene said, "thank you for comin'. Bob loved you so much. He never got over you 'n' Bud breakin' up." She broke down for a moment, hugging Sissy tightly, then almost got control again. "He said you were both just too hardheaded, too much alike. I don't know what I' gonna do with . . ."

"Mama, don't cry," Willie said. "Mama . . ."

"I better go," Aunt Corene said. "Thank you again. Com'ere Willie."

She picked up Willie and moved on toward the car. Lou Sue walked on with her mother and brother. Bud wanted to go with them but he could not bring himself to without saying something to his wife. He felt like saying something hard, but he couldn't, not here, not now, not after what his aunt had said. He said the only thing he could think of to say.

"Thanks for comin'," he mumbled.

Sissy nodded. They stared at each other.

"He was sort of my uncle, too," she said. "Still is by marriage. Divorce ain't final yet."

Pam stepped closer to Bud. She took a firmer hold on his arm. Her clear brown eyes stared at Sissy and Sissy's bloodshot blue eyes stared back.

While the two women glared, Bud looked from one to the other. Pam's nose was powdered, Sissy's was red. Pam's eyes were outlined in black, Sissy's had scarlet rings. Pam's complexion had the perfect even tone of paint, Sissy's was blotched. Pam had not been crying, Sissy had. But all Bud, in his present state, saw was how much better Pam looked than Sissy.

"I got the papers your lawyer sent," Bud said. "Ain't had time to look at 'em yet. But I will."

"That don't matter," Sissy said. "I guess all that matters

is just what Uncle Bob always wanted. For you just to be happy. I hope you are. Are you?"

"You bet," Bud said too defensively. "You?"

Her coming had thrown him off balance emotionally, now his aggressiveness unbalanced her.

"Sure," Sissy said, "I finally got just exactly what I wanted. A real cowboy."

"Me too," Bud hit back. "I finally got what I wanted, too. A real lady."

Pam smiled ever so faintly in spite of herself. She tugged gently at Bud's arm.

"Bud," Pam said, "the family car is waiting."

He nodded.

"We've gotta go," Bud said. "Sorry."

With Pam on his arm, he started toward the black limousine that the mortuary had provided for Uncle Bob's family. Soon their backs were turned to Bud's wife, who watched them go.

"We're gonna be leavin' right after the rodeo tonight," Sissy announced.

Bud stopped walking, and Pam stopped a half step later. He turned and then she turned. He started to ask a question but decided not to.

"Wes says there's no life for him here," Sissy answered the unasked question. "He cain't get no decent job, so he's just gonna win the rodeo and we're gonna leave."

Bud stood there looking puzzled. He wanted just to go but he had to understand.

"How's he gonna do that?" Bud asked. "He cain't win the rodeo. He runs the bull."

"No," Sissy said, standing all alone. "They got in a big fight last night. Gilley thought he was bein' too rough on the customers. Hurtin' too many of 'em. So he fired his ass. And Wes said, 'Okay,' took out his wallet, put down ten bucks, and entered. He's gonna win five thousand dollars." She made it sound like all the money in the world. "Says we can get deep into Mexico on that."

Pam could not help a small smile once again. She was involuntarily amused by Sissy's naïveté about money. And she was pleased by the thought of her rival disappearing into Mexico. Yet Pam was in a graveyard, trying to play the part of a mourner, so she bit her lip. She put on a solemn face as if it were makeup.

"Good luck," Bud said.

"I don't guess you'll be there," Sissy said, "will you, now?"

"No," Bud said. "I'm gonna stay close to my Aunt Corene tonight."

Feeling a small tug at his arm again, Bud turned and walked toward the family car. After he had gone a few steps, he glanced back over his shoulder. Sissy had not moved. She stood there with her feet planted wide apart, her cowboy boots sinking into the wet earth, her hands on the hips of her black jeans. Bud thought she looked like the outlaw at the funeral.

When they reached the family car, Pam got in, then Bud. The doors were closed quietly. And the family drove away, leaving Sissy alone with Uncle Bob.

44

The Backyard

Bud stood in Uncle Bob's backyard, gripping the top of the chain link fence, the sharp ends of the wires biting into his palms. At regular intervals, he would hear volleys of laughter coming from the house where the wake was being held. He had come out here to get away from the laughter that haunts every wake, to escape the crush of people, to be alone. If he had been at home, he would have climbed his windmill. He never missed it more than now. Climbing it now in his mind, he gripped the top of the fence harder, as if it were his ladder, and hurt his hands worse.

Hearing the back door open, Bud turned his head. His Aunt Corene was coming out to him. She was still wearing her black dress. He was still in his black wool suit. The weather had cooled off some and he was more comfortable in it now. Aunt Corene moved across the lawn, which was just getting started. The backyard was covered with little circles of grass that the builder called "sprigging." The sprigs were finally reaching out to each other, but the yard still looked polka-dotted. Reaching the fence, Aunt Corene touched the sleeve of Bud's new suit.

"Darlin'," Aunt Corene said, "I've got somethin' for you."

Bud saw that she was holding something in her hands wrapped in tissue paper. The paper rustled softly. She had had trouble keeping her hands quiet ever since it happened. She started to give the gift to him as it was, then pulled it back, confused, unable to make up her mind, deciding finally to unwrap if before she parted with it.

"Bob told me just last Monday," she said while her unreliable fingers were busy with the tissue, "think it was Monday, that he wanted you to have this. And wear it in the rodeo. For good luck."

Bud looked from his aunt's hands up to her face. Strangely, he thought she had never looked prettier. Her mourning became her. If only his uncle could see . . .

"I ain't goin' tonight," he said in a thick voice. "Just cain't."

The gift was unwrapped now. The uncertain hands held out the silver buckle that Bob Davis had been awarded for winning first place in bull riding at the Mesquite Rodeo in 1964.

"Please take it, Bob," Aunt Corene said. Then she realized her mistake. "I mean Bud. Oh, would you listen to me?" Not knowing whether to laugh or cry, she did a little of both at the same time. But she did not give up on her mission. "Please, Bud, take it for good luck."

Bud let go the painful fence to take the buckle in his hands. He studied it for a moment, trying not to break down. If he broke down, he was afraid she would, too, and he did not think he could stand that. He tried to focus on the silver bull-rider.

"I'd be proud to take it," Bud said. "But not for good luck. Not tonight."

Aunt Corene stood up straighter. Her eyes were still blurred but they were also determined.

"Bob had kinda forgot his rodeo days till you come along," Bud's aunt told him. "Even forgot where he put his rodeo buckle. I had a helluva time findin' it."

"I'll bet you did," said Bud, risking a smile.

"I did," she said with an echoing smile, which quickly changed back into a sad determination. "And now that it's turned up, I don't want it retired again. I wanta give it to somebody who'll use it."

"All right," Bud said almost soundlessly.

The two of them stood there, not saying any more, looking away from each other to the horizon that was lined with refinery towers. Bud would wear the buckle later, but right now he wanted to put it away. It made him too sad and self-conscious. He slipped the heavy piece of silver into a pocket in his wool suit.

"I got to go back in now," Aunt Corene almost whispered. "Good luck."

When he was left alone again, Bud reached out once more and grabbed hold of the top of the fence. The sharp points dug into his palms again. The sun was going down. In the fading light, Bud studied his hands on the fence, the petroleum stains that had almost washed out, the small cuts, the missing finger. He was thinking about his Uncle Bob, but he was also thinking about himself. The first time he had really felt his mortality—felt it in a personal, frightening, undeniable way—had been when he lost his finger. This loss had proven to him that he was perishable. Flesh of his flesh, bone of his bone, body of his body had died and been flushed down the drain without even the benefit of a decent burial.

Now Bud had suffered a second loss, which served as another overwhelming reminder of his own mortality. He had lost his Uncle Bob. And he knew that one day he would lose himself.

Glancing up from his hands, Bud focused momentarily on the horizon with its towers. Then he looked back down at his hands again, but the lingering memory of the towers caused an idea to begin to form. Raising his eyes once again, Bud stared past his hands, past his crippled finger, past his own crippled immortality, past himself. There was something he had to do for his uncle.

45

The Flying Red Horse

Bud climbed into the sky wearing his rodeo cowboy clothes and his new rodeo belt buckle. The rungs of the ladder were cool in his hands as he mounted higher and higher into the night. He felt as if he had practiced this climb many times before—every time he climbed his windmill. But now he was not climbing to be alone, not to think. The wind seemed to rise as he rose, which bothered him, but he kept on going higher. Bud looked up to where he almost expected to see a sharp, bladed wheel but found himself staring instead at the flying red horse that hovered over the refinery.

Around his cowboy waist, like a gun belt, as he climbed, was his tool belt. On one side, his hammer hung heavily, occasionally bumping into his leg. On the other side, a hacksaw was suspended. The pouches of the tool belt held wrenches and screwdrivers. He had armed himself with these tools because he knew he would need them when he reached the top.

Pausing in his journey, Bud looked down at his world. Way out there, he could see Gilley's Club. The saloon was easy to find because it was so well lit at night, especially the parking lot, which was already full and overflowing. He could even barely make out Wes's trailer standing there by the corner of the honky-tonk. Focusing on this tiny blue matchbox in the distance, he tried to imagine the life inside it, but he found that he could not or did not really want to. In the other direction, he recognized Pam's apartment building, which reached up so high so far away. Then he tried to find his own trailer park, but in the night he couldn't.

Looking around at closer range, Bud saw a refinery that looked like a ghost town. The actual distilling of petroleum products from crude oil was almost entirely automated, so at night the plant could be run by a handful of operators. And they were all indoors. No one moved on the face of the ugly steel landscape. So there was no one, for the moment at least, to see or care what he was doing. And even if a stray night watchman should pass, he probably would not be able to see the cowboy climbing toward the flying red horse. The night was too dark and Bud was too high.

Of course, Bud could not help looking down at the burned-out tanks, number six and especially number five. He thought they looked like bomb craters, but he did not really know what a bomb crater looked like. Actually, at that height, they looked like blackened coffee cans. Uncle Bob had died at that edge of the can right there.

Looking away from the memory, Bud's eyes scanned the parking lot until they found his black truck. He thought he might be able to see Pam inside it, but he couldn't. Still he knew she was there, waiting nervously for him. She would be staring through her window, trying to see him, but he doubted that she could. He felt totally invisible—a part of the night. He had not told her what he planned to do, just that he had to stop by the refinery to take care of something for his uncle.

He had rested long enough. Looking back up at the horse, he started climbing again. The night seemed to grow colder as he mounted higher. Shivering, he wished he had thought to wear something warmer. He told himself that he would never learn, but that he should stop thinking about it. The horse grew larger and larger as the real world grew smaller.

When he reached the platform beneath the hooves, Bud moved extremely cautiously. He knew he was prone to accidents at great heights. Trembling in the cold wind, he crawled slowly to the first of the cables that held the flying horse like steel ropes. There were four cables in all, each one running from the horse to an eyebolt, each eyebolt anchored to one of the platform's four corners. Bud got out his hacksaw and went to work. The teeth scraped and grated against the steel fibers of the cable. It was a struggle. Steel sawdust sprinkled down onto his boots. Working so hard, he soon was not cold anymore.

When the hacksaw finally bit through the first metal rope, Bud rested for a moment. The freeing of the flying horse had begun. But it had taken Bud over ten minutes to cut the cable. This job was going to take longer than he had thought. And it was going to take more out of him than he had imagined. He hoped that he would not be too late for the rodeo—and that he would not be too tired.

Crawling cautiously again, Bud made his way to the next steel lariat that held the horse where it was. Before he went back to work, he peeked over the edge at the world that waited for him. Then he shrugged his shoulders to relax the muscles, took a cold breath, and sawed. He was soon perspiring. Revenge was work. He cut through this cable a little faster. Like any job, it took some time to learn to do it right.

While he was sawing the third cable, Bud felt a blister begin to rise on his right hand. He was glad he rode with his left. He shifted the saw in his hand, which helped a little, and kept on. He could smell how hot the blade was getting. Now he wished he had brought an extra in case this one broke. The third rope snapped.

The blister burst while he was sawing the last cable. It made his palm feel wet and sticky. His shoulders began to ache. The blade smelled hotter and hotter as it wore deeper and deeper into the steel rope. If his hand and the saw would only hold out, he was almost done. With every stroke, he started repeating to himself, *please*. He pushed, *please*. He pulled, *please*. He pushed and pulled and pleased until he finally cut the iron horse's last iron tether.

After a brief rest, Bud ducked under the steel horse's steel flank as if he were going to geld it. Actually, he was preparing to attack the place where the animal was bolted to a pipe that held it aloft like a lollipop on a stick. He fumbled in the pouches of his tool belt for his wrenches. Withdrawing two crescents, he adjusted them to the right size. There were only two bolts. This part of the job was much easier than the sawing had been. Since he was no longer working so hard, he began to get chilly again. The wind was cold on his body, which was still damp with perspiration. Bud removed one bolt and then the other.

Taking a deep, freezing breath, Bud stepped all the way under the steel horse. He placed his back beneath the steel belly and lifted with all his strength. Slowly, the flying red horse rose up off the pipe that had supported it all its life.

Now Bud supported it. Standing on top of the 200-foot tower, he held it aloft on his shoulders. The iron horse rode the cowboy. Straining hard, Bud took a couple of steps toward the edge. He had been worried all along about how he would part with the horse. He kept imagining that he would somehow become entangled with it and share its fate. He "saw" himself riding the flying horse down and down out of the sky . . .

Giving one enormous heave, Bud finally threw the flying red horse off the top of the tallest tower in the refinery. He watched the horse's fall. Its iron wings did not save it.

46

The Rodeo

The cowboy hurt but he enjoyed the pain. His blistered right hand was so sore that he cradled it in his lap while he drove with his left. His back felt as if he might have strained it, reinjuring the same muscles that the same tower had injured once before. The top of his shoulder was scraped where the iron horse had given him one last kick as it fell. But his night's work had left him so exhilarated that he did not mind the aching. Bud felt just enough like an outlaw.

Sitting next to him, the oilman's daughter was excited, too. She was also beginning to think of him as an outlaw. At first she had tried to hold his hand, but he had explained to her that she was hurting it more than she was helping it. She sat with her shoulder just touching his.

Bud had never seen the parking lot so crowded. It was already full, and the field across the street was full, too. This was by far the biggest mechanical herd ever driven to the doors of the old saloon. Still afraid he was going to be too late, Bud worried that he might have to park miles away and then walk. Pulling into the parking lot, which clearly had no room, he kept looking for any opening with no real hope of finding one. And then up ahead he saw a camper backing up and pulling out. He considered it a good omen for the night.

Filling the camper's vacated space, Bud turned off the engine and then the lights. When he closed the door, he forgot about his burst blister and so hurt his hand, winced, and then smiled. Damn, hadn't that been something? He heard the

267

crash in his memory as he walked toward the rodeo with his gear bag slung over his sore back.

Pam took Bud's arm just as he was glancing over in the direction of Wes's blue-and-silver trailer. A light was on in the back. It was probably a bedroom light. Once again, he tried to imagine life behind those tin walls, but his imagination flinched before it imagined too much. He looked straight ahead at the entrance to the saloon. He was walking a little stiffly.

"Are you going to be all right?" Pam asked.

"Uh-huh," Bud smiled.

When they reached the saloon door, they had to wait in line to pay their money to get in. There was often a line but never before one this long. Bud was still worried about being late. While there were still a dozen people in front of him, he called ahead to the woman who was taking money at the door.

"Minnie," he yelled, "the bull ridin' start yet?"

"Nope," she called back. "That's last. You got plenty a time. Hold your horses."

As soon as he walked into the saloon with Pam, Bud saw Sissy standing on the other side of the long bar smoking a cigarette. For some reason, he was glad she was not there under the light in the bedroom of the blue-and-silver trailer. He glanced down at Pam to see if she had seen Sissy. She hadn't. Looking back across the bar, Bud realized that he hadn't either. The cowgirl with the cigarette looked a little like his wife, but she was not Sissy. She had dull eyes.

Looking around for Sissy, Bud could not find her, but he did see a crowd gathered around the punching bag. This event had already started. The machine's siren went off so often that that part of the saloon sounded like a firehouse.

"Let's go look at the punchin' bag," Bud said.

Pam clung to his arm as they moved through the dense cowboy crowd. As they drew closer, they could see the blood on the bag. When a new fist slammed into the bag, the blood splattered. The bag looked as if it were bleeding. It appeared to be wounded. It seemed to be losing the fight. But it wasn't. The machine was soggy with cowboy blood.

Just beyond the mechanical bag, Bud saw Sissy. She was facing away from him, but he recognized her hair. Then she turned. She wasn't Sissy either. His wife probably was out there under the bedroom light, after all.

Bud led Pam to a position behind the judges' table, which had been set up for the event. A skinny cowgirl sat at the table in front of long lists of names and numbers.

"Number twenty-seven," the cowgirl at the table called, "Ben Goodnight, from Texas City."

A heavyset cowboy, whom Bud had never seen before, stepped up to the bag. On his back, he wore a white square of paper with a big "27" printed on it in red. It looked like a large date from a large calendar. All the contestants wore numbers on their backs as if they were in a real rodeo. Number 27 measured the distance to the bag with his arm, thought it over, measured it again. He backed up a couple of steps and then ran forward as he delivered the hard overhand punch to the machine's jaw.

The siren went off. The light went on behind the picture of the girl with no clothes on at all. And the machine rocked on its iron legs. The big crowd gathered around the punching bag cheered loudly, boisterously, happily, drunkenly. While they were still yelling and whistling, a rodeo judge in a red vest stepped up to the dial to get an exact reading.

"Three hundred forty-five," the red vest called out. "Three four five."

"Three forty-five," echoed the cowgirl at the judges' table. "Our new leader is Ben Goodnight with a score of three hundred forty-five. Nice goin', Ben." She looked down to write the score after his name and then looked up again. "Number ninety-six, Norman Tucker, from Abilene."

Tall, thin Norman, who stood like an S, replaced the heavyset cowboy in front of the punching bag. He didn't really live in Abilene. He lived just down the street from the saloon. But he had been born in Abilene twenty-two years ago.

"Come on, Norman," Bud yelled. "Show 'em how it's done."

He whistled and clapped at the same time for his old friend.

"Go, Norman," cried Pam.

Hearing her, Bud smiled. He knew that she did not know Norman. She was cheering for him because Bud was. It somehow pleased him.

"Do it, Norman!"

"Come on, Norman!"

Norman measured, gritted his teeth, and swung. He was

not as big as the Texas City cowboy. He wasn't as strong. But he had had a lot more practice on this machine. He knew it was good to come down on the bag a little, knew the angle, knew the sweet spot. The big crowd cheered and clapped and whistled.

"Way to go, Norman," Bud called.

"Nice one, Norman," Pam cried.

The judge in the red vest stepped up to take a good look.

"Three hundred sixty," the vest called. "Three six oh."

There was more cheering.

"Three sixty," said the cowgirl at the table. "Our new leader . . ."

Then Bud saw Sissy.

Bud thought he saw Sissy again on the dance floor during the dance contest, but he was wrong once more. He wondered why he kept thinking he saw her. He told himself that it wasn't because he wanted to see her. He even went so far as to remind himself of all the reasons why he did not want to see her. He didn't want her to flip him the finger again. He didn't want her to tell him once more that she had found a real cowboy. He told himself that he was relieved that she was nowhere to be seen.

In the dance contest, dozens and dozens of couples with numbers on their backs turned in circles within circles. They all had on their fanciest clothes and did their fanciest steps, more and faster spins, little side skips, dips. Bud and Pam watched for a while but he soon lost interest. His mind was on his own approaching event. He leaned down to Pam.

"Let's go on over to the bull," Bud said. "I wanta start gettin' ready."

"All right," Pam said.

Lifting his gear bag once again to his shoulder, Bud led the way. They skirted the dance floor, passed along the long bar, and then walked between tables toward the bullring. The saloon had set up new bleachers all around the bull that really did look like rodeo stands. They made Bud a little nervous. In his thinking about the rodeo, he had never imagined that so many people would be watching.

Circling around behind the stands, Bud and Pam entered an area behind the bull master's table that corresponded to the area behind the chutes in a real rodeo. This was where the contestants got ready, warmed up, made one final check of their equipment, did all the little things that kept their hands busy until their hands really had something to do. Bud put down his gear bag and unzipped it. Uncle Bob had helped him pick it out the week before. He was rummaging through it when he felt someone looking at him.

Glancing up, Bud saw the coyote eyes staring at him. Sissy had seen him first, after all. She had been standing a few feet away and he had not even noticed her. She stood between Wes and a rodeo clown in baggy pants, a big bow tie, a whitewashed face, and a painted smile. Sissy wore a hint of makeup, too, which irritated Bud because he thought she had made herself look better for the rodeo than she had for the funeral.

While Bud watched, Wes bent over his gear bag. It was older and more seasoned than Bud's. Wes took out a pair of spurs and spun the rowels. They were still spinning when Sissy bent down and took them in her own hands. Kneeling, she began strapping the spurs to Wes's boots. Bud was surprised to see her in this position. It seemed so unlike her.

Pam saw Sissy, too. Bending down, Bud's new girl friend copied his wife. She found the spurs in Bud's gear bag and withdrew them. Uncle Bob had also helped to pick these out. Pam touched the points of the rowels as gingerly as if they were pins. Then she spun them slowly. They looked like tiny windmill wheels going around and around in a gentle breeze. Pam knelt in front of her cowboy to buckle the spurs to his boots.

Sissy pulled something made of black leather from Wes's old gear bag. The black leather was rolled into a tight bundle with a leather thong tied around it. She untied the thong and unfurled a pair of black chaps that looked like pirates' flags. The outlaw's initials were stitched in white leather near the bottom: *WH*. Like the gear bag, they were well worn and weathered. They looked like old, comfortable armor that had endured many campaigns.

Like an echo, Pam lifted a tight roll of brown leather from Bud's new gear bag. Hurrying to catch up, she unfurled brand-new brown chaps that smelled like a new saddle. Pam held up the chaps with special pride, for they were her gift to her cowboy. His initials were stitched in black leather: *BUD*. His armor was unscarred by any previous battles.

Sissy held up the black chaps and buckled them around

Wes's waist like a leather apron. Then she knelt to strap the chaps to his legs. First, she buckled the bottom strap, which was located just above the knee. Then, she worked on the second strap, which came mid-thigh. Finally, her hands busied themselves with the top strap, which embraced the top of the thigh where it joined the crotch. Watching his wife minister to Wes, Bud could almost feel the touch of her hands. As she pulled tighter on the outlaw's crotch strap, Bud's own crotch winced. As she tried the strap to see if it was tight enough, he himself felt the tug. Before his eyes, Sissy's dressing of Wes seemed to be turning into a public seduction.

Feeling another tug at his crotch, Bud realized that Pam was strapping on his chaps while his wife was attaching the outlaw's. She proudly pulled at the new leather, feeding it through shiny new buckles, tightening and arousing at the same time. And Sissy watched—her own nerves pulling tighter and tighter.

Bud alternated between watching the other bull-riders on the bull and withdrawing into his own thoughts about his own coming ride. He would worry about the others and then he would worry about himself. He would concentrate on the others' style and then he would concentrate on his own. He would look around and then he would look inside.

When he worried about the others, Bud worried not only about Wes but also about a group of real rodeo cowboys who had been attracted to the saloon rodeo. They were different. Their hair was even shorter than the saloon cowboys' hair. Their jeans were even tighter. Their manner was even cockier. But the biggest difference was their hats. The rodeo cowboys wore none of the store-bought decorations that the saloon cowboys liked to pin on their hats: tiny gold eagles, miniature saddles, gold initials, buttons with funny sayings. The rodeo cowboys would have none of that but simply adorned their hats with a single feather. These real bull-riders condescended to the Gilley's bull-riders. And the Gilley's riders, in turn, seemed to view the professional riders as bandits who had come to steal the prize money that was rightfully theirs. Bud was not the only one who was worried. Nor was he the only one who watched closely when the first rodeo rider was announced.

"Number eighty-nine," Steve Strange, seated at the bull master's table, boomed over the microphone, "J. R. Jones, out of Big Spring. Says here that J. R. is a member of the Rodeo Cowboys Association, the good ol' are see ay."

Bud resented this swaggering outsider who walked across the mattresses in chaps even more beat-up than Wes's. His spurs jingled as he vaulted onto the bull's back. He fussed over his grip and then slapped himself in the face. He was ready.

When the bull leaped, number 89 raked the unfortunate machine with his spurs. But the bull—wide open on its highest speed—soon had its revenge. It spun to the right, then whirled back to the left, leaving 89 still on its back but off balance. And the bull never let him catch up. It spun and bucked and hurt 89's balls and delighted all the Gilley's regulars who cheered not for the cowboy but for the bull. The buzzer sounded, *burrrrr*!

As 89 staggered back toward the sidelines, the red-vested judges compiled their scores. The scoring was done exactly as in a real rodeo. There were two judges, one on the left side and one on the right. Each judge scored not only the rider but also the bull. The rider could earn up to twenty-five points for his ride, the bull up to twenty-five points for its bucking, from *each* judge. Then the two judges added their scores together to come up with the final score, which meant that a perfect ride, if one of those ever occurred, would receive a perfect score of 100.

The judge on the left gave the rodeo cowboy twelve points for his ride. He was more generous with the bull, giving it twenty points. The judge on the right gave the RCA member ten points and the bull nineteen. The scores were totaled and written boldly on a blackboard, which was held up to the crowd. The blackboard said: "61."

"Sixty-one," Steve boomed over the mike. "J. R. Jones scores sixty-one points on his first ride."

The contest would be composed of two rounds. Each rider would get two rides. The winner would be the rider with the highest combined score on both rides. If a rider got bucked off, he was out of the competition.

"I thought he'd do better," Bud told Pam. "Wonder what went wrong."

He was puzzled but not displeased. He grinned as he rubbed his hands on his new chaps.

"Number fifty-six," Steve announced, "Buba Sailors, from Austin. Let's go, Buba."

Bud did not exactly root for Buba either, but at least he did not resent him, did not root against him. Buba lived down the road, worked at Mobil Oil, and came to the saloon almost every night. Bud even managed to clap his hands. Pam clapped, too.

Buba rode pretty well. He would never have known how to ride a real bull, but he knew how to ride the bull at Gilley's. He knew just where to sit, just how fast the bull would spin, just how high it would buck. He also knew what not to do. He wasted no time watching the bull's head to see which way it was going to turn because he had long since learned that it had no head. When the buzzer sounded and he slid down, his score was posted on the judges' blackboard: "76."

"Seventy-six," boomed Steve. "Nice goin', Buba. Our new leader in the bull ridin' is Buba Sailors with a score of seventy-six. Now he's the cowboy to beat."

The crowd in the bleachers clapped and cheered just like at a rodeo. Bud clapped, too, but not very enthusiastically. He had not wanted Buba to do quite that well.

The next rider was another member of the Rodeo Cowboys Association. He swaggered out to the bull, jingled aboard, and got bucked off.

"Too bad," said Steve's amplified voice. "All right, folks, let's give him a big hand because your applause is the only pay this cowboy's gonna git."

Bud realized that he had lost track of Sissy. He was not sure why he wanted to know where she was, but he looked around for her. He saw Wes but not Sissy. Wes was standing in an aisle between two bleachers—standing alone. Bud could not help wondering where Sissy had gone. He was still looking around for her when he saw her approach her outlaw from behind carrying a shot of tequila and a beer. She handed them to him one after the other. Bud was not the only one who noticed.

"Would you like anything to drink?" Pam asked. "I'd be glad to get it for you."

"No, ma'am," Bud said. "I can barely ride that thing sober, much less drunk." He chuckled. "You wanta get me killed?"

Bud saw Sissy looking over in his direction. He tried to imagine the life behind the gold eyes, but he could not. Her look told him nothing of what she was thinking. Tonight her eyes did not take sides. He felt Pam's hand on his arm. She took sides.

When the crowd roared, Bud looked to see what they were laughing at. Two rodeo clowns were carrying off a fallen bull-rider. They were pretending to be on his side, to be taking care of him, but they were really using him to their own comic ends. The cowboy struggled to get away from the funny-faced Good Samaritans.

"Number eighty-seven," Steve announced, "Bud Davis, from Spur."

47

Bud and Wes

As Bud walked toward the bull, his new chaps rustled noisily and made him feel funny. His spurs jingled cheerfully as if they were laughing at him. He needed to block out the sound of the chaps and the spurs and fans in the bleachers, so he reached up and pulled his hat brim down lower over his eyes. Coming up to the bull, he put both hands on its back and jumped. In midair, he heard his chaps rustling louder and his spurs laughing harder than ever before. Then he was sitting on the bull's back, looking around at all the tiers of people. With all the shouting and screaming and clapping and other spurs jingling on the sidelines, Bud heard above the din: *Stay in the well*.

When he raised his right hand into the air in front of so many people, Bud was never more aware of how crippled it was. He made his hand into a camouflaging fist but knew this was no way to ride and relaxed it. He leaned his head one way, then leaned it the other, practicing staying in the well. Or so he told himself. Actually he simply had to do something, anything, because he had never been more nervous than at this moment. It was that terrible moment just before. He was shaking. He could not have said his name.

"You think you're ready?" Steve Strange asked over the microphone.

Bud nodded. His head was still moving when the bull began to move, too. It bucked and spun to the left. And he heard the familiar voice yell: *In the well! In the well!* Tilting his head to the left, he knew he was making the correct move, knew he was riding it right, knew he was doing just what he had been taught. With this motion, all the awful nervousness drained out of him. He could no longer worry about the ride because he was too busy riding.

When the bull spun back to the right, Bud tilted his head to the right. *In the well*! *Atta boy*! He no longer felt as if the earth had suddenly started to spin the wrong way. The change in direction seemed natural. He rolled with it. He could feel himself maintaining his balance and it felt good.

Lifting his spurs high in the air, Bud could no longer hear their merry jingle. He could barely hear the crowd. All he could hear clearly was the blood in his ears and the voice saying: *Rake it*! *Rake it*! *Rake it a coupla times*! His boots with their spurs moved in a circle, out, up, around, and down with a crash. The iron rowels raked the iron bull. Then the spurs moved through another circle that was not completed until they dug into the bull's back once again. One spurring circle grew out of another grew out of another grew out of another. *Rake it*! The spurs landed! *Rake it*! The spurs landed harder! *Rake it*! The spurs landed harder still!

Bud saw Sissy. If he had been able to imagine the life on the other side of the coyote eyes, he would probably have imagined that she was impressed. And he would not have been wrong. Sissy was surprised that Bud rode so well. She wondered where he had learned to spur. She found herself wishing she could rake the bull like that, too. In the middle of this wish, Wes bent down to her.

"Bud's been practicin'," he said.

Sissy looked over at Pam, who was clapping and cheering the way she had at so many football games. She had been a cheerleader in high school. When she went east to an all-women's college, she had had no team of her own to cheer for but she had cheered enthusiastically for her dates' teams. Pam had never seen Bud ride the bull before, so she had no idea how much he had improved. But she was still impressed and excited by the ride. It never occurred to her to wish she could ride the bull like that. Cheering was enough for her.

When the bull cut back in the other direction this time, Bud felt the force of the spin pulling him out of position. *Stay in the well*! The remembered voice was louder than ever now. *In the well*! *In the well*! He pushed his head over hard and his hat came off, but he saved his balance. Now he could concentrate on his style again. *Rake it*! But he could not afford another mistake. *Stay in the well*! Everything seemed to spin faster, to blur, *rake it, in the well, rake, well, rake, well, well, well* . . .

The buzzer surprised Bud and the cheers startled him even more. He kept on raking the bull even after it had stopped bucking. When he realized what he was doing, he slid down a little dizzy. Glancing at the judges, he started for the sidelines and Pam. Before he reached her, the judges' blackboard was raised aloft.

"Seventy-eight," Steve Strange announced to the crowd. "Our new leader is Bud Davis with a score of seventy-eight. Nice goin', Bud. Ain't seen you around here for a while. I figured you'd forgot how to ride that thing."

When he reached the edge of the mattresses, Pam kissed him. He opened his eyes in the middle of the kiss and saw golden eyes watching him.

"Number thirty-four," Steve told the rodeo fans, "Jessie LaRive, from right here in Houston. Show 'em how, girl."

As Jessie headed for the bull, Bud looked over at where Sissy had been, but she was gone. He wondered where she had wandered off to this time. He looked around for her, but when he didn't see her, he returned his attention to Jessie, who was just vaulting aboard. Feeling Pam tighten her grip on his arm, he looked down at her. And there, standing next to Pam, was Sissy. He felt a sudden surge of energy.

"Hi," his wife said.

"Hi," Bud said.

Sissy had come over to compliment her husband on his ride, but now that she was there she found herself saying something quite different from what she had planned to, and in quite a different tone.

"Thought you weren't comin'," Sissy said almost accusingly.

"I'm here," Bud said in an equally hard voice.

He had noticed something new about her brown felt hat. It was decorated with a gold pin that had not been there before. It was a number: 13½.

"Where'd you get the pin?" he asked.

"Wes," she said. "He gave it to me."

"What's it mean anyway?"

"What's it mean that he gave it to me? Or what's the pin mean?"

"The pin."

"Wes says it means the people who sent him to prison. A judge, a jury, and a half-assed lawyer. Says lotsa convicts wear 'em."

The three of them—Sissy, Pam, and Bud—stood together watching Jessie adjust herself on the bull. None of them knew what to say. Sissy wished she had not bothered to come over. She had not said what she had intended to say and she was not feeling the way she had intended to feel.

The bull started and Jessie stayed right with it. She had on chaps, too, which flapped against the bull's sides. She had spurs, too, although she did not put them to much use. The crowd cheered wildly for the first cowgirl to ride in the rodeo.

"I thought you might enter," Bud shouted above the cheers.

"Me, too," Sissy said, "but Wes wouldn't let me."

Bud glanced down at Sissy with a curious look on his face. He could not understand why she seemed to obey Wes so readily when she had never obeyed him. He had no way of knowing that she was afraid of Wes. Her outlaw had told her that he did not want her making a fool of him the way she had made a fool of her husband—so she had not entered the rodeo.

"Jessie looks pretty good up there," Bud said.

"Yeah," Sissy muttered.

When the buzzer sounded, Jessie got down with an excited grin on her face. The judges did their arithmetic and wrote on their blackboard.

"Seventy-two," Steve called out. "Not bad, Jessie."

The stands cheered as if she had just taken over first place.

"I'm gonna go say congratulations," Sissy said.

"Number one oh six," Steve announced, "Wes Hightower, from Amarillo. Now don't hurt it, Wes, okay?"

Wes winked down at Sissy and stepped onto the mattresses. He walked slowly toward his ride. Bud thought Wes's old chaps spoke with quiet authority. His spurs jingled like prize money. He seemed to sway less on the mattresses than the other cowboys. When he swung up onto the bull, his chaps, which almost seemed a part of him, flapped like giant black wings.

"Wes used to run the bull," Steve chattered on into the microphone, "so he oughta know how to ride it. You ready, Wes?"

"Let's go."

Wes rode the machine like a machine. His legs pumped with the regularity of pistons. He turned when the bull turned as smoothly as if he revolved on ball bearings. He handled the bucks as if he had inner shock absorbers. The human machine was more than a match for the merely mechanical one.

Bud looked over at Sissy, but she was watching the bull-rider, so he looked away. He imagined her pride in Wes and Wes's ride. He really did look like the cowboy she had always wanted. Sissy looked over at Bud, but he was watching the bull-rider, so she looked away.

Bud looked down at Pam. She seemed to be impressed by the ride, too. He looked back at the rider.

Doubling up his fist, Bud pounded it into his own thigh. It hurt. For the first time since his name had been called, Bud remembered his burst blister. And he remembered other aches and pains and strains. Watching Wes ride the bull, Bud began to feel like a cripple again.

When the buzzer sounded, the great black wings flapped again as the outlaw dismounted. The crowd roared when the judges' blackboard was hoisted into the air.

"Eighty-one," Steve Strange told the saloon. "Our new leader is Wes Hightower with a score of eighty-one. Nice goin', ol' buddy."

48

The Second Round

The chaps hung heavy as Bud waited to ride again. As slow time passed, they seemed to weigh more and more. They were beginning to feel like real armor. With his legs wrapped in leather, he did not quite recognize himself. He did not look like himself. He did not walk like himself. Wearing chaps, Bud somehow felt like a cowboy—a real cowboy—whom he did not quite know.

Shifting his weight nervously as he waited, he felt the leather tug at him in an almost sexual way. Something about this sensation made him look down at Pam. She smiled up at him warmly. Then he looked for Sissy, but she was missing again. Bud discovered her at the long bar. She was buying another shot of tequila. As she was carrying it across the saloon, she stumbled but recovered. The golden drink seemed to buck in the shot glass. She spilled a little of it on her hand, but she still reached Wes with most of it. She had been buying him one after the other. Wes swallowed this one like the others, in one motion.

"Number hunderd and six," Steve Strange said into the microphone, "Wes Hightower, of Amarillo. Wes, you're up again."

Wiping the last tequila from his lips with the back of his hand, Wes stepped onto the bull's giant bed. After an intermission, the second round of the competition was now well under way with all the remaining bull-riders—the ones who had not been thrown—riding in reverse order. This time, the

soft footing bothered Wes more than it had when he first
walked to the bull. He swayed like everyone else, maybe a
little more. When he reached the bucking machine, the black
wings did not fly quite so gracefully but rather settled onto
the bull's back a little too much like a wounded buzzard.

Bud glanced over at Sissy, who stood with the empty
shot glass in her hand. She was frowning. Then she licked the
inside of the glass absentmindedly.

"Ready?" Steve asked.

"Yeah," Wes said in a tired voice.

"You sure?"

"Sure."

Once again, Wes rode the bucking machine like a riding
machine, but now the human machinery was a little out of
tune. Its timing was slightly off. The piston legs moved a little
more sluggishly. The ball bearings in his waist were corroded.
His shocks absorbed less of the punishment. The machine
was not running at its best, but it was still a machine. It still
made all the right moves with an approximation of mechanical precision. Raking the bull's sides, the rowels of his spurs
were like cogs turning in a rusty but still reliable engine. A
drunk Wes rode better than the other cowboys sober.

Bud's hopes had risen when he saw how much tequila
Wes carried to the bull with him. But now they were coming
down again. The alcohol had crippled Wes but not enough.
Watching the black wings flap with every buck, Bud felt his
own chaps growing heavier and heavier still. While Wes's legs
seemed to fly, Bud's felt more and more leaden. He told himself that he had preferred the first round when he rode before
Wes. Now he would have to go to the bull with Wes's ride
still spinning in his memory.

Bud looked over at Sissy, who was licking the inside of
the shot glass again. She turned the glass lazily while the bull
whirled at top speed. Bud was not sure she was even
watching, even interested, but then she put two fingers in her
mouth and whistled.

The longer Wes stayed on the bull's back, the better he
seemed to ride. All that confusing bucking and spinning were
somehow sobering him up. Even slightly impaired, he still radiated confidence. It was a measure of his confidence that he
felt sure he could win the rodeo drunk. And this self-assurance would probably influence the judges. They could not
help being impressed by the presence as well as the tech-

nique. Bud looked down at Pam and saw that her nipples were hard.

By the time the buzzer sounded, Wes was riding almost as well as he had ridden in the first round. When he dismounted, his chaps once again flew through the air with the grace of a black eagle. He walked slowly away from the bull, but he was no longer unsteady. When the judges posted his score on their blackboard, the bleachers roared almost as loudly as they had the first time.

"Seventy-nine," Steve Strange announced. "Wes Hightower is still our leader with a combined score of a hunderd sixty. Congratulations, Wes, you're way out in front, ol' buddy."

Bud's chaps tugged at him again, but this time it was not a flirting feeling. It was more menacing. Something seemed to have hold of his manhood.

"Number eighty-seven," Steve Strange told the stands in his loud electronic voice a few minutes later, "Bud Davis, of Spur. Well, looks to me like Bud's about the only rider left with a prayer a catchin' my ol' buddy Wes and winnin' this here event. Yeah, Wes's just too far ahead a ever'body else. Don't mean to make you nervous, now, Bud, heh heh heh heh heh."

As he walked toward the bull over the cotton quicksand of the mattresses, Bud could feel that his back had had time to cool and stiffen since his first ride of the evening. Now it hurt the way it had on the night he had broken his arm. Remembering that other bad-back night, Bud glanced over at Sissy. She was standing next to Wes, examining his hand, which he seemed to have injured during his ride. Looking back at the bull, Bud tried to walk a little straighter, to wear his pain like a badge he was proud of, as if anyone could see it.

"Lemme see," Steve chattered on electronically, "Bud scored—where is it now?—a seventy-eight on his first ride. Now Wes's combined score is one sixty. So Bud'd have to score—one sixty take away seventy-eight—lemme see, lemme see. Bud'd have to score a eighty-two to tie, a eighty-three to win. That's right, ain't it? Looks right."

When he reached the bull, Bud placed both hands on the bull's back, about to vault aboard. But he felt a stinging in the palm of his right hand where the burst blister touched the machine. Rather than flinch, he pressed harder. He was still enjoying his pain, still felt pride in his pain, was even beginning to cultivate the pain like a crop. Bud's sore hand lifted him onto the bull.

"Yeah, that's right. Eighty-two to tie. Eighty-three to win. Uh-huh."

It was that terrible moment before, once again. His nerves were screaming like the rodeo fans in the bleachers. Raising his right hand over his head, he felt the scratch on his shoulder complain about the movement. The hurt somehow helped to calm his nerves.

"Ready, Bud?"

"I guess."

When the bull bucked the first time, Bud hurt all over. The second buck hurt him less. The third buck did not hurt him at all. The anesthesia of action had quieted all the pain for as long as the ride lasted. Bud rode without thinking about what he was doing to his body. He had at least that much in common with the machine beneath him—neither of them felt the blows.

The bull went into a dead spin, which was the hardest ride of all. Listening to the remembered voice, Bud tilted his head into the well and raked the bull with all his might. Looking down the length of his legs at his spurs was like looking way up twin windmill towers, the cruel rowels spinning brightly like cruel, bladed wheels in a high wind. And the bull itself whirled on and on like a windmill in a storm. Dizzy from the endless circles, Bud rode the windmill with windmills on his feet.

Lying back, his boots poised for the attack, Bud saw Sissy for a moment in the space between his raking legs. Her golden eyes stared at him between his ringing spurs. He raked. Then his wife spun by and he saw Wes. He raked harder. Then the outlaw spun by and he saw Pam. He raked again. And then here they all came once more. He seemed to reach out for Sissy with his spurs, then he spurred Wes, then Pam. They whirled before his whirling eyes. Sissy and Wes and Pam, Sissy, Wes, Pam. SissyWesPamSissyWesPam . . .

Suddenly the machine came lurching out of its dead spin, reversing directions, trying to outsmart him, but he went with it. There was Sissy again. He leaned into the well. The bull changed directions again. There was Pam. He leaned the other way. When the bull circled back once more, Bud leaned once more toward Sissy, who had her two fingers in her mouth, whistling.

Once again, Sissy was surprised at how well Bud rode, his second ride much better even than his first. In a sense, she felt as if she were seeing him for the first time. If she had not known him so well, she would have wanted to ask him: *Are you a real cowboy?*

Sissy had moved away from Wes, not far, just a step and a half, but they were both aware of the space between them. Sissy could not help comparing the two rides, Bud's and Wes's. Where Wes's moves had been mechanical, Bud's were spontaneous and fluid. Where Wes had been a machine on a machine, Bud was a dancer on the bull's back. Where Wes's legs were pistons, Bud's feet seemed to be doing intricate dance steps as they spurred. He kicked as if he were doing the cotton-eyed Joe. He spun as if he were doing the whip. He moved his feet faster and faster as if he were doing a hoedown. His jingling spurs played the music to which he danced.

Sissy somehow felt that Bud was riding his dancing ride for her. It didn't make any sense, but that was how she felt. She remembered feeling the same way the very first night he rode the bull. It was as if his worst ride and his best ride were somehow dedicated to her. Wes could feel this connection between the cowgirl beside him and the cowboy out there on the spinning bull. He reached out and took hold of Sissy's arm. His hand felt as cold and unforgiving as a handcuff.

His mind and body spinning, Bud saw the long bar whirl by where he had met Sissy. He turned around again and saw the bar where he had lost her. He turned and saw the punching bag where Sissy had hurt her hand on the night he proposed to her. He turned and saw the dance floor where he had danced with Sissy and where he had danced with Pam and where Sissy had danced with Wes. Around and around and around, his memories whirled by him on a merry-go-round. Sissy memories chased Pam memories chased Sissy memories. The bull-rider lurched in Sissy's direction, then lurched back toward Pam, who stood clapping and cheering, looking beautiful and out of place.

Even Pam, who knew very little about bull riding, could tell that Bud's second ride was better than his first. She did not need any special knowledge to appreciate its grace. She admired his arching body, his driving thighs, his dancing feet.

Pam liked Bud—even loved him—as much as she ever had. She had this thing about cowboys, as she liked to say. And Bud was proving himself to be even more of a cowboy than she had ever realized. Every buck, every spin, every rake seemed to make her like him more.

Pam and Sissy and Wes—they kept spinning before Bud's eyes as if he were dancing with them all. He seemed to be whirling them all around and around and around, turning this way, then that way. His whole world seemed to spin, like the bull, like windmill wheels, like the rowels of his spurs, like couples on a dance floor.

When the buzzer sounded and the bull stopped, Bud's world seemed to keep on turning. He just sat there for a moment waiting for it to stop. Then he got down in a daze and walked toward Pam with the cheers making him feel even more disoriented. When he reached her, Pam hugged Bud— and they waited. The compiling of the score seemed to take longer than usual. The judges were evidently double-checking their arithmetic.

"Eighty-three," Steve Strange roared over the speakers. "My, my, my . . .." He paused. "Sorry, Wes, ol' buddy . . ."

Pam reached up to kiss Bud, but then she changed her mind. He was staring across the bullring at Sissy.

49

The Shoot-Out

Jessie came in third, Wes placed second, and Bud won the bull-riding event at the rodeo in the saloon. He never felt more like a cowboy than when he went up on the bandstand to receive his prize money. The honky-tonk, which had always had a flair for the dramatic, paid in cash. After all, the management did not want the prize to look like just another paycheck. It wanted a memorable ceremony. And it knew that the ceremony would be remembered best if the money was counted out in hundred-dollar bills. Fifty of these bills were counted out and handed to Bud. It was a winner-take-all contest. Second and third place were not worth anything. Jessie at least came and stood on the bandstand with Bud, but Wes was not around. As he came back down again, Bud's eyes searched the saloon's vast indoor spaces.

"Looking for someone?" Pam asked.

"What?" Bud asked.

"I wanted to know if you were looking for someone."

"No."

"You were looking for her, weren't you?"

"No."

"She went out the side door. She left."

"Shit, I wanted her to see this."

They stood at the foot of the bandstand. Bud clutched more money than he had ever held before in his crippled right hand. Cowboys were coming up to congratulate Bud.

Cowgirls came up, too, but not the one he was looking for. He thought he was angry at her again.

"Let's go over there," Pam said, nodding, "where it's less crowded."

She led the way between the tables. As they walked, Bud kept looking around. Once they were out of the crush, Pam stopped by an iron pillar under a light. She faced Bud.

"You did it for her, didn't you?" Pam said in a voice that was accusing, hurt, hard, vulnerable. "Practicing, winning, all that, didn't you?"

"I . . ."

"Because you sure didn't do it for me."

Pam seemed to be near tears in the happy honky-tonk—tears of anger, tears of frustration, but mostly tears of pain. She was trying to hide her hurt. She wore her pain not like a badge but like a blemish that she was ashamed of.

"Look, I'm a shit," she said, "but I'm not that big a shit. I have to tell you something."

She paused as if she were trying to decide whether or not to go on. Staring at her, Bud hardly recognized Pam. She seemed as strange wearing these emotions as he seemed to himself wearing chaps. She had always been a woman whose feelings were as well ordered as her bedroom, but now she was just as confused as anyone else.

"Remember when you came back that day and the trailer was cleaned and vacuumed," she went on. "Well, I didn't do that. Sissy did. She was there. She was the one who took the vacuum cleaner out of the box. And she left you a note asking you to phone her, but I tore it up. Because . . ."

Pam wanted to reach out for Bud, but instead she leaned back against the iron pillar. It was hard and cold against her body, but it would have to do. She shivered.

"Well, because I was sort of jealous, and I wanted to keep my cowboy."

Most of all, Bud was surprised. Staring at Pam, he realized that he really did not know her, had not known her. He was angry at her for deceiving him, and yet still pleased that she cared enough for him to do it. He wanted to punish her and comfort her at the same time. Emotionally, his world was spinning again, turning him this way, reversing directions, turning him that, trying to disorient and confuse him.

"That's the kind of lady I am. I don't suppose you could . . . No, I don't suppose."

Bud stopped staring at Pam and looked again for Sissy. His eyes searched in every direction, moving faster now, in a hurry, becoming almost frantic, everything whirling before his eyes again because he was turning his head so fast, this way and that.

"But I tell you what," Pam said, breaking the silence and closer to tears than ever, trying harder than ever to hide the blemish of pain on her face, "if you ever want to make her jealous again, you know where I am."

Bud studied Pam one last time, this stranger. He wanted to kiss her, but he wanted something else worse.

"I gotta go," Bud said.

Pam did not let the first awful tear—another blemish—escape until after he was gone. She watched his back, with the big red "87" pinned to it, running through the crowd. She saw him dodging cowboys and cowgirls, sometimes bursting right between cowboys and their cowgirls, heading toward the back door. Even when his number disappeared in the crowd, she still followed his hat as it bobbed hurriedly by the other hats, picking up speed all the time. More tears had run down her reddening face by now, which really was beginning to look blemished.

"Hey, cowboy," Pam said.

She spoke to a rodeo cowboy who was passing nearby. He wore a feather in his hat, tight jeans, and a self-assurance that seemed uninjured by his failure to place well in the rodeo. He knew he was good-looking and he knew he was a real cowboy. Still he was surprised to hear the beautiful, crying lady calling to him. He stopped and looked her over.

"Yeah, you," Pam said, "when're you going to take me home and rape me?"

Taking his hand, she looked back one last time. Bud was just reaching the back door. He hit it as hard as if he were mad at it. The door slammed open, and he ran out of the body-heated air of the saloon into the waiting coolness of the outdoor night. Then he stopped. Standing there in his chaps and rodeo number, Bud searched the parking lot as if he expected to find Sissy loitering among the cars. Not finding her so easily, he looked in the direction of Wes's trailer. Lights were burning in the living room as well as the bedroom. Suddenly he realized that he was still carrying $5,000 in his right fist. He doubled over the bills and shoved them in the hip pocket of his jeans.

Then Bud looked back at the outlaw's trailer. Before, his chaps had made him feel as if he were wearing heavy armor, but now they felt like no protection at all. He seemed almost naked before his enemy. For now he could imagine at least a part of the life beneath the trailer lights. He imagined weapons. And his imagination frightened him, paralyzed him, left him standing there feeling foolish.

While he stood there, Bud looked from the trailer to his truck. He studied its black outlines. When he had seen enough of them, he stared back at the silver-and-blue box. His eyes grew more and more restless. Trying to make up his mind, he kept looking back and forth from the pickup to the fortress to the pickup to the fortress. He felt like a coward until he finally did decide.

Walking quickly now, Bud headed for his truck. He dodged between the closely parked cars and pickups and vans, moving faster all the time, finally trotting. Occasionally, he would look back over his shoulder at the trailer as if he were afraid of it. When he reached his pickup, he opened the door on the driver's side and leaned all the way across the seat. He opened the glove compartment and took out the miniature license plate that said:

Texas
SISSY

He swiveled and put it back on the rear window opposite

Texas
BUD

Then he reached behind the seat. His tool belt was familiar to his touch. Pulling it out, he strapped it on over his chaps.

Closing the door of his truck, Bud walked toward the blue-and-silver trailer. With his hammer knocking against the side of his right leg, he felt a little foolish, but he kept going. He also felt afraid. Now, as he made his way between the vans and trucks and cars, he moved more slowly. He kept staring at the trailer as if he expected it to do something threatening. A shadow moved on the bedroom window.

The closer he came to the outlaw trailer, the sillier he felt—in his chaps, in his tool belt. He suddenly realized that he was still wearing his number. He tried to tear it off, but it was hard to reach. He decided to leave it. After all, it did not make him look much funnier than he already looked. He glanced around to see if anyone was smiling at him—and his fears—but no one in the parking lot seemed to be paying any attention to him at all. It was late and they were intent on getting home.

When he reached the blue-and-silver trailer, Bud climbed the five wooden steps to the front door and then just stood there in his chaps and his tool belt and his number. His pounding blood seemed to carry all sorts of fears to his brain. He was afraid of Wes, afraid of being embarrassed, afraid of guns, afraid of rejection. What if Sissy just laughed at him and refused to go with him?

Bud knocked on the door and waited. He was even more nervous than he had been on the bull just before it was switched on. He heard someone coming and hoped it was Sissy. It was. She looked out the porthole in the door with a puzzled expression on her face. She opened the door.

"Bud, what're you doin' here?" Sissy asked, staring at him. "Why you're wearin' your . . ."

"I gotta talk to you," Bud interrupted her.

"I cain't. I gotta pack. We're leavin'."

"I know you're leavin'. But I gotta tell you somethin'. Let me in. No, you come out."

The initial surprise at seeing Bud at her door was wearing off, giving way to nervousness. She had her own fears, just as Bud did. She looked down, not at him.

"No, I just cain't," Sissy said in a voice that begged him to understand. "Wes's in the bedroom. He's waitin' for me. I gotta go."

She was more nervous than ever now, but she didn't close the door. Bud gave up on trying to get her to come out to him. He would talk to her where she was.

"Look, I'm prideful and hardhead," Bud told her in a voice that strained to maintain control. "I know that. And I wanta apologize clear back to when I hit you the first time."

Sissy was surprised again, stunned. Now her world spun, turning one way and then another. Now she was disoriented.

"Don't matter," Sissy said in her confusion.

Staring at her, Bud was afraid he was going to cry. Here he had just won the rodeo at Gilley's, here he was supposed to be the toughest bull-rider around, here he was in his chaps and his spurs, here he was with his eyes filling up.

"I put your name back on the window," Bud said in a thick voice. "I love you, Sissy."

Sissy's world lurched again. She stood there in the doorway trying to understand what was happening and what she was feeling. She saw that her cowboy was about to cry. And suddenly she came rushing across the threshold at him, throwing her arms around him, hugging him, crying.

"I love you, too, Bud," Sissy choked.

He pressed her to him and kept fighting against crying.

"I didn't know you cleaned up the trailer that day," Bud told her, all in a rush to fix everything right now. "I woulda called you, but she tore up your note. You can ride that bull anytime you want, it don't matter no more."

"You were great tonight," she wept. "Really great. I was hopin' you'd win."

"Well, I did, so just screw Mexico. I got five thousand dollars. We can go anywhere we want. We can go . . ."

"To Spur. You still want to?"

Suddenly Bud was not paying any attention to the conversation anymore. He did not even hear Sissy mention his hometown. He was staring at her face. The right side was red and puffy. And now he could see that her nose had been bleeding. There was still dried blood in the nostrils and in the little trough leading down to her mouth. Her upper lip was beginning to swell.

"What happened to your face?" Bud asked angrily.

"Nothin'," Sissy mumbled.

"What happened!"

"I got hit."

"Did he hit you?"

Sissy nodded slowly. "I didn't wanta go to Mexico."

"I'll kill him!"

Bud rushed past Sissy into the trailer.

"Bud, don't!"

Paying no attention, Bud charged into the tiny living room. By the coffee table, he slowed up just long enough to look around for Wes. Bud saw the outlaw through the bedroom door, sitting on the bed, cradling a pistol in his hands. What the intruder did not realize was that Wes was cleaning his gun. Seeing the outlaw with a revolver, Bud reached for his hammer as he rushed the bedroom.

Seeing Bud with a hammer in his hand, Wes began hurriedly trying to shove .38-caliber bullets back into his gun. As he ran through the cramped kitchen, Bud kept expecting the pistol to go off. He still did not understand that it was not ready to fire yet. He did not even know he was in a race.

"Bud," Sissy shouted behind him, "this ain't a game no more! Stop!"

Wes's gun came up. Bud's hammer came down. The pistol was knocked across the cell of a bedroom. It hit the wall and fell to the floor. Bud had won a race he did not even know he was in.

Leaning back on the bed, Wes lifted one boot. He kicked Bud in the balls. When Bud doubled over, Wes hurried to his gun. He picked it up and pointed it at his victim, but it was broken. While Bud was trying to straighten up, trying to raise his hammer, Wes took his pistol by the barrel. He used the gun like a hammer. The first blow hit Bud on the neck and dropped him to his knees.

Sissy came rushing into the bedroom to try to stop the fight, to try to help Bud, to try to save him. She grabbed Wes's right arm, but he elbowed her in the stomach and sent her crashing into the wall. Then he stood over the kneeling Bud, beating on him with the gun. Dodging some blows, absorbing others, Bud drew back his hammer and swung as hard as he could at Wes's ankle. The hammer struck about halfway up the outlaw's boot. Wes cried out in pain. Sissy was clawing at him again, but he brushed her away with a backhand blow to the face that sprawled her across the bed. Then he aimed the butt of the gun at Bud's head. The impact knocked one of the plastic grips off the handle of the pistol.

When Bud regained consciousness a few minutes later, Sissy was bathing his face with a wet cloth from the tiny bathroom. It took him a moment to remember why his head hurt so bad. Then he looked around for Wes.

"He's gone," Sissy said. "He took your money and my car. He's goin' back to Huntsville for sure."

Bud just groaned and raised a hand to his head. Sissy bent down to kiss him. That was when Bud noticed how bruised her own face was. Her left eye was swollen. He could feel that his right eye was swollen even worse. The two injured faces kissed each other. Pam had loved Bud for riding so well and winning the rodeo, but Sissy loved him now, as she had always loved him, for how badly he had been hurt.

"How come you to do a fool thing like that anyway?" Sissy whispered.

"I dunno," Bud whispered back. He thought about it. "Guess I thought I was a cowboy."

"You are."

"No I ain't."

Sissy gently dabbed his face again with the rag. Bud reached up with his right hand and gingerly touched the bruises on her face. She kissed his littlest finger.

"I don't want no cowboy," Sissy said. "I just thought I did."

"I don't want no lady," Bud said, smiling. "I just thought I did."

LATHAM ON LATHAM

Before our daughter was born, my wife and I drew up family trees for our doctor. He wanted to know what everyone died of. My wife's Massachusetts ancestors generally died of heart disease and cancer. My Texas forefathers were dragged to death by horses, hanged, shot, knifed. One of my great grandfathers was killed in a knife fight following a quarrel in a saloon. His widow remarried. But her second husband was killed in a second fight in the same saloon. I was naturally brought up with a healthy respect for saloons.

In 1978, I first visited what is surely the world's largest saloon, Gilley's Club, in Houston. Although I had been warned against such places all my life, I more or less moved in. As I got to know the saloon cowboys, I realized that they came to Gilley's for the same reason my ancestors had come to Texas: to escape. Since a young man trapped in a boring job can no longer go West, he goes to a Western bar.

When my grandfather on my father's side came to Spur, Texas, it was literally an escape. He had been living in Central Texas when he got into trouble. What made it worse was his being the son of a former Texas Ranger. The Ranger's son was out riding one day when he came across a stray cow. He roped it, tied it to a tree, and went to get his brothers to help him drive it home. When he got back he found a crowd. The cow's owner and a posse of his friends offered my grandfather a choice: get lynched or leave the county. He headed for Spur.

I was born on Main Street in Spur in a hospital that has been torn down. I grew up in a lot in Texas towns: Munvay, DeLeon, Huntsville, Abilene. And then I went east to Amherst College, where I got my B.A., and Princeton University, where I got my Ph.D. I worked for the *Washington Post, New York* magazine and *Esquire*. I wrote a couple of books, *Crazy Sundays,* about F. Scott Fitzgerald's Hollywood days, and *Orchids for Mother,* a spy novel. And then I went back to Texas after a long absence to study the urban cowboys there. When I first walked into Gilley's, I felt, on the one hand, like a native son, and on the other hand, like Margaret Mead stepping ashore in Samoa for the first time.

RELAX!
SIT DOWN
and Catch Up On Your Reading!

☐	13098	**THE MATARESE CIRCLE** by Robert Ludlum	$3.50
☐	12206	**THE HOLCROFT COVENANT** by Robert Ludlum	$2.75
☐	13688	**TRINITY** by Leon Uris	$3.50
☐	13899	**THE MEDITERRANEAN CAPER** by Clive Cussler	$2.75
☐	12152	**DAYS OF WINTER** by Cynthia Freeman	$2.50
☐	13176	**WHEELS** by Arthur Hailey	$2.75
☐	13028	**OVERLOAD** by Arthur Hailey	$2.95
☐	13220	**A MURDER OF QUALITY** by John Le Carre	$2.25
☐	11745	**THE HONOURABLE SCHOOLBOY** by John Le Carre	$2.75
☐	13471	**THE ROSARY MURDERS** by William Kienzle	$2.50
☐	13848	**THE EAGLE HAS LANDED** Jack Higgins	$2.75
☐	10700	**STORM WARNING** Jack Higgins	$2.25
☐	13880	**RAISE THE TITANIC!** by Clive Cussler	$2.75
☐	12855	**YARGO** by Jacqueline Susann	$2.50
☐	13186	**THE LOVE MACHINE** by Jacqueline Susann	$2.50
☐	12941	**DRAGONARD** by Rupert Gilchrist	$2.25
☐	13284	**ICEBERG** by Clive Cussler	$2.50
☐	12810	**VIXEN 03** by Clive Cussler	$2.75
☐	14033	**ICE!** by Arnold Federbush	$2.50
☐	11820	**FIREFOX** by Craig Thomas	$2.50
☐	12691	**WOLFSBANE** by Craig Thomas	$2.50
☐	13017	**THE CHINA SYNDROME** by Burton Wohl	$1.95
☐	12989	**THE ODESSA FILE** by Frederick Forsyth	$2.50

Buy them at your local bookstore or use this handy coupon for ordering: